VOICES OF ROME

There will be bodies
death on the Tiber

VOICES OF ROME

Four Stories of Ancient Rome

Lindsey Davis

HODDER &
STOUGHTON

The Spook Who Spoke Again © 2015 by Lindsey Davis
Vesuvius By Night © 2017 by Lindsey Davis
Invitation to Die © 2019 by Lindsey Davis
The Bride from Bithynia © 1991 by Lindsey Davis (originally
published by Woman's Realm/IPC magazines)
This edition first published in Great Britain in 2023 by Hodder & Stoughton
An Hachette UK company

1

Copyright © Lindsey Davis 2023

A CIP catalogue record for this title is
available from the British Library

Hardback ISBN 978 1 399 72133 2
Trade Paperback 978 1 399 72134 9
eBook ISBN 978 1 399 72135 6

Typeset in Plantin Light by Palimpsest Book Production Ltd,
Falkirk, Stirlingshire

Printed and bound in Great Britain by Clays Ltd, Elcograf S.p.A.

Hodder & Stoughton policy is to use papers that are natural, renewable
and recyclable products and made from wood grown in sustainable
forests. The logging and manufacturing processes are expected to
conform to the environmental regulations of the country of origin.

Hodder & Stoughton Ltd
Carmelite House
50 Victoria Embankment
London EC4Y 0DZ

www.hodder.co.uk

VOICES OF ROME

CONTENTS

INTRODUCTION

Some time in 2014, I was approached to write 'a short story'. It would be for Amazon's e-book platform, the Kindle, and the lure was that my mainstream Flavia Albia novel that year would then receive special publicity. Naturally it was hoped that I would write about Falco or Albia. I didn't want to, because on the infrequent occasions when I write something extra I always prefer a change. It's more refreshing. I offered a compromise, a spin-off from my spin-off, which would be narrated by Albia's brother, the weird child Postumus.

That started a short digital series, three stories that were originally available only in e-book and audio versions. It turned out that 'short story' meant something quite long, almost a quarter the words in my novels, so I've always called them novellas. My natural length is longer, which gives me the space I like in order to investigate every wrinkle of each new plot and to develop its particular characters. But in my two series I was creating the baroque sweep of a grand family soap opera, with people we can sometimes only glimpse because there are so many; I quite enjoyed these three chances to explore minor characters in more depth than usual. They sit with Falco and Albia, available for readers who want a little more while they wait for a new full-length book.

Readers begged me for print versions, so I kept begging

my editor and now we are putting the downloads together in print. You see, we do listen! To round off the bundle, I have added a Mystery Extra to the expected extras.

THE SPOOK WHO SPOKE AGAIN

'Then you can be the only boy in history who,
instead of running away from home to join a circus,
has to run away from a circus to go home.'

When Falco and Helena were travelling in Syria in *Last Act in Palmyra*, they joined a travelling theatre company. Disguising himself as a jobbing writer, Falco wrote a new play, *The Spook Who Spoke*. This heady drama is clearly the ancient New Comedy prototype for *Hamlet*. Its existence was later confirmed in *Alexandria* when Falco looked himself up in the pinakes, the Great Library's catalogue. Yes, they have him: *Phalko of Rome, father Phaounios, prosecutor and dramatist. His writings are: 'The Spook Who Spoke'*. Phalko ranks an author because his play has been publicly performed on stage, even though that was in a one-night-only disaster at a Roman fort in the Palmyra desert. My readers love it and some dream of finding the script . . .

The Spook Who Spoke Again, my download, features the play's proposed second performance in Nero's Circus in Rome on the eve of Domitian's Triumph. Here, the sinister adopted son of Falco and Helena wreaks havoc as he tries to exact revenge on his birth mother, the absurdly colourful snake-dancer Thalia, who has (he thinks) allowed her monstrous python Jason to eat his pet ferret. Alexander Postumus is a boy convinced of his own intelligence and

2

superiority, although he is only twelve, or perhaps eleven, and we can see he is more vulnerable than he thinks. Carried off to work with Thalia's animals and to be taught acrobatics and acting, after his ferret vanishes he has nobody to discuss problems with, so he confides in us. He deems the slinky pet's disappearance to be murder, so it must be avenged even if that means executing his birth mother. Seeking justice for Ferret, he sets out to investigate, in a parody of what Falco and Albia do for a living. He gets it all wrong. It's not his fault. He never means to be bad.

Postumus was supposedly fathered by Falco's father Geminus, another colourful character who is wonderful or tiresome, depending on your point of view. Falco and Helena suspect a deliberate deceit by Thalia to obtain an inheritance; at the end of *Nemesis* Thalia dumps the newborn baby on them and in *The Ides of April* Albia tells us Falco has formally adopted him, in his own sneaky scheme to safeguard the family fortune. When reclaimed by Thalia once he seems old enough to be useful, Postumus first wonders about a mysterious 'zoo-keeper' for the role of his father, then sizes up another possible culprit; this man – accidentally – becomes a fatality. Though chastened, Postumus also destroys most people's relationships, nearly ruins the intended play, is almost squeezed by Jason, starts a riot in a monumental arena and sets it on fire. Thalia despatches her terrible child back to Falco and Helena. He seems sweetly unaware of the damage he has done, but does he welcome a return to his comfortable home and safer parents? . . .

I was surprised how many readers wrote to query, or even to congratulate me, on the portrayal of Postumus as someone 'on the spectrum'. This was never in my mind. The Romans don't appear to have identified what we call autism; Helena

Justina only classifies him as 'unusual' and I follow her. I know this child; I recognise the way he acts and thinks. I even wonder if I myself may have acted and thought in the same way. To me, Postumus only exemplifies an intelligent but insecure youngster; in *A Comedy of Terrors* I was to stress that he wants to be a gladiator, like any other Roman boy. His anxieties are understandable: he has two mothers and several possible fathers, while Thalia's request to uproot him for her circus only confirms that his insecurity is real.

What might he become in later life? His obsessive curiosity about the world masks more shrewdness than we may think. Think about how competently and uncomplainingly he knuckles down to mucking out the circus animals (gleefully aware that people don't expect him to cope). Think about how he boldly reorganises ticket sales and then lectures tourists. Postumus has a future. I suspect he will one day run the auction house, the circus, or even both – and he will do it well. People may view him as a bit of an odd personality, but that will suit his double careers. He won't care. He'll just doggedly get on with it.

I would find it a strain to write a whole novel about him. But Postumus is very sweet. I enjoyed giving him this outing of his own.

VESUVIUS BY NIGHT

All that crud is going to come down on us.

After *The Spook Who Spoke Again*, I warmed to shorter pieces somewhat. My next was something I had always said I would never attempt; it's about Vesuvius erupting. I had

4

even slowed down my main series to avoid having to face this and, I admit it made me cry to write about it. Yet the Vesuvius eruption of AD79 is also one of the cracking great stories of history.

The first reason for *not* tackling the eruption was that it would be inappropriate for my lighter romps featuring Falco and Albia. Secondly, Pliny described everything. But people asked me 'What happened to Larius?' and I was ready to answer. Inevitably, because we do know in advance the fate of Falco's much-loved nephew, his novella had to be tragic. Albia has revealed that Larius and all his family were lost when the volcano erupted. I couldn't change that.

We first meet Larius as a wide-eyed teenager who reads Catullus and saves people from drowning in *Shadows in Bronze*. He reappears in *A Body in the Bath House*, by then transformed into a hard-partying lad-about-town who has bunked off from his wife and young children to behave *very* badly, especially in dark British bars. Urged on by the equally reprobate Camillus brothers, he drinks, swears, fights with men, flirts and worse with women. Why is he in Britain? Professor Barry Cunliffe thinks fragments of wall plaster at Fishbourne Roman Palace resemble work at Stabiae, where Larius trained and, according to me, the new frescos are going to be painted by him.

In planning the novella, I did have new material. Even though Pliny's descriptions have long been used by vulcanologists, the truth about pyroclastic flows was only accepted after the Mount St Helens eruption. Then in archaeology, three key locations had been either recently excavated or studied: first, the House of the Chaste Lovers in Pompeii and the adjoining House of the Painters at Work gave me the elegant designs Larius is working on, providing also

5

vivid details like the spilled bucket of sloppy wet plaster that is upset when the painters run away, and even the roadworks outside in the street. Next, although it was long believed that everyone who lived in Herculaneum escaped, boatsheds on the original shoreline have been dug out and visitors can see upsetting replica skeletons inside. These tragically show that large numbers of people of all ages – including children, a soldier and women with their jewellery – took shelter together; while hopelessly awaiting rescue, they were killed in the night by a huge wave of heat. Finally, at Oplontis, home to the imperial villa that has always been my favourite site on the Bay of Naples, further buildings have given up evidence of life at the time and long-lost bodies.

For me, there was still no justification for reprising the event as mere entertainment; it had to have deeper reso-nance. As I said in a Newsletter when the novella was published, *the cruise ships disgorge, coachloads of touring visitors criss-cross about led by guides with lurid umbrellas, and the young take their inane selfies without even looking at the ruins.* So the best way to make people think about these sites, which are still, in effect, graveyards, was to make characters we care for experience those terrifying last days. Lest it be too heartrending, I brought in the sub-tenant Nonius who, in his ghastly way, decides flight is for fools and makes the best of his chances for robbery, murder and rape. As we crime-writers say, human nature never changes. Fate, as Falco and Albia might add, is rarely fair. Yet some-times it can be. In another plotline, I ensured that the wife of a faithless husband has her satisfying revenge.

It might have been attractive to let my own people escape, but in *Enemies at Home*, Albia anticipated me: Larius, she

6

says, 'was the kind of fixated artist who would have tried to finish his wall, even though the whole house faced violent destruction. As soon as we heard about the eruption, my father went to see if he could find Larius, though he never did. Falco spent weeks there, in anguish as he tried to dig down through twenty feet of mud or ash. He could never find any trace. We decided the whole little family must have tried to escape too late; Larius was killed, along with many other people, most of whom were never found.'

At least in writing *Vesuvius by Night* I was able to show where he and his exhausted daughter took their last rest, and where his wife and other children went to sleep too, all taken in an instant by those pyroclastic flows.

My title came from the kind of painting Larius is prevented from producing. There is one example by Joseph Wright, in the Barber Institute in Birmingham.

INVITATION TO DIE

Titus Flavius Domitianus Augustus Germanicus,
conqueror of the Chatti and Dacians, in the ninth year
of his tribunitian power, fourteen times consul, imperator,
pontifex maximus, princeps and Father of the Country,
invites your attendance at a banquet on the Palatine.

The Emperor Domitian awarded himself a double Triumph in (probably) AD89. If this really happened, he had never actually fought against the Chatti because a frozen river thawed before they made it across, then the Dacians were bought off. In *A Capitol Death* I was to have a lot of fun with the subsequent Triumph being cobbled together. It's the same festivity that brought Thalia's troupe to Rome in *The Spook Who Spoke Again*, but here we'll see political stirrings about an emperor whose paranoia is becoming too dangerous for Rome. As part of the celebrations (probably) Domitian devised his macabre joke, the Black Banquet, supposedly to honour the fallen in Dacia and cruelly meant to terrify members of the Senate.

I had touched on this dinner in *Master and God*, where I examined the life and reign of Domitian and tried to explain, if not to excuse, the man he became. In that book my protagonists stayed outside (Gaius and Lucilla, quarrelling madly . . .) It now struck me that having become senators in the Albia series, Aulus and Quintus would receive invitations to the far-from-festive feast; unable to refuse, they must have been right there inside the dining room, eating funeral food and being danced at by unpleasant naked boys. Sometimes you do get lucky with ideas!

I knew I would enjoy writing about the brothers in their own right, exploring their domestic lives and social positions, then watching how they handle serious danger. Falco's influence must be there in their responses to the Emperor's threats. We know more than the Camilli have ever been told about their uncle's plot. Did they ever understand that while they were young men away on foreign service, Publius' daughter Sosia Camillina, the cousin they had been brought up with, died at the hands of Vespasian's maverick younger son? In *The Silver Pigs* Sosia gave me my first shocking murder, my first unusual weapon, my first evidential proof – and my first occasion when an investigator is driven inescapably to seek the truth. Because of Domitian's relationship to Vespasian and Titus, of course Falco and Sosia's family have been denied full justice for her murder. Now Domitian holds supreme power. When their imperial master greets them at his banquet, those events long before have a sinister resonance for those of us who remember why he and Falco are enemies. Will Domitian now recall that he has a reason to turn on the brothers? They do know their political careers have been blighted and like us they must fear that this will be more than an evening with a difficult host . . .

We have known Camillus Aelianus as the grumpy one and Justinus as the handsome one through both Falco and Albia. We have seen Quintus devastated by romantic love and Aulus as a faithless betrayer. They both have awkward marriages which it was good to examine, with glimpses of the six lively children Quintus and Claudia have produced. I was especially happy to show more of Meline, who had previously been a background figure. In the novella I was able to give her thoughts, fears, and at last a voice. Aulus, too, comes out of their second relationship well. They were among my choices for Falco's three failed attempts to run a detective agency with partners, so we have watched him training them to be practical and street-wise. (Unlike more pampered, less experienced senators, after the Black Banquet these two can safely find their own way home.) I think at the banquet they show their full maturity. Here are Aulus and Quintus on the alert yet restrained, while displaying their wit, humanity and courage.

At the conclusion, another handy device cropped up for me: when the party seems safely over, unwelcome imperial 'gifts' arrive: it's Domitian's warped version of taking home a balloon and a piece of birthday cake. I wanted to imagine what might happen to those black-painted dancing boys who, with their suggestive gestures and warped upbringing,

9

would surely have been a trial in any respectable household. If the Black Banquet really happened, several hundred aristocratic homes must have been lumbered with those posturing human handouts. My solution for one pair is that they are swiftly passed on by the Camilli, whose wives deposit them with Albia, saying that she is scary enough to cope. Well, that supplied new characters to send into a sad encounter with a serial killer in *The Grove of the Caesars* . . .

The Camillus brothers are left to ponder how Rome should face up to the Emperor. Might Falco's training lead them to become assassins? Will the Camillus family ever seek retribution for Sosia? Even if I'm speculating, as ever I won't plan. I showed some historical answers, in *Master and God*. If it ever happens that characters from the Falco series play some part in Domitian's demise, that must be another story.

THE BRIDE FROM BITHYNIA

*I have to confess, I drove here a great deal
faster than you said you would allow.*

Finally, a little extra. This was written for a different purpose and to some extent in a different style. When I was first trying to become a published writer, Sally Bowden, the Fiction Editor at *Woman's Realm*, commissioned several romantic serials from me. Not only did this help me survive financially for several years, but Sally had a son who became an archaeologist. Will, now an eminent professor, was to help me visit Nero's Golden House before it was open to the public and, famously, to descend into the sewers below the Forum of Nerva, a nerve-racking research experience that would be immortalised in *Three Hands in the Fountain*.

Only one of my early magazine serials had a Roman time period, when I was just beginning to find my way tentatively into the ancient world. Commissioned by Sally just before she retired, my two-part offering overlapped the first Falco novels but was sneakily drawn from an earlier, unpublished novel that didn't quite work, even for me, although I was fond of its protagonists and interested in their situation. With its brief mention of Vespasian, the original must have dated to immediately before I seized on him as a potential hero; next I wrote *The Course of Honour* and then I turned to Falco. I find it interesting that this had been my jumping-off point.

By 1991 I had definitely 'found my voice', as they say about authors. I was writing with more confidence and authority. I had started to feel at home in the Roman world and to portray it without worrying that my audience would feel too challenged by the unfamiliar. In the earlier work, for instance, I used English place names, which grates on me horribly now. We have left them alone as the serial is offered to you as an item of interest, just as it was – which of course is more than thirty years ago in my writing career. I notice that although some scenes are set in Rome, there is really no description of the city; how that would change!

I have suggested *The Bride from Bithynia* be included here because it is another story of the Camillus family and in fact introduced them. Aelia Camilla is more than Helena's aunt. She is a typical 'Lindsey heroine': a little at odds with established society, sharply observant, witty, practical, and resolutely brave. Perhaps she even foreshadows Helena herself or, when Helena seeks refuge after her failed first marriage, perhaps she becomes her scratchy niece's more serene role-model. Aelia Camilla's brothers, the well-meaning senator Decimus and reckless Publius, gave me a significant element of my plot in *The Silver Pigs*. Of course we would come to know them well. Decimus would be an enduring, endearing figure in my series; Falco would expose Publius as a traitor to Vespasian, then have to dispose of his corpse – a gruesome task where the Camilli may never have cottoned on to the details.

Gaius and Camilla had a life in my imagination beyond their serial. They would survive the Boudiccan rebellion and stay in Britain to help remedy Roman mistakes and rebuild the newest province. Their lovemaking on the eve of the battle produced the first of several children: Flavia, who has a role in my series more than once. When Falco first meets Helena Justina in Londinium, the way that she and Flavia interact gives him his first inkling that Helena may have a human side; some years later, in *The Jupiter Myth*, Flavia and her young siblings will show friendship and kindness to the angry street child, Albia.

But this couple of diplomatic ex-patriots came to have a vital role for me. At the start of my long series, Falco is gruff, antagonistic, and seriously opposed to the wealthy and often worthless aristocrats who run Rome and the empire. He bitterly distrusts the senatorial class; however, he admits to us that he has never really encountered the middle rank at close quarters. When he visits their home, Gaius and Camilla shock him with their civilised attitudes, not least their visible affection for one another. He recognises in them a strong sense of duty and ethics, to which he, as a fighter for justice, has to respond. As he battles

12

corruption, with ambitious men and their willing stooges plotting shamelessly, Falco can see that Gaius Flavius is absolutely straight. They will be friends. I love their discussion of London Bridge in *The Jupiter Myth*. When, eventually, Falco wants to improve his own social position in order to provide a better life for his family than in horrid Fountain Court, his experience with Helena's aunt and uncle must be a factor in reconciling him to a promotion he would once have rejected.

This was important for me too. Having abandoned my own career in government employment, I did want to show that I had believed in decent public administration; so, it was a deliberate act to create a 'good civil servant'. We may laugh a little at Gaius when he dives into being the obsessive bureaucrat, but to me he remains an ideal.

Then of course there is my little theme of women driving. Aelia Camilla needs to do this if she and her companions are to escape being massacred in the Boudiccan Rebellion. She later teaches her niece. This will lead to one of my favourite exchanges: Helena has bravely ventured to the silver mine (the same one where Camilla and Gaius spend their early married life). Falco has been nearly killed there. She manages to extract him, but he is seriously hurt and ill after months as an undercover slave, plus they need to escape from a dangerous situation. Helena puts the half-dead hero into her uncle's pony cart and as they, too, race away to safety, she chivvies him: 'Tell me if I go too fast and frighten you.' Falco growls back, 'You go too fast – but you don't frighten me!'

We know then, and they will soon realise, they are both in safe hands for the rest of their lives. It comes directly from the moment, at the start of this serial, when bad-boy

Publius Camillus lets his eleven-year-old sister take the reins in his chariot.

I like to think too that the brother's words apply to my own position as I began what is now a long career. I had learned what I *wasn't* going to write, or not anymore, and was setting out on a braver, more original, much stronger course. Camilla and Gaius will always be special to me, not least because out of their story came their outspoken niece and her dogged partner. Once Helena and Falco arrived, for me it was as if those Bithynian grooms had loosed the horses again: *'Just decide you're going to do it, and we'll go.'*

The Spook Who Spoke Again

Rome:
the Circus of Gaius and Nero
in the Transtiberina
August AD 89

I

As soon as I got there, my mother said, 'We must put on a revival of Falco's old play to celebrate.'

It sounded as if she was trying to make me feel at home, but now I had no home. She had come and removed me from where I lived with my other mother and Falco, and taken me to Nero's Circus, where her troupe of entertainers had arrived to work for a season. I think it is wrong that a very intelligent boy should have to live in a tent. Especially if he must share it with his mother and a large snake.

My change of circumstance came as no surprise. I had met her, the mother who bore me, because she came to our house every few years to have a look at me. She was very tall, with bulging muscles. She never wore respectable dress, only theatrical costumes. She must have decided what size to wear many years ago when she was smaller, so I could see parts of her that I had never been able to inspect closely on other women, even on statues, squeezing out of her tiny costumes. The clothes were bright coloured and trimmed in exotic ways. I keep lists of interesting things and after several visits I had written down: glass spangles, feathers, fur, braid, gold cord, silver beads, and leather fringing. The feathers were from peacocks, ostriches and parrots, all birds she had owned herself in her menagerie, though some had pined away and had their feathers plucked after they died, she said.

According to her, she visited my family out of affection for me, to see how I was getting on. My other mother, the one who brought me up, let out a snort as she said that affection had nothing to do with it. Thalia, my mother, wanted to see if I was useful yet. I was twelve now, or so she claimed, although my other mother muttered that I was probably eleven because Thalia fudged my date of birth as part of her daft scheming to disguise who my father was.

I am not supposed to know about that. Why does my father need to be disguised? Is he a god who visited earth one day? That would make me a demigod, like Hercules.

I am good at listening so I have discovered three definite things. Number one: I am Marcus Didius Alexander Postumus, son of Marcus Didius Falco, yet Falco is not my real father, he adopted me. When I question him, it sounds as if he did not want to do that, yet I have to admit he treats me the same as the others, except of course I am a boy so I have special rights. According to Falco, who is a rather dry person, my special rights as a Roman are to be bullied by my female relatives and to eat porridge, the dish of our ancestors. We never have porridge at our house so this cannot be right.

If my father had the kind of son he likes, it would be someone boisterous who makes a lot of friends, and who is pally with his father all the time. They would go fishing off the Bridge and wrestle each other around the house, damaging vases, while my mother asked them to please grow up. This is not me.

The second and third things I have found out are as follows. Number two: my mother who bore me always says that my father was Didius Favonius, the auctioneer who founded our family business. I mean the business in my adopted family. Favonius, who was also known as Geminus because he liked to cause confusion, died before I was born. He was Falco's father so this is why an obligation to take care of me was imposed on Falco. But when Falco and my other mother speak together in private, which they often do although I can find a way to listen if I want to, sometimes they allude to a man in Alexandria. He is Number three. I do not know his name because they just say 'the man in Alexandria' in hinting voices. They appear to consider he occupies a position of importance, though they also call him a zoo-keeper. That is interesting, though not something to be proud of. I do not know how I can go to Alexandria to ask him anything, so I generally pay him no attention. Being my father is a demanding honour which cannot be left to someone in Egypt whose social rank and occupation seem mysterious.

If I ever find out he really is a person of importance, I shall hasten to him in order to take up my rightful place. 'Don't do that,' says my sister Albia; 'I met him, Postumus; he is a philanderer, despite being married. Like most of the bastards.' My sister is an embittered woman, even though she denies it. But she has an unusual past so can therefore expound on many subjects in a firm tone of voice.

My other mother is Helena Justina. She nearly had a son of her own, but her baby died when he was born, so she had to have me instead, because I had been dumped on Falco to be taken care of. Helena and Falco had adopted Albia before, but that was from choice because they found her running wild in horrible Britain and she looked intriguing. Sometimes I feel that Helena does not like me as much as her daughters, but she hides it well. Most people do not take to me, I know, which was why I valued Ferret.

When my real mother came to fetch me from home, my other parents sat down for a council and gave me the choice of whether to go. Legally I belong to them, but morally Thalia has a claim on me. Falco and Helena asked very kindly if freedom to decide for myself worried me, but I set their minds at ease. I decided the experience would be one of value to someone with an enquiring mind, as I have.

My other mother sternly told Thalia that if I went with her, there were conditions. Helena Justina is good at conditions. Falco says it is her natural gift, yet he still loves her.

Helena's conditions about me are cleverly thought out, which is what she is like: first, if I ever want to return home, I must be allowed to do it straightaway. Second, Thalia is not ever to take me outside Rome. Third, I must be sent over the river to have dinner at Falco's house once a week. I suppose then they will quiz me about whether I am happy living in a tent with circus performers and animals, or do I want to be a boy in a respectable home again. Their concern is unnecessary because if I want to go back I shall just do it of my own accord, using a map I have drawn to avoid asking directions from any strangers who might be unreliable. Fourth, I can have my ferret.

The fourth condition was breached on the first day.

What I am writing down here is the conversation that I would have had with Ferret, if I could still talk to him, about my life with the entertainment company. In the time that I owned him, which was one year, seven months and three weeks, we had many exchanges in private. Talking to Ferret helped me explore my ideas about the world. I found him an excellent companion, who never made a fuss about listening to me. He did not try to put forward ideas of his own. When you talk to other people, unfortunately they are prone to joining in, as if they think you want to hear an alternative to your own theories, but their ideas are mostly inferior to mine so I don't.

You are wondering why I could not speak to him now. I regret to report, Ferret was no longer available to be my companion. A huge snake called Jason had eaten him.

My mother Thalia, who is Jason's owner, claimed I was mistaken and Ferret would turn up. I knew she was lying.

I was extremely annoyed about this. If nobody else cared about knowing what happened, which they obviously didn't, it was up to me to investigate, as my father and my eldest sister do in their work as informers. I have watched how they go about it so I know what to do. When I had proved who was to blame, I must then impose justice. Father and Albia have explained this. Murder is a capital offence. The cruel person who commits murder has to die. This is the law. Superior-quality murderers are told to commit suicide with their own swords in order to save state expense, says Falco, while inferior ones are sent to the arena lions and gobbled up. That provides public entertainment and a warm sense of well-being in criminals who have managed not to get caught, says Albia.

Being devoured as a punishment would be appropriate for the python after he ate my ferret, but I was not sure how to arrange it. I have never heard of a snake being condemned to the arena. Or even put on trial first. Of course, if my father was a god and I was a demigod, there would be no problem. Hercules strangled two snakes in his cradle, so I should be able to manage one python.

Jason behaved as if he thought himself superior quality, but I doubted whether he would commit suicide on my orders. He didn't own a sword. Thalia says he is easy to train, but only by her because he is used to her. If I wasn't a demigod, I might not manage to execute him myself, because I could see he is too strong. When Thalia does her rude dance with him, even though she is large she can barely carry his weight on her big shoulders. However, those of us who investigate guilty acts must go beyond the mere explanation of what happened, my other mother, Helena, says. We have to ensure justice on behalf of victims, to help their grieving relatives and friends. Also, there has to be social order.

So I decided Thalia was to blame because she owns this snake, and she kept him loose in her tent. If Ferret was to be properly avenged, I must apply the penalty. I would have to execute my mother.

2

The first thing you have to do when you investigate is make notes about the crime scene. This depends on being able to gain access, because the guilty parties or other annoying occupants may try to keep you out. Inspecting the scene of my ferret's death was no problem, however, because I was living there. And so I can easily describe it.

My father has told me how to write up an enquiry. I don't have a paying client to report to, but I still have to be specific, to help any poor barbarians who might read my account one day. So pay attention, hairy barbarians: the death of my ferret took place in the year of the consuls Titus Aurelius Fulvus and Marcus Asinius Atrantinus. Do not ask me who they are. Nonentities who won't annoy the Emperor, says Falco. Ones who like risk, adds Albia. It happened in the city of Rome in Italy, Europe, the World. It was August and scorchingly hot.

A famous fact is that Rome is built on seven hills, but I know there are more. I have been making a list in my geography notebook and so far I have counted twelve hills, if you include the Oppian, Janiculan, Vatican, Cispian and Velian. While Mons Testaceus is a hill too, it consists of broken potsherds so I have decided that it doesn't count. I believe the real ones are called: the Capitoline, Palatine, Aventine, Esquiline, Quirinal, Caelian and Viminal. As you can see, the hills of Rome are very badly organised. If I have identified the real Seven Hills correctly, they are all on the other side of the river from where Ferret was killed. They are in the main part of the city, where I grew up.

The river I mentioned is the famous River Tiber. It is the most important river in Italy, though it is full of brown mud and its flow is often sluggish. Don't fall in or jump in because you may catch horrible diseases. It goes right past our house (where I used to live before Thalia collected me), which is on the Marble Embankment, a favourable position where you can look out and watch ships. Before the embankment was properly built, the house flooded every year. I have never seen that happen, I am sorry to say, but our downstairs rooms all have strange patches on their plaster and in winter they smell peculiar.

From our roof, which my father has cluttered up with flowerpots, you can look over the river at the Janiculan Hill. That is one of the extra hills of Rome that have been incorrectly added in by people who are not methodical. Lying below the Janiculan ridge is the Transtiberina district where many colourful foreigners live. It is the only official district of Rome on that side of the river. I was brought up on this side in the Aventine District, which is number thirteen. Thalia had taken me across to the Transtiberina, number fourteen, which is where Ferret was going to have his fatal meeting with the python. It was the first time Ferret and I visited the Transtiberina properly because I am not allowed to cross any of the bridges on my own.

Sometimes rules like that are imposed on me by Falco or Helena, who say it is for my safety. Usually I just pretend I have forgotten them telling me, and then I do what I want anyway. The rule about the bridges had managed to be followed correctly, mainly because I had not yet examined the lifestyles and character of any foreigners, a subject I was saving up until I could study them properly. I believe there are rather a lot of them and it will take a long time to place them all in categories.

I was interested to be taken across the river now, though as we made the journey many of the people we passed stared at us, which I found unpleasant. Thalia had clearly never heard my father's rule, which he endlessly tells us, of do not draw attention to yourself. Her tiny clothes and the way she bulged out of them caused much excitement. She could never have gone on surveillance anywhere, if she suddenly spotted a villain who needed watching. The villain would notice her at once. She was in front, riding a donkey and carrying my luggage, so I lagged behind as much as possible hoping that nobody thought I was with her. Some whistled. Some called out rude words. I tried to remember the words, to add to a collection I keep.

From other occasions when Thalia had visited Rome, I had worked out why she set up camp in the Transtiberina. A lot of the people who worked for her and all of the animals were foreign, so they fitted in over there. Another reason was that the entertainments they gave to the public generally happened in that location. At the far end of the Janiculan Hill, the north end, the Emperor Nero had built a Circus, when he wanted to race in chariots with people watching and cheering his expertise. It's called the Circus of Gaius and Nero because the earlier Emperor Gaius began it, only he was killed for being a crazy madman. He sounds an interesting subject for study. Later, Nero thought it would make a good place for chariots. He was also a crazy madman so went well with Gaius. I could say *like someone else we*

27

know, but I had better not in case our Emperor kills me. He is fond of executions.

Close by is another arena that was built by the first Emperor, Augustus, who was horribly sane, a building which is called the Naumachia because it can be flooded with water in order to be used for mock naval battles. Once a year, Thalia and her people put on shows in Gaius and Nero's Circus and in the Naumachia, though not when it is full of water.

When we got there I found that the entertainers were living next to the Circus. They had created a village of tents, alongside which were cages and pens for their menagerie. I could hear barking and roaring from some distance away. The tents were all sizes and made of different materials, such as skins, felt, leather and hemp. Most had fancy swags or banners hung on them so the effect was untidy but cheerful. On average, the tents had long ridge poles and straight sides, like temples, but some were round with pointed or domed roofs, like the famous Hut of Romulus on the Palatine Hill to which I had once been taken as an educational visit. It is made of sticks and smells bad inside.

Thalia had the largest tent, a long dark red one that I saw at once was luxurious compared to the others, so this showed that she was the most important person here. I was glad that I was not expected to live in an inferior tent.

Her tent had a fine round entrance with a domed roof. When we arrived, Thalia said, 'Stay here for a mo' in the pavilion and don't touch anything.' Adding, 'I know what men are like! Juno, don't I know it . . .' I hoped she wouldn't tell me anything embarrassing about why she said that.

Left on my own, I stood in the doorway, letting my eyes grow accustomed to the dim interior. Soon I made out that

28

the inside roof of the first part was decorated in moon and stars designs. This formed a reception area. Beyond it lay one long private room, but big enough for Thalia's bed, and many piles and baskets of stuff. There were wooden supports at various places, which you had to dodge around. Thinking about it afterwards, a furious chase could happen around those tent poles if somebody was trying to rush away from a dangerous antagonist. No antagonist would come after Thalia, they would be too scared of her.

She had dumped my possessions on the ground while she went off to stable the donkey. I noticed that its welfare was more important than seeing to me, which was because Thalia is good with animals. In my experience, she is less good with boys. But she thinks she is. When she came back, I was still standing in the doorway. She gave me a suspicious glance as if she thought I probably had gone in and touched things, though of course she found no evidence. I am very good at not leaving a trail.

'Come in, don't be shy, Postumus. Nobody's going to eat you,' she said. Then 'Oh!' she exclaimed, showing that she is an alert woman. 'I ought to have said something about my snake – I suppose you met Jason?'

Yes, I had.

While I was by myself, waiting for her to come back, I heard a sudden rustling noise. There was a large pile of cluttered up garments and what looked like curtains close to the doorway. I was rather surprised when I saw that the tangled mound was moving. Out of it slid Jason. He had come to have a look at me. I looked right back, which he seemed not to be expecting.

I knew who he was. I had heard about him. My father

hates him. Falco tells us anecdotes. He has known this snake for many years from encounters with Thalia. He always says Jason looks for a reason to run up inside his tunic and bite him somewhere painful. I knew that pythons can bite; they really overpower their prey by squeezing tight until they are suffocated, but snakes do have teeth, which are sharp, to help them fasten on to their prey while they start constricting.

You probably wonder why a boy who was brought up in a nice home in Rome knows all the facts about snakes. We have a library, which contains an encyclopaedia. I am allowed to read whatever articles I like, so long as I don't drop ink or parts of my lunch on the scrolls, also if anyone else has left a slip to mark their place while they are working, I must never remove it. I don't, although sometimes for fun I add a lot of extra slips to confuse people, poked in beside articles no one would ever want to read, for example on Theological Syncretism or on the Sieve of Eratosthenes. I wish I had my own sieve, the Sieve of Postumus.

I looked up snakes. As soon as I was told that I had a mother who owned pythons and who danced with them in public, I thought I had best know what I had to deal with. So I knew what to expect from Jason when he slithered out of the garments and curtains. Sections of him kept coming until he was six feet in length. That meant he was fully grown. If he seized hold of me, I would find him powerful and hard to escape.

His markings were mainly shimmery gold, with irregular patterns of dark brown and sometimes white, as if his skin had cracked and deeper colours were leaking through. He had dark eyes, so I could tell he was not shedding his skin, which I had learned would make his eyes turn blue. His

30

head was shaped like a trowel and I looked at his mouth carefully because I had been told that a large python can eat a small boy. Only a very sensational encyclopaedia would inform you of that, but I heard it from Katutis, my father's secretary. Katutis comes from Egypt and likes to tell me amazing nonsense to see if I foolishly believe him. It is a very annoying habit. Why would a person want to be a nuisance to somebody else?

Sizing up the situation carefully, I could not see how I would fit in, even though snakes' mouths are specially hinged to enable them to eat large things. My sisters call me chubby, which would now be very useful if it protected me from Jason.

I wondered if he would let me take hold of his jaws to test how wide his mouth would open. It might be premature to try so I would observe him more, before I did any experiments. Experiments need to be thoughtfully planned. I have learned that by having them go wrong.

He reared up and swung about, taking a good look at me. His tongue was flickering. That is so they can smell you. A nervous boy might have been frightened but I decided not to let him think it. My father had always told us Jason was a bully. Father says you have to stand up to bullies because they will be very surprised. Sometimes for a joke, he adds they will be so surprised they'll hit you harder. But you will feel better in yourself, he adds comfortingly.

I folded my arms and said in a clear voice: 'My name is Marcus Didius Alexander Postumus and I have come to live here. Thalia is my birth mother so I shall have certain privileges. I expect you believe you are king of this pavilion, but all that is now changing. Don't give me any trouble or I shall be compelled to assert my authority.'

He hissed at me.

'I presume you are insecure and nervous,' I replied calmly to the presumptuous python. Falco had warned me he had a nasty attitude. 'But that's enough nonsense, Jason.' I thought about picking him up and putting him back in his pile of curtains, but I could see he was too big. If he was stretched up vertically by his pointed tail, he would be one and a half times as high as I am. His body was fat and round, indicating he would weigh a lot if anyone tried to lift him and put him away to make the tent tidier.

To subdue him I would have to use my superior status and personality. 'Behave yourself please. I am the young master and you will just have to put up with it.'

Jason immediately became cowed. He curled up in a ball as if he was trying to hide. That was when my mother came back.

'I'm glad to find you getting on so well together,' she remarked. 'If you have an old tunic you don't want to wear, we can put it near his nest so he can get used to your scent.'

I did have an old tunic in my luggage, because when Helena was packing for me she had said, 'I shall put this in, darling, so you can make a bed for Ferret where he will feel at home.' She had not said she was relieved to be getting rid of him because of him scenting his territory all around our house, although I knew she must be. Mothers are a little fussy about smells. He also jumped out at people unexpectedly while he was busy exploring.

Anyway, instead of complaining, Helena Justina stroked his fur and told me she would miss him. 'Though not as much as I shall miss you, Postumus.' This was an example of her being a kind and loving mother, which she is. I decided I should jump into her arms and hug her in case Helena was feeling miserable about me going.

Look after your mother, Father always says. Of course I am a dutiful boy. Still, it was going to be rather time-consuming, now I had two.

Thalia told me some more about Jason, who remained curled up. 'He'll soon unwind his daft self and come nosing out to see who I've brought to live here. Snakes are inquisitive and they love to explore.' I informed her that the same is true of ferrets. Mine would be popping his head out of my sleeve any moment to look around the place where I had brought him. He likes expeditions, though I have to keep hold of him in case he runs into any dark places and I can't lure him back out.

'Hmm,' answered Thalia, in the kind of voice people use when you have just asked for permission to go outside and watch two drunk men fighting one another on the embankment. I now realise she must have been thinking Ferret might pop inside Jason for a look around in him, and Jason would eagerly let him become lunch. 'Don't go upsetting my big boy, Postumus; pythons easily go right off their food if they are worried about anything. Next time someone catches a rat I can show you how I have to tempt this big softie into eating.' She had a thought. 'As for your ferret, I suggest you keep him close with you, where you can supervise what he gets up to.'

She did not say why. She must have known what was likely to happen.

3

I was allocated bedding and a pillow, which I was to stow neatly in daytime. This seemed silly, since the tent was full of clutter, but I bided my time about mentioning what I thought. We ate a meal with other people then I went to sleep in my mother's tent, with no idea it would so soon become a crime scene. If I had known, I would have made a drawing of where everything was, especially the position of the python.

Next morning, everyone got up as soon as there was any light. I was still sleepy. Thalia explained that they all had to look after the animals, a task with which I must help them now I was here. She did not ask whether I agreed. I saw what my family had always meant when they said she would want me to be useful to her. I was to be shovelling out fouled straw.

I discovered my job when I was taken to meet the menagerie keeper. Lysias was a thin man with a weird expression and long hair tied into a rat's tail on top of his head. I saw that he preferred being among the animals to enduring people. He had chosen to be an eccentric character. I respected him for that. I tried to see how he had arranged his hair, thinking I might grow mine long and do it the same, but I could tell he did not like me looking.

My mother left me at the menagerie while she went to

rehearsal with some acrobats. Lysias inspected me, sniffing the air, just as the python had done yesterday. He introduced his two assistants, Hesper and Sizon, who were busy throwing raw meat to the animals. They were low-grade, crude men, not minding if they got blood on their tunics.

'Thalia's boy,' said Lysias, meaning I was important.

'She's got a weird one there,' replied Hesper. 'He does a lot of staring.' Staring is one of the things people usually notice about me.

Sizon made no comment, only handed me his broom with a gesture that made a statement: he had done the menial tasks until today, but now he was glad it was my turn.

Lysias became extremely stern as he explained that I was never to go into any animal's pen or cage unless the others had moved out the animal to another cage for safety. None of them ever went into a cage on their own. Once a man called Fronto had been eaten by a panther when he accidentally let himself be trapped with it. Nobody who had heard him screaming or who helped gather up his bloody remains would ever forget. Not that there were many remains, declared Lysias with a cruel laugh. 'Don't mention Fronto to Thalia. It's old history but she still gets weepy. She made us keep that panther for years, out of respect, in case part of Fronto was still inside.'

I asked had she been very fond of Fronto? Hesper chortled no, only being humped by him. I worked out what that meant, so I nodded wisely. Lysias told Hesper to watch it, without specifying what needed to be watched.

The animals they had were: a wild boar (very grumpy), antelopes (who huddled together and kept trembling), a camel, two young cheetahs who had long legs and unpleasant manners, a bull, a kennelful of trained dogs and three

35

ostriches who caused a lot of trouble. 'Watch out, they peck.' The best was a half-grown lion called Roar.

They had had a giraffe until last week when it had died. I was sorry to hear that, I commented politely. Hesper sniggered that I hadn't minded eating a steak off her for dinner last night. I think he was trying to upset me but I agreed it had been tasty and there was no point being put off eating a creature I never even met, so then Hesper looked disappointed.

He and Sizon were disappointed again when they moved the wild boar out of his cage for me to clean up after him. They thought I would refuse to do anything, or that if I tried I would be useless. They were ignorant people. I just went in and got on with sweeping out the poo and stinky old bedding. I knew how to take responsibility for animals. I had Ferret, after all. I had to look after him myself; it was one of Helena's conditions for me owning him at home.

We had also once had an extremely old dog who was prone to accidents. She belonged to all of us, though mainly Father. Anyone who saw a mess on a mosaic had to run and clean it up at once, to stop Father becoming miserable because he loved that dog and could not bear her becoming so old and helpless. Uncle Lucius Petronius came to gently 'help her on her way'. I don't know how he did it, because although I wanted to watch he shut the door.

After that Father buried the dog at our other house on the Janiculan Hill, where my dead grandfather and baby brother are. He didn't give her a tombstone but he told us if he had, it would have said: *Nux, best and happiest of dogs, run with joy through all Elysium, dear friend.* We all liked to talk about her jumping up on ghosts. I wondered whether

36

they would squeak with spooky surprise if Nuxie came up behind and sniffed them with a cold nose.

After I got the boar's cage nice and clean, I asked where to put the sweepings, so Sizon led me to a barrow; I just sensibly picked up the straw on a shovel, loaded the barrow then wheeled it to the midden heap. Straw is light. It was not onerous. I cheered myself along by an incantation of 'O pigshit, pigshit, pigshit, pigshit!' which is a famous saying by my grandfather, Geminus. He must have been jolly. My marching song seemed to impress Hesper and Sizon.

The whole job was smelly and dirty. Luckily I was wearing the old tunic Helena had given me to be Ferret's bed. I had left him asleep in my best tunic instead, which would be nicer for him. He had tried running around all night, exploring, and in the morning he was so dozy he only wanted to stay behind so that is why I left him in the tent. Jason seemed to be a nocturnal creature too, and Thalia snored, so it had been quite noisy in the tent. But when I left in the morning, Jason was asleep and I forgot he might pose a danger.

At the menagerie, I decided I would make scientific notes about the different kind of droppings that the animals deposited. I explained to Hesper and Sizon how this would need to be done, tomorrow when I brought a note tablet for making descriptions and a ruler for measuring the pieces of poo. I have a surveyor's folding measure that Father once brought home from the auction house, because he thought I would like it. This was correct. I use it all the time. I could tell that Hesper and Sizon failed to see the seriousness of my planned experiment.

At lunchtime my mother came along. They tried to hand me back to her but they had no luck. Announcing that she

37

was glad we were all getting on together so nicely, Thalia went off again, saying she had to have a meeting in her tent with a man called Soterichus, a dealer in exotic animals. The meeting was private. Lysias would have to look after me that afternoon. I was given strict instructions not to go along and interrupt. 'I suppose you know what "strict instructions" means, Postumus?'

I nodded. 'Strict' ones are where it is best to wait a long while before you ignore them, so it will seem better when you pretend that because you are only a little boy, you forgot being told the instructions.

Having diligently mucked out the cages, I found myself at a loose end. This often happens to me. When I am allocated a chore, I carry it out methodically. I never waste time gossiping. What is the point of that? Brooms are not for leaning on. I never have much I want to gossip about anyway. I keep things to myself for future use.

If I can invent a better way to do a task than other people use, which I generally can because I am more scientific, I usually speed up the process, whatever it is. Soon my task is completed, and to a good standard. Then I have to find something else to do.

When Lysias inspected my work he seemed both surprised and impressed. That was what I had expected. 'Of course it all has to be done again tomorrow, young Postumus.'

'Of course it does,' I agreed calmly. 'Animals poo out their bowels every day, just as you do, Lysias. Unless you have constipation.'

'That's my business,' said Lysias, with a guarded expression.

'Or if you can't go, it isn't!' I jested merrily.

38

He just glared, but this was a good conversation with him.

To while away the rest of that afternoon while Thalia was having her meeting, I looked around the menagerie and inspected how it was run. Members of the public were being allowed in to look at the beasts. A very beautiful young woman called Pollia was taking their entrance money. She was dressed like an acrobat in a short skirt that showed her legs a lot, at least as far as her Diana the Huntress boots. I could tell she didn't really want to do that job, so I offered to take over. I like to be helpful, if I have nothing else to do.

Pollia rushed off happily. Before she went, I saw her giving Hesper a squeeze and a kiss. I made a note that Hesper must be her boyfriend or her husband. In my opinion anyone that beautiful could have done better for herself.

Although I was not yet investigating a crime, I knew that in any new circle of acquaintances you should take notes of who belongs with whom, because it may be useful to know if anyone is cheating on someone. You then don't say the wrong thing at social gatherings. That is easily done unless you concentrate hard. So I decided that once I had access to my note tablets in the tent again, I would devise a chart of people who were linked to each other. I could write down all those I met. Once I learned their names and something about them, I would draw lines between the ones I noticed were particularly friendly with each other.

While I was taking the menagerie's entrance money from the public for Pollia, I realised that the entertainers ought to charge a larger ticket price. I had several times visited the imperial vivarium at Laurentum, where a collection of wild elephants roam about the sand dunes; Laurentum is a coastal town not far from where we have our seaside holiday villa. The point is, I knew how much it costs to be admitted to see the imperial elephant herd, so I reasoned that we could ask for almost that much money. Not quite as much, because these were not the Emperor's animals. On the other hand, nobody had to travel anywhere to see them, they were conveniently here in Rome.

I didn't ask Lysias, but when I took over I just raised the ticket price myself. It wasn't written anywhere. When people arrived they were told what they had to pay. Nobody argued when I said my new cost. I told everyone they must now apply my new price. Although they looked surprised, they seemed to accept what I said.

The entertainers were lucky to have my expert knowledge. To make the increased price good value, I gave visitors a short lecture on the animals they were going to see, and I showed them around myself, making sure they learned as many useful things as possible. People ought to have an educational experience, not just stand by the cages with their eyes popping, waiting to squeal if some wild beast roared at them. That is no benefit at all.

Roar did roar. His body was half-grown but his roar was already stupendous. I liked him.

As the afternoon wore on, the public stopped coming. I was tired and growing bored. I really wanted to go to get my note tablets, to start all the new charts and lists I had invented. Also, I thought it was high time someone kept accounts for the menagerie ticket money. Thalia still never appeared again, so I wandered closer to her tent. Perhaps she had just forgotten to come and fetch me.

I had asked Lysias who Soterichus was and what my mother was discussing with him.

'He's an animal importer from North Africa. He supplied

the damned giraffe that sickened on us. Thalia will be having a go at him over that, then trying to extract a refund. We know he wants us to take a crocodile off his hands as quid pro quo. Nightmare. Can't be trained to perform and they are too bloody dangerous. She won't fall for it – at least I damn well hope she doesn't.'

As I mooched about looking at the tent, I noticed the door flaps to the round entrance part had been lowered, though the tapes down the edges were not actually tied up. I was thinking about squirming close and peeking through the flaps to see what was happening inside.

While I was planning my move, I had one of my big ideas. North Africa is where Egypt is.

I went back to the menagerie and asked Lysias what part of North Africa the beast supplier had come from.

'Alexandria, I suppose. They all do.'

So that was when I solved the mystery. Soterichus must be 'the man in Alexandria' that Falco and Helena Justina spoke about. I knew then why I was forbidden from inter- rupting. Thalia wanted to stop me meeting him. The man who was in her tent with her must be my real father.

4

I assumed Thalia and Soterichus must be doing 'what men and women do' which is what my sisters say to keep it a secret from me. I think I know what it is, though I have never seen it happening. Julia and Favonia explained that this is how people make babies, so I wondered if my mother would have another one. Since I had three sisters already, two of them very annoying, I didn't need more and even though silly people sometimes suggest I must want a little brother, they are wrong.

I decided to go in and put a stop to this.

I strolled up to the tent humming, so it would seem as if I was breaking the strict instructions by accident, while very busy thinking about other things. When I went inside, I saw that what men and women do is to sit on cushions with a low table in front of them, containing little drinks cups for visitors, like the silver ones Father has for dealers at his antiques warehouse when he is trying to make them pay too much for items. There was also a large bag of money and tablets of lists. I had not known that making a baby is a financial transaction, though I suppose it makes sense. Father is always saying that bringing up his children costs him a lot of money.

I might ask my mother how much she paid Soterichus for me. She seemed too busy at the moment to ask. She wasn't taking much notice of me coming into the tent because she had Jason coiled around her and he was fidgeting.

I was disappointed in Soterichus. He was an unhappy-looking man with a big belly and a red face. Although his beard was stubbly, otherwise he had very little hair, with what remained being crinkled and greyish. He was dressed in a long brown tunic, with deep, brightly coloured braid on the hem. He wore battered old sandals through which big ugly toes were visible, with thick snagged nails, and he had several bangles on his hairy arms. All his skin was the colour of burnt wood and he smelt like the menagerie.

Thalia didn't seem too bothered by me appearing in the tent. She was still trying to organise Jason more suitably around her. 'This is my lad. Say hello nicely to Soterichus.'

'Hello,' I said, not nicely because I was so displeased to learn I had been fathered by a glum man in horrible sandals. 'My name is Marcus Didius Alexander Postumus. Postumus is supposed to mean I was born after my father had died.' That was if my father was my grandfather Favonius.

I was watching Soterichus closely, but he made no reaction to being told he was dead (if it was him). He just gave me a nod, as if a no-account person had been introduced to him, then he seemed to be waiting to return to his transactions with Thalia. She looked put out; she was concentrating on the python. You would think if he was arranging to have another baby Soterichus would want to inspect me, to see how well the first one had turned out. Or perhaps he could instantly tell from my impressive demeanour.

I decided to bide my time before letting them know I knew he was my father.

'Do you want to fetch your ferret, darling?' asked Thalia,

43

in a kindly voice. By this she was indicating to Soterichus that she was a good mother. It was the first time she ever said 'darling' to me, though Helena does. Falco calls me Scruff although I am not scruffy at all, but a neat person unless I have happened to get dirty. He says his nickname is ironic.

I nodded and started looking around the tent; then came the horrible moment when I began to realise Ferret was not there. Thalia and Soterichus continued their meeting. It involved a tense conversation about the giraffe. They were pretending it was all trading banter, but I could tell they were just saying routine things, not meaning anything real. He claimed he would persuade her to have the crocodile eventually, because he knew she wanted it really. She said he was smooching as usual but he could forget it. Crocs were lethal. She did not have the staff or the facilities. He said yes but the public adored them. She called him a rude word.

I had not heard that word before; it was obviously very bad. I would have to write it down.

While Soterichus was spluttering in surprise, I said loudly, 'My ferret's gone!'

'Cough up, Soterichus,' Thalia ordered him. 'The giraffe was piss poorly from the off and you bloody well know it. You pulled a fast one when you passed him off, more fool me for believing you . . . Postumus, dearie, I shall help you to look. He can't have gone far. He must have burrowed in somewhere.'

She jumped up, pretending to help me, though I could tell it was only to show she would definitely have no more to do with Soterichus' offer of the crocodile. She still believed nothing had happened to Ferret.

As Jason slid off her when she leapt to her feet, I felt a terrible premonition creeping over me, like when you have accidentally stood in a very cold pond. I looked at the python. He smirked back at me. He was the kind of guilty criminal who stands there and dares you to accuse him, saying ha, ha, you can't prove anything, while he's laughing.

I said, in a quiet voice, 'I wonder if Jason has eaten my ferret.'

'No, Postumus darling, of course he hasn't. Jason had a rat two days ago, he won't be hungry again yet.'

'He has eaten Ferret! I know he has.'

'Don't get yourself worked up.'

I wanted to scream and create like a very little boy, but I was twelve, or more likely eleven as Helena would say, so I knew better. I wanted to cry big tears, because I had lost my friend Ferret and also I was afraid he must have had a frightening experience when the snake attacked him. I hated to think of him in that predicament. He must have been horribly surprised. I always looked after him as nicely as I could, so he was not used to anything bad happening. I hated to think of him slowly going down inside the python, at first perhaps still alive. I wondered what that must have felt like.

I wished we had never come here. I wanted to go home. Sometimes I imagined that if I could just run home, I might find Ferret sitting up on his normal bed there and it could be as if none of this had happened to us. But I knew that was no good.

I went back to searching, madly throwing things aside while I looked everywhere again.

Thalia went out to Soterichus in the round part of the tent. I heard her say in a low tone, 'You had better go. I

45

need to see to him. His pet is lost and you can see his poor little heart is broken.'

I did not say goodbye or watch Soterichus leave. Even if he was my father I had no interest in him now.

Thalia helped me hunt for Ferret. She was very methodical. She said she had had to hunt for lost creatures before. I bet she meant Jason. Our searching made him agitated, so Thalia wound him up and fastened him in a huge basket. She didn't think I noticed, but as she fed his coils into it, she ran her hands over his body, which I guessed was to check if she could feel Ferret inside him. After she tied down the lid of the basket, we could hear Jason thumping about and trying to break the container so he could escape and cause havoc.

I had once thought a python would be an interesting pet to have, but now I just hated Jason. He was a killer. I hid my feelings, which I am very good at, but I was already deciding I would prove what had happened to Ferret. If I could find any bits of him, I would hold a proper funeral. And then I would make those responsible pay for his death.

5

Thalia kept refusing to admit that Jason must have killed Ferret. We searched the whole tent and even went to those next door, asking if anyone had seen him. Nobody had.

I didn't want any dinner. I went to bed. I was pretending not to mind as much as I did. Thalia tried to soften me up but I stayed quiet and private. My father and sister say you should never consent to be drawn in by people you need to investigate. Trust nobody. People are all devious. Suspect them all. So I played the brave boy and agreed whatever was said to me. However, I was not talking. I kept my thoughts to myself.

In the morning Thalia sat down with me saying, as if she cared, that we would keep searching when we had time. I was not to worry about it. He was bound to turn up again.

She knew nothing. Well, she wouldn't admit it. Classic, as Falco would say. She would be found out. I would do it.

At least now Ferret was officially designated a missing person, so I was allowed to write up posters in order to describe him and to seek information.

LOST: Sable ferret, guard hairs dark, mask white, tail dark, paws dark, eyes black, nose pink, expression sweet, character lively, answers to Ferret. Useful info to MDA Postumus care of Thalia, finder's fee. No timewasters, please.

Thalia had offered to pay a small reward for anything that led to his return. That was easy for her to say. She knew she would never have to cough up.

I wanted to go to the vigiles and make a report, but Thalia would not let me. In the Transtiberina I didn't know where the cohort lived so I couldn't just go by myself. She claimed they had better things to do, saving peoples' lives in fires, letting burglars run away and harassing innocent performers about their entertainment licenses.

When someone goes missing you have to consider whether they have recently been anxious over anything. I supposed Ferret might be worried that he had come to a strange new place. I didn't think so, because I was here with him. In the past he had visited the coast with me and came along if anybody ever took me on an outing. Albia took me with her to Nemi to bring me out of myself, though it didn't. It never bothered Ferret. He just wriggled inside my tunic during the journey and became madly excited when he could explore a new place.

Lysias said if Ferret was a dog or some other kind of animal he might run off and try to find his own way back to what he thought was his real home. I should send a message to Falco and Helena in case he turned up. I didn't know who would carry a message for me, but if Ferret appeared at our house on the Aventine, they would know I needed to hear he was safe and to have him back immediately. My parents have thoughtful natures. But I couldn't see how he would travel through the streets to their house without some other boy deciding to grab him to have as a pet of his own.

Hermes and Sizon asked if Ferret had a girlfriend he might have eloped with. They were giggling about their suggestion, trying to annoy me. 'Has he run off to have a fling, or is he unlucky in love and has gone into hiding to get drunk and mope? Ooh, you don't think he could be suicidal, do you, Postumus?' I ignored them.

On my own I thought about that. The menagerie had plenty of animals but no female ferrets he could have fallen for. Anyway, he was loyal to me. Or, as Helena Justina would announce to nobody in particular in her special voice, as a male, he knew when he was well off.

The next question was, did he have any enemies? Only Jason. Normally, when they belong to a responsible boy, captive ferrets have nothing to be afraid of.

I could not remember who told me this but I knew in the wild ferrets are attacked by large birds of prey, badgers and foxes. If he had gone into the lion's cage to look at Thalia's half-grown lion, Roar, that might have had fatal consequences but nobody I spoke to had seen him heading towards the menagerie, let alone Roar's cage. In any case, I had been at the menagerie myself all that morning and much of the afternoon, so he would have seen me there and come joyfully to jump down my tunic-top as usual. He could have poked his head out and looked at the lion from there.

I could find no witnesses to anything that happened in the tent. Unless somebody went in secretly, only Thalia and Soterichus had been there after I left Ferret behind that morning. Thalia vouched for Jason being on good behaviour all the time she was there with Soterichus.

49

She didn't go back until the afternoon. Her python must have done the dirty deed by that time. When she arrived with the animal trader, Jason smarmed up to her looking all innocent. That was good enough for Thalia. She would never hear a word against him. She never gave a thought to my pet.

It was deadlock.

Well, I usually win situations like that.

Today I had to go and clean up after the animals again, though only the most dirty cages. The entertainers loved their beasts, or at least took care of them because they were valuable, but did not muck them out every single day or it would cost too much in new bedding. About mid-morning I had finished, so the head keeper, Lysias, said I should go to the Circus and see the rehearsals which might cheer me up. He couldn't bear me hanging around all moody. Frankly, I myself had had enough of him complaining about my attitude. When people suffer a bereavement, others should show them consideration.

Hermes took me along to the Circus, though the building was large and right beside the tents so I was hardly going to get lost. I asked if he had come with me because he was hoping to get another kiss from the beautiful young woman called Pollia, like yesterday. Hermes jumped at that. He looked at me sideways and said no fear, because Pollia was married to one of the acrobats. They would be practising together and only a fool would touch her.

I must have seemed surprised. Hermes warned me to keep mum. I said that would be a lot easier if I had a fig pastry to take my mind off the secret. I had noticed a sweetmeat seller with a tray, right outside the entrance gate.

Hermes congratulated me on not being as dumb as I looked, then he bought me a cake.

Some things are just too easy.

The Circus of Gaius and Nero lies along a large road called the Via Cornelia. It is a very pleasant situation in the Gardens of Agrippina, who was Nero's mother. Helena Justina says bringing up Nero was nothing to be proud of; she tried hard to do much better with me. I consider I have brought myself up, but to save offending Helena I don't say so. I am generally a credit to my upbringing. Sometimes I accidentally do something bad, but if I am careful she doesn't find out.

Agrippina owned the land between the River Tiber and the Vatican Hill, where this Circus had been built. Like the Circus Maximus near my own home, it is a long, enclosed monument for racing chariots, with ranks of seating balanced on many fine arches. It has a solid barrier running up the centre, called the spina. The chariots dash up one side as fast as they can, career around the turning point at the end, and zonk down the other side. Each time they complete a circuit, a marker is removed to signify how many laps. Most races are seven laps. Removing markers helps drivers to pace themselves and to know when they have finished, assuming they avoid crashing. Of course everyone hopes chariots will come to grief, with huge splinters and wheels flying all over the place and someone screaming horribly as they die.

In the middle of the spina at this Circus I saw a huge obelisk. Hermes informed me it had been brought to Rome from Heliopolis in Egypt. It was of a red colour, covered with signs that are called hieroglyphics, with a big metal ball on top. Falco's secretary Katutis was trained at a temple in Egypt, the land of his birth, so he can read hieroglyphics. I was sorry he wasn't here to tell me what these said. I might try to draw them and ask him later, though there were rather a lot. Now I was investigating the death of Ferret, I might not have time.

On one side of the track, Thalia and her people were doing various kinds of acrobatics. She was trying to train the half-grown lion to walk along two ropes from the top of the spina to a special stand where someone stood offering him food. Roar didn't want to do the trick so he just stayed still, with one big furry paw on each rope, while she called to him. She saw us and gave up, grumbling as she arrived, 'I must have spent half my life trying to get one beast or another to perform this trick. I had an elephant who refused to do it for years and now here's Roary playing me up the same. He will do it, sir. He will be ready by September.'

Then I saw she wasn't saying this to me, but a man who had been waiting quietly. He was Sir. He wore a heavy toga over a white tunic with purple stripes to show he was very important. Thalia had to be polite him. And she was hardly ever polite to people.

Hermes ignored the important person; he insisted on interrupting, telling Thalia how he had brought me along to be cheered up. As soon as the important man heard me mentioned, he started across to where I was standing on the track (because we had come in through the main gate at ground level). When I recognised him, I immediately said hello nicely, without being told to. Thalia rushed up too, muttering to me not to bother a magistrate.

He said, smiling, that it was all right. 'Postumus and I are old friends.' It was Manlius Faustus, the aedile I had seen a few times with my eldest sister, Flavia Albia. She is an informer and knows all types of people, even disreputable ones.

Thalia looked amazed, then seized on the connection eagerly. She said I should sit with my friend Faustus while the company performed for him, because he was reviewing their acts as one of his official duties, seeing if any were good enough for the Roman Games next month. 'You can help him decide to have us!' she said to me, winking heavily.

Albia had told me this Faustus was a man who never said much, but when he walked into a room, he had better find you doing something he approved of. I knew for myself that he had a strict attitude. He once told me off, for being out in the streets on my own at night, because I needed to observe the proceedings of the Festival of Ceres on the Aventine. Albia said he meant it for my protection, then she told me off too.

Last month he saved my sister's life when she was very ill, so all her family had to be grateful to him. I was prepared to take the lead and schmooze him, as my father calls it. I was the family representative.

Faustus and I walked up steps and found ourselves seats from which to watch the acts. While we waited for them to start, he said in a friendly tone, 'I am glad to see you, Postumus. I need to ask you a favour, if you don't mind.'

I replied, ask away then.

'Flavia Albia is bringing me to dinner at your house. Your parents have invited me, to meet everyone.'

I was surprised because Albia didn't want us all to inspect Faustus and ask him nosy questions. Albia thought Father would stomp about complaining about her new boyfriend, which he usually did, so when Father dropped hints about how it was high time he met this Faustus, she just looked as if she was very busy thinking about something else and she did not answer him. She was good at that. I had studied how she did it, so I could follow her method.

'Naturally I am apprehensive,' said Faustus. 'Since you and I already know one another, I hope you will be there to give me kind support.'

I promised I would, adding that we were all intrigued, since we had thought my sister would never find anybody to suit her because of her difficult standards. 'There are bets that you will run away when you find out what she's really like. My other sisters are saying, "Albia is such a terror; even if he is wonderful, she will soon throw him out".'

Manlius Faustus winced. 'Is it inevitable?'

'No, we think she likes you.'

'Really?'

'Don't worry, we have ordered her to be nice to you. By the way, on behalf of our family, Manlius Faustus, thank you very much for rescuing Albia when she was having the squits and dying on the floor.' My mother, Helena Justina, thought somebody ought to say this and get it done soon, or he would think we had no manners. And Helena said it wasn't enough for Father to take him for a drink, to which Father replied obediently, all right it could be a drink with three kinds of olives in nicknackeroony bowls.

'Your mother wrote to me very touchingly,' Faustus told me.

That was when I felt I should explain to him my state of having two mothers, one of whom was Thalia. She was at that moment winding Jason around her body and preparing to show off her famous snake dance, which Falco called an eye-watering cultural experience. I believe Faustus had already heard all about my situation, probably from

54

Albia, because he wanted to discuss whether I was happy here with the entertainers. Albia must have told him to check up.

He confided to me that he had lost his own mother when he was young and had missed her badly ever since. So I was lucky to have two. Then he said, I should probably view Helena Justina more favourably. Not only had she brought me up from a baby, but she was the best choice for a boy who might go far in life. Helena was a senator's daughter which could be an advantage.

I agreed with that, but said I had thought coming here would be a useful experience. Fair enough, replied Faustus. Enjoy it for the time being. He seemed a reasonable man, for a friend of Albia's.

I explained about having to go home once a week for dinner, so we could make it the same day as he had to go; he said that would work neatly. 'There is something else I could ask you to do, Postumus, if you were interested.' I said again to ask away. 'I may be organising a wedding soon.'

'Is that another job an aedile has to do, sir?'

'No, this would be a family occasion. If it happens, I shall need a sensible boy to be the chief torch bearer, in the procession afterwards. It is quite a responsibility,' said Faustus, looking sideways at me. 'Apart from the religious aspects, the other boys who hold the torches – you know it's obligatory to have the groom's snivelly little nephews and the bride's horrible cousins – they all have to be supervised carefully, in case they set fire to anything.'

I liked the sound of that. I mean supervising horrible little cousins. I don't mean setting fire to stuff. If you burn someone's house down, they can sue you for compensation. This had been explained to me. Several times, actually.

'So it will be the real works with all the nuts, including relatives?' I had heard Helena Justina describe weddings in that way.

'Yes. A big public show.'

So lots of people would see me with the torch. Excellent!

Then we ended our chat, because Manlius Faustus had to evaluate the acts that Thalia was announcing. I wanted to take a good look at the performers, just in case one of these had gone to Thalia's tent yesterday and seen something, or even stolen my ferret. This rehearsal turned out to be a good chance for me not only to be on good terms with my sister's important new friend, supposing he managed to last with her, but also to size up suspects.

6

Even though they had known that the aedile was coming to watch them, the performers took a long time to sort themselves out. While we waited, Faustus said the demonstration was for the Roman Games, which take two weeks in September. They are the oldest, most famous Games in the calendar and this year it was his task to organise them. Of course he needed to do that well, to obtain a fine reputation afterwards. I thought it might be good to be an aedile myself one day, as I am sure I could organise people, though I might find it all a worry.

When Faustus reminded me what happens, I remembered going to the Ludi Romani with my parents on past occasions. There is a good procession of chariots, which then do races, and horsemen, and also drama. Thalia wanted to be in the theatrical events. She now showed Faustus her snake dance. I had never seen anything like it. From his face, neither had he. Thalia and Jason swayed together while the python wound himself around her in curious ways, though he was so heavy she could hardly support him slithering. I wondered how she had thought up this dance? And however she trained Jason to take part? asked Faustus, sharing my amazement.

Flutes were played at the same time. Other musicians then played tibias, drums and lyres to which acrobats tumbled, walked tightropes while twirling batons and para-sols, and juggled with a large variety of things. First a few people at a time, then slowly everyone joined in.

Manlius Faustus sat still, watching. He showed no sign of whether he liked anything, just sometimes wrote notes on a waxed tablet. All the performers were watching him to see what he thought, but nobody could tell. His slave Dromo had brought along a whole bag of tablets for him; when I asked to borrow one, Faustus gave me one at once, making sure it was nice and waxy, and also a stylus like his own. I tried to see what he was writing but he used short-hand symbols that I didn't know.

I wanted to make a list of all the performers but there were too many. They moved around so much I lost track of them, which was annoying. Sorting out my suspects would be hard.

I saw Pollia being thrown in the air and caught by two men, so one must be her husband, but which? They were called Laurus and Pedo. Pollia could stand on her hands and bend entirely backwards until she grabbed her own ankles. Then they picked her up and threw her between them again, while she remained in the form of a joined hoop. And they rolled her along.

Another very beautiful young lady called Silvia came skipping up to them, doing a cartwheel as she arrived, then she and Pollia were both tossed to and fro for a time, before they climbed onto the men, with a small woman called Sassia bounding up to jump on top as well until they made a pyramid of bodies. Then someone flipped some coloured balls up to Sassia, which she juggled, only dropping one; a golden crown was thrown up to her too, which she caught right on her head.

They all jumped down. They landed lightly, pointing their feet elegantly. This time, Faustus applauded, so I did too, assuming it was etiquette. I saw Thalia mutter something to Sassia, after which she came to us and put the crown on the aedile's head with a fancy gesture. He allowed her to do it, though I thought it was really not correct to involve him like that. He politely wore the crown during the next act, then took it off again and placed it on the free seat on his other side from me.

We watched more performances. I had lost track of the people's names. While we sat, I found myself thinking about Ferret. That saddened me. I wished I had him down my tunic now. He would have enjoyed looking out at the performances, twitching his whiskers. I could have talked to him about it.

When there was a pause while equipment was wheeled in for a balancing act, Faustus asked me quietly why I was feeling unhappy. He may have thought it was being with Thalia instead of at home. I hoped he would not tell my parents since I had no wish to cause trouble in their minds. So that he would understand, I decided to tell him what had happened to Ferret. He listened in the same way he had watched the acts, still not speaking. He seemed a thoughtful person. This is very unusual.

The next time we were waiting for something to happen, I asked whether, being a magistrate, Faustus could help me investigate. He replied rather regretfully that his remit didn't really cover that, because apart from organising public festivals it was more about patrolling markets and bath houses. Rome has a lot of those. Some are disreputable. And brothels, I suggested, since I had heard my two younger sisters giggling over it when they were discussing our Albia's new friend.

59

'Unfortunately, yes; brothels,' agreed Faustus in a solemn tone. Clearly he was a man of duty. I knew these were rare so I was pleased to have met one.

The next thing that happened was that a new group of people arrived. Thalia loudly greeted them. They were actors. Their leader was called Davos. Thalia had only announced the names of the other performers when it was their turn, but she brought Davos right over and introduced him. His troupe was here to show Faustus their acting in the hope he would accept them for a play at the Roman Games.

'I've known this fellow for years,' Thalia said in a glowing voice. 'You will find him the best – and I'm not just saying that because he happens to be my husband!'

That made me jump. Davos was a solid man with straight grey hair. If he and Thalia were married, surely that made him my father? Another? This was rather complicated. I took a good look at him, finding him preferable to the animal-seller, Soterichus. But when he noticed me staring he gave me a strange look, not friendly.

In other respects, Davos seemed at ease. He tossed the golden crown at someone standing on the track, then sat himself down right alongside Faustus. He began explaining their play, a comedy which he said he had just dug out of their chest of scrolls in honour of my father, Falco that is, who once wrote it. He writes things but we try to avoid having them read out to us because we think they are terrible.

Faustus said that he was a new friend of Falco's daughter, Flavia Albia, so he (Faustus) hoped he (Falco) would be pleased if his play was accepted for performance. 'I'm being judged – don't get me into trouble here!'

'He's a mad bugger,' answered Davos, as if this was a compliment. 'Don't worry. He'll be thrilled we haven't dumped his piece of nonsense on a midden-heap.' That sounded as if disposing of the play might have been a possibility.

'Make your pitch then.' I noticed Faustus gave such orders in an easy way; he was comfortable with his importance and people seemed to take it well. I would like to be like that. He listened patiently while Davos confessed that the scrolls had become rather jumbled up since the last performance; in fact, he said with a chortle, to be honest *The Spook Who Spoke* (which was the play's strange title) had always seemed jumbled even in performance. Mind you, that was in the Palmyra desert, which explained a lot. The night had ended in a riot, though he assured Faustus that had nothing to do with Falco's play's noble lines or vibrant theatricality. If Faustus liked the sound of it, the actors could unscramble the scrolls in a twinkle. Something could be made of it.

I wondered if we would see a riot here in Rome?

Davos began describing the play. He had a deep, powerful voice that was lovely to listen to, even though his conversation was crude. 'You get the usual comedy banalities. Innocent, slightly dim adolescent is passionately in love with a gorgeous girl in a brothel –' I glanced at Faustus who smiled at me. 'I can't remember offhand whether loverboy's dad is a soft touch or a scheming miser, but he's lost at sea, until he turns up alive and well. The mother's a harridan in a fright wig. Always gets laughs. A ghost pops up to put the mockers on everything, everyone pairs off and we have a sing-song with a folk dance to send the audience home in good spirits.'

61

'Any extras?' asked Faustus. He seemed to know what to ask. I wondered how you learn to be an aedile. Perhaps there was an instruction book.

'As many as you can take. A young woman – well, she's got five children and isn't as young as she looks – plays the water organ. That usually follows on its own, because getting the organ on stage is a palaver. If Thalia's still got her donkey who does tricks, we'll write him in for extra light relief.'

'The crowd generally likes "business"?'

'Absolutely – if Ned's dead, the lads can mess about with a rope. We once tried to use Jason as the rope – you know, he starts stiff, the rope wrestlers don't notice what they've picked up, suddenly they get a big surprise that it's a live snake, so they run off screaming while the audience hysterically wets itself – sadly, the scaly bugger was too unpredictable on stage.'

'Hmm,' commented Faustus, who now knew from me that Jason was a murderer of ferrets. 'Is this python dangerous? I have a remit to deal with marauding wild animals.'

'Oh Thalia has him under control. She loves the thing. Owned him for years without incident.' Davos continued talking about the acts, in ignorance that the question was asked for my investigation. 'Originally old Falco wrote in a pair of stand-up clowns who commented –'

'Clever cook and boasting soldier?' asked Faustus, raising an eyebrow. He looked tired.

'Got it in two! You may be glad to hear we have Congrio, who is all the rage. Very big star. I'm lucky to employ him. You must have heard of Congrio.'

'A barber, a fisherman and an intellectual went into a bar . . .?' suggested Faustus.

Davos winced. 'Hilarious, trust me. It's the way he tells them.'

'Hmm,' said Faustus again, making a short note on his tablet.

'Would you like to hear him do his set about the man from Kyme?'

'Too Greek. Make it a place that people in Rome may have heard of, Davos.'

Davos waved up the comedian who was a thin ugly person with bandy legs, very sure of himself. After a huddled discussion, Congrio announced grumpily, 'Ditch Kyme then. For you, legate, it shall be the man from Ostia.'

'Thanks,' answered Faustus instantly. 'I come from there.'

'Shit!' muttered Davos. 'Quick! Think up another town, Congrio, for god's sake! Any damned town, so long as it's not famous for libel lawyers . . .'

'Ostia is fine,' Faustus soothed him. 'I was having you on. I grew up at Fidenae.'

'Too many comedians here!' Davos commented, pretending to be hard done by. I could see that insulting a magistrate didn't really bother him. This was like Falco, so if Davos was my real father, I would know what to expect.

Davos saw me looking at him again, so gave me another suspicious frown. Faustus saw that. 'Davos, this is Marcus Didius Falco's adopted son.'

Davos groaned. 'Oh, you're Thalia's unexpected little bundle, are you!'

He didn't seem pleased. I told him in a stiff voice, 'I am Marcus Didius Alexander Postumus.'

'Very nice!' Davos didn't sound as if he believed that. He wasn't interested in me either, and went off to organise a rehearsal of *The Spook Who Spoke* for the aedile.

I took the chance to ask Faustus an important question. If Davos and Thalia were married, did that mean Davos was my father? Faustus replied, not necessarily. Then he assumed a kindly expression, adding that Flavia Albia was bound to say, he was almost certainly not. My sister Albia is famous for her wise experience of life.

'You mean, Albia will ask, was any handsome wine-seller passing by, ten months before my birth?'

'That would be like her.'

'I don't know. I wasn't here.'

'And that,' said Faustus, 'sounds like the punchline of a joke about the man from Kyme.'

I said I hoped then that the man from Ostia would be funnier. He laughed easily.

The actors performed a scene, which I found dull. It had a lot of talking and nothing happened. Afterwards Faustus took me down to Thalia and Davos on the race track. He gave orders that the full script of the play they intended to perform must be sent to him tomorrow at the aediles' office so he could try to get to grips with it. Then they would not be allowed to vary a word after he approved it. He said he liked the acrobats, but he had to view several companies, so would only confirm whether Thalia's were chosen for the Games once he had seen the others.

He gave some money to his slave Dromo, a sneery, spotty young man, who I could see was jealous of me being on such friendly terms with his master. Faustus told Dromo to run to the sweetmeat-seller and buy me a cake.

'Can I have one?' demanded Dromo; he was like the cheeky slave in Falco's play.

'All right. Just one; no more, Dromo.'

I think Faustus intended me to go along with Dromo on the cake errand but I stayed behind. I didn't like the look of Dromo and I was hoping to hear what his master said to Thalia if it was about me. It was. The magistrate stood with one hand on my shoulder like an uncle. He suggested that Thalia should consider how I was a boy with potential, but if at some point in the future it ever became known I had worked with entertainers that would be a certain career impediment. She knew the legal situation.

Thalia gave him a nasty look but said quietly she would bear it in mind. Dromo came back and gave me a cake he had bought with the aedile's money. He tried to pass me the smallest, but I pointed out that I had seen what he was doing so he had better swap them over.

After they left, Thalia changed her attitude. She told me in private that maybe Faustus was right. If I wanted to be a big rissole one day, I had best stop mucking out the menagerie animals. I asked what kind of rissole I could be. Thalia said, sounding less cross than before, that since Didius Falco was an equestrian and Helena Justina's family were senators, the menu was mine to choose. As a Roman, I could be any kind of exotic rissole I wanted, with whatever fancy gravy I liked on it and a side dish of radishes. And I was not to worry because Falco knew what he owed me so he would pay for it. With fish pickle on the radishes.

From what I knew of Falco, that seemed a rash claim. He often said to his children that we shouldn't raise our hopes because he intended to spend everything and only leave us his good wishes and a pair of old boots.

Thalia did not know about me taking visitors' money for the menagerie. I decided not to mention that, because I was halving the new increase in the ticket price with her, in case I needed any petty cash for my enquiries into Ferret's disappearance.

7

I felt that my enquiries were bogged down. People in my family say this happens. You have to go home and rave about, groaning like an ogre, while everyone keeps out of your way. If you start throwing your boots at the walls too noisily, Helena comes in and settles you. She says, calm down, darling, you don't frighten me but you are scaring your poor innocent children. Tell me what the matter is, please. Nothing is the bloody matter. I know, just tell me about it, sweetheart. You growl that the case is impossible, you wish you never took it on, why don't you ever learn, you are going to sack the client and bugger it.

I see, says Helena.

Next day you get up, have a bright idea, and solve your case.

You can't get bogged down on the first day, that's too soon to lose heart. You have to do spadework first. Spadework or legwork. I couldn't do legwork because I wasn't allowed to walk off on my own, I was supposed to stay in the tented area or at the Circus track. So I did more spadework.

After the aedile left, the acrobats milled around. They were stretching, balancing and practising sleights of hand, juggling and manipulating. The kennelful of trained little dogs were running around pulling miniature chariots. Faustus had not witnessed this, which was a good thing because only half of the doggies did it, while the others broke out of their reins and scampered about, yapping naughtily.

I announced loudly that I would not tell my sister's boyfriend, the aedile Faustus, that the company's performing dogs were hopeless, so long as someone helped me find out what happened to my ferret yesterday. They all pulled faces, as if they were impressed.

You have to identify where everybody was when the crime happened. So I walked around asking each person whether they had been in Thalia's tent yesterday morning, or if not, where? I made a list on my tablet, the one Faustus gave me (he had told me I could keep it unless he ran out of them). There were two columns, one column for people who admitted they had been in the tent and one for those who hadn't, but when I finished asking, all the people were listed in the same column, saying they had not been there. This was no use. But at least I had now learned their names.

They all knew me too, so if anyone remembered anything helpful, they could come and find me easily.

I then made a third column for anyone I believed had lied to me. This was one: the tiny woman called Sassia. She had a face like a monkey and I could see all her bones. The reason I thought she was lying was that she was now wearing a green costume with fringes on it which I knew I had seen in the pile of clothes in the tent. It was a crucial clue.

On the other hand, it would be very dangerous for Sassia to go into that tent because if Jason thought she was a little monkey, he might make her his prey. But if she had badly wanted to fetch her costume, she might have shown him Ferret as a distraction from her.

I could not really remember when I saw the green costume. Was it before Ferret disappeared, or afterwards?

68

Luckily it wasn't my job to remember things, because I was not a witness. I was the enquiry agent. We don't come under suspicion. We are in command.

If Sassia collected the costume this morning, she would be in the clear for the crime, which happened yesterday. I didn't ask her that question. I was biding my time. I could make it a dramatic moment in my revelation of the suspect's guilt.

You have to do that in public, gathering together all the interested parties so you can discount them or discredit them. Don't forget that someone may own up who hasn't really done it, because they are protecting someone else. There is generally someone with a long-lost lovechild they have not dared to name, or another person has been blackmailing someone to force them to keep quiet about a terrible thing that happened twenty years ago. This is life. Especially when it's death. Especially murder, because nobody would kill another person just because they lost their temper, would they?

The acrobats were rather strange. When I was asking questions and working out who they all belonged with, Pollia was sitting across the lap of the one called Laurus; she looked extremely comfortable there so I asked if he was her husband. I knew it was wise to check. I carefully didn't mention that I had seen her kissing Hesper yesterday. On no, said Pollia with a silly laugh, her husband was Pedo. I couldn't understand it because Pedo at that moment was snuggling up to the other woman, Silvia. They were murmuring to one another and giggling the way people do when they are being all lovey. I didn't know how to show all this on my chart of which people were linked to each other. These acrobats did not even try to make my job easy.

After I had made a whole lot of notes, I noticed the scene-shifters were bringing in the water organ that Davos had mentioned. I had only seen one from far away before, so I walked up to watch.

'Oi, oi,' said a young man called Theopompus as they were setting it up. 'Here comes the supervisor! Watch your backs.'

I gave him a sickly smile, saying I hoped they knew how to do this without me helping.

A nicer one called Epagatus stood aside with me and discussed how they put the organ together. That left Theopompus with all the heavy lifting, which did not please him.

I knew something about this because in our library at home, I mean Falco's house, we had a scroll with drawings of inventions. It included a hydraulus, which is the official name of a water organ. There is an octagonal base with the pipes on top, twenty four (I counted) in decreasing sizes. The big fat longest pipe was twice as tall as me, so it was a very imposing structure. The force of the water descending somehow makes air rise up from a chamber into the pipes which creates sound. A double keyboard is used to choose which pipe, and so which sound comes out. Epagatus tried to explain the works, but I could not follow. He was not a good explainer.

I wasn't going to hear the hydraulus playing because Sophrona, the musician, had to look after all her brood instead that morning. Epagatus said that as well as five children she had a useless husband she couldn't get rid of and also a lover, Ribes, the orchestra conductor, whom Epagatus called as dim as muck, and who was in fact the father of all her children. Theopompus called out scathingly, not too dim to have it away whenever he wanted, then let another idiot have the expense and trouble of his brats. Sophrona specialised in twerps. You wouldn't think she was also capable of playing sublime music.

'Does Sophrona's useless husband know he's being made a fool of?' I asked.

'Oh, no. He's extremely short-sighted, is Khaleed. Nobody knows the number of times he's glimpsed Ribes making a fast getaway from their tent with his tunic still halfway up his arse, and not realised it was him, let alone what he must have been up to!'

I was cross because that was another very complicated link to draw in my chart.

As the organ wasn't playing, I wandered off to where a properties controller from the theatre company was sorting out equipment. Large baskets had been delivered, which he was emptying out and exploring. He had a fake baby wrapped in a moth-eaten shawl, enormous rattly cooking pots, a shaggy coil of rope, bags of wooden money and a very old home-made snake with spangly eyes. He waggled the snake wildly, hoping I would scream though I didn't. Sand fell out of it.

They had some cracked leather armour for the boasting soldier to wear and a couple of wooden swords that any suitable character could use. I picked up one, struck a few attitudes and tried the edge. It didn't feel sharp. 'Would you be able to kill a person with this?' I was thinking about my task of bringing retribution on whoever was to blame for my loss of Ferret. I really meant, would *I* be able to kill someone. Someone such as Thalia.

'It's blunt. That's intentional. It wouldn't go in, but if you

71

ran at an opponent fast, you could inflict a really cracking bruise. Believe me, that has happened. Actors are always involved in deadly rivalries so they whack one another "accidentally".' I pricked up my ears, in case I had discovered more murky situations to investigate, then I reasoned that the acting troupe had only arrived this morning so none of them were relevant to the death of Ferret. While I thought about that, I swished the wooden sword about, frowning seriously.

'What are you thinking of, Postumus?' demanded the props man in a suspicious tone. His name was Dama. He seemed a better class of person than the acrobats, though not much better.

I gave him my mysterious smile. That normally settles a conversation. Most people who receive my mysterious smile go away in a hurry.

I had got the hang of investigating, and the next stage would be something that always happens to annoy the investigator. That was clear because of what Dama said: 'Ho, ho!' He sounded alert and stern. 'Don't tell me you are looking for a means to protect yourself, young man?'

8

This is what I mean about the next stage of the investigation. I know from my father and sister that when you have stirred up everyone sufficiently by your penetrating enquiries, the suspects and conspirators believe they have to defend themselves by trying to block you from asking any more questions. This is likely to involve some kind of violent attack on you. Suspects are always dim people who imagine you will be frightened off. They never reckon on courage and grit.

What it tells you is that you have touched a nerve and are worrying them by coming too near the truth for comfort. This confirms you are being successful. You can take heart – though you must also be extremely careful and keep looking behind you wherever you go.

Although Dama had suggested it was me who might need protection, I knew he must be bluffing. Underneath his question was a threat. What he meant was: 'Are you wanting protection? – Because I am going to lure you down a dark alley and thump you horribly until you are covered in blood and can barely crawl home to be bandaged up and given hot soup.'

Of course there were no alleys in the Circus of Gaius and Nero, though threateners who were small enough could crouch down and hide between the seats, ready to jump out at you.

I gave Dama my thoughtful look, the one Albia says means I am considering whose head to put a hatchet in. Normally people who receive that smile then make themselves scarce. Sometimes I hear them muttering. If they complain to my parents, it used to be that Falco or Helena had a little talk with me, but they have now stopped bothering.

'Oh,' I replied coolly when he failed to leave the scene. 'I am a boy, Dama. Naturally I like to pretend I am a soldier thwacking the enemy. I do it every day until my mother says, Alexander Postumus, do stop damaging the furniture and making such a racket. Please may I borrow this sword while nobody else is using it, so I can march around being a legionary in my imagination?'

'No,' said Dama.

'It's only a game, Dama.'

'The theatre props are not toys, Postumus. Put it back immediately and don't touch anything else.'

I put back the sword tidily as soon as he told me to, like a meek obedient boy. This time I gave him my saddest look, all downcast and big brown eyes.

'Cut it out,' said Dama. 'Now hop off and irritate some-body else.'

I walked off as he had told me, still pretending to be well-behaved. I went far enough for him to think he had safely got rid of me, then I turned around. I was still in hearing distance. Of course I was, or there would have been no point.

'Just one other thing, Dama, if you don't mind.' This is called tactics. Dama scowled. I ignored that. He was pretending I had not spoken to him. You have to carry on

74

anyway, to catch them out. 'What was the reason, please, why you thought I might need to protect myself?' He wasn't going to answer me, but I made myself look horribly anxious about it. 'Am I in some kind of danger that I don't know about?' I sounded as nervous as I could. Since I didn't know of any danger, I wasn't really.

Dama still made no answer but he stopped looking angry. I waited a little then walked back slowly until I was close up again. I was showing I trusted him utterly, so it was his duty to be kind to me. I sat down cross-legged beside one of the props baskets. Then I waited. I am an extremely patient person.

'You're not in any danger,' Dama said, after he had fiddled with the props for a while. Obviously I then knew I *was* in danger. That was a surprise.

He went on with what he was doing, though it looked as if he was drawing it out to avoid speaking. He had a huge cloth costume, like a gigantic circular sheet with holes for eyes, which I guessed was the ghost's robe. Lots of plays contain a ghost though in the ones I have seen it never does much. People tell you that you will like the play because it is really exciting with a ghost, then it never is. They are just trying to persuade you to go to the play with them, so we can all be together as a family for once. It's best to go. That keeps them happy and they will hand around a lot of sweets.

The ghost's eye holes had grown tattered so Dama was sewing around them neatly. He had a basket of stuff for mending jobs, with glue pots, shears, hammers, thread and different kinds of wire and string. I would have liked to investigate these things, but decided not to. Or not while Dama was watching.

He put the costume material over his own head to try it

75

out; most people would have made woo-woo noises and waved their arms spookily but Dama didn't bother. He must be a man of the world. Anyway, I had the impression he didn't believe in ghosts.

I had waited this long time, because I could tell he was not a bad man, but one who wished me well. So I asked in a little voice, 'Who doesn't like me, Dama?'

Finally Dama gave me a straight look. 'I can't comment on who likes you or doesn't like you, Postumus, but you need to be aware of your position, boy.'

'What position, Dama?'

'With the other company. You are Thalia's lad. They have been an established performing group for two decades. Everyone thought they were a communal troupe, each with joint interests. Shared fates and shared fortunes. But now suddenly you arrive. Some people are bound to suspect that Thalia brought you in to be the heir.'

Did that mean I would own the menagerie and the tents, and I could give orders to the acrobats?

'I am only twelve.' I didn't confuse him by mentioning Helena's theory that I might be eleven.

'Well, you're twelve now,' Dama told me in a dark voice. 'You will grow. Some people might not want to stick around to watch.'

'What do they think is going to happen, Dama?'

'What always bloody happens – injustice and ingratitude!'

'Oh will that happen in the theatre group as well?'

'Who knows? It doesn't bother me. I can always go home to the hills and keep pigs in my old age. That's assuming I can stand the rural life and my foolish bloody relatives.' He had thin grey hair, a beaten-up manner and he looked quite old already.

'So,' I asked carefully, 'do you think the acrobats believe I am a threat to them?'

'Well, they are all mad buggers. Some of them can't think. Even the ones that can do seem to leave their brains behind when they put on rosin and take hold of a balance pole. The animal trainers are the worst misfits in the universe – and I say that after working with bloody actors. But look closely, Postumus, and you may catch a tiny whiff of discontent about how you popped up as Thalia's pride and joy. Word has already run around about you reorganising the gate money at the zoo like some little eastern king in a turban. It would hardly be surprising if there are those around here who are worried. They could well be hoping to get rid of you.'

'So what do I need to do about it, Dama?'

'Keep your head down and try to stop annoying people.'

I promised him I would stop being annoying. It was easy. People are always making me say that.

9

I am brave. I was not worried. If any of the animal-keepers or acrobats were coming after me because I was the unwanted heir, I would thwart them with my cunning. All I had to remember was to look behind me when I was going anywhere, listen for sinister footsteps following me and watch out if any door handles began to open silently. That would be when I was sitting still indoors, probably absorbed in writing up one of my note tablets by the light of a whickering lamp.

Of course in a tent there are no door handles. To enter a tent secretly, you have to untie the door tapes. That takes too long for you to creep up suddenly, because there is a long row of tapes that are tied up in bows all the way down the door flaps. They are not just to keep out unwelcome visitors while people inside are doing private things such as sleeping or nose-picking, they are to stop wind and rain. Weather is very insidious, Thalia had told me. I thought that was a silly thing to say in Rome in August.

Of course a bad person with murderous intentions wouldn't wait around untying a lot of tapes. They would simply cut through them in a trice, one big swoosh with a brilliantly sharp dagger that they had honed for days in readiness. Then they would have the dagger ready, for coming to get me. I must find a weapon of my own to use to kill them first. While they were looking everywhere in the tent for me evilly, I would jump out from behind Jason's basket and take them by surprise.

That reminded me about Jason. I still had to deal with him.

Nobody at the Circus of Gaius and Nero was bothered about me, they were all too busily rehearsing and practising. I went by myself to the stone armchair seats and sat a few rows from the front. I spent some moments thinking sad thoughts about Ferret.

These front seats are reserved for senators, so it was an appropriate place for a boy who might eventually become a big rissole. I would have explained this to any ushers who came to ask me to move off, but there were none that day. I was free to get used to the armchair seats, which I did almost immediately. They had an excellent view. They would be better with cushions, but a rissole would bring those, or have his people carry them in for him.

I had saved up the cake Manlius Faustus bought for me so I ate it now, rather slowly because it was not long since I ate the other one that Hesper had provided. At one time I did see Thalia stand up straight and look around, as if she wondered what had become of me and whether I was doing anything she wanted me to stop. I waved, giving her my innocent look. That's the look Father says is about as innocent as a nicker's nadger. He never explains what a nicker is, nor the purpose of his nadging tool. That's Father. He has wild ideas. We are all used to it.

Thalia was too far away to tell whether I was up to something. My innocent look satisfied her. She just waved back cheerily and went back to what she had been doing. She didn't know me as well as Helena Justina, who would have come over to check more carefully.

After I licked the stickiness of the cake off my hands and as far around my face as my tongue would reach, I spent the whole of the rest of that afternoon sitting in the senators' seats and thinking. I did an extremely large amount of useful thinking. A lot of people would have been very scared if they had known the thoughts I organised.

One idea that came to me was this: if somebody wanted to scare me away, so I would go home and no longer threaten them by being the unwanted heir, they might have chosen the well-known wicked ploy I had heard about, the one where you don't actually harm the person you are aiming at, but instead of that you do awful things to somebody else they care about. Had someone deliberately killed my ferret so I would take their hint?

If that is what they tried to do, they must be a person who didn't know the rules. You are supposed to leave the body on display in public. This is to send a visible message. Also, the person who has to receive the message must be able to understand what it is.

If I had found Ferret's limp corpse nailed on a big tent pole with his paws outstretched and his fur bedraggled, and with his dead eyes looking at me, I would have been very upset. I felt quite upset just imagining it. Even so, I would not at first have realised it meant, Get lost unwelcome newcomer, don't steal our rights because Thalia is your mother. Or anyway, she's one of your mothers.

When it was time to leave the Circus, Thalia came to collect me so I asked her straight out. 'Did you bring me here because I am intended to inherit your company?'

'No, I bloody didn't!' How angry she was! I understood what was going on. It happens among people who are in

80

charge and therefore occupied by many anxieties. Thalia had had a long day of people and animals not doing what she wanted. She sounded tired. Being tired had made her cross. 'I brought you to muck out the cages – and look where that's got me!' She had a rant, while I listened politely. 'It's all very well looking forward to the day when I can say, "That's my son, the Consul; he's my boy!" You will have to be forty years of age, so what will that make me?' I decided not to ask her. Mothers are old to start with, while according to Helena, having children puts many extra years on them. 'Gods in Olympus, Postumus, I'll be a hundred and long past caring.'

'I see,' I said.

'Well, if I've got to stick it out that long, I just hope I keep my libido and all my teeth.'

I had never heard of a libido. Since Thalia was so fond of it, it must be some exotic creature that I had not met when I was sweeping out the menagerie. I wondered if it ate ferrets.

I still thought Jason was my chief suspect. That meant Thalia was responsible for him doing what he did to Ferret. So as we went to have our dinner, I thought further about ways I might be able to impose retribution on Thalia.

10

We went over to where the theatre people had pitched their tents; we were having dinner with them that evening. It was supposed to be all friendly and festive. That means people who really despise one another are pretending to be best pals, although you can see they are not trying hard. Terrible music is played while you eat, on whiffly flutes and twangy string instruments of country design. People sing miserable songs about other people leaving home. The food is delicious though nobody notices; they all tuck into the wine flagons, then pretty soon some fights start.

As a sensible boy who had been properly brought up in a good home, I would have to be the peacemaker, which I would achieve with my impressive oratory. I had learned it from a grammar teacher I was sent to once, until he asked to be relieved of the burden. But I was not sure the actors and performers would have been taught to respect the power of oratory.

When we first arrived, Davos' actors and Thalia's acrobats and animal-keepers greeted one another as if they had not met properly earlier in the day. Some sounded quite cheerful and welcoming. A few groaned and muttered, though they did it in an open way that was meant to sound as if they didn't mean it. 'Oh it's you again, you worthless lot. We heard you had all been thrown in jail in Arriminium!'

'Was it your group who put on *Medea* at Neapolis and only two people came, both of them by accident because they thought it was to be fighting cocks?'

'And with a blind rat who left at the interval?'

'No that was in Bruttium and it was a three-legged dog. The two men had been promised naked women in the chorus. They all stayed to the end, but only because someone had given them free tickets which they wouldn't waste.'

'Did you do the show?'

'Yes, but we cut half the play so we could go for an early supper. And we put up the understudy as Jason.'

I was confused by this, since why was Thalia's python in *Medea*? Then I remembered it was another Jason, the hero of the play.

'That understudy of yours needs some practice, by all accounts!'

'But he's a pretty boy. He can just recite a laundry list and the women start fainting with pleasure. Any magistrates they are married to are so pleased the wives start taking an interest in sex again, they give us an extra night in the programme . . .'

And so forth. I didn't know how to converse like that so I just kept quiet. Thalia had introduced me to a group of the actors, then she left me with them while she went and sat beside Davos. I presumed that since he was her husband and she had not seen him for a while they wanted to talk privately about their adventures in the meantime. In fact for most of the evening they said nothing at all to each other; I know people who would say that proved they were married and had been for a long time. I looked at them in case they were quarrelling, but they were just taking no notice of each other, side by side. It did make

83

them look as if they were jointly the king and queen of the feast.

It was all rowdy but good-natured. Everyone there seemed colourful in some way. They were used to having open-air dinners like this. Quite a few had not been at the Circus track that day so they were new to me. I also noticed children, though none of them came and spoke to me.

Some of the actors I had been left with got up and walked over to another place, but three stayed with me as if they did not mind having been asked to look after me. These all had real names, plus names of the character they were to be in my father's play and titles of the kind of character that was. I was flummoxed about all these; when they tried to explain it they decided to stick with their characters' names.

'So I am Moschion,' announced the young man. He had unruly yellow hair that should have been cut about a month ago, but he let it tumble around in a way I wished mine would go. He looked like a wild brigand. 'I'm the young hero. He is dim and cowardly; he cannot bestir himself to action, so he needs prodding.'

'I am the clever slave who has to prod him. I do everything to sort out the plot,' said another man, who was older but equally untidy and exciting. 'I am called Bucco.' That meant Fatso, but he was very thin. He told me this enabled him to show off his powers of acting.

'And I play the Virgin, traditionally so-called – always a laugh as she works in the brothel,' added a young lady. 'She is Chrysis and is very beautiful –' I didn't think she was. She had a big wart on one cheek and her mouth went down at the corner in an ugly way, though I realised she couldn't help it. Helena would say, she probably made up for it with

84

a lovely personality. I think that was true because Chrysis kept picking out nice morsels of food and feeding them to me in a dainty way as if I were her little pet sparrow. 'I never get any stage time even though I am supposed to be the prize the men are all wild to get. Moschion is in love with me, but he is too useless. The Spook has to pop up and order the idiot to get on with it.'

'Who plays the Spook?' I asked with interest.

'Anyone who isn't doing much at the time. He's covered up. He has no words. You can just throw his sheet over your other costume and prance on.'

That sounded like a good disguise.

'Who is it the spook of? Who is dead?'

'No one is dead, Postumus,' the Warty Virgin corrected me sternly. 'This is a comedy. Relatives are lost at sea, lovers are thwarted by mean parents, partners argue over a bag of gold, the jokes are terrible, but nobody can die or it would depress the audience. On comedy nights people come for pork scratchings, feeling up their neighbour's wife and happiness.'

'Until they go home very sick from too many snacks,' added the Cowardly Hero gloomily.

'But they smile through their vomit, darling!' sneered the Clever Slave.

That sounded a good trick. Next time something made me sick I would see if I could throw up while smiling.

'It was supposed to be the ghost of Moschion's father.' Chrysis was musing, as if she remembered the play when it was performed before. 'For reasons of his own, the actor-manager they had at the time, old Chremes, decided the father was only lost at sea so Falco had to change it. He was doing so many re-writes he got lost at sea himself over it.'

85

'So you were there?' I asked.

'A mere child, Postumus! Falco's big idea was this: the ghostly father would tell Moschion that he, his father, had been murdered by his uncle, who had then married his mother. Well, everyone poo-pooed that. In comedy mothers are always loyal to their husbands, that makes it so poignant when they deplore the men's bad behaviour, especially when the father goes chasing after the Beautiful Virgin that the son is in love with.'

'I see,' I said.

'And of course a son will always be true to his pa, even if his pa is an idiot and has paid money to the brothel-keeper to buy the son's girlfriend to have her himself. Still the son stays loyal and respectful. This is how theatre works. You have to have known elements. The audience needs to feel secure.'

Chrysis insisted that Falco had wanted Moschion to be a respectful son to his missing father in the play, which she thought reflected Falco's views. I corrected her because everyone knew Falco and Favonius had been estranged for many years. Falco still says Grandpa was as painful as piles. But Chrysis insisted you have to have a happy ending.

I asked what about someone who had several fathers in his life? I was thinking of me. As well as Falco, who had adopted me, I had his father Favonius and perhaps three others: Soterichus the animal-seller, Davos who was Thalia's husband and the mysterious 'man in Alexandria' that my parents spoke about, if he was someone different from Soterichus. I did not name all these men to strangers, but I said there were a lot of possibles. The actors giggled and said, knowing Thalia, that was all too true. Bucco reckoned there were bound to be others too. Chrysis thought to be on the safe side I had better be loyal and respectful to them all. That would keep me busy.

Moschion was still laughing; he decided this would make a very good plot for a play. You could have the different fathers running in and out of the three doors that are always on a stage set while he, Moschion, tried to keep them from meeting each other. I complained he wasn't taking my predicament seriously. Bucco apologised for him and said that now I could see that the Young Hero was indeed an idiot. It sounded as though Bucco was jealous of Moschion for always getting the best part.

They had poured wine in my beaker whenever they took some themselves so I seemed to become unusually talkative. I didn't intend to mention anything secret but I did tell them about Hesper and Pollia and Pedo and the other acrobats. They guffawed. I then asked if they could point out Sophrona, so I could see if the water organist was very beautiful; Chrysis said Sophrona was nothing special (apart from being able to make all Hades of a noise on a hydraulus). I explained that I wondered how she had ensnared both her idiot husband Khaleed and Ribes the sneaky orchestra conductor who was the real father of all her five children. Bucco guffawed loudly, then he jumped up and strode off to another group of people to tell them what I said. Chrysis and Moschion muttered to each other that for a Clever Slave, he was never clever. Chrysis pointed out the five children, who were scampering around in a happy fashion.

Then I started to feel very sleepy and stopped talking.

The next thing I remember about that evening is that while the feast seemed to be going on for ever, Thalia came and took me back to her tent. She said she was going to stay

87

with Davos, but I would be all right on my own. She helped me lay out my bed, and tucked me in, though she did not tell me a story, which Helena Justina does.

'You can have Jason for company.' Thalia must have seen me pull a face, for then she said if that worried me, she would fasten the python into his big basket. He didn't want to be put in the basket; he rocked it from side to side as much as he could, but Thalia lifted a heavy cooking pot on top to hold the lid down.

I yawned a lot and made sleepy noises, so off she went, leaving me alone.

If I had had a sword, I could have lifted the pot off, raised up the lid of Jason's basket, then sliced his nasty head off as he came out to have a look around. I didn't have a weapon. But when I was sure the coast was clear, I squeezed out between the ties on the tent flaps and went to get one.

I I

Away from the feast it was extremely dark. Nobody had wasted lamp oil by leaving lights in their tents. I couldn't really see the Circus of Gaius and Nero, though I sensed where it was. In the dark it felt as if a giant had made it grow even larger so the huge long building stretched away endlessly.

I tiptoed through the other tents, though they all lay quiet. Only when I came near the Circus was there a faint light at the entrance. Torches were attached either side of the gates. They were too high up for me to lift one down. I had feared the Circus would be all locked up, but when I approached the two great gates through which processions entered, I found they had been left open a small crack.

By this time my eyes were growing used to the night. I edged through the gates and entered the deserted Circus silently. At this moment I remembered being told that you should never go to an empty building on your own without telling someone first, in case an accident befalls you, or some wicked person is lying in wait to tie you up and murder you after hours of gloating torture. You are bound to drop your oil lamp and be plunged into pitch blackness. But there was nobody at the Circus, they were all having their dinner.

Besides, you only have to worry about an ambush if a

dangerous person that you are trying to catch has drawn you there with a fake message. The best thing is if you have worked out their whereabouts using your super intelligence, so you can jump on them suddenly. You just have to keep looking around for their brutal henchmen. But that is all right if you have secretly brought your own loyal assistants who are lying low, disguised as bushes and statues. You can summon them with your special whistle, then you all burst out and beat up the bad people. Then they cry, Oh Jupiter Best and Greatest! Postumus, you clever swine, we never expected that!

I knew this from Helena telling me stories.

Because it was summer, the sky had a little light still. It was past the time when swifts squeal about, though I heard an owl out in the Gardens of Agrippina. I could discern the long empty space inside the Circus. The banks of seats and the spina were shadowy shapes and the track looked a slightly different colour from them so I could see where it was. But when I walked forwards I couldn't really see the ground, so I was scared of falling over. I made my way very carefully and slowly. The dry sand on the track was slippery underneath my sandals, though it made no crunching sounds. Nobody would hear me coming. Of course I wouldn't hear them either.

I knew that when the acrobats finished for the evening they had left all their equipment propped against the spina, a little way down from the entrance. Most were small items for balancing or juggling, though they also had ladders and towers. The actors had brought less baggage. Davos had explained that if Manlius Faustus, the aedile, agreed to let them perform in the Roman Games, they would be allocated a proper theatre which would have its own permanent stage and backdrop. However, since they never knew what disreputable place they might have to work in, they did drag around with them a portable set with three doorways. It was so dilapidated they must have owned it a long time. It would be here, along with the props baskets that Dama had been sorting out. Those were what I wanted to investigate for weapons.

The first thing I stumbled into, to my surprise, turned out to be an animal cage. I could tell from the smells and snuffling sounds whose cage it was. I remembered how Thalia had been trying to make Roar, the half-grown lion, do a tightrope walk. After she became exasperated with his refusal, she had him left here so she could try again with him tomorrow.

I thought Roar must be lonely out here all on his own. Perhaps he was being punished for being naughty. He had to stay in his cage by himself until he apologised. I murmured hello to him, since we were acquaintances. I had met him at the menagerie when I was sweeping out the cages and I made him the high point of my tour for the public. He had not been appreciative of visitors, just padded about looking superior. Despite his attitude, people were really impressed to see a lion close up, even one who still had some growing to do.

I heard Roar come right up to the edge of his cage, where I was standing. He grumbled in the back of his throat because a lion always has to make out that he is dangerous. He then gave a huge yawn full of smelly breath. I wasn't frightened of him but I stood back, because Lysias had warned me never to get too close or Roar could grab my arm through the bars and pull me in to eat me up.

When I walked on I could hear Roar prowling as much as he could in his travelling cage. Then he did a gigantic lion pee. It sounded like a big burst pipe from an aqueduct. I did a little pee myself against the spina, to keep him company. If it had been a competition, Roar would easily have won the prize.

I went on further, only to find that another enclosure had been built with hurdles; inside it were the nasty little performing dogs. One of them was digging a tunnel so they could escape. They had been provided with a lantern, a nightlight so they could find their food bowls and the bedding that they slept in. They all rushed up to the edge of their pen when they saw me, yapping their stupid heads off, because they hoped I was bringing them more dinner. But I only stole their lantern.

After that it was easier to walk along to find the baskets and baggage that had been left piled up. I started to investigate these things, which took a long time. I could not remember exactly which was the props basket with the swords and stage armour. There were several, all looking as if they could be the one I wanted. None were labelled. If it had been my job, I would have made sure they were.

Their lids were fastened down with extremely stiff old leather straps or roped up with complicated knots. Fortunately I am known as a determined soul. I stood the mutts' lantern on a bale of straw so it shed light where I wanted, then I began to open the containers one by one. If they were no use, it seemed polite to do them up again, so that made everything take twice as long. I knew you should never make a mess of other people's property then expect some slave to come along to tidy up for you. Or your mother. She has better things to do. Helena Justina is very good at explaining this, and never even loses her temper, except one time when I had completely destroyed the salon and her brother was coming to dinner with his smart new wife. The wife soon divorced Uncle Aulus, same as his previous one, so what I had done didn't matter as much as Helena had thought. But by then she had had a volcanic fit that quite impressed me.

In the end I did find the weapons. I made sure not to take the sword I had tried out earlier, the one Dama had told me to put back and not play with. I chose a different one that he had not given instructions about.

The baskets' hard leather straps had made my hands hurt. While I stopped to massage my fingers, I thought I heard voices. Being a boy of quick thinking, I curled up small behind one of the sets of steps that I had seen the tumblers jump off onto a see-saw. It flung them up to the sky, so they did somersaults as they flew through the air until they landed on someone else's shoulders. I wished I could do that. If I stayed with Thalia long enough, I would ask to be trained. I felt sure I could master it easily but if someone was going to give me lessons, first I would have to remember whatever I was supposed to have done that made my visits to the oratory teacher end badly. I believe that after the experience of teaching me, he left Rome unexpectedly. Father claimed the man had fled to become a hermit in the Tripolitanian desert, but Helena told me he just went to start a school in a new town. That was far enough for him to feel safe again.

There were definitely people here in the Circus. They were too far away for me to see them or tell who it was, but near enough to know that it was a man and a woman, who were arguing. Whatever they were quarrelling about must be important, for their words rang out bitterly and they kept at it for a long time. Sometimes they seemed to move around, as if they were pacing angrily up and down like Roar.

They seemed to be working their way towards me. If they came any closer they were likely to discover me. I wanted to avoid that in case they noticed I had taken a sword as part of my retribution plan and for protection as the unwanted heir. Never let the opposition know that you are armed, at least not until you have cleverly worked out who the opposition is and how you will dispose of them.

By now I thought the people I could hear sounded like Pollia and Hesper. I would have expected her to be rowing with her husband, Pedo, but perhaps he was busy doing something else. Besides, Pollia and Pedo could argue in their own tent, they wouldn't need an assignation in a secret location after dark. Probably the argument would be short too. Once people get past 'I cannot take any more of this!' and so forth, someone storms off in a huff. If the children are crying, the other person will calm them down saying, 'Don't worry; they will come back as soon as they are hungry'. If it's raining they come home sooner than that.

This arguing upset me. I decided I wanted to leave, so I had a good idea about how to escape. I wriggled among the baskets until I found the ghost costume Dama had mended. I pulled it over my head, tucked the sword I had come to get tightly under my arm, held up the many long folds of cloth, and went out towards Pollia and Hesper, weaving to and fro like a ghost. I couldn't take the lantern with me, because I had my hands full of costume. Anyway, it would have made me more visible.

Pollia screamed at my sudden spooky appearance. Hesper let out a huge exclamation and I heard his heavy footsteps coming towards me. I could not see out of the costume properly because the eye holes were not where I thought they would be. Hesper was angry. As a crude man, he might not know the rule that nobody may lay violent hands on a free citizen of Rome. So I ran away as fast as I could, hoping I could find the right direction for the gates.

Hesper was easily gaining on me. The cloth of the costume tripped me up. I fell down with a mighty whack. Luckily it didn't matter because I heard Hesper fall over as well, because the little dogs had finished making their tunnel to freedom so they all come pouring out from their pen and ran into him. He crashed to the ground as they scampered under his feet.

Holding the sword tight, I made a fast run for it, managing to reach the gates. Behind me was a horrible sound of Hesper yelling curses. Some were very bad words. Behind him in the distance I heard a woman weeping inconsolably. The dogs barked. Roar let out a huge roar. And when I looked around, pulling the eye holes into place, I saw that the lantern had toppled over on the bale of straw and set fire to it. Hesper had got up and rushed back to put out the fire. That was lucky for me.

Quickly I squeezed back through the Circus gates, wrestled my way out of the ghost costume which I dropped on the ground, then ran furiously fast back to Thalia's tent, flew inside and jumped into my bed.

There I lay like a good boy. I was so tired out that I was falling straight to sleep. But just before I nodded off, someone came into the tent.

12

Someone was coming to get me.

The person sounded different from Hesper, heavier and more blundery. Anyway, Hesper must be still putting out the fire in the Circus. The first thing I noticed was this new person fumbling with the ties on the door flaps. I knew it wasn't Thalia. She had gone back to the theatre people, to spend the night with Davos, who was her husband and she hadn't seen him for a long time so they would have many things to discuss. Anyway, she knew how to deal with the ties quietly. They were her own knots.

Whoever it was came inside and began blundering around the pavilion. He was making noise as if he was a clumsy person.

I didn't know what to do. I put out my hand and tried to feel if I could burrow under the side of the main tent to get away secretly, but the leather was pegged down too firmly for me to pull it up to wriggle through. You have to make a tent secure from rats or thieves and barbarians reaching in to grab your kit or the hunk of bread you are saving for breakfast. Also you have to keep out mud and dust or floods if there has been a downpour. I know the laws of camping from my father (I mean Falco) and his great friend, Uncle Lucius, who love to describe how they were in the army once.

96

I thought I had better get away from here, but I must do it in some other way. I would have to get up, move quickly from my end of the tent through the round outer part, then run like mad. I had to go right past this man, before he saw what was happening.

I decided not to put on my sandals, which might make a noise and tell him he was not alone. I picked up the wooden sword, though. I crept to the curtain that separated the tent rooms. I was being perfectly silent, which I know how to do. Many people have commented on how well I can creep up on them. I am not allowed to creep up on Falco, in case he spins around and instantly kills me, thinking I am an assassin.

As soon as I slid through the curtain, I saw a large man. He did have a pottery oil lamp but very small and faint. He was also shielding the light with one hand so it illuminated the tiniest area, but then he turned from the place where Thalia had her bed and looked right at me.

'Oi!' he yelled. 'Come here, you!'

He was going to grab me. He smelled of wine, which I knew meant he would be hard to reason with. It would be no use asking what he wanted or begging him not to hurt me.

I ran straight at him, with the sword held out in front of me. It hit him at waist level. Dama was right, the point would not go into him, but the man nevertheless wobbled right off balance.

I ran out past him. Hearing cries and struggling noises, I looked back through the doorway. Straightaway I recognised that the man was Soterichus, the animal-seller.

Soterichus had barged against the big basket. He knocked it, so hard the heavy pot on top fell off, clanging. The basket lid dropped off too. Jason the python instantly shot his head out. He seemed highly annoyed at having his sleep disturbed and his basket knocked over while he was inside it. His tongue was flickering more wildly than I had ever seen and he was making a strange noise.

Soterichus lay on the ground, waving his arms about and rolling, trying to stand up again. He was definitely drunk so this was very funny. One of his flailing arms hit Jason in the eye. I could see it was an accident. Jason, that dumb snake, thought it was on purpose. He was mightily displeased. Oh dear.

Jason slithered all the way out of the overturned basket in one long smooth uncoiling movement. Before we knew what was happening, he wrapped his strong body around Soterichus. He began squeezing. He was tightening as hard as possible.

Soterichus went very red in the face. His mouth opened, though he was too busy being squeezed to say anything. He couldn't escape from Jason's coils. I could hear him breathing in horrid jagged gasps.

I decided to address the unfortunate situation. 'Jason is suffocating you,' I said in a stern voice. 'He is too strong for me to stop him, so I will go for help.' Fetching someone to rescue the man was a polite thing to do. I didn't say that I wanted to save Soterichus because I needed a discussion with him about whether he was my father.

I scuttled as fast as possible over to where the theatre people had their own encampment. In the dark I had to be careful not to get lost and I had no sandals on, so I was held up when I trod on stones and had to hop about squealing. Everyone was still having their dinner. I ran to Thalia, telling

98

her at once what was happening to Soterichus. She leapt up. Bowls and cups scattered in all directions. Faster than I would ever have thought she could run, Thalia pelted off. Davos and lots of other people saw that this was an emergency so at once followed, leaving their food bowls and beakers behind. I limped in the rear, until I was suddenly seized by Lysias, who saw I was barefoot. He kindly picked me up and carried me all the way back to Thalia's tent, although when we arrived, he kept me outside while other people went in.

Not long after, two men dragged out Soterichus by his feet, with his head lolling in the dirt. They pulled long faces and told us he was dead.

13

I felt extremely annoyed. It was bad enough that I might need to execute my mother, once I could organise it, but now by hitting him with the sword I had helped Soterichus to fall against the snake basket, which offended Jason, who killed this man who might have been my father. How fortunate I was that Falco and Helena had adopted me. Otherwise I would soon be all alone as an orphan. I felt a worry I sometimes have: who would then take care of me?

'He was carried off by shock,' announced Davos. 'The snake hadn't finished; his heart gave out.'

People were fussing around me, so I pulled my sad little boy face. As I hung my head looking frightened, they asked gently what I had seen before I ran out of the tent. I replied in a brave tone that while I was sleeping in my bed where my mother had tucked me in, I heard an intruder. Startled by me and seeming drunk, Soterichus fell over. Jason escaped. I ran for help.

People sniffed at the corpse and remarked that yes, Soterichus must have had a lot to drink; he reeked of it. Apparently he was known for it, too. Lysias patted me in approval for having been so observant.

'Coming to sell you his crocodile!' rasped Davos to Thalia, with a snooty look. 'Still negotiating sales on your back, are you?'

'Rubbish!' Thalia threw back at him crossly. 'Why do you think I made sure I was not in the tent when he toddled up?'

'Because you know you can never resist temptation! Yet you left your boy there.'

'I left my python too, may I remind you – I thought if Soterichus wandered by, he would just put his head in, see I wasn't there, and bugger off. He would only be after one thing and it didn't involve either Postumus or Jason.'

Somebody had found the wooden sword. Dama, the props man, asked me in a dark tone whether I had taken it. Thalia snapped that of course not because I was tucked up nicely in my bed by her, my loving mother, a poor little soul innocently waiting for an intoxicated livestock merchant to crash in and spoil my happy dreams. Dama backed off, looking nervous.

Hesper arrived. I was sure I would now have to confess about the sword, but Hesper told a story that he had been to the Circus because he smelled smoke and heard the little doggies barking. He made no mention of Pollia. While he was there, he said, he was terrified by an apparition that suddenly jumped at him, a man wearing the spook's costume. Hesper reckoned it must have been Soterichus. Everyone agreed that Soterichus had no reason to steal a wooden sword from the props basket, so he must have been at the Circus for some other bad reason. They decided it was because he knew Roar was left there. Soterichus was hoping to kidnap our lion.

So that was all right. It served the lion-thief right that Jason constricted him.

'How is the poor python?' Hesper asked Thalia. Apparently it had taken lots of them to haul Jason off Soterichus, coil by coil. Once he started constricting, he wanted to finish the job.

'Highly agitated. He never attacks people. He must have felt threatened to do anything like this. It's going to take weeks to nurse him through it.'

Everyone then told me what a brave boy I had been. I was not to worry about what had happened. As the body of Soterichus was towed away somewhere else, even Davos was kind to me, taking me back to my bed and saying he would sit and keep me safe until I fell asleep again.

I would have fallen asleep quite fast, only Thalia replaced Jason in the big basket, which took her some trouble, aided by Lysias and Hesper. Jason did not want to be there. He kept me awake for a long time, bumping and banging as he tried to escape again.

14

Next morning everybody was subdued. Thalia had to go and tell the people who belonged to Soterichus that they would not be seeing him again. When she came back, to our surprise she brought the crocodile that he had been trying to sell her. She said it was compensation for him dying at our camp. Anyway somebody who knew what they were doing had to volunteer to look after the reptile. I watched its arrival at the menagerie. They had one rope tight around its long scaly snout and others on its body. He was struggling wildly. It took five men to drag him into the enclosure where they meant to keep him.

The menagerie would be closed that day. I offered to do dung-sweeping but Lysias said Sizon would do it today. That would teach him to drink himself into a stupor at the feast. Hesper wasn't being much use. He was moping. Someone had given him a big black eye. I whispered to Sizon was it Pedo? To which he answered no, Pedo couldn't hit a fly if it landed on his nose; the gorgeous Pollia whacked him.

Since nothing was happening there, I went to the Circus. I had asked Hesper if he would give me money for another fig pastry as my reward for keeping his secret. He said, no he bloody wouldn't since it wasn't a secret now, was it? He continued that if he found out what vicious bastard had snitched to Pedo, he would string them up and disembowel them with a rusty knife, extremely slowly. I was glad it was Moschion who snitched. I assured Hesper that it wasn't me, so he snarled to get out of it. That was when I went to the Circus of Gaius and Nero, so as not to annoy Hesper any more.

The cake-seller wasn't outside anyway. Instead, I found a public slave, the one who was supposed to sweep up, lock up and look after the torches. He liked to do anything that wasn't work so he showed me his little equipment hut, where he kept his broom and had his lunch when anybody gave him any. I apologised for not being able to share a pastry with him.

The hut also contained the torches, with their pitch and the flint for lighting them. Remembering that the aedile Manlius Faustus had asked for my help at a wedding, I asked if I might borrow one of the torches. I wanted to practise carrying it, as if I was in charge at the wedding procession. The slave said as I was so nice to him, of course I could.

The torch was large and quite heavy. I was glad I had conducted this experiment, because now I could advise Faustus to supply lighter ones. I did it well, but the snivelly little cousins and nephews he had mentioned would not be able to manage.

I took the torch with me into the Circus. There I saw Pollia, who had as big a black eye as Hesper's. None of the acrobats were practising, so I went up to another young lady, the one called Silvia, who was sitting cross-legged against the barrier around the track. She looked rather gloomy. She said it was because Thalia had forbidden them to perform today.

'Oh why is that, Silvia?'

'Too dangerous when participants are having an enormous fight. You cannot risk dangerous throws when your life is in other people's hands. There has to be complete trust. At the moment someone is likely to get dropped – on purpose.'

Silvia pointed out Pollia's eye, so I mentioned that Hesper had one the same, which Pollia had given him. Silvia snorted. She said it was Hesper who bopped Pollia, though no one knew who hit out first. Pedo, Pollia's husband, was sporting *two* black eyes, one each from Hesper and Pollia. That would teach him to weigh in while his wife was disagreeing with her lover. What had it got to do with him anyway?

The little woman Sassia was limping, but she had refused to say how or why that happened. Silvia herself looked unscathed. I asked if that was because she led a moral life, and she replied, no it was because she knew how to hide what she was up to.

'Will the quarrel be sorted out, Silvia?'

'Better be. If not, our group will have to break up. Everyone will lose their job. Then Thalia will be short of acts and will have to sell her animals. She won't get work – and so it goes on.'

I said I was sorry to hear that, then I left her so I could march about to do more practice with my torch.

Thalia called me over. She asked how I was after the upsets yesterday evening. She had been sent a message that my father, Falco, would be coming to the Circus later to watch a rehearsal of his play, *The Spook Who Spoke*. Afterwards he would take me home with him to dinner, because I was supposed to go every week according to Helena's conditions and tonight they had the aedile Manlius Faustus coming.

'Why does he need to see the play if he wrote it?'

'Re-writes. Plays are all about re-writes. To see if he can twiddle with the script to make improvements. Don't tell him the best improvement would be to start all over with a decent new play. I remember he's very touchy about it . . . Helena has written me a note "Tell Postumus little dumplings". What's that about?'

'Yum! My favourite dish.' I was not surprised, since if Helena Justina knew I was coming to dinner she was bound to order this for me specially.

Thalia gave me a look as if she thought I might be criticising her as a mother, because she did not know my favourite. It is scrumptious roast chicken served with very little parsley dumplings floating in the juice. Well, I would have told her if she had asked me.

'Now then,' said Thalia then, in a tone of voice with which I am familiar. She seemed to have had second thoughts about me being tucked up in my bed all last night. I prepared for a talking to. 'Can you assure me, Postumus, you were never in the Circus yesterday evening? You did not wear the ghost costume, or loose the dogs, or set fire to the straw? How did you feel about Soterichus dying in our tent like that?'

Albia says you should ask one question at a time, otherwise your suspect will only answer the easiest, where they can safely tell the truth. Nobody can have explained that to Thalia.

'I was sad about Soterichus being constricted by Jason,' I answered perfectly honestly.

'Well, you know it's a horrible way to die.'

106

'I suppose so.' The man had looked more puzzled than horrified. He seemed too bleary to understand what was going on. 'But I didn't want any harm to befall him. I was upset because it was important to have a discussion with him. I had been told he came from Egypt, which has a connection with me being born, so I specially wanted to ask him if he was my father.'

'Bloody hell!' exploded Thalia. 'Only if he was a magician – I didn't know him until five years ago. Anyway he came from Memphis, not Alexandria, which I can assure you was your place of conception. Mind you, it was on a ship I first met that filthy rogue Geminus so we can call you a sea-baby. Juno, you are a strange little tyke, Postumus!'

Oh good, she was so surprised she forgot her other questions. That saved me having to own up or to be a bad boy who tells lies. Helena and Falco have a rule that I must always tell the truth, which I have solemnly promised to obey, but that is in their house so it might not apply when I was with another mother. Thalia had not thought up any rules for me. If I stayed long, she might get around to it.

The only other thing that happened that morning was that Thalia got in a bate because no members of the public had paid to come inside the Circus. Apparently the usual thing was that after sightseers went to the menagerie they were offered cheap tickets to watch a rehearsal as well. Lysias, who was attending to Roar, told her that now visitors had to pay my new price for the menagerie they wouldn't part with any more money afterwards.

Thalia and Lysias stood with their arms folded, looking across the track at where I was. They didn't say anything to me, so I just continued to practise my walking in a torchlight procession.

I had some thoughts there on my own. I was considering this Circus that Nero had completed for chariot races. Afterwards I had been told it was convenient for the cruci-fixion of many Christians who had confessed to causing a great fire that nearly burned down Rome. This shows that you should never take confessions on trust because it is perfectly possible Nero started that fire himself to clear land to build his Golden House, or that it was simply an accident.

Confessions can be beaten out of people. That was a fact worth remembering. I had not forgotten my investigation into the python's crime. Sometimes you must pretend to be busy doing something quite different, to lull your quarry into a sense of false security. Any boy knows how to pretend to be playing happily, while he is planning to do something else.

15

Lunch was on the hoof, which only meant flatbreads in the hand and carry on with what you were doing.

Since the acrobats were barred from performing, they just huddled by the racetrack so I went to sit with them. Hesper came slinking up to Pollia.

'Don't come whining around me, Hesper. You have ruined my marriage!'

'You ruined your own marriage!' snarled Hesper, trying to stop the others hearing, especially Pedo, Pollia's husband. He was watching with a faint sneer. 'I thought you were true but you ruined my life!'

'Get lost, waste of space.'

'Oh shut up, the lot of you!' shrieked Sassia, the tiny woman. Everyone looked shocked. Questioning looks were passed between them. Sassia jumped up and strode off by herself, aiming a kick at Hesper as she passed him. I had no idea what that was for, though the others looked as if they had just twigged something.

The play rehearsal was starting, so I left them and went to sit with the actors. I looked around for Falco but I could not see him. That made me worried, in case nobody came to fetch me for dinner that evening.

★

The Young Hero was to play Moschion, the Prince of Chersonesos Kimbrike.

'Wherever in Hades that is,' muttered Chrysis, who was elegantly lolling in a seat alongside me. I tried not to look at the wart on her face, for I know that is rude.

'Chersonesos Kimbrike is in the far, far north,' I informed her. 'We have a Map of the World on a wall at our house, so I have learned all the places.'

'How clever you are! Plays always have to have exotic settings, Postumus. You couldn't set a comedy in Italy or Greece, it's too familiar.'

I didn't recognise the Young Hero at first because he was wearing a black wig to show he was youthful and virile (even though dim and cowardly).

First Davos came on as the old father, in a long white gown with a staff. A short prologue explained to us that he was sailing off to Sicily.

'Why is he going there?' I whispered to Chrysis.

'Absolutely no bloody idea, pet.'

'To get him out of the way so he can come back,' explained Davos, as he came off stage – which was actually off track, of course, since we were at the Circus of Gaius and Nero, not at a proper theatre.

Davos plumped himself down, holding a copy of the play, so he could write notes on it. He seemed to get bored with that quickly so he gave me the scroll to help me follow. It was not much help.

The play continued like this:

Mother: Stay with us, Moschion, my son. Do not go
              to Germania Libera!
Pause. Even longer pause

Davos:	*rushes back on stage*
	Bloody hell, I'd already left for Sicily . . . No, wife, he shall go to Britain.
Mother:	Why, they are all mad in Britannia, and painted blue.
Father:	Then nobody will notice that Moschion is mad too. He shall be escorted by our loyal slaves, clever Congrio and wily Bucco.
Mother:	Then take good care of him for us, wily Congrio and clever Bucco.

Moschion, Prince of Chersonesos Kimbrike, then did not go anywhere, though his father did. Perhaps Moschion had stayed at home because he was supposedly going away to be educated at a university, even though he was clearly too dim. Besides he was busy pursuing the Beautiful Virgin so he had no time for study. There are no universities in Germania Libera, it is all huge forest.

Word then came that after two days at sea a warlike pirate sailed up and set upon Moschion's father and killed him. I felt sad for Moschion.

Congrio, the thin old clown, was to appear next and tell jokes to cheer us up. I had seen him already on the sidelines, huddled with someone wearing the ghost's costume. The ghost seemed to be telling him a new joke, which they were busy writing down. Congrio was clutching a large scroll that Chrysis told me was his joke book. If anyone tried to borrow or steal it, Congrio would kick off in an apoplectic fury. Sometimes if they ever found it unattended people moved it for a game, though they never moved it very far, nor owned up who did it. That was very funny.

Presumably because he had no time to learn the new

joke, Congrio brought the scroll on stage with him and read it out. First he explained what had happened to the old man, Moschion's father, who had ended up missing at sea. I said it to you in one sentence, but Congrio spouted on endlessly. If this was meant to be amusing, I failed to see why. Facts should be told in a plain way and get on with it. Then he did his joke.

Congrio: Three intellectuals went into a bar.

Bucco: *aside* Jupiter, who writes this stuff? You just can't get the poets nowadays.

Congrio: When the waiter came to greet them with offers of refreshment, the Platonist decided that since the three parts of the soul are Wisdom, Courage and Temperance, he would wisely ask for bread to line his stomach, bravely try a high priced wine, but restrain himself to a half flagon.

The Aristotelian disagreed. He thought the perfect form of the human soul is reason, separated from all connection with the body. So he would try to get extremely drunk on anything the waiter brought him, until his body had no idea where it was and his mind lost all capacity to reason.

The Cynic claimed the highest good is to spurn every kind of enjoyment, so he would order the terrible house wine then not even drink it. The kindly waiter took pity on him, offering to supply the primal substance identified by Thales of Miletus – which is water.

Bucco: This is tedious. Get on before we all pass out!

Congrio: The waiter brought their order, then the three intellectuals spent a pleasant afternoon at the bar, engaged in discourse of the finest kind, each one drinking according to his personal philosophy. Eventually it was time to leave. The waiter had been keeping a careful eye on them, for he had met intellectuals before. He jumped in to present their bills, pointing out that in the spirit of Pythagorus, the world is perfect harmony depending on number, and the most perfect number would be the price of their drinks plus a large tip for him.

The Aristotelian at once replied that the aim of human activity is happiness, for which material goods are unnecessary – so he had left his purse at home.

The Platonist responded with a smile that the waiter would not lose by this, for Wisdom, Courage and Temperance are united by Justice, so he would cover his friend's bill as well as his own.

The Cynic wasn't there by then. Needing to relieve himself of much primal substance, he guessed it was time to pay the bill and since cynics are shameless, he went out to the lavatory, dived down the alley and never came back.

Bucco: The Spook claims this rubbish is not what he wrote. Let those who are to play your clowns speak no more than is set down for them.

113

Congrio's joke had caused a lot of winces among the audience. They were making restless movements.

Congrio: The other intellectuals thought the punchline needed more work. But the waiter said, what can you expect? Falco wrote it.

I had had enough of drama, so I slipped away quietly, taking my torch for more practice. It had gone out, so I went outside the Circus gates to the little hut. The public slave was asleep but he woke up and said since I was using the torch so much, I ought to have the bucket of pitch. He showed me how to dip the torch and replenish it so it would go on burning.

I spent some time by myself, marching, then I was bored. The torch was still burning well since I had used a lot of pitch on it. I had no way to douse the flame. Since I am a sensible boy, I did go and look at the cage where Roar was kept, because I thought he would have a bucket of water in which I could plunge the flaming torch with a huge fiery hiss, but the half-grown lion must have been thirsty that morning and had drunk it. I left the torch and the pitch container safely outside his straw-carpeted cage. I leaned the burning torch against the stonework of the spina where it could do no damage

Roar wasn't in his cage. Thalia had taken him out earlier, hoping once more to entice him onto the tightrope, though he kept refusing. He was still over by the equipment, fastened with a rope on his leg, looking lonely. I went to speak to him. He was lying with his paws together, looking around with a sinister, snooty expression. It looked safe to go up and stroke him but I decided not to. He began chewing at the rope on his leg. I would have mentioned it to Thalia but she was too far away. Nobody else was nearby because they had all gone to stand around laughing at the play.

When I myself returned to watch more rehearsal, the action had moved on. I could not tell easily what was happening or why.

Chrysis: Methinks I saw your father by the port.

Moschion: Beautiful and virtuous Virgin, how can this be, for he is lost at sea, murdered most foully by a warlike pirate. Alas poor ghost!

Chrysis: No ghost. Not dead.

Moschion: *amazed* Not dead?

Enter Father

Moschion: *amazed again* Father! Not dead! Mother, here is my father. Seasick, I think, coming from Sicily.

Mother: *amazed* Oh Moschion, speak no more, for I believed him dead and I am married!

Pollia: *off stage* More fool you then!

Father: *amazed* Wife! Married?

Mother: Husband!

Chrysis: Help, ho; she faints!

Moschion: Mother, mother, mother.

Father: Attend your mother.

Moschion: Father, father, father.

Enter Spook

Chrysis: Here's one who can explain all this. Speak, speak, Spook, speak to me!

The Spook was a good character. I liked him very much. I think the actor enjoyed playing him. He loped on stage in a wild manner, swaying from one side to the other, waving his sheeted arms and swooping. Even when asked, he did not speak. His not speaking was the scariest thing about him.

That was when new things happened, which interrupted the rehearsal. Over by the acrobats' equipment, Roar must have gnawed through the rope holding him. He stood up to stretch his legs, then decided to go to his own cage where he felt comfortable and he might find a piece of bloody meat left over from his breakfast. He couldn't get into the cage though. With a grunt, he jumped on top, which people noticed, then when they began shouting, he came off again with a grand flying leap. He was a rather clumsy lion. The half-grown beast landed on the bucket of pitch, which fell over onto a spare bale of straw, where all the contents rolled out. Roar took one sniff then sprang back. His next mistake was to knock into the torch even though he could see I had left it standing upright to be safe. He pushed the torch over too with one curious paw, so it landed in the overflowing pitch. That started a big whoosh of fire.

Roar was so scared by what he had done, he ran away. First he fled straight into the scene where the play was being acted. When he saw the Spook, he spun around with catlike tread towards the other actors. They all jumped in terror, screaming.

Exit pursued by a lion.

With one mighty bound, Roar then cleared the barrier by the track that was supposed to be protection if a chariot team crashed. He took off, jumping up the rows of seats to the very top of the Circus, where he stood on guard, roaring proudly.

Despite this, I noticed people pointing elsewhere. Gulp.

The overturned pitch was now a big wild fire, sheeting all up the spina which appeared to be burning even though it was stone. The effect was spectacular. This only lasted a short time, luckily, because all the men who worked for both Thalia and Davos went running as fast as they possibly could to put out the flames that were burning down this famous monument. But it had set alight the dry old wood of the temporary set with three doors and was licking over the baskets and hampers, with their ancient desiccated wicker. The men had to spend a long time working to rescue things and dampen down the raging flames. I could hear horrified exclamations at the damage.

This was not my fault, and unintended. Nevertheless, it seemed a good idea to go away while I could do so. I foresaw a lot of being talked to. I was just setting off quietly, when somebody scary stood in front of me. He was wearing the ghost's costume.

At last the Spook spoke. It was a surprise. 'Hold on there, Scruff!'

From the ironic nickname, then I knew that the Spook was Father.

16

Me:	Father!
Father:	Son!
Others:	Aah . . .
Father:	Come, some music!

Stagehands bring up the enormous hydraulus

Sophrona: *plays very loud music*

Father: *aside* Oh horrible! More horrible! Most horrible!

My father pulled off the ghost costume, which he shook out and folded neatly, then handed to Dama with polite thanks. To Thalia and Davos he said that his play seemed to be holding up well, to which Davos answered, yes it was holding up as well as it had ever done. He sounded as if he meant something different from the words. Falco just gave him a huge grin, the grin that looks as if you might not be able to trust him, even though he is pretending he is utterly dependable.

I felt my hair being scuffled up. I normally complained about that but today I liked it. My father said to Thalia, 'I hear you just acquired a crocodile. That brings back terrible memories!' His hand on my head now felt heavy and still. In a changed tone, he asked, 'So, do you see anything of Philadelphion these days?' Thalia gave him a narrow look. I knew nothing of any Philadelphion, so I leaned heavily against my father's hip, wriggling to imply I was bored by the adults' conversation. 'Time I took this one home to face my daughter's fancy man. He will have to stay with us tonight. Are you finding him tough to cope with? Shall we have him back permanently?'

'Why? He is only a gossip-mongering, commerce-busting, death-dealing, sinister staring little arsonist. I can manage!' Thalia exclaimed, before she looked around at the havoc in the Circus and faltered. 'What do you want to do, Postumus, darling?'

Suddenly I decided I would like to live at home again. It was one of Helena's conditions that I could.

'Go and catch your lion,' continued Father in a lenient tone, being kind to Thalia. 'You know the child is in good hands. Helena never finds him a handful – after all, she's used to looking after me. Say goodbye then, Postumus.'

I did as I was told, adding nicely, thank you for having me. Thalia crouched down to hug and kiss me, wiping away a fond tear. Above her, Falco secretly winked at me.

He and I walked pretty fast from the Circus of Gaius and Nero to the tents. He grabbed my things and made a bundle which he shouldered easily. I ran back to fetch my best tunic, knowing that with a guest tonight I must have it on at dinner. That was when I had a huge surprise. Curled up fast asleep in the bed that I gave him, alive and well, was Ferret.

'Titan's turds,' observed my father in amusement. 'I thought you lost him?'

At his masterly voice, Ferret awoke. With a joyful squeak, he jumped straight down the tunic I was wearing, then slithered around inside furrily, exploring. We were both thrilled to have found one another.

'Time for a fast getaway,' urged Father, as if he feared someone might come and stop us. 'Let's go home, Scruff, for porridge, the dish of our ancestors.'

I gave a wise smile, for I knew it would be chicken with little dumplings, my favourite.

So we set off back to the Aventine. My father was carrying my luggage with one hand, while his other firmly held one of mine to stop me getting lost. I felt a warm feeling of relief. I was going for dinner with Didius Falco, going home like brothers who had been out all day on an adventure. Also I was looking forward to seeing Helena, and hearing her cry happily, 'Ah here he is! My littlest has come home again.'

Best of all, I had my ferret.

Vesuvius by Night

I

Our introduction to
Nonius the scrounger.

The girl had gone. It was no surprise. Leaving was what girls did. Few of those that Nonius brought home stayed until he roused himself from stupor, even though they had to be very drunk to come with him in the first place.

The night before, his voice would have been loud in calling for the wine, although he knew how to absent himself just as the tavern bill was brought, leaving others to pay up. A wink to some equally sly waitress, who had been serving whatever party he latched onto, would bring her back here with him at the end of the night. It might not be for his sexual prowess, which most bargirls derided on principle, but because he could offer a bed. For him and for them, this was better than dossing down in a stable with the beasts.

It was normal for such companions to skedaddle before he woke up. They had to be back at the places where they worked, seamy wine bars down by the Marine Gate or raucous hovels around the amphitheatre. These scrawny women in their off-the-shoulder tunics were needed to give the marble-patched counters a cursory wipe down and start selling snacks to morning customers, however groggy they felt. Most of the Empire was fuelled by street food.

They rarely bothered to say goodbye. Most couldn't stand the thought of daytime conversation with Nonius. Once in a while, some scrupulous woman might even feel ashamed of herself for accepting his invitation. It never affected Nonius. He had no conscience.

At least if his partner had gone before he dragged his eyes open, his incoming landlord would not see her. There was an unspoken rule that Nonius could bring back visitors, since it was difficult to stop him, but only so long as nobody threw up and he left the sheets clean. Nonius preferred any of his overnight companions to make themselves scarce early or inevitably they looked at the new arrival with much more interest than they showed him. His landlord was a tall, fine-looking lad, still in his twenties, who retained traces of the carefree adventurer he had been when younger. On returning home after work, he was generally tired out, yet he could summon up a twinkle for a barmaid, especially if he found her naked in his bed.

The landlord was married, but his family lived in a different town. The kind of women who came home with Nonius would view a wife who lived elsewhere as no hindrance, indeed her very absence would encourage them to cosy up, counting the landlord as unattached. They saw a subtle difference in status between a man who worked and his disreputable subtenant who never paid for anything. Girls knew what they preferred. Nonius might pretend not to care, but he liked his floozies to leave the scene before they decided there was better available. Let the landlord find his own women. Nonius told himself, the one vice he never had was pimping.

In fact that was simply lack of opportunity. Any women whose life he had tried to manage had laughed in his face. And oh yes, he had tried it. Nonius had tried most things.

The landlord took over the room at night; that was an absolute rule. It was, after all, his room. He returned in the evening, grunted, turned Nonius out of the bed and fell into it himself. He would leave again at first light, sometimes still in the dark if his current job was any distance away. Nonius paid him a small fee to use the bed by day, while the other man, a painter, was out creating frescos.

'Pornographic?' Nonius had asked, with interest.

'Double portraits of staid married couples,' lied the painter. There were many erotic pictures in Pompeii, and some were commissions done by him. But from what Nonius could gather, he was mainly a landscape artist.

Nonius initially viewed this as a mimsy occupation, so he was surprised at how businesslike the other man could be. His landlord was wily enough to extract the room fee in advance, and he never loaned any of it back, however much Nonius pleaded.

'No, sorry, you'll have to cadge off your mother again,' he would say, even though he had no idea whether a mother existed. 'Oh, I forgot,' he then joked annoyingly, 'you sold her into slavery! Well, maybe your grandad will mortgage his farm to help you out, Nonius. It's no good asking me, I have three daughters' dowries to find and four no-good sons who won't leave home.'

Given his age, this was clearly untrue. Any children he had must still be infants. Artistic types were full of fantasies, Nonius thought, and this mean bastard was polishing them up deliberately to tease his penniless tenant.

'You heartless turd,' Nonius would respond glumly. He expected to live off other people. It never struck him that someone might see through him and fail to go along with it. Life had taught him that people were idiots.

Unbeknown to him, the painter did have five children, all born in the last eight years, plus a belief that he probably ought to provide for them. Sometimes – not in his wife's hearing – he called himself stupid for bringing this upon himself, but in fact he was extremely intelligent. He knew he needed to take care with money and believed he could handle Nonius. Nonius thought otherwise.

Their different attitudes to cash coloured their relationship and could yet cause it to come to grief. The painter earned a good screw, Nonius believed; he must do. He worked all hours, apparently enjoying it, and was said to be a good artist, his skills much sought-after. Earthquake damage from nearly two decades ago, followed by further seismic upheaval, meant Pompeii was full of opportunities for a decorator with a reputation. The landlord must be saving up his wages. Nonius had yet to discover where he kept his stash, which he planned to steal. It was best to wait as long as possible, so there would be more money. Also, once he lifted the moneybag, he would have to vanish, which was always inconvenient. If he needed to hole up away from the action, Nonius wanted his haul to be worthwhile.

Action, for Nonius, did not involve work as the rest of us know it, merely the slick separation of other people from property they thought theirs. Whether earnings or inheritance, he liked to show owners that their money and valuables were meaningless baubles; they should not grieve if these were lost to them. Ideally, they should acquire more so he had a second chance to rob them.

Nor should they be enraged about their sweet daughters and willing wives, should Nonius happen to run into these other 'commodities' while they were plying looms or having their hair done. Women were his (he believed) as much as bronze household gods, chalices, gold finger rings, coin hoards, or any ivory cupboard knobs a carpenter had carelessly left while he went for better fixing-screws. Nonius had been known even to tickle up arthritic old nurses and vague-eyed grandmothers. Pompeii was famously dedicated to Venus and, he said, he must keep in good fettle.

As he romped his way through the female population, there were rarely complaints. He claimed they liked his attention. However, it could be because any woman who thought of complaining tended to find that Nonius had vanished like a mouse through a knothole.

He knew when to flit. Having a nose for danger was a key skill. He could tell at a glance if a house was too dangerous to wander into 'accidentally'. His preferred tactic was to saunter inside, wiping his feet on the Beware of our Dog mosaic, admire the place like an invited guest, search out a fine silver cup or tray that was crying out to be carried off under his none-too-clean tunic, then grope a startled woman as he left – before she realised what was happening. If he could slide out without causing an alarm, the slaves copped the blame.

Nonius had seen every variant of the mosaic doggie doormat. He knew all those bristling creatures, black ears pricked, big collars stiff with spikes, eager to have your leg off with their bared teeth, yet harmlessly stuck in tile limbo. He knew from experience that homes guarded by motto mats with silent barks generally did not have a real dog, but relied on nothing worse than a half-asleep porter who spent too much time in the kitchen. If someone banged the big bronze seahorse knocker, the porter would drag himself to the door to insult them and, if possible, refuse them entry. Nonius therefore did not knock. Why invite problems?

Sometimes front doors had locks. Often, in fact. This was a bustling seaboard town, full of sailors, traders, horny-handed fisherfolk, the occasional soldier, runaway slaves, and countryfolk with straw in their hair who had been sent down from the hills to make money any way they could. Windows that overlooked the street had heavy bars too. Nonius had ways around that. He carried a big metal ring full of different latch-lifters. Most locksmiths sold picking tools for people who had lost their keys, and many had encountered Nonius making obviously false claims about 'his' house key having gone missing inexplicably. But his favourite method was simply to wait until some oversexed young master popped out for a secret tryst with a prostitute, or a careworn kitchen-maid was sent running for more bread rolls in a hurry; if they left the door slightly ajar to assist their return, he weaselled in.

When he strolled out again, perhaps carrying a filched pillowcase that he tightly wound to stop its contents rattling, he liked to close the front door properly behind him. He had a mischievous streak.

These days, however, Nonius maintained that his burgling career was over. He was moving up.

The crunch had come while he was first badgering his landlord to agree their rooming arrangement. The painter refused to share his doss with a sneak-thief. This unreasonable attitude ought to have been the first sign he was no airy-fairy soul with stars in his brain, but so hard-headed he was positively ethical. He could be stubborn too. When he would not budge, Nonius firmed up an idea he had for branching out. Pompeii was a town full to its battered old defensive walls with businessmen who thought they knew all about commerce. Nonius planned to convince them that they needed his financial know-how to help make even more money. He was going to help rich people get richer quicker. At least, that would be the claim. Certainly a hunk of what they already possessed would be withdrawn from an armoured bankbox to find its way to Nonius in advance of whatever 'rock solid' investment he proposed. When the mad scheme failed to materialise, he would be long gone.

Nonius had explained his sparkly new career to the painter, calling himself a financial adviser, which he insisted was so much more worthy than being a thief. The painter suspected it was much the same thing, but felt other people must take their chances. They were free to exercise choice. So was he, and since hiring out his bed would help pay his rent, he chose to take Nonius at face value.

When Nonius moved in, his meagre luggage included an awning pole he had filched from a schoolmaster, which left a class of seven-year-olds sitting out in full sun while they chanted their times tables. This stolen pole could be threaded through the top of a smart tunic and hung up to keep the garment nice. The tunic was a pleasant emerald-coloured number he had picked up from one of the clothes-mangers in a bathhouse changing-room; it had red braid around the neckline, extended down the front in go-faster-to-the-top stripes. In his new business outfit he could pass himself off as acceptable in a better class of bar, where men with cash to invest could be singled out as potential clients, otherwise known as victims.

The routine was one he had always used: Nonius quietly attached himself to their party in a way that made them feel they had known him for years. He wormed his way in with screamingly funny, very raunchy jokes and an offer of drinks all round, while he generously called for more olives and nuts. He stuck with them all evening. Along the way, he sold them the dream. They paid for the wine out of gratitude.

Greed, Nonius knew, overcomes natural intelligence. Men who were perfectly capable of managing estates or industries complained with dreary predictability that the big earthquake had damaged their livelihoods. These were Pompeii's wine-suppliers, perfumiers and fish pickle brewers; statue importers and bronze vessel manufacturers; not to mention accountants, auctioneers and lawyers who serviced the other businessmen. To Nonius' mild surprise, the latter class, advisers themselves, were the easiest to bamboozle.

It was true Pompeii had been devastated by that earthquake; the damage was so bad even the Emperor, Nero at the time, had paid for some repairs. Not many; just enough to make him look good – not *enough*, griped the businessmen routinely. A second earthquake two years later happened when Nero was performing a harp concert for what he viewed as his adoring public; he insisted on continuing to the end of his recital, then the theatre collapsed moments after it was evacuated. That barely dented his local popularity, especially since his gorgeously beautiful, fabulously rich wife Poppaea came from these parts.

Money counted here. Though they were still prosperous in fact, townsmen of substance hankered for the better days they believed they had known before the quakes. Such men were ready to fall for a promise from Nonius of easy returns; even the astute among them – those canny few who, like his landlord, doubted his probity – even they would eventually follow their colleagues like sheep. No one wants to be left out.

Nonius possessed no investment experience. All he knew was how to bluff. He had noticed that most advice on any subject is handed out by people with no practical knowledge, only the ability to sound good. Self-assurance happened to be his chief talent. He had also reached a time of life when he looked as if he had kicked around the world enough to have gained special insights, so his lived-in features and silver-grey sideburns made him very persuasive to men who were on their fourth flagon of mellow Vesuvian wine. They loved to think they caroused with other men of the world. They were blind to the fact that the world of Nonius was a stinking midden.

Perhaps Nonius sensed that time was running out; some day he would lose his luck. Clumsiness already threatened his touch as a thief, and his slippery trickster skills might start to waver too. So he was aiming for a different existence, one with fewer risks of exposure. The Bay of Neapolis was the best place in the world for leading a life of leisure. Nonius planned to make a quick killing, then retire on the proceeds.

The first trial of his business plan had been convincing the potential landlord that his new career was a goer. Fortunately the painter had vaguely considered having a roommate. Daywork tradesmen often bunked down together, for company and to save money; as a worker in the building trade, sharing was nothing new to him so winning him over had merely been good practice as Nonius tried out his spiel.

That was how the new career would operate too: identifying a perceived need in a client, then saying that he, Nonius, was here to satisfy the need. Mutual advantage.

Good as my word. Utterly reliable. Grasp this wonderful failsafe opportunity, honoured sir, for it cannot be kept open much longer, I am cutting my own throat as it is. I, Nonius, through my private contacts have secured a risk-free privilege, which is available for a limited period only. Don't tell your friends or they'll all want it. I would jump in myself, but I am heavily committed elsewhere at the moment. I like you. There is no need for the tiresome burden of documentation, I trust you, simply give me your deposit and the deal is clinched . . .

Part of his skill would be to sell solutions to clients who did not even realise, until he told them, that they had a problem.

Really, the painter had grasped that all the flash talk was rubbish, but Nonius was well able to ignore others' scepticism, so long as he got what he wanted. So now they rubbed along in the shared room, more or less in harmony. When the painter fell into bed after a long day creating frescos, Nonius went out in his sharp tunic to gain clients. He picked them up as they enjoyed relaxation in the better class of bar – larger establishments that offered space inside as well as counters on the street, and with secluded gardens. Most had a pricelist on the wall that included 'Falernian', which might even be the real thing.

Wine – 1 *as*
Good wine – *2 asses*
Falernian – *4 asses*
Fellatio – *anything between 1 as and 7*
Tips – *at your discretion, sir*

Plus bar staff who didn't pick their noses, or at least not in front of you.

When Nonius had tickled up a new prospect successfully, or better still a consortium of these idiots, he would come home and change into his grubby clothes, then go back out to the lower class of dive to drink himself silly in celebration, until dawn broke and the painter took his brushes out to work. Then Nonius, with or without female company, could come home again and have the bed.

The room was a small bare space above a cheap front shop that had been carved out of a once-fine large house. In Pompeii such remodelling was rife. One-time gracious mansions were divided into upper-storey apartments and ground-level bakeries and laundries, fitted with street-side workshops, and flanked with booths and bars. Even their exterior walls were hired out for advertisements and electioneering. This situation both provided for, and in itself encouraged, a shifting population. Families and businesses came and went in the refurbished properties, while a whole new range of entrepreneurs flourished through leasing real estate. Many were freed slaves, flexing their financial muscles and not caring that trade was supposedly dirty. Some were merely from families that had once been kept down socially by an older and more snobbish local élite, but who, since the earthquake upset everything, were emerging into confidence, status and power.

The entrepreneurs lived in better houses than they rented out, homes which they decorated fashionably. This brought continual work for painters. And Nonius was sure, if he himself could offer the right temptations, it would bring a fortune to him.

He had noticed his landlord wore a sardonic expression while this was explained. Jupiter's jockstrap, that dauber thought a lot of himself. He was not from around here. It was said he had been born and bred in Rome. It damn well showed. He was a cocky sod. While he was listening to his customers' generally daft ideas for décor, this supposedly brilliant artist might appear mild-mannered enough, but clearly he believed himself superior to anyone in Campania. He must set customers straight without them noticing he thought their own taste dire. Presumably the wiser ones just let him get on with it. He preferred to be given a free hand; he knew that when they saw what he painted they would be delighted. He was very sure of his talent.

In the opinion of Nonius, this arrogant, tight-arsed young *Roman* was just ripe to have his self-assurance pricked, by Nonius helping himself to all the money that painter had saved up. It was going to happen. When Nonius was ready. When – and even he had to admit this was proving difficult – when Nonius had managed to find out where the painter's savings actually were.

In his mind, the future loot had acquired colour, substance, and ludicrous bulk. He had been thinking about his landlord's money so much that he had lost all sense of proportion. He was now imagining a silver hoard so glorious it needed to be guarded by mythical beasts. He believed that men in the building trade were generally paid with coinage but that sometimes, when a customer had a tricky cashflow, they were offered rewards in kind. Nonius, who could be just as imaginative as any of the best fresco painters and mosaicists around the Bay, now pictured more than mounds of glimmering sesterces; he dreamed of unexpectedly fine works of art, antique Greek statues and vases, tangles of curiously-set jewels . . .

The tight-fisted swine had hidden his hoard too well. It was not in the room. Nonius searched everywhere, taking up floorboards one by one, then hammering them down again. Since he had the place by daylight, he could see what he was doing so knew he hadn't missed it. Nothing was here.

The landlord did get paid. Nonius had observed him obsessively. The painter always had money in his purse, a little corded leather bag he kept around his neck, from which he took coppers to buy a flatbread or an apple from a street stall. He could pay his way (a concept Nonius viewed askance) and never seemed troubled by financial anxiety in the way destitute people were. Nonius could spot that. He had been there.

Nonius would get him. In the meantime, until the particular day in question dawned, life continued for them both with its gentle cycle. Like a plumb-bob in motion, they came and went in their terrible bleak room, one swinging in, one swinging out, passing each other with barely a nod, never sharing a meal or a philosophical conversation, yet constantly linked by a mutual thread of existence.

When Nonius took his turn in the bed, once he finished with any female companion – assuming he could be bothered, and assuming she didn't order him to screw himself and leave her be – he would sleep like the dead, or at least the hungover. Since being hungover was so regular for him, it passed without too much pain, normally around the time the light began to fade at dusk. He usually woke and was ready to decamp when his landlord's weary feet climbed the stone steps from the street.

But on the day in question, it was different. He woke much sooner than he wanted. Nonius abruptly reached consciousness while there was still sunlight streaming through the broken shutters at full intensity. His body sensed it was only about midday, though sounds from outside seemed not quite right.

Nonius lay spread-eagled, face down. He had ended up diagonally on the mattress, tangled in the sheet, unsure for a few moments where the ends and sides of the narrow bed were in relation to him. He felt a fear of falling out. He would have groaned, but could not summon the energy.

He thought he knew what was going on. He realised that what had woken him was a peculiar sensation, a sense of his bed shifting beneath him during unnatural reverberations. Anyone who experiences this, even for the first time, knows it must be an earthquake. Even in places where earthquakes have never happened before, the occurrence is so strange it is unmistakeable. It ought to be unsettling, yet Nonius had lived through seismic activity, so he felt neither alarm nor surprise. People said, 'This is Campania, what do you expect?' Earthquakes regularly happened. In the past, the street level in Pompeii rose or sank by several feet. The shoreline changed. On the way out to Cumae lay fiery, sulphurous fields and lakes whose dead air killed birds overhead. The earth was rocky and barren there; it stretched and heaved, spewing hot fumaroles of steam or gas. Poets wrote of it as the entrance to Hades.

For the past four days minor tremors had been felt. Locals cursed, but were used to it. Noises cracked and grumbled deep underground. The credulous believed giants were walking the earth. The racket was growing louder but as the days passed people took less notice.

Was there now to be another significant earthquake? Nonius knew that when the ground began rippling in waves, as if solid earth had turned to water, the sensible rule was to leave your building. Best not to be indoors when your house falls down. Even if somebody eventually dug you out, if anyone bothered, you might be dead of fear and suffocation by the time they pulled off the rubble.

He still felt too hungover to move. He just thought about it. Staying put was the way to get killed. Nonius ought to evacuate. Still, he told himself that being out in the open was dangerous too. This particular house had survived in the past. It was shored up, with walls and ceilings patched, but the fresco painter, who knew about building stability, had once said it only needed maintenance; he reckoned it looked safe for the time being.

Nonius must have slept through some upheaval. The noise seemed to have ceased now, yet he guessed what had been happening. Sod it. If it was midday, he had not yet rested long enough to want to rouse himself. Last night's girl had gone. She had raided his purse, damn her; with one eye, he could see it lying on the floor, obviously empty. If he went out he would only get a bite to eat if he cadged off some old acquaintance, and most of them were wise to him.

So Nonius stayed where he was, prone on the bed, not troubling himself to go outside.

So far, he had no idea that this time everything was different.

2

Next the painter, who regards himself as a less raffish character. However, he has had his moments.

The painter witnessed what happened. He had left the room where he was about to start once the plaster was ready, and walked outside. The tremors of the past few days had unsettled him. Though he pretended to ignore his tension, the recent subterranean activity had been growing worse.

'Come and see!' his daughter had called from the street doorway, sounding more curious than alarmed, yet excited. 'Father, look at this!'

He had been standing back from the main wall of the big room, taking the measure of its central panel where he was ready to paint a mythological scene. The new top coat of plaster was just reaching its critical stage. Even so, he went to find out what she wanted, after first encouraging his junior, Pyris, who was putting a black wash on a panel. It was well within the boy's competence, so the painter could leave him to it.

Hylus, the other man in their team, was crouched down

by the dado touching up a merry scene of cupids racing in chariots drawn by little goats. 'Fresco cupids have a bloody hard life. I hope this bunch are grateful I'm letting them be boy racers. They're constantly at it, working their wings off, making perfumes, weaving at looms, being gold-smiths. I bet their pay stinks too,' joked Hylus, who often wittered on while he was working.

'One's got a boil on his bum,' commented a plasterer. He was up on the scaffold, annoyingly. That ought to have been done by now, way back when the coffered ceiling and coves were put up and painted. They were supposed to finish first so the decorators could move top-down. Anyone other than a crack-brained plasterer would see that was the sensible way to programme a job.

'Shit, it's a drip; thanks, Three Coats. Fetch me a rag, will you, Pyris?' Hylus was clearly thinking only a plasterer would make such a big deal of pointing it out. Three Coats, named for his endless lessons on how to build a fine surface, smirked. A sound wall in fact had six coats, three in the rough and three smooth with marble dust, but the painters, who were competent plasterers themselves, never let him finish telling them.

That smirk from Three Coats had irritated the painter more than usual, so it had been a good idea to move away. Popping out to see what his daughter wanted avoided snapping at the other man. As team leader, he liked to keep the peace.

He could not afford to disappear for long. Frescos must be painted at the right moment. Now that Three Coats had filled in his panel and its design was roughly marked out, he had to work fast, before the wet plaster went off. In fresco, colours were not simply laid on the surface but were sucked into the glossy final layer of the finish while it remained moist. This made the paint survive household knocks better, and it could be washed down without losing colour. They always assured their customers it would last forever.

Sometimes they completed details dry, but that was for a reason, or so they claimed. Actually they might not have finished in time and had no wet cloths to keep the plaster workable. They pretended to be using a 'specialist technique'. Painters knew how to preserve their mystique.

The recent shudders from deep within the earth had disturbed and annoyed the team leader. He possessed a sense of danger, though he could live with risk. He just worried about their work. The current site had suffered before; next door, where they had also been working this month, the bakery oven had sustained major cracks in the big earthquake and was now being repaired yet again. Most of the flour mills were completely out of action. This morning, when he and his team turned up here, they had anxiously inspected all the walls; having to check every day for overnight disturbance made him depressed, even though everyone who worked in Pompeii routinely endured their work being damaged. At least the townsfolk tenaciously rebuilt; shockwaves meant a surge in property renovation, which was excellent, although you never knew if what you finished for your customer would survive the next upheaval.

An artist who cared could end up having a breakdown. At this point in the job, any flying dust was a nightmare. And what was the point of putting your soul into your work, if your efforts might be cracked apart or even brought down? If people liked your style they would call you back for repairs, but creating a scene for a second time was unsatisfactory. You could get tired of constantly redoing jobs. Artists dream that what they produce will last for generations – small hope in the Campanian earthquake zone.

Anyway, when customers had something done twice, even if the fault was unavoidable, there was always a niggle about the extra payment. He hated the stress.

So these past four days of tectonic agitation had left him restless. The uncertainty had made him surly and unable to paint well. He needed to settle before he started the new panel. As team leader, he did not need to ask anyone's permission. He had moved away from his paints, as if to take a pee or find a bite to eat from his knapsack.

In reply to his young daughter's call he stepped right outside the building. For a moment he stood quietly and looked up and down the side street. It was being dug up in several places: there was already a long trench for what seemed like endless work to the water supply, god knows what engineer had thought that up. And now, next to the house, a cess-pit had been excavated, its ghastly contents piled up everywhere. That made the third in the side street.

Householders would be glad if their indoor toilets stopped smelling, but they were not pleased about the haphazard dungheaps. This was even worse than normal. Pompeii's streets could be foul. Sometimes a frustrated householder put up a sign on his exterior wall, saying *Do not shit here, stranger, move on!* It only gave passers-by ideas, and if it didn't work for individuals, it was hardly going to deter the dead-eyed, cack-handed, bloody-minded workmen who carried out civic contracts, not when they had mounds of stupendously ponging sludge to store somewhere while they dug a big hole.

He stepped around the piles carefully and went in search of his daughter. She wasn't to be seen on the main road, so he turned and cautiously retraced his path. He had to go right to the other end of the side street before he found her, standing stock still at a corner, balanced on a stepping stone. Unlike the more sedate town of Herculaneum where his wife lived, Pompeii had no proper drainage; the town sloped steeply down to the sea so when it rained, surface water just dashed along its streets towards the port, carrying every kind of rubbish. The stepping stones were handy, though a magnet to children. One more worry . . .

'What have you seen, chuck?'

'There's a fire behind the mountain.'

His daughter Marciana, eight years old, was the original reason the painter had rented a room of his own. She stayed with him sometimes. It gave him an excuse to limit how much he fraternised with his colleagues, being something of a loner. Even before he decided to sublet, his daughter had camped out downstairs at the lodgings. Now, no way was he having her come into contact with Nonius. Nonius, with his various unpleasant habits, had no idea Marciana even existed.

When he found her outside, the curly-haired little girl was rapt, staring towards the dramatic view of Mount Vesuvius; the tall local mountain, beloved of Bacchus and one-time refuge of Spartacus the rebel slave, dominated sightlines, elegantly framed by the distant city gates. Lush to its familiar high, craggy summit, packed with prosperous farms and vineyards, Vesuvius was one of many peaks in the area, yet it stood slightly isolated from the rest, with special charm. That must be why it had its own name. Five miles from the sea, it was always touched by threads of incoming cloud, dreaming in sunlight as it had done for generations.

'Come out of the road!'

Many a child in the Empire was killed by an accident with a cart; drivers were madmen, utterly thoughtless, often drunk or dozing too. Anxious to retrieve his moppet, the painter was nevertheless distracted by what had so fixed her attention.

Behind the mountain as they saw it from Pompeii, clouds of grey smoke were filling the sky. If it was a forest fire, this was a strange one. The painter remembered hearing a sharp bang, but it had been distant and at the time he'd been concentrating on mixing a paint colour.

Nobody had ever suggested Vesuvius was volcanic, as far as he knew. If that had ever been true, it was long extinct. Most hills in the Italian landmass looked similar in form, from the long barricade of the Apennines to this circle of ancient peaks around the Bay of Neapolis. The Apennines were unstable, with regular landslides, rockfalls, mudflows and sinkholes. But the painter believed Italy had only one active volcano, the legendary Etna in Sicily. He dreamed of going south to see it, so he could paint Etna spewing fire, with the philosopher Empedocles throwing himself into the crater in order to prove he was immortal – while the mountain contemptuously hurled one of his sandals back to show he was not. The possibilities for contrast between dark and fiery light, the chance to show violent activity, were seriously alluring. Well, one day . . .

Not here though. Not here, despite recent warning signs. When, this very week after the Rustic Vine God Festival, growers had returned to town after inspecting their Vesuvian grapes before harvest, they claimed to have seen the ground bulging and even seen fumaroles like those that boiled and steamed in the Phlegraean Fields. They reckoned their vines were being scorched, ruined by unusual ash deposits.

Many chose to disbelieve them, which was the convenient response. A straggle of nervous folk did take fright. Everyone else said they were only looking for an excuse to visit relatives or to escape nagging spouses. Many of their neighbours were trapped in inertia, because if they left, where could they go? People had to live.

As the painter looked at the smoke, now almost draping Vesuvius in a grey fog, his mouth went dry. He felt his heart lurch. He reached for his daughter, intending to bring her back onto the pavement, when a new event happened. They heard it and felt it: a terrific rolling bang, the movement of air hurting their eardrums, panic striking the soul. It was so strong the painter staggered, almost thrown off balance. Clutching at him, the child cried out.

'Hades,' he said to himself. He often talked out loud to nobody. He recovered. He grasped his daughter by the hand, feeling her cower against his leg, hearing her whimper.

What he and the child saw next was utterly unexpected. Rooted to the spot, he could not believe what he was watching. It was momentous. The top of the mountain had blown right off.

He was a fatalist. He knew straightaway that he would not paint the waiting wall panel.

3

So the painter and his daughter sensibly decide what to do.

The painter's name was Larius. Larius Lollius.

Everything had begun for him twenty-three years before, in an upstairs room high over a forlorn back alley on the Aventine Hill in Rome. He was born the first child of hopeless parents, who claimed they had wanted him, but never sounded persuasive. His mother, Galla, was a floppy, washed-out woman, exhausted by life even before she produced too many offspring; his squint-eyed father, Lollius, was a Tiber water-boatman, a feckless predator on such as she, yet a man who would never resolve his family's distress by decently abandoning them. He vanished whenever things got tough, but always returned to cause more upset and land Galla with yet another child. Off again when the bills came in. Rollicking home once more, just when his children were learning to prefer the peace of his absence.

Galla belonged to a large family and when Larius was fourteen, better-off relatives had kindly brought him on holiday to the Bay of Neapolis. It was the most beautiful spot in the Empire, perhaps the best in the world. That huge bowl of enclosed water, surrounded by cliffs and mountains, bewitched him. The call of ships and the sea turned his young brain, until his entrancement took the form of falling in love. First love. His first mistake in life. The fatal one.

At the same time, he had seen local fresco-makers at work and realised he wanted to be a painter. This at least was no mistake – o gratitude, all you wondrous gods – but what he had been born for. His family reckoned he was 'going through a difficult phase', by which they meant he was an adolescent boy who read poetry and had high ideals. Ideals were no use to working people in Rome. Poetry made them fear they could no longer control him. But his choosing a career in art was useful. Having a 'career' at all was a hilarious novelty, which meant they could stop wondering what to do with him.

When his relatives went home, he stayed. His parents would be furious, but he knew they lacked the energy or resources to come and fetch him. He was free. He had taken charge of himself. He was having a good time, too.

He stayed in Campania with his true love, Ollia, who had been a nursemaid to some children in the holiday group he came with. A podgy, acne-ridden lump, she was a year older and a little dimmer than Larius realised. She was his first girlfriend; somehow he'd wrested her from a brawny local fisherboy, who had caught her eye by throwing nets around attractively. He never caught much.

That boy's family had hoped he would get Ollia pregnant. They thought that insisting on marriage would allow their lad to adopt a better life in Rome when Ollia went home. Everyone in Rome did well – everyone else knew that. Relatives might gain material advantages from the fisher-

146

boy's lucky transferral to this city of magical prosperity; they might even follow as hangers-on . . .

Eight years had passed. They were still waiting for it to happen. Even though Ollia lived with Larius, they thought the marriage would come to nothing. One day fate would work for the fishing folk. Slow people, but bizarrely trusting.

Larius and Ollia still saw them occasionally, when they wanted a day by the sea and a fish supper. The lad, Vitalis, hung around; hanging around had always seemed to be his main activity.

For Ollia, marriage turned out dismally. She now knew that she was permanently stuck right here with Larius or, worse, without him. Even if he left her, she would never get away from the life they had foolishly chosen in their teens.

So Ollia was still the painter's wife and, unless she died in labour, he accepted that she always would be. Their children were Marciana, Ollius and Lolliana, Galliana and Varius. Ollia had named them. Larius would never have foisted 'Ollius Lollius' on anyone. She had to do the naming because after their first, which scared the boots off him, Larius managed never to be with her for the births. The last four comprised two sets of twins. He could not even begin to think how ghastly those labours must have been. It was almost enough to put you off sex. Almost.

Marciana, the eldest, was Larius' favourite. Now eight, she even wanted to paint. She had talent and he was teaching her; it was theoretically impossible for a girl to do this professionally, but if it was what she wanted he would let her work with him. She was in Pompeii now, already able to bind a tint for him, or speak knowledgeably of Egyptian Blue and how a pinch of it sneakily added to chalk white would make the white brighter.

Marciana was regularly driven from Herculaneum in a neighbour's rackety cart, when the neighbour came to the Saturday market. She brought her father clean laundry, food and news of the family. She would then remain in Pompeii for a few days while the neighbour consorted with his mistress; Marciana stayed with Larius' landlady, not one of Pompeii's grand entrepreneurs but a timid widow who lived in her own space on the ground floor, just across a courtyard from where Larius and Nonius slept upstairs.

His room was a dump so drab that Larius told his daughter she was not allowed there. For him it was merely a place to sleep, but if Ollia found out how bad it was, there would be ructions. Marciana understood. She never gave him away to her mother. The child bunked down with the widow, close enough for Larius to keep an eye on her; instinctively, even though she knew all about Nonius, she kept out of his sight. Marciana fed the old woman's cats, sometimes fed the old lady, who was growing pathetic, then came to the site where she mixed paints and watched her father working. Learning, learning. When their neighbour from Herculaneum, Erodion, had had enough of screwing his secret ladylove, or when the bamboozled husband inconsiderately reappeared, Erodion jumped in his cart, returned to his own wife, and took the painter's child back to her mother.

Marciana had a battered old basket that she carried to and fro with her. Her dolls poked out of it, a mixed collection made from terracotta, wood and rolled up rags; the rag doll had an arm missing, the wooden one was whittled for her by the other painter, Hylus. She hankered for a fully articulated ivory beauty, styled in the latest fashion; she knew such things existed, although they were too expensive.

Every birthday and Saturnalia she hoped. A bright child, she knew it would never happen. Larius, who thought his children were heading for enough disappointments, was wise enough never to be drawn into a promise.

Marciana always had the cranky dolls tucked under an old, moth-eaten napkin in the basket as if they were lined up in bed. While travelling home in the neighbour's cart, she kept the basket on her lap, solemnly talking to her dollies. Larius had been told their names often, though he forgot. It was hard enough remembering those of his own brood. Well, he knew, though not necessarily which name went with which child. Tough little tykes, they scoffed at him, accepting his vagueness yet perhaps storing up future resentment. *You never loved me, you're a terrible father, you couldn't even be bothered to remember what my name was!*

Hidden under her dolls in the basket were the wages Marciana took home for her family, after carefully deducting an allowance for her father. Nobody ever robbed her. Nonius, the dreadful sub-tenant, had no idea this gap-toothed little girl even existed, so that was how they thwarted him.

Marciana, very observant, had Nonius figured out as soon as she first saw him. 'You'll have to make sure that person doesn't steal all your money, Father.'

'Right!'

'I shall take charge of it.'

Larius knew that the women in his family (except for his woefully useless mother) tended to take this line – though not normally at eight years old. He followed orders.

She was a good daughter. It was always a surprise to Larius that he, who could not be called a good father any more than his own was, somehow acquired this sensible, warm-hearted, talented, highly likeable child. And that she loved him.

He knew he did not deserve it. He could be too much like his own father. For instance, there was a gap of some years after Marciana and the first twins, before the second set. It happened when Larius accepted a call for trades to go overseas for a large prestigious building project in faraway Britannia. He was eighteen. At the time, they already had Marciana, and Ollia had just found out from the local wise woman that she was probably expecting a multiple birth next. Larius had matured, enough to see how he had trapped himself in misery, yet not enough to deal with it. Strife and fear for the future darkened his marriage. Good money was promised for the British adventure and he was feeling desperate. He had been working in the huge holiday villas of the very rich that lined the cliffs above Stabiae, fantasy palaces which only emphasised the squalor of his own life.

By then he knew his art. A good artist, who saw his talent, had trained him. Generously gave him chances. Pushed him forward to be noticed by clients. After four years, Larius was no longer an apprentice but an independent painter, specialising in exquisite miniature details. His pictures would sit in the middle of panelled walls to draw the eye and stop the heart. On the strength of his skills, he was accepted for the fancy British job, which was financed by the new Emperor, Vespasian. He didn't tell Ollia he was going. He just left a note.

'How lucky I can read!' she said grimly.

Larius claimed he needed to earn extra; in truth, he was going on the run from his wife, who knew it. Ollia feared he would never come back. It was a reasonable fear, because he himself dreamed of escape.

He worked abroad for a couple of years, telling himself he had got away. But the climate and provincial limitations of Britannia eventually made him homesick. The Palace of King Togidubnus at Noviomagus was nearing completion so he was about to be laid off, then Larius had failed to organise himself to slip anyone the right bribes to obtain contracts on the new public buildings up in Londinium, the only other place in Britain offering work for an artist of his calibre. The south coast, his stamping ground, was becoming a tight spot for him. He had too many feuds with men he had drunkenly beaten up. Various women were after him. He came back to Italy.

He could have gone to Rome.

He should have done.

It was the terror of Ollia's life that Larius would one day slide away to Rome, without her. Although they both had family there, neither kept up contact. Since they married he had never been back to his birthplace, because he knew that Ollia's fears were correct; if he returned home, he would be permanently sucked in. Lovely Campania would see the last of him. He would never send for his wife and children; they would become ghosts to him. Larius would be subsumed into the hard drinking and hard living that made his father so repulsive, swamped by the demands of his extended family, taken over by the easy deceits and the fast bright hum of city life.

He was a loner here. It suited him.

On leaving Britain, the allure of the sea and the sunlit skies on this perfect bay drew him. Warmth, colour – and rich patrons wanting top quality décor. He returned to Ollia. It surprised them both. He stayed with her. Which was even more strange.

There were regular quarrels but even so, Larius suspected yet another birth was imminent. He had made things easier by installing his wife in rooms in Herculaneum, a town which was small and select and could be passed off as a good place to bring up children. He normally took jobs elsewhere. Close, but not too close. It stopped the squabbles. Since his return, he'd sobered up as far as he thought reasonable, took a grip on his life as far as he could be bothered. He accepted that what he wanted to do, all he wanted, was to paint.

The rest sometimes felt like a nightmare, but Larius conceded that the nightmare affected Ollia too. He was not blind to her situation. He was contrite, if not excessively. They got by. She believed he loved the children, which she thought must make him happy; ultimately true to her and to the infants they had foisted on the world, he himself never analysed his emotions. Happiness was a mental conceit; he dealt in spatial excellence. He loved the execution of his work and his power to provide pleasure even to strangers; that gave him an easy nonchalance. Within himself he was stable, relaxed, more or less content. Certainly he applied himself.

> *When things are troublesome, always remember,*
> *keep an even mind, and in prosperity*
> *be wary of too much happiness.*

Horace.

> *A picture is a poem without words.*

Horace again – maybe a bit fanciful to someone who actually produced pictures.

Larius knew other poets but had absorbed a lot of Horace. For instance, that quote his filthy subtenant Nonius would choose:

Money first; virtue after.

Larius had grown up, but he still read. Ollia no longer did. During their adolescent courtship, they had bonded through endless discussions of elegiac love poems. The intellectual aspect of Larius was what attracted her, so much that it enabled him to supplant Vitalis the fisherboy, at Oplontis, even though he could show off a fine naked chest, toned muscles, a slick shoelace moustache; he was a virile hunk who obviously knew what to do with his body – which Larius in those days, being fourteen and painfully shy, did not. However, Larius liked reading and thinking; Ollia had thought him so very sophisticated and romantic.

Now, Ollia said she had no time for poems. Presumably it saved her many bitter feelings.

For such a fine artist there would always be employment. At the moment, Larius had this contract for a big building complex close to Pompeii's main street. Work had been going on here for several years. The residential spaces were empty, with the garden currently in use as a materials store, though a busy street restaurant still operated on one corner and a large integral bakery remained in operation – a positive bread factory, with four querns trundled round and round by half a dozen mules, at least when the querns were working. They were currently idle due to earthquake damage.

The decoration scheme was to be modern yet not completely ludicrous. Larius understood clients. These

153

would not want the most traditional style, which merely consisted of representing in paint other materials, mainly marble; nor would they take to the over-the-top fantastic grotesquery popularised by Nero. *'But Larius Lollius, what is this supposed to be? . . .'*

Larius himself loved swirling and smearing colours to create mock-marble, but his designs had to meet the desires and prejudices of the persons who paid. Fair enough. His task was to win them over. Make them believe they chose what in fact *he* had chosen to give them. So he kept faux marbling for a private hobby, nor did he try to force-feed customers the very latest ideas, the kind of crazy perspectives that drove critics to apoplexy.

Larius, who enjoyed a bit of theory when he had time, did his research; he had chortled over that curmudgeonly old architect Vitruvius letting off steam:

images which were used by the ancients are now tastelessly laid aside: monsters are painted rather than natural objects. For columns, reeds are substituted; for pediments, the stalks, leaves, and tendrils of plants. Candelabra are made to support representations of buildings, from whose summits many stalks appear to spring, with absurd figures thereon . . . such forms never did, and never can exist in nature. These new fashions have taken over, until for lack of competent judges, true art is little esteemed . . .

Let it out, Vitruvius old man! Try not to burst a blood vessel.

When in doubt, centre a panel with a finch, pecking at a fig. Just too cute. *'Oh Larius Lollius, the little bird's adorable!'*

There you are. No self-respecting craftsman listened to an *architect*. Painters and the other trades had all been treated to far too much waffle and nonsense, told too many times to rip out good work on a whim, denigrated in front of a client, blamed for faults that the fancy-arsed arrogant twerp with the note-boards had brought about through his own ignorance. How much better any site would run with a project manager who understood logistics: install a clean latrine, supply beakers of hot mulsum, voice respect for proper skill and experience, pay wages in full and on time – then let your painters do their stuff.

Simplicity, legate.

In the current house, he and his team were now working on a grand reception hall. Pompeii was overrun with guilds, religious cults and political schemers who wanted to control the place. Campanians were diligent plotters. All the best homes had a large, formal reception space where ambitious owners could hold court. A meeting place for the funeral club to get tipsy. A super setting for tasteful soirées where civic votes were rigged.

This saloon would be an impressive one. Other reception rooms had already been painted in white, Larius' favourite colour-scheme, divided up into panels by the kind of dainty candelabra and ditsy flower garlands that made Vitruvius and others shit splenetic bricks. Each tapestry of elegant sections contained one dramatic black panel at the centre, within which was a scene of polychrome fine art. Larius painted those himself, small pictures of historical scenes, architecture or rocky country views. He was famous for his seascapes. He based them on what he saw here in the Bay. Figures were never problematic for him either.

The team had already had fun on this project. Next door in the bakery, they had turned out conventional still-lives of fish, floating figures with spears or flowers, and couples lightly intertwined as they danced on air. There were scenes of people glimpsed through doorways. Clients always liked fake doorways, with their hints of mystery. Hylus had painted a superb brightly-coloured cockerel pecking at a half-devoured pomegranate beneath a shelf of untouched fruit. Hylus was really shaping up these days; he must have a good career ahead of him.

Their best effort was a dining room. Larius had taken the lead on that. Stuck awkwardly between a stable and the flour mills, the bakers hired out the room commercially to bring in extra cash. In keeping with its purpose, it now held witty scenes of banqueting. The women had been made to look as if they were hired-in professionals, though in one scene these caterers were not professional enough; a serving maid was tottering and having to be supported, drunk. Meanwhile one of the young male guests had collapsed on his couch. In another picture all the girls looked as sloshed as their men; one seemed unaware she was upending her winecup, though in fairness, although one of the males was raising a drinking horn with panache, his crony had fallen back on the couch with one arm dangling. He was very, very far out of it, assuming he could feel anything at this point of the night . . .

'Wishful thinking!' Pyris had chortled. The wide-eyed young trainee, a gullible boy, was in constant awe of the lives he believed his elders enjoyed, based on their wild boasts. He ought to have known better: he went around with them, so had seen for himself that the whole team had fairly restrained habits. After a hard day, they were too tired for debauchery. It was the plasterers who drank themselves silly and went at it like rabbits with as many women as they could get their hands on. Plasterers, according to painters, were utterly notorious.

Painters, according to plasterers, were worse.

'All based on intensive research!' Larius had answered Pyris, with an exaggerated wink. He deliberately made much of figuring in a nipple on one of the party-boys' courtesans. Then Marciana brought him lunch, so he quickly had to pretend he was only touching up the goodtime girl's diagonal garland.

Today the big room they were working on, being more formal, had lush red and gold panels rather than white, alternated with dramatic black. Half finished, the work was on schedule. They had reached Larius's favourite task, the pictures; he loved this stage, beautifying a room as if it were hung with framed art. He was ready for the significant scene – a nice bit of mythology. Always proper in a public room.

He was all set up. He had lightly scribed a basic scheme, measured out with compasses. He had positioned his brushes. On the floor and on a scaffold for the higher work, he had stationed pigment pots of various sizes, each small enough to be held conveniently in the hand while he worked; the pigments were ready, with spatulas, water, and eggs and oil for binding. Marciana would come in and help him with that. He would work rapidly but thoughtfully, changing pots unhurriedly, then painting with fast, sure brush strokes.

He had been about to start when his daughter called him.

As soon as he saw what was happening to the mountain, he thought dryly that the mythical painting was done for.

Myth was occurring here. No one alive had experience of such natural force, so Larius could not have predicted that the biggest event in Campania for a thousand years was about to happen. But he was bright, and sensitive to what he saw. Foreboding struck him at once.

Jupiter. Jupiter and all the gods in the Pantheon.

A column of debris was being pushed up into the sky above Vesuvius, higher and higher, at enormous speed. Incalculable to those on the ground, masses of it hurtled up for miles. Eventually the dense pillar broadened out at the top, disseminating like the branches of a stone pine or the cap of a gigantic mushroom. Pulsating clouds of fiery material writhed like the steaming entrails of some huge beast when its belly was slashed open in the arena.

All that crud is going to come down on us, thought Larius.

He lifted his face. The wind was blowing this way. Pompeii was what, five miles from Vesuvius? The choking clouds would land here.

He tugged Marciana's hand. 'We have to leave, chuck. We must get away.' She looked up at him, verifying his decision. 'Trust me,' he said. *Trust Father. Even though he's terrified.*

She nodded. 'How can we go?'

'I'll find Erodion and his cart.'

Then, before he could stop her, Marciana snatched her hand from his grasp and was off up the street. 'Dollies!'

'Stay at the widow's. I'll come and get you!' yelled Larius. It would take time to rootle out their lugubrious neighbour from his Pompeian mistress' bower, in order to persuade him to produce the cart unscheduled. Erodion was not known for rallying in emergencies. His wife handled any crises.

Larius strode back indoors. Standing in consternation,

158

the lads looked to him to say what was up; they had heard the stunning explosion but were scared to go and look.

'Drop everything. Just leave it. Shit on a stick; this is a big one.'

Conscientious, they still stood, unsure. Hylus could not help letting his eyes go to the main panel, gauging the state of the plaster. Young Pyris quavered, 'What about the client?'

'Let me square it with the client. Don't bother with your stuff. Get going; save yourselves, lads, before it's too late.'

Their stuff was here; they slept on site. Larius telling them to abandon their things made them jump to. This was serious. They put down their pots and brushes. Even Three Coats began struggling down from the scaffold; his joints were swollen and crippled, so he had to take it gingerly. He knocked a whole bucket of slopping wet plaster all down the newly painted wall but Larius, who would normally have been enraged, gestured to forget it and just get moving.

They could run for the port. A boat would take them off, assuming there were any boats. Hylus grabbed money for fares or bribes. Or they could head out of town, inland, putting distance between themselves and the coming catastrophe. It would be all right. They had enough time. Even if Larius couldn't find Erodion and the cart, so had to travel with his daughter at her little legs' pace, all of them at that moment still had time to escape.

4

Nonius properly wakes up and grasps what wonders this may bring for him.

Slowly it dawned on Nonius that the street noises were unusual.

He must have dozed off after his first awakening and could not tell how long had passed. Had he slept through another bloody big earthquake? Six hundred sheep slaughtered in the fields by poisonous gases? Upper floors of houses damaged so badly they would simply be bricked up and never used again? Temples tottering, granaries groaning, columns smashing down in pieces? Some buildings destroyed so completely they had to be demolished and their plots given over to agriculture? People killed?

Hades, it had better not be any of the clients he had carefully sweetened up for his financial projects! Don't say his efforts had been for nothing. Nonius hated waste.

He jumped out of bed.

Sudden motion was an error. He sat back down on the mattress edge, allowing his sore head to normalise before he stirred again. Once the room slowly stopped spinning, he found last night's tunic, his scruffy one, which was scrubbled up on the floor where he had dropped it. He pulled on the garment, automatically straightening the folds to hang well. He was so vain, he stayed to comb his hair. Too befuddled to find his nitcomb, he used the painter's. When he had finished, instead of putting it back on Larius's small bedside tray, Nonius dropped it into his own luggage pack.

Only then did he finally drag himself down the steps into the street outside. As he opened the door, the light beyond seemed hazy. Nonius coughed. People were walking or running downhill towards the port. There was constant movement through the streets, like when the amphitheatre disgorged its audience after the games and everyone went home at once. Hundreds of people were flowing in one direction, purposefully. Some carried bundles, some hoisted small children on their shoulders so they could move faster. He saw wheelbarrows, piled with household goods. There were cries of alarm, even screams of panic. But most walked as fast as they could in grim silence.

A pattering sound was everywhere, a sound like heavy rain in a Mediterranean storm. It was unceasing and regular, though occasionally broken by a loud crack. When Nonius ventured over the threshold, he jumped back, exclaiming. Bloody hell, it hurt! Small pebbles, like hail but harder, were showering from a darkening sky. There were gusts of a really bad smell.

Nonius, who was still woozy, took his time to gather what was going on. The rain of stones, ash-coloured, cinder-like, stinging and biting, filled the air. He wanted to hide, to cover up bare skin, to duck his head, to flee back indoors. But even half asleep, Nonius soon saw that sheltering was not for him.

Seeing his puzzlement, someone named the mountain. 'Vesuvius!' Vesuvius had blown up? Jupiter Best and Greatest.

He had to be out. He had things to do. He would be extremely busy. This was his great chance. The foolish people of Pompeii were leaving their homes. Stupidly or not, they believed it was a temporary evacuation, after which they would come back. So they left most of their possessions behind.

Let them flee. Flight was for fools. Not Nonius.

He understood at last. Fabulous. For him, this was the best opportunity ever.

Bracing himself, Nonius went out into those streets, where anxious escapees were following each other full of uncertainty, whereas he was full of purpose. Trying to dodge the battering lapilli, the crowd hurried frantically yet seemed to have little idea where they were going. Wailing and selfishly trying to save themselves, while getting in his way, people had no idea. Nonius had to use his chance. Some wore cushions tied on their heads, or were huddled in cloaks, too muffled up and much too scared to see where they were running – and nor did they notice what Nonius was doing. As if he had been born for it, Nonius was making the most of this situation. He worked with joy in his heart.

A middle-aged woman was struggling with her doorlock. 'Oh madam, let me help with that!' insisted Nonius, shoving her on her way in a fluster, while palming her latch lifter.

A man left his keys in their usual hiding place, under a plant pot. Nonius observed. After the householder scurried off, Nonius retrieved them.

A pregnant woman had trouble carrying treasured possessions; Nonius offered to help her, seized the bag manfully – then vanished in the gloom.

A slave who had been left behind to guard a place, answered the door to Nonius' urgent knocking. He sounded official. 'You have to get out! Everyone has to leave now. Don't stop for anything, run for it!'

Soon he was madly gathering silver dinnerwares, bronze household gods, gladiator figurines, coins, male and female jewellery. Glass was too fragile, more's the pity. Bankboxes were beyond him to force, he was in too much of a hurry and had no strong tools; cupboard doors eventually gave way.

A young female slave who had been hiding in a backroom came to investigate the noise. She had the bad luck to run into Nonius, to his delight. Already terrified by the eruption, she could not escape. 'Well, *hello there, darling!*' Her lucky day.

It wasn't rape.

Rapists always say that though.

She really wanted it. She was a slut, a slave, she made me do it. She shouldn't have screamed. She was screaming because she enjoyed it. She knew I couldn't help myself. It wasn't rape.

Hades. This was the most exciting event in this town. Nonius was more thrilled than he had ever been. The spoils were his. All of it, everything. What else could anyone expect?

5

In Herculaneum, the painter's wife attempts to cope.

It was one of the twins who first noticed that something was happening. Varius, the two-year-old boy, had gone out of doors, crying, after being told for the umpteenth time he could not have any more nut-custard, because there was no more. There would be none until Marciana brought money home, whenever that would be. Ollia was reasonably certain Larius would send something, yet since he had once absconded without warning, she never felt entirely secure. She kept an old cooking pot of coins, buried in the garden, a bit of money collected in better times and hoarded, in case she was suddenly destitute.

Those had been hard years for her, when Larius was in Britain. On her own, she'd had to scrape a living. When she could, she took in other people's children to mind, but most folk around here had families for that. She did mending. Some women spun wool, a Campanian cottage industry but Ollia, who grew up in Rome, had never been taught. Patching tunics or strengthening their necks where seams often tore was tedious and only brought in a pittance.

In summer she could get horrible temporary work serving

in a bar, or helping out in kitchens as extra banquet staff when the rich descended on their holiday homes, but then she had to find somewhere to park her own infants, who resented it and played up. She hated having to plead, the risk of being fondled by men she despised, the hostility from others who were equally desperate for the work. She missed her children.

Larius did return, with money, but then she had to fight down her anger against him. He wasn't naïve; he must have realised, when he left, what his absence would mean. Ollia had been furious. When he turned up again, she could so easily have sent him packing, but she had to think about their children. She had to pretend.

Things were better now. She was here while most of the time he worked away in Pompeii, but they counted themselves a family. In some marriages separation is a good idea. Larius had always been a one for ideas. Their children, who only saw him when he came jauntily bearing presents, adored him, never understanding his faults. They saw their mother all the time and each one had her measure, so her role was more difficult. Plus the struggle to look after them was every day and unrelenting.

Angrily she called Varius back. Screaming no, he ran to hide. She left him to it.

He was more of a handful than any of her others, a defiant little tyrant, but she knew where he would be. He always crawled into the hencoop. He would come to no harm there. When enough time had passed for him to calm down and start to feel he was missing things, Ollia would waddle out to fetch him. She and her toddler would have a little chat as usual – he smelling of poultry shit, whimpering and hiccupping, while she too settled down as she cuddled him. She would sigh, and maybe shed a tear or two herself. Holding her hand, he would then come indoors meekly.

She was tired. It was still barely noon, yet she felt she had been on her feet all day. Sultry weather was not helping. She knew she was expecting again. If it was more twins, she would kill herself. Maybe she needn't bother: nature would do it. Her mother had carried triplets once. They all died in the birth, including her mother.

No, it mustn't happen to her. Somebody had to look after these. She had to take care of herself, make sure she was always here for them.

She liked children, fortunately. Hers, with their dark curls and attractive features, were generally a pleasure. They had good times together, at least when there was enough to eat and none of them were sickly. If Ollia had to choose the memory she most cherished, she would pick a lazy day when she took them along the coast to Oplontis for a picnic, sat on the beach there, gazing out to sea. In her mind, this scene took place when Larius was away. It was just her and them. One child lolling against her, the others playing quietly. The blue of the sea meeting the uniform blue of the Neapolis sky, while the hot sun made everyone drowsy. The scent of newly landed octopus cooking on skewers over a fire right there on the shore at sunset. Friends she had known since before she was married, who treated her like family.

The fisherman, Vitalis, her old flame.

Would he have been a better choice? It was too late now, and Ollia had enough folk wisdom to know you should never waste time on regret, not for a man. Well, bloody hell, Ollia; not that one!

166

Vitalis had never married. A fool might imagine the bronzed, muscular lump was pining for her, but Ollia was too wise to think it. More likely he remained alone because other girls had been wary of his roving eye and, let's face it, his laziness. When his father and then his uncle died, he took over their fishing boat but he never changed. It was a hard life, so not ideal for Vitalis. He would never put himself out unless he had to, yet he seemed surprised when he then did badly.

Ollia was not surprised at all. Long ago she had palled up with his mother, two wise women shaking their heads over him.

When Larius left her that time, when he went off to Britain without saying a word, Ollia could have had her chance with the fisherboy, She was too taken up with little Marciana and her newborn twins, so she never did anything about it. Nor did Vitalis. His inaction was not due to respect for her married status, nor fear of the burden of children, but just because Vitalis never did anything about anything.

That was life. She knew to this day that Larius might well have stayed away, so she would really have been stuck. But the fisherboy was no better.

Larius did come back, though he was rarely here with her. But since then, he sent money almost every week; Marciana brought it, and there was plenty. Figure painters were well paid.

One thing you had to say for him, Larius worked hard. He loved to paint. He loved that more than he loved Ollia and the little ones, she had to accept it. But this was probably how it would be now, this was probably permanent. To drive him away entirely she would have to make his life very miserable indeed, so she would not do that; it was tempting to nag when they came together, but she resisted. They would survive somehow. And Ollia felt safe that she was no longer alone; in any real emergency, Larius would come to help.

Varius was a child who looked around him, hoping for an excuse to yell his head off in exaggerated terror or disgust. Today he noticed Vesuvius looked peculiar, so after a second of bafflement, he began screaming. As she went out to her little boy and saw what was happening to the mountain, Ollia's first thought was Larius. He would come for them, he would tell her what to do.

One of her neighbours called out, hurrying away. 'Have you seen it? We are all leaving, Ollia. Grab your tots and come along with us.'

She was grateful for the offer. But Ollia, wife of Larius the painter, gazed at Mount Vesuvius as it spewed a plug of ash from the depths of the earth and sent clouds of fine material flittering all around the peak, and said no, no thank you. She had to wait here until her husband came, because he would need to know where to find them.

The first emission looked like forest fires smouldering on the side of the mountain. That continued for some time, covering the peak entirely. Ollia went out to watch occasionally as she tidied up after giving the children lunch. Then came a huge noise as if all of Campania was breaking apart, so she ran out of doors again, and witnessed the beginning of the first big eruption. Horrified, she watched a massive column of molten rock and gas climbing ever higher from the peak, desperately close to Herculaneum. The pulsating cloud was grey, with lighter and darker parts as different materials were thrown up. She noticed fires on the mountain itself, then bursts of flame amongst the rising column and flashes like lightning in the dark clouds that were reaching into the sky. The very air felt hot on her face; it seemed to reek of poison.

It was ten miles for Larius to come, even if his journey was not impeded. Logistics were not Ollia's strength. She did not immediately grasp that to reach his family he would have to travel up the coast road through Oplontis, approaching much closer to this vigorous new volcano. Larius, who had their eldest daughter with him, would want to find safety – and, for him, that lay in the opposite direction.

6

People begin to make their escape if they can.

The painters Hylus and Pyris, accompanied by Three Coats the plasterer, reached the harbour outside the Marine Gate. In a tight group, with plenty of attitude, they were able to push their way through the other fugitives. In the terrible gloom, people were losing each other. Friends and family called out in panic.

'Ione!'

'Glaucus!'

'Bloody Greeks,' muttered Hylus as he tripped over a young girl who seemed to be blind; grasping her by the shoulders, he set her facing the right way but then left her.

At the shore, ships owned by wealthy men had been laden, ready to transport them and their possessions to safety; they might take others on board if their crews were decent and had room. However, these vessels were all trapped, prevented from launching by a strong onshore wind. The sea was whipped up unusually. Further out, the painters could see a small number of boats heading into the coast in a rescue attempt, including one large military trireme that must have been sent from the naval base at

Misenum. These were held up for another reason: when pumice from the eruption landed in the sea, it floated. Pieces started small. However, they cooled rapidly once they hit water, then welded together into large solid plates of debris. Awkward bobbing barriers crowded the shallows. Chunks of this crud blocked inbound shipping. While the men watched, even the oared trireme gave up and veered away, heading instead for Stabiae. For the crowds who had hurried to the shore in hope, escape by sea looked impossible.

Hylus and Pyris glanced at each other. After summing up the chaotic harbour scene, they did not hesitate. Others were milling about the moorings indecisively, but the painters set off on foot at once, turning south towards the River Sarno which they would cross, away from the town and its turbulent mountain. The constantly increasing layer of ash was making it difficult to walk. They were already wading through it, hot between the open toes of their work boots. The coating of fine cinders on buildings and roads was rising steadily so the two painters, with their professional knowledge of physical materials, understood their situation was highly dangerous. They needed to travel fast.

Three Coats, who like so many old workers was very severely crippled, had told them to go on ahead and leave him. If and when Larius came by in transport, the plasterer could rely on being picked up. Hylus and Pyris felt some uncertainty, but let themselves be persuaded. That was how it was that day: no time for debate. Every man for himself. In their hearts they knew that if Three Coats had been a painter they would probably have carried him, but all the prejudices of their trade worked against him now.

He had been the butt of secret jokes for a long time. Like

many, years of heavy work had brought arthritis on him; his was much worse than normal wear and tear. He was bent over, hook-backed, his lower limbs twisted. He walked only with a painful hitch and roll. How he managed to do his work at all was a miracle, yet somehow he scraped together the energy and will. The other plasterers had left him with the painters to relieve themselves of the responsibility, then they went off to another job.

He was still a good plasterer, though agonisingly slow. Larius had tolerated his frailty, knowing the elderly man had no other way to make a living. His team looked sideways at Larius sometimes, wondering if the time had come for him to tell the project manager to hire a faster worker, one who would be safe on ladders. So far Larius had never broached it. Instead he carried buckets for Three Coats, sometimes even hauled the disabled old man himself up a scaffold, pretending it was horseplay.

Three Coats normally liked to pretend he was no different from anybody else. But today he knew his failings had finally caught up with him. He could not walk through the ash that lay in a deep fluid carpet like soft blizzard snow. He had to watch Hylus and Pyris set off through the knee-high sludge, in gathering murk, heading down the coast road towards the Surrentum peninsular. They would have the choice of turning inland or moving along the far side of the bay. Resigned, Three Coats stayed at the Marine Gate. There were arched tunnels, a high central entrance for vehicles with two lower ones for pedestrians. He sat down on a stone bench outside one of the pedestrian arches, waiting for Larius to come along and give him the lift he so badly needed.

Larius never came. Hindered by his physical condition, the plasterer would make it no further.

7

Erodion, his mistress, her husband, his horse and his fate.

Larius found his neighbour from Herculaneum, Erodion, at the house where, he knew, Erodion stayed with a fruiterer's wife if the fruiterer was away. Tending his orchards, presumably, while somebody else was gaily plundering his plums.

She was a buxom piece, that Nymphe, shameless and up for mischief. She kept her house nice and herself smart. Fashionable hair. An air of understated bossiness that feeble men like Erodion found swimmingly attractive. Popular in the neighbourhood, Nymphe had her own style and was comfortable with it. She was also, it suddenly transpired, pregnant.

This had come as a big surprise to Erodion, whose wife in Herculaneum, Salvia, had never given them children despite his vigorous attempts to fertilise her. He thought offspring would give Salvia an interest – that is (so the idiot imagined), she would then be too busy to question what he got up to on his trips, suspiciously sniffing his clothes for strange perfumes, interrogating Larius and Marciana, generally nagging in a wifely way. He was a pain, and Salvia knew it.

Erodion reckoned himself an expert in wives and their

ways, due to his frequent observation of two of them. One his, one not. This allowed him to be both personally prejudiced and entirely disinterested when he discussed women. He ran the full gamut of misogynist thought. He enjoyed holding forth, imposing his opinion on others in a merciless, dolorous way. On anyone who put up with it, at least; Larius tended to give him the elbow once he started.

Erodion was a market gardener so he prospered. Campania, with its famous three or four harvests a year, had the most fertile soil and the best climate in Italy. His leeks and cabbages were stupendous, his onions exquisite, his artichokes and asparagus made eaters weep with pleasure. Whenever Erodion came to market in Pompeii – *when I'm allowed out of the house*, he would mutter bitterly; *when the sly worm wriggles off*, his wife would say – he went home afterwards with enough money to allay her curiosity, even after he had provided lavish presents for his mistress. Salvia received smaller, fewer presents than the fruiterer's wife – except a pair of superb snake bracelets, which became hers the time Erodion accidentally mixed up his parcels. Nymphe's loss, that week.

Even when he came up with the right gift, it was hard to know what Nymphe saw in him, for he was a lax-bellied, big-headed, puffy-faced swine with swollen legs and a pointy nose. It could be she had her own problems. That the fruiterer, Rufius, was so often away himself suggested to Larius that *he* might be embroiled with someone else's wife at Nucera or Capua, venues to which Rufius assured Nymphe he must journey frequently to dispose of his own juicy produce in *their* markets. Since the complex arrangement apparently kept them all happy – Erodion, Nymphe, Rufius, Salvia (well, maybe not Salvia) – Larius merely smiled over it to himself and never commented.

Larius might have laughed about it with Ollia, who of course knew Erodion and the badly neglected Salvia in Herculaneum, but he had not discussed their neighbour's behaviour lest it gave Ollia ideas about what he, Larius, might be getting up to while he was working away in Pompeii. Why invite trouble? Domestic distrust would be all the more unfair, given that Larius never got up to anything.

Well, pretty well never. And if he did, it was not important.

He knew where Erodion's lovenest was, so he hastened there, knocked loudly, pushed past a slave who opened up; talking tough, Larius demanded that his neighbour come out at once and hitch up the cart so they could leave town. 'Otherwise I'll have to pinch your horse, Erodion!' It was a knock-kneed, foul-breathed ancient beast; Larius wished Erodion had stopped wasting his money on Nymphe and bought a better one.

But there was chaos in the fruiterer's house. When Vesuvius blew, Erodion had offered to take Nymphe to safety, Larius discovered; but she'd refused to travel. He'd been gallantly insistent, but she'd cut him off and stated why: she was expecting. Running away from the explosion wasn't an option.

Erodion innocently assumed the baby was his. Some men would run from such a predicament. Erodion, it turned out, was the kind of reckless sentimentalist who immediately wanted to desert his legitimate wife; he took the instant decision to acknowledge this child, unborn though it was, with Nymphe barely showing yet, and that he, she and their little one should live in bliss.

Nymphe wailed aloud at this terrible idea. Erodion beat his head in frustration that she could not see what was being offered – not merely escape but the subsequent bliss. Neither of the lovers was paying real attention to the erupting volcano, too close for comfort.

Actually, Larius, the father of five if not six, reckoned Nymphe's condition was obvious. He was astounded Erodion had not noticed before. As for bliss, in Larius' experience that was a myth, and not the kind of myth he could paint.

Plunged into this daft scenario, thinking fast, Larius suggested that Erodion might be wise to wait before busting up two homes – or even three, if the fruiterer also had a complicated relationship in Nucera or Capua, some fraught affair which might be altered by his dutifully taking on his wife's baby. Also, said Larius as wisely as if he had in truth been there for the births of those twins, pregnancy involves many dangers and uncertainties; besides, he pointed out, unless Nymphe and her husband had never engaged in intercourse there was no way to be sure who had given her a child. Rufius might genuinely be the one with rights.

No use. Whether from honest good-heartedness or a paternalistic desire for possession of what he saw as his goods, Erodion was still laying claim to this foetus that, a few beats of time before, he had not known about.

'Stop being an idiot, Erodion. Just get lost,' said Nymphe. Clearly she was a practical woman. Nymphe had flair. Larius wondered if his neighbour wasn't the only lover she had been stringing along when her husband went to market.

Erodion was about to burst with stress when a voice – the fruiterer, Larius assumed – was heard at the front door, loudly calling to Nymphe. He must have returned from fruit-selling and fornication (if he did that) and when he saw Vesuvius erupt, he rushed to his house to comfort his expectant wife. 'I am here; love. You are all right now!'

He had a deep voice, that of a burly man. He sounded

forceful. Larius, a veteran bar-brawler when young, judged that Erodion was about to be laid out cold.

If he had come home quietly, Rufius could well have marched in to find an agitated stranger needing to be punched in the teeth. Nymphe, however, seized the moment while Rufius (a well-trained beast domestically) was bent over on the threshhold, taking off his outdoor shoes. He had to beat the soles together to knock off cinders, which fortunately delayed him.

Nymphe opted for Rufius like a loyal wife, or at least one who knew that husbands who follow house-rules are to be treasured. She ordered Erodion to exit by the back way – and get out fast. To make sure, she kicked him from behind, while Larius pulled him from in front. She slammed the door after them and they heard her cooing, 'O Rufius, I am so glad you've come, I am so frightened!'

'Two-timing bitch!' snarled Erodion. That was no way to speak of the mother of his child, if it was his, but Larius kept mum.

Other things were on his mind. Now he could haul his sullen neighbour away to prepare the cart for urgent travel. As they whipped up the tetchy old horse to go and collect Marciana, Larius decided to take the reins. Erodion sat sunk in gloom. His life had changed. He had lost his lover, been deprived of his unborn heir; life was brutal, fate was cruel . . .

'Erodion, we have worse changes ahead! The whole bloody world's exploding. We may be going to die today. Shut up, will you?'

'You're heartless. I've lost everything!'

'Don't be daft, you still have Salvia.'

Not the right answer. 'Barren bitch.'

'Bollocks, she's a perfectly nice woman.'

That was debateable, for Salvia possessed a sharp tongue (she needed it), but Larius had his hands full trying to forge a passage down a narrow street against an oncoming tide of people, while the ever-descending lava fragments were darkening the world to near-impenetrable gloom. Nevertheless, since he was philosophical, he could not help reflecting.

Many a tricky situation would be exposed today. Not the duplicity of Nymphe and Erodion perhaps, though that had been close: Rufius could so easily have rushed in to find his wife, wearing fancy ear-rings that he had not bought for her, enjoying a light lunch with a strange man, who was so much at home he had brought his own comfortable house slippers. The small staff of slaves would have been disloyally hoping they could watch the post-prandial gropes. Probably the intruder would have been gulping up his egg salad from the favourite bowl of Rufius . . .

Narrow escape. Let's hope we can all manage another one and get out of Pompeii.

They passed the house where Larius had been working. He jumped down, ran indoors and picked up his set of best brushes. These were British badger and squirrel hair, lovingly cleaned and cared for, each marked with his initials on the stock. Tools of his trade. The one thing you save. All over Pompeii doctors were catching up surgical instruments, surveyors were packing their measuring equipment in custom-designed satchels, priests were running away from temples with valuable objects of obscure religious design. Votive bowls were flitting mysteriously all over town.

Coming out, Larius nodded to the baker, who was standing on his doorstep looking impatient. His was the largest bread-making firm in Pompeii. He seemed to be alone now; he must have despatched his staff, slaves and freeborn, to safety. 'Aren't you leaving?'

'Got a piglet and a bird half done on the cooking fire.' The man shook himself so clouds of flour dust flew off him, mingled with fallen ash that he had acquired from standing outside among the volcanic lapilli. He coughed.

'Madness!' called Larius, back on the cart. 'Forget lunch. Don't expect us to help you eat it, not today! You need to leave.' He had worked for this man; they had a good relationship.

There was nobody at the street bar on the corner, except his ghastly subtenant, Nonius. Nonius was working his way along all the beakers of wine that customers had abandoned half-full on the crazy-paved marble counters. He was so busy emptying saucers of olives and washing them down, he did not see Larius, who made no attempt to call out.

At the widow's house, he turned the cart with some difficulty so it would be ready for their flight, and left Erodion in charge of it.

He ran indoors, calling for his daughter and the widow, his frail landlady, whom in kindness he intended to bring along with them. He found Marciana in a state of tearful panic. 'She won't leave without her cats!'

'Oh hell. She must, chuck. It's not safe to stay.'

The timorous old woman appeared, then began wailing. Once, she had been respectable. These days, she looked like a hag in a cave from some legend: wild strands of hair, mad eyes, a dirty tunic that she never changed, hands like claws; yet ultimately pitiful. Larius agreed to have a quick look for her pets, so with a muffled curse he started searching. He felt a professional obligation; he had drawn them from life a couple of times, since cats prowling after birds were a popular motif.

The garden was filling up with deposits; lapilli were finding their way in through open windows, ash even working under closed doors. No doubt agitated by the eruption, the damned cats were nowhere to be found. Soon Larius abandoned that crazy quest, then ran outside, back to the street with his heart bumping; breathlessly, he climbed upstairs to his room to fetch an old cloak in which to wrap up his daughter to protect her from the falling missiles. On the way he noticed several sacks of goods, a candelabra sticking out of one, which he knew must be treasure stolen from houses by his unscrupulous subtenant.

While Larius was back inside the widow's apartment, collecting Marciana and failing to persuade the old woman to flee with them, Nonius came along the street.

He was here to pick up his plunder, pondering how he could possibly transport it. When he saw the cart outside, he thanked the gods, even though they had inconsiderately left him with a problem: what to do about Erodion? Oblivious, Erodion was still perched on the driving plank, where Larius had left him. He had the reins in his limp hands, bitterly sunk in his misery at the faithlessness of Nymphe. All around him fell the endless shower of lava, now in much larger fragments.

The widow's house needed maintenance more than it had shown. With the weight of fallen cinders, its roof began to creak; rafter batons bowed, on the verge of failing; a loose tile slipped and fell. This heavy terracotta pantile smashed down on Erodion, gashing his head open. As he started from his trance at last, bemused by being struck so painfully, he tried to staunch the pouring blood.

Nonius picked up the heavy tile from the road. He jumped up on the cart. There, he smote the woozy market gardener

180

again and again, holding the rooftile two-handed to batter his skull, until his victim stopped moving.

It was irrelevant now whether Erodion had fathered Nymphe's baby. Nonius had killed him.

Nonius heaved the lifeless body off the cart, then quickly fetched his sacks of treasure and drove off. When Larius came out of the house with his daughter, who was carrying her precious basket, they saw their neighbour lying in the street. Erodion was already partly buried by a thin blanket of pumice. A pantile covered with brains lay beside his corpse.

'He is dead,' Marciana pronounced, hard of heart. 'Don't cry, dollies; he's no loss!' Larius had been dithering but he stopped and gazed down at her. He loved her at this age: old enough to be cheeky, though still young enough to sometimes need him. The cart they were relying on to save them had vanished yet she seemed insouciant. 'Someone took the horsey. They won't get far.' Of her own accord, Marciana spun away quickly inside the house, returning without her basket. 'Less to carry. Maybe we can come back for them . . . So, Father, the old lady is hiding in her pantry. It's just you and me – time for us to get out of here!'

8

Ollia acts.

Slowly, slowly, the painter's wife reached her decision. She recognised that she must not rely on Larius. She had to deal with this herself.

In Herculaneum, they did not have, or not yet, the constant fall of pumice that had been landing further south. With the wind still blowing away from them, only a light covering of ash lay here. But there was alarming geological activity, with swirling clouds of noxious gas and violent underground shudders, accompanied by constant loud noises. Ollia had always hated earthquakes. This was more extreme than anything she had ever known; it made buildings sway and threaten to come crashing down. Vesuvius was in such flux that the mountain itself was re-shaping, while the land heaved under huge pressures. Although the sky-high column of debris still held up in its enormous cloud, Ollia became terrified.

The noises were unearthly. When they lessened, her neighbourhood had an eerie quiet. Most people had left. Only invalids, the old, or the very pregnant had remained this long in their houses. Even they, if they could, had begun shuffling slowly to what they prayed was safety.

Very soon the whole town would be empty. Ollia must go too.

Her sudden sense of isolation scared her. Normally people were working, singing, chattering. Wheels creaked. Donkey bells rang. In this unsettling absence of daily clamour, her few chickens in the yard that passed for a garden were audibly agitated. With the children's help she collected her anxiously fluttering hens, penning them in the coop. While she was outside, she dug up her cache of emergency coins. Dealing with this gave her a last chance to consider what to do. In Herculaneum that day, a woman with small children and no transport had few options.

She put an amulet on each child to avert the evil eye. Subdued, they complied.

'You may take one toy each. Varius, I said one; bring your chariot. That's your favourite.' Though innately disobedient, Varius clutched his miniature quadriga, with its mad-eyed driver; it had moving wheels, well sort of, though Ollia often had to fiddle with eyebrow tweezers to get them to go again for him, when they seized up. Lolliana and Galliana had collected a doll each; Ollia was a conventional mother. Lolliana really yearned for a toy sword but Ollia had pooh-poohed that. Ollius brought his pottery pig moneybox. He liked to persuade his siblings to put any coppers they had into his box through the slot, then would not let them have their money back. The family all joked he would grow up to be a banker.

'Now everyone use the potty.'

'Everyone use the potty,' they mimicked, though without malice. *'Tinkle, tinkle!'* Chorusing Mother's instructions had become a new routine lately. When they went on an expedition it was a joke they enjoyed, including Ollia in their

glee. To look after this large group of children, she had to be organised; they accepted her methods, were even proud of how she managed.

Now she tried not to let them see how fraught she felt, while they pretended not to notice, which was their way of helping. They lined up and weed as much as they could. She gave each a kiss for being good. Then Ollia took the younger twins each by the hand, while the elder twins went on the outside, grasping their younger siblings' free fists.

'Stay together.'

'Stay together!'

'Are we going to the seaside?' For them that meant Oplontis.

'Wait and see. It's a surprise.'

How true. She had no idea where they should go. To safety – but where was safe?

Automatically, Ollia set out in the direction she had seen her neighbours hurrying earlier, which was downhill along one of the main roads, towards the shore. Escape by boat. That made her nervous, for even after living near the ocean for almost a decade, Ollia could not swim, nor could these children. Larius, whose oarsman father on the Tiber in Rome had long ago taught him, was himself teaching Marciana, but he never saw enough of the others; he promised, but it never happened. Ollia wouldn't let them go on boats, except the fishing smack owned by Vitalis when it was safely hauled up on dry land.

By now only a scatter of fugitives still made their way along the streets. She glimpsed a few dark figures down side alleys, but the place was ghostly. The civic area lay behind her, the basilica and theatre. They passed through pleasant residential parts of this well-ordered town, until they reached the area where rich people had commandeered the seaward approach for enormous coastal residences, fabulous second homes with swimming pools, libraries, breezy terraces to walk on while gazing out at grand views. Below those high-end resort properties, a row of vaulted sheds had been hacked into the cliff, sometimes used for laid-up boats, sometimes for storage. Ollia and her now frightened group of infants ended up among a crowd there.

She had done the right thing, clearly. She had chosen what hundreds of others also thought best. Nobody could criticise her. Mothers are so often afraid of being blamed.

Someone said the fishing fleet had gone out at dawn and not returned, but other boats were coming. It was unclear where this information originated, though for the desperate it had a ring of truth. Standing at the choppy water's edge they looked out to sea and wanted to believe.

Tension was high, yet people stood there patiently. Everyone was frightened, but they did not know what else to do. They would wait to be rescued, and if no boats came by nightfall, they would all shelter in the boatsheds.

A fishing smack rocked in. It was empty, no catch today from those teeming waters. The man said shoals of fish were floating out in the bay, all dead, as if the sea had poisoned them.

The crowd surged forwards, but the fisherman waved an oar aggressively so they pulled back. He took off a small group, people he knew, though when he plied the oars again his boatload seemed to lack direction, he himself rowing with an air of hopelessness.

Herculaneum grew dark very early, and it was very dark indeed. All afternoon people stood waiting, in a kind of ghastly twilight. Nobody spoke much. Behind the town, loud terrible sounds continued from deep within the earth, which seemed no longer solid but boiling. As the mountain kept hurling molten rocks and ash ever skywards, people eventually began to move under cover.

'When can we go home?' pleaded a sad, scared child.

'Not yet,' said Ollia. She did not know that they might as well have done.

9

Larius and his daughter fleeing.

Earth tremors shook Pompeii too, with noise and clouds of sulphur. The ash lay so deep, Marciana was tiring by the minute; she had no hope of wading far through the filthy material, which had landed in such quantities that roads showed only as dips, making the mounded walkways featureless deathtraps. The famous Pompeii stepping-stones, the bollards protecting fountains and altars, the worn ruts in the road surface now lay treacherously buried.

Ash and small lapilli kept falling. Doorways were blocked. Balconies held piles of the grey-white stuff. Some frightening alteration meant the debris shower now contained larger lumps of rock. These cinders were three times as big as when the eruption started, and they felt hotter. Larius saw someone struck so hard they fell and could not continue. A child might be killed outright. He was afraid *he* would be killed and his child left to fend for herself in this nightmare.

The terrible darkness was increasing. Ash coated them so they felt sticky with it, tasting grit, breathing in particles that clogged their lungs. Every few moments they had to shake themselves, to ease their clothes.

This was not going to work. Nobody who tried to escape on foot would make it. They had left it too late. They had too far to go.

Larius started considering whether to take shelter and simply wait for the emissions to finish. He did not like the idea.

They reached the house with the bakery; the baker was just coming out, bringing a panniered donkey. He was about to lock in his others. They were valuable animals. He used them to turn the flour mills or for deliveries. He still imagined he was coming back, to continue with his thriving business.

Frantic, Larius caught at his tunic sleeve. 'Lend me one! I'll pay for it. I'll give you anything . . .' He gestured wildly to his struggling daughter. The baker liked her. Marciana looked up at the man, a natural little actress, putting it on. *I am young; it is your choice, but please save me, kind soft-hearted sir . . .*

It worked. 'Have the hinny. You'd bloody well better bring him back for me, Larius!'

Each animal was desperate to leave the stable anyway. They could hear whinnying and kicking. When the loaned beast came crashing out of doors, Larius had to jump to hold him before he bolted. This one was wild, tall though, part donkey, part small horse. Larius put Marciana up in front of him so he could hold her, dug in his heels heartlessly and rode. He rode for some time behind the baker himself, who had also decided to mount his delivery beast, until they became separated, losing each other; in those terrible streets full of dangerous blackness and flying debris nobody would expect a friend to stop and search.

Larius stayed up on the pavements, because of the roads'

hidden potholes and stepping-stones. At every side street he had to encourage their mount to drop down its front hooves and cross, unable to tell where the road was, or how high the next pavement up which it had to scramble. The hinny panicked; *he* panicked, but they had to go on.

In places they forced their way through groups of other fugitives, but sometimes there was no one about, and they felt they were the last people on earth. Their hinny, fearful and keen to escape, was wading, sliding, staggering. Larius leaned forwards, over Marciana, talking in its hairy ears, encouraging, soothing. Hell, he was soothing all of them. He and the child were equally scared.

'Are we going to die?'

He made a reassuring noise. With neither saddle nor stirrups, he was constantly struggling for balance. Any father knows how to pretend he is concentrating on the job in hand too much to answer a hard question.

Any daughter knows how to interpret that. At least we are together, thought Marciana. Doggedly brave, she would not have wanted her loved papa to be here in trouble on his own.

Still fairly innocent, she wondered what this adventure would be like. Larius, whose heart had never stopped sinking since the crisis kicked off, did not want to find out.

His first idea had been to follow his mates, travelling down to the Marine Gate. He and Marciana were starting from the very centre of the town. No direction would be quicker than any other, except that if they continued towards the water they would be on the main street, which was wider and more familiar, then eventually pass through the Forum. That would be a clear open space for the hinny to cross

189

on level ground. Though Larius wrestled with the idea, he decided against it. Most of the civic buildings were in a state of renovation. Pompeii was in the throes of a really big rebuilding project: a huge new temple of Venus half completed, the old Temple of Jupiter decommissioned and its statuary dismantled, bath complexes under repair, markets being reorganised. He knew the Forum had been obstructed with building materials which must now be partly hidden under erupted detritus, hard-edged clutter that would be tricky to manoeuvre around. It could bring the horse down.

Besides, people had rushed towards the sea. Pompeii had disgorged a multitude, who would be clogging the jetties and the roads to the south. He envisaged chaos. If there were any boats, they would be full. And, Larius guessed, maybe there were none. People might hope in vain. If there turned out to be no sea transport, everyone would rush away hysterically overland, causing hideous congestion on the roads.

No one would regulate an evacuation. Larius did not know, but it wouldn't have surprised him, that even the commander of the fleet at Misenum only rowed over to help a personal friend, with no apparent thought for the ordinary populace. A managed fleet of triremes and local shipping could have achieved something. No such plan was initiated.

Save the rich and sod the poor. What changes?

Still thinking, Larius knew where one possible boat existed, a boat owned by a crack-brain so bone idle he would probably be sitting on the beach right now, watching the mountain's pyrotechnics, dimly chewing an anchovy. Vitalis.

Larius made up his mind. He would struggle up to Oplontis, then make Vitalis row him up the coast. If not, he'd pinch the boat and row it himself. So Larius turned off before the Forum, then rode the hinny out by the Herculaneum Gate.

He was heading towards the volcano, but also to the town where his wife and other children were. He had a ridiculous hope that he might somehow collect them. Ollia, he knew, would trust him to try. Dear gods, they were both barmy; he hoped Ollia had had the sense to get away without waiting.

Even so, he was going there. He felt an unexpected focus; his wife and the twins seemed oddly remote from his own immediate predicament, yet they were tugging at his heart. A desperate concern was the daughter in his arms. Always prone to sickness, she had begun coughing and spluttering scarily. Marciana might boss him like an adult, but now Larius felt acutely aware of how slight her body was, a father's dread of how a young child's hold on life can suddenly become fragile.

Ollia must have experienced this many times when her children were sick in their feckless father's absence. For the first time, Larius felt genuine sympathy for her troubles.

You are helpless. You do all you can for them, but nature ignores your desperation. You cannot let your own burden fall on them, or your fear communicate; you must conceal your pain. They may live or die; you are unable to do anything except watch as they stay or go from you.

Now it was his turn to cope. Now Larius was alone with it. Jupiter, this was a disaster.

10

In the boatsheds.

'It's smelly! I don't want to go in there.'

'Just a bit of seaside pong. Don't make a fuss.'

'When will it be over?'

'I don't know, it's no use asking me. We all have to be patient. Just be a good girl, will you?'

A soldier was directing the crowd taking shelter. 'Let's keep it civilised – put the women and children right inside. The young men can stay out on the beach, if there's a shortage of space . . .' Ollia felt grateful for his guidance, grateful for any. 'Come further along, there will be more room in the next shed.'

Aged about forty, he was in uniform, armed and carrying a toolbag. Had he been on leave or on a mission? He was making himself useful. He helped Ollia, lifting one of the younger twins against his shoulder, scooping the other under his free arm as they found a shed that still had room. 'Are these all yours?'

'All mine, and another on its way,' she answered firmly. She could see him eyeing her up, hoping she was just their nurse. Ollia made it clear she was a married woman, respectable, unavailable. Larius wouldn't want her getting friendly with a soldier. Anyway – for heavens' sake!

Ollia had long ago learned to complain about Campanian men, overlooking what those in her home city had been like. She let him help, but only because suspicion of a stranger kept Varius quiet. Ollius was staring at the man's sword. So was Lolliana, but the girls shrank against their mother shyly.

Once inside the dark boatshed, the soldier subtly moved on, taking his unwelcome overtures. Probably he just wanted a companion to take his mind off his own fear. Maybe he would be lucky, find some other young woman to flirt with.

After she rebuffed the soldier, Ollia listened and was surprised by how freely her companions were talking to strangers in this shared nightmare. 'I was just fetching in my bedcovers from airing as if it was any ordinary day! Then this happened. It's terrible . . .'

'Terrible,' Ollia sympathised automatically, not wanting to be reminded how bad it all was. More than usual, she was conscious of being from Rome where people were brusque and private. Ollia needed to see what was going to happen before she commented on any of it.

She was hungry. They all were. She had brought no food. They must do without – she would have to find something tomorrow for them. She was tired too, desperately weary after this awful day and her fear of what was yet to happen.

From inside the sheds, which faced out to sea, those sheltering could no longer see the mountain's fiery outbursts, though they heard and felt reverberations from endless explosions inside the deep magma chamber. Under cover of the vaulted roofs, with a whole escarpment above them to muffle the outside commotion, people might feel a little more secure.

They were packed in, hundreds of them, including the elderly and invalids. Many were women and children, as if the male population had selfishly made off earlier, leaving their dependents. But that was unfair. Most men would have been elsewhere this morning, going about their normal business out in the fields or on the water. If they had not rushed home, perhaps they had been simply prevented by events.

Maybe, thought Ollia with a shudder, her Larius had been struck down and was lying hurt. Dear gods, she hoped he had got Marciana with him. She wanted her daughter, but she had to trust that Larius would look after her. He was strong, capable, sensible enough beneath all the painting and poetry . . .

'Ollius, stay here; don't wander off!' The little boy would vanish if she took her eyes off him. Always curious. No idea of remembering where the others were. The last thing she needed was a lost child.

Somehow, they found space to lie down. Ollia tucked the children beside her, leaving room for other people, keeping her own within close reach in the dark. The twins were silent, deeply subdued by today's strange experience, aware of the adults' fear. Eventually her youngest slept, though they whimpered in their dreams. Her six-year-olds lay motionless, but they were more conscious of danger; heads close, they had been whispering together. Now she knew they were tense, listening, on the verge of crying.

Outside it must be night now. Smoke and ash created utter darkness. A few lamps and lanterns had been lit in the boatshed interior, sparse pinpoints of flame that barely touched the intense blackness. The people around her were quiet, though not completely still. There was a constant faint shuffle of movement. Adults, unable to sleep, talked together in low murmurs. They struck up a muted camaraderie even though they could not see one another. Some were in family parties. Others simply sat or lay, frozen in misery.

Ollia felt like that. She was a mother being brave for her children. Nevertheless it was so dark she could let tears trickle unseen. Holding in sobs, she closed her eyes. Soon, surprisingly, she drowsed, soothed by the warm presence of her babies against her, somehow falling into sleep because she was so exhausted and shocked.

It helped that she was not alone here. It helped that she was surrounded by other people, all feeling lost and traumatised, all waiting out this dreadful night in shared terror. A woman stepped carefully over the still forms of her companions. Excusing herself if she disturbed anyone, she murmured, 'Must get outside for a bit. I'm desperate for fresh air . . .'

Outside, the air had no freshness; it was sickly with gas and turbid with ash fragments, but she steadied herself against a wall, head up as if searching for the invisible sky. Around and above Vesuvius, bright lights were flickering like sheet lightning, though the flames were much larger.

As the woman had expected, as she had even subconsciously planned (surprising herself), she soon heard a quiet footfall. It was the helpful soldier. She had made sure he heard her say where she was going. He found her by instinct in the blackness. He was tall, she remembered. Sturdy, but he had a bad leg, legacy of a wound, an accident, a kick from a horse. She had noticed his equipment; sword, dagger in its scabbard, the ornamental metal belt that symbolised the military, with its sporran-like hanging chains to protect his manly tackle.

Soldiers had their way of avoiding a complete unbuckle; in the pitch black, the woman heard quiet chinks as he shifted his belt, hauling it sideways around him, out of the way. He's had practice, she thought, liking to know; tonight she was desperate for competence.

She did not want endearments, let alone softening up in the way her ludicrous husband thought he must bring presents. She had her own jewellery with her. She wore both the emerald bezel ring and a carnelian engraved with a hen and three chickens; she carried safe a further collection, two snake-headed gold bangles, pearl ear-rings any noblewoman would be glad to wear . . . Gifts of love, pretended her faithless husband; gifts of guilt, she realised – though she took them. Never underestimate the earning power of a betrayed woman.

The soldier was no catch; she had already glimpsed by lantern light that he had three teeth missing, which she guessed was not from battle but brawling.

There were people all around them on the beach but it was dark and anyway, all inhibitions were dispensed with tonight. It was understood why they had sought each other out. They shared a snatch of conversation, sizing one another up before proceedings began.

'Is this worse than war?' the woman asked, meaning the commotion around them.

'No,' he answered frankly. 'In war you will always have someone to blame, and normally someone to hate too.'

'Can't you loathe nature?'

'No point,' he said.

Without a word more, they reached for each other.

Later, while they were still outside, standing and gazing at the volcano's pyrotechnics, for some reason the soldier asked, 'Are you married?'

'Somehow I don't think that matters tonight!' replied Salvia.

The wife of Erodion, sneaky market gardener and serial adulterer, was neither bitter nor enjoying a sense of revenge. She felt a lot better, actually. Better than she had felt for years. So if these were her last moments of existence, for Salvia tonight was satisfactory.

She and the soldier moved apart but they both stayed outside on the beach.

Everything was altering.

Above Vesuvius, the column had rocketed up all day, pushed out by the mountain and then sucked upwards by atmospheric pull; now it reached its greatest height of nearly twenty miles. Large missiles shot upwards, destabilising the lighter contents. The stupendous elemental cloud mass collapsed. Everything aloft fell back upon itself, down into the fiery caldera that had been throwing up white-hot gases and molten rock from the earth's crust. Immeasurable forces fought, causing a new stage of activity. Abruptly, with more power than anything on earth, the volcano's violent contents welled up and overflowed.

I I

Larius indomitably reaches Oplontis, where the fisherboy is as useless as he has always been.

On a clear day the journey from Pompeii to Oplontis is not far. In his time, Larius had driven, ridden or walked this coastal road, enjoying a chance to absorb the natural beauty of the bay, while his thoughts went off into their own freewheeling. Sometimes he had to curse an obstructive carrot cart; but sometimes a bonny farm girl would offer distraction if he pretended interest in her olive oil. Even if she snubbed his chat, there would be a stall of fish pickle to tempt a purchase, fishing boats to watch, or his own hopes and dreams to polish up. He had always liked this road.

Once, on the same journey, his uncle, Falco, had given him a strange heart-to-heart, explaining contraception, such as it existed. Five, going on six children later, Larius was the first to admit the discussion had been wasted on him. Still, today he thought of his uncle, a man with a reputation for problem-solving. *Well, get out of this one, Falco!*

The sight of the volcano ahead kept Larius resolute. As

long as he could, he rode the baker's hinny. With its fairly willing cooperation, he had passed out of Pompeii through a necropolis, a street of noble tombs outside the Herculaneum Gate. Later, other fugitives would simply give up their flight right there, so near the town, overcome by fumes, heart attacks or pure exhaustion. But Larius had gone through early enough; had made it to open country, travelling out on this shore road that he knew so well, though today it was unrecognisable under the rising deposits of magma, viewed through a choking veil of smoke.

He managed the couple of miles to Oplontis. He was not sure how he did this; still, although Larius seemed a dreamer, he had always been stubborn. Maybe dreamers have to be. Besides, he felt desperate. He had a wife, four distant children, and this other child to save, let alone himself. He would not give up.

He was not ready to leave his existence. He had pictures to paint. He unexpectedly wanted a chance to make things happier between him and Ollia; he also wanted to watch their children blossom into fine young people. His girl might defy convention and be a famous woman painter. The others were promising characters too. He would be a better father, if only it was allowed. Hell, he might even be a better husband. He definitely wanted to be a better artist.

He knew he was good. He believed he still had more in him.

Oplontis was a hamlet. It was dominated by a huge imperial villa that once belonged to the family of Nero's wife, though for years no one imperial had stayed there. The Flavian emperors preferred to holiday in their own Sabine hills. If they ever turned up in Neapolis, their chamberlains imposed upon some hapless senator. Larius had once been in to look, so he knew that even though the long swimming pool in Poppaea's place was being used by locals as a fish-pond, the statues in the gardens were extremely fine, while indoors it had gorgeous, innovative art on its walls.

A couple of families had smaller villas, the kind used for a mix of pleasure and rustic industries, but mainly Oplontis was a dead hole these days, all mullet nets and battered scallop creels.

Larius had guessed right: down on the beach, all the sensible fishermen had left, taking out their families before the sea became impassable; only the hopeless Vitalis had dallied. There must have been others who felt trapped by their own indecision, but they had taken to their heels now. This man had always lacked motivation. He must have sat here, hoping the volcano would simply shut down, or that the ghastly scenes around him were all a puzzling dream . . .

Larius arrived at crunch time. Finally, even Vitalis had accepted he should make a move. He had spent time plug-ging holes in his boat and hunting for his favourite oar. He had gathered up his free-range cousins and his vague-eyed mother, who was all of ninety. They had packed their fishing smack, which was not large, with a crazy collection of barrels and baskets, then all squashed aboard. The boat sat unnerv-ingly low. Nevertheless, Vitalis was now posing on the end, plying the long oars with his chest out-thrust, as if he were still showing off his body to girls. All the sneering local girls had gone, hours earlier.

Larius hailed him. Vitalis backed the oars. Any excuse to stop moving. He had barely travelled any distance; they were still in the shallows. A couple of his relatives were batting at monstrous mats of floating pumice, trying to clear a path.

'Who's that?' called Vitalis, although he knew.

'Me, Larius, Ollia's husband. I've got Marciana, can you take us with you?'

One of the cousins shouted out that no they bloody couldn't, they were bound to sink. True. If Larius climbed in, the weight of a strong twenty-three-year-old would make that craft capsize. It was the same one he first saw a decade ago, which Vitalis had barely maintained. Even if it stayed afloat, the ramshackle old thing was too laden to be rowed far. Only Vitalis had oars anyway, the cousins were half-heartedly wielding poles and brooms to push aside the welded pumice and other flotsam that cluttered the sea.

The waves looked rough. They had shipped water. One of them bailed morosely. As a water boatman's son, Larius assessed the situation with grim, professional eyes. His father would say, don't touch it.

The old woman, who had always been kind to Ollia, squawked that they could squeeze in the little one. Ruled by his mother, Vitalis even fixed his oars and trod danger-ously forward, teetering among his relatives who grabbed at him dangerously. Though terminally hopeless, Vitalis had always been good-natured. He held out his arms to take Marciana, as Larius picked her up and began to paddle out with her.

She clung to her father. Struggling wildly, Marciana refused to go. She had never been a screamer, but she screamed now. It was too heart-rending. Larius gave in and returned to the beach where pumice scrunched beneath his feet as he floundered and nearly lost his balance. Had he failed Marciana? He kept her, kept hold of her; wept with frustration, yet accepted his own unwillingness to send her off alone on a risky vessel, with people he regarded as feckless and a man he had never liked.

So he and his child remained together at Oplontis. They watched the fisherboat slowly leaving for as long as they could see it, though it was soon lost from view in the darkness. Vitalis rowed, not with the strong, seated pulls of trireme oarsmen, but with the standing method used all over the Mediterranean, a kind of leisurely sculling that appeared inadequate, yet which took the boat out steadily until only a short time later it was far from shore.

Night seemed to fall. Maybe it was still daytime, but this seemed like night. Was there a moon? If so, it was completely blotted out.

Larius was too exhausted to continue. He sat down against an old hut that had half collapsed under fallen ash. More ash rained down.

He would rest. He would give his daughter a night's respite. Tomorrow they would try to travel on to Herculaneum, foolish thought. For now, they would stop here.

Deep inside the volcano something must have changed. The ceaseless fall of white lapilli altered. Larger, blacker tephra descended in hot chunks three times bigger than before, now inches across, among a new shower of terrifying heavy rocks. These fell with stunning speed. Nobody was safe outside. So, leaving the hinny on the beach, Larius abruptly picked up his daughter; carrying her tight in his arms, he put his head down and ran for his life.

When he crashed into one of the lesser villas, the first place he came to, he was amazed to find its once-gracious rooms were full of people.

A dirty tide of humanity had fled, some like himself from

Pompeii though others were local. Sometimes during earth-quakes people took to the fields to avoid the risk of being crushed under falling masonry. Now, after the all-day punishing descent of volcanic matter, these wanted a good roof above them. As night came, fugitives were reconciled to staying here.

If the villa's owner was present, Larius never saw him. Maybe the place was not in the possession of people of substance, or maybe they no longer used it for the high-life. Still, there were oil lamps and someone had lit a few.

Rustic equipment was everywhere. One room contained an enormous pomegranate crop, the ripe fruit spread evenly on mats. Not having eaten or drunk for hours, Larius and Marciana helped themselves.

'Tuck in. Don't expect snack-vendors coming round with hot sausage trays . . . We can leave a payment in a dish.'

'I don't think so, Father!' Smeared with juice and enjoying this snatch of banter, Marciana perked up. 'Shall I look for their cutlery canteen with the antsy-fancy pomegranate seed-picks?'

'Daft beggar. Use your fingers.'

He licked one of his and tried to rub smuts off her white little face. It merely spread the dirt. Larius stared at his pigtailed tot, still swathed in the cloak he had wrapped around her at the widow's house, feeling his love well up. Something caught in his throat. Aware, but ignoring paternal sentiment, Marciana went on eating pomegranates.

They poked around, searching for somewhere to rest. Everyone else seemed to have gone to the basement, as if it might be safer. Among their fellow fugitives, dimly viewed in near darkness, they discovered a subtle hierarchy. The rich, clutching jewel caskets and cash boxes, shunned those who might turn on them and rob them. They clustered in one room. In another, the rest eyed everyone darkly. Neither group wanted anyone else to join them.

He and Marciana came back up to the reception area. Plebeian to his soul and still a city boy at heart, Larius cursed the country bastards hogging the space where he wanted to settle his daughter for the night. The child was utterly done in. Hell, *he* was. If humanly possible, he would not have them spend this night huddled by a spiky bankbox in the godforsaken atrium with volcanic hoggin and rocks dropping through the roof and the risk that Campanian clod-hoppers would trample them in the dark. Nobody would give him an oil lamp, or he would have gone in search of an empty bedroom.

They wandered hand in hand to the huge double-height courtyard. The centre space was deep in volcanic debris, which had even buried a mass of upended amphorae that had been waiting to be filled. The intended grape or olive harvest must be lost in the fields, choked or burned.

Tentatively feeling for stair treads, they climbed to the upper storey where they cleared the deep ash by shoving it off the balcony. Marciana was by now so tired and drained, she dropped asleep immediately against a remaining drift of debris. After making sure she would not sink in and suffocate, Larius went for a short mooch, wading along the dark upper verandah. Fathers have to check the house. Fathers prowl the perimeter, on guard. When a long day ends, fathers wander off by themselves, looking up at the stars while perhaps they fart quietly to show that they don't give a damn, while they think about their responsibilities.

There were no stars. But if you could ignore the constant volcanic commotion, there was time to think. Indeed, there was nothing else to do. This was when Larius Lollius the painter took stock, having an enforced pause in his desperate journey. Sheltered with his daughter at least temporarily, he assessed their plight.

Now, Larius faced the likelihood that he would not survive this. Standing alone in a peristyle of somebody else's villa as it slowly filled with still-hot magma, he wondered whether they would be forced to simply stop right here. It felt too unsafe. What choice was there? As far as he had seen downstairs by wavering lamplight, this place once possessed fine decoration of the kind he had spent his adult life creating. It had been turned over to industry and barely lived in, or at least not used for the leisured life its first owners must have planned. But it was being swallowed up in filth, filth he could taste, filth that had made his daughter cough her lungs out, and which was stifling him too. He felt the grit in his teeth, dust sticky on his skin, and clothes, debris clustered in his hair. Oplontis was slowly being buried. Anyone who stopped moving would be buried too.

Now, looking out and up, Larius could see Vesuvius. The coast below the mountain was shrouded in impenetrable dark, while huge flames of different colours rent the high slopes and the sky above the volcano. Sometimes there were single streaks of light, sometimes a snaking trail, sometimes whole showers of pyrotechnics shaken out through the billowing blackness. All around grumbled the noise of what-ever was happening far underground. Innumerable farms must have been destroyed. Crops and vineyards were buried, hundreds of animals were dead. People too. Even those who had managed to stay alive until now were facing cataclysmic danger.

This was when Larius cursed his fate, and he cursed

from his soul, using the worst words he knew. Here he was, an eyewitness. He wanted to paint this. Generations of painters would strike awe in viewers with their *Vesuvius by Night*. For them would be movement and torment, fire and darkness, horror and suggested noise. They could position tiny figures, stricken by fear, contrasted against the enormity of ungovernable natural forces. Many would achieve this from imagination alone, for you cannot force a volcano to erupt when you need a model. He could have done it from life. But Larius knew, recreating this dramatic scene would never be for him.

He could only stare, as he thought of his own short life and his family – then in his wry way accepted the aching pain of so much wasted opportunity. He was a fatalist. He knew, tonight, this was the end of everything for him.

He went back to his daughter and squatted beside her, elbows on knees, face buried in his hands. All over the area people took that pose. It was a position in which they could rest – but also the posture of despair.

12

Nonius proceeds towards magnificent prosperity. Can a man with no conscience really be happy? Of course he can.

B ack in Pompeii, there had been a lull caused by the combination of nightfall and the increased ferocity of falling pumice. No one now ventured onto the streets. Pale ash lay to chest height; it was rising several inches every hour. If, from his resting place at Oplontis, Larius had given any thought to his former subtenant, he might have assumed Nonius would still be tirelessly attempting to rob people. But Nonius had gone. It was what men did, those with an instinct for self-preservation – or those protected by the gods.

The good people of Pompeii had entrusted themselves to many deities' protection that day. Venus Pompeiana, their town's chosen dedicatee, whose huge half-built temple towered over the Forum, stared out dramatically to the turbulent sea. Bona Dea, the Good Goddess, received many frightened pleas. Egyptian Isis. The goddess Fortune herself, who leaned on a rudder with which she governed human destiny. Apollo, light-hearted, talented past patron of the city. Giant phaluses that symbolised life, small ones with ridiculous wings or hanging bells. Jupiter the king of all . . . Despite amulets, signet rings, statuettes, pleadings, vows and prayers, the gods with their heartless, ruthless neutrality lent no help.

Fortune helps those who help themselves, thought Nonius, the cheery villain who had been so tenaciously helping himself to other people's property.

As the eruption started he had worked, harder than ever in his life, continuing through as much of the day as he could. Treading the ash, peering through the murk, forcing open half-blocked doors as he battered his way in to find secreted riches. Luckily in the best houses, their valuables had been displayed in the atrium, easy to find unless owners had snatched up their treasure and inconsiderately run off with it – ignoring the need to supply Nonius.

Enough was left for him. People had locked up, intending to come home tomorrow. People buried stuff, yet left behind their spades. People dropped things as they ran. As the day had grown worse and those who remained from choice or helplessness cowered in ever deeper hiding places, Nonius coughed and staggered, yet he obtained many delightful sets of silver drinking wares: trays, jugs, pairs of cups, mixing bowls, snack saucers, spoons and ladles, little tripod stands to place your drink upon, even egg cups. He gathered dishes and jugs that were designed for religious offerings. He snatched bags of coins. He took jewellery: chains, ear-rings, bangles, finger rings, pendants, brooches, filigree hairnets. If he found no gold, he did not reject silver, alloys, even iron if it looked to have a value.

Then as the day went on, before ash filled gardens and

made doors quite immovable, before he was brought to a standstill, Nonius departed from Pompeii. His sense of timing remained sharp. While roofs and balconies began to collapse all across the town, he was travelling out. He saw fires – and saw the falling pumice quench them. He heard screams and cries for help but he kept going. He was safe by the time the ceilings smashed down in the house where Larius had once worked. By then so much ash had descended, the newly decorated plasterwork landed not on the mosaic floor but on fully four feet of debris that had already poured into the house, the bakery, the garden, the stables full of panicked beasts. The baker's hog and poultry were still on the cooking bench, definitely overcooked.

While others were trapped inside buildings or buried in the streets, Nonius escaped. While people and animals died in Pompeii, he lived. It could have been different. If Fortune was fair, Nonius would have been stuck in the doomed town. He might even have found salvation. If endings were truly cathartic in real life, he could have carried out some great act of selfless sacrifice. He might have saved someone else, or at least offered comfort to somebody deserving.

Alternatively, if the Fates had taken another view of his despicable past, for retribution he could have been made to suffer. The Fates could have trapped him in a building collapse, perhaps quite accidentally, then left him there to await death – with its coming certainty a painful punishment.

Not him.

Nonius left. Erodion's raggedy knock-kneed horse took him and a heavy cartload of plunder safely inland. Worse, far worse for those who like justice, Nonius was even at that stage planning to come back. Once the hot slurry cooled in the devastated town, Nonius would be there again.

He would find his way amongst the buried buildings, remembering where the best homes were, digging down to salvage statues, stripping out expensive marble, grabbing any portable plunder that remained. Other looters would be killed by further building collapses, but not him.

For him, what did the future hold? One day a man of great wealth would turn up in another town, under another name. Even 'Nonius' had never been his own. He had been born somewhere north of Campania, making his way from one town and one scam to another, evading detection, escaping the law, ducking the authorities' notice, playing the nobody; whenever he could no longer pull it off, he slickly moved on, like any corrupt crook with blood on his hands who never left a forwarding address. He had passed through one location after another, always slipping away at the right moment, until one day in Herculaneum he had seen a benefactor's statue near the Suburban baths. Master of acquiring power by association, he stole the name as his own validation. On leaving Pompeii he would do the same again, 'Nonius' becoming 'Holconius'.

'Are you related?'

'Distantly, I believe . . .'

He would not return to live amidst ruination. Economic blight never attracts such men. So, after making huge wealth, the compulsive survivor would head towards retirement elsewhere. He left the cart to disintegrate in someone else's orchard. Towards Erodion's horse he felt no gratitude; for the wheezing beast there was no rewarding pasture in its old age. He handed it in to a knacker's yard. Still, rather than being worked to death by Nonius, that horse may have welcomed being turned into pies.

The man himself would live frugally, conserving his cash

as those whose wealth does not reside in land tend to do, from fear it may slip from them. He had wondered whether to apply for land, when estates that had belonged to disappeared residents were officially redistributed. There was a killing to be made there, but with his instinct for self-preservation, Nonius/Holconius chose not to subject himself to the narrow-eyed stare of a commissioner sent by a hard-headed Flavian Emperor.

With old age, he would become known as a miser. The sparse number of slaves who cared for him would lead pitiful lives, beaten and barely kept alive. He would never try to bribe them into anything that passed for loyalty, even though he was terrified of being left alone. Suspicion of others' motives would govern him. After all, he himself had lived as the worst of men, so he expected to be cheated.

But he would stick it out for years. When the time came to take to his bed finally, it would be nothing like the bed he had once shared with Larius Lollius. That had had uneven legs, hard slats for support, a lumpen, flea-ridden mattress, one thin pillow. The retirement bed of Nonius was to be a stately wide antique, with bronze fittings (stolen) and ivory inlays (bought with loot). His mattress would be well-corded and evenly stuffed with fine Campanian wool, his pillows made from softest down, his laundered sheets smooth and his coverlet embroidered.

Nonius would die in his sleep peacefully, there in his own bed.

13

The next volcanic stage.

For others it had been different.
The peril that not even Nonius could have survived occurred close to midnight. That was when the vast cloud's weight collapsed back into the volcano's chamber. Super-heated material then churned with new energy into a different reaction. Mud and steam, heated to a primeval temperature, were sent rolling out of Vesuvius at ground level. The first surge headed straight for Herculaneum.

This was not a slow creep of lava, like those in other eruptions from milder mountains, that local people come to view as it gloops like red-hot porridge over slopes and fields. This was a devastating torrent that rushed at incred-ible speed, white-hot, yet not even a fireball for it contained too many compressed solids. The avalanche crashed into buildings, either smashing them apart or pouring through windows and doors to fix them in an eternal mould. It covered two miles from peak to coast in moments, destroying all. Battered and splintered material was caught up and carried. Where buildings spontaneously burst into flames, those flames were immediately smothered by rock, mud and detritus.

With the surge came heat. This heat was four times greater than that of boiling water. As it punched across the countryside it carbonised wood, cooked fat, evaporated moisture, desiccated bone. No living thing survived. Uprooted trees were swept away. Any cattle that had escaped previously were lost now. All the birdlife that Larius and other painters loved to portray perished, along with fish and shellfish, snails, insects, worms, mice. The few people in their homes, the many collected on the beach all died there, and they died at once.

Out of doors, the soldier may have glimpsed the surge's approach. He may have heard its roar approaching. Before he even gasped, that heat killed him. His corpse pitched forwards, face down, fracturing bones, while his skull split open as his brain boiled. Further along, Erodion's wife Salvia fell dead on the beach too. Inside the boatsheds, the heat took everyone. Ollia, the watchful mother, opened her eyes instinctively as the noise exploded, yet she and her children took no last breath but were lost, while the sleeping still slept.

This death is terrible to us now. Then and there, nobody realised. No one felt terror or had time to panic. There were no cries. It came too fast for pain or understanding. They were gone. All gone.

So much physical rubble pushed across Herculaneum that the coastline permanently moved out more than a thousand yards. Meanwhile in the normally tideless bay, the sea behaved differently. Shocks deep under the ocean floor caused a great movement. Salt water was suddenly sucked out for a long distance, exposing the seabed, stranding marine life, revealing long-lost wrecks – and creating new ones. Silently, the same sea then gathered into a tall, swelling wave that moved at awesome speed as it returned again, thundered inland, then retreated to its natural place.

Captured in this was Vitalis. His labouring boat was tossed end to end, and everyone thrown out. Drowning is said to be an easy death. For those who have to endure it, it cannot be easy enough.

No one would know how many were lost in that most beautiful of bays. No one could count the people who drowned helplessly out there in the terrifying dark.

Larius would never learn that his decision to keep Marciana with him was as good as any he could have made. Oplontis was buried deep by that first pyroclastic flow, along with Herculaneum. The same unstoppable avalanche of molten mud and rock spread out over the near coast, with its immediate intolerable heat. Larius Lollius died with his eldest daughter almost at the same instant as his wife and other children. Like them, he never knew what happened.

A consequence of such intense heat, well known to fire-fighters, is that human tendons suddenly contract. In death by thermal heat, an involuntary spasm causes corpses to clench their fists and bring them up defensively. This might have pleased Larius. In his wry way, he would appreciate that when he was taken, he looked like somebody defying fate.

14

Afterwards.

During that night, the cloud above Vesuvius rose up and collapsed repeatedly. Massive surges continued, six in all. Herculaneum was buried seventy-five feet deep. With the third or fourth surge, the direction changed; it became Pompeii's turn. One pyroclastic flow reached the town's walls, its molten contents swirling around them though not entering. Anyone who attempted to flee as the surge came towards them managed only yards. Anyone who had made it outside the gates, died there and was buried. Everyone left in the town was killed by heat.

The next flow surged right over the walls, on top of the dumped deposits of its predecessor. This one rolled through Pompeii, entering buildings where anybody who had remained there already lay dead.

Even when morning should have come, a cloud of utter blackness rolled out and smothered the whole area around the bay and inland, terrifying people. Although it was possible to survive, many begged for death to end their terror. Destruction continued around the coast to other towns such as Baiae and Stabiae, burying the fine holiday resorts that had once been beloved of the wealthy. Deep ash covered everything, as far as Surrentum and Misenum, and out to the islands. The effects went further. Dirt and atmospheric darkness easily reached Rome. Taken high into the skies and carried by the wind, spewed filth was to blight crops and cause pestilence in countries far from Italy. Traces would mark the ice at the earth's poles.

But on the second day the eruption ended. Convulsions continued underground as the land settled, but the fiery chamber had completely emptied. Weak sunlight tried to break through a wan haze. Slowly the expelled material began to cool and harden. Its forlorn crackle could be heard, but otherwise there was silence. Nothing else moved.

People would come searching. There would be official and unofficial salvage through the ensuing centuries. Pompeii and Herculaneum might be lost to the memory for a time but they would be found again. From the best and worst motives, people would be drawn to the bay. Traces of the dead, material items, and surviving art would strike generations with curiosity, awe and excitement. Scientists of all disciplines would find work. Writers would speculate, salaciously or with compassion. Unthinking people, poorly inducted, might fail to show reverence. Many would not linger. Yet in those places where thousands of the dead once walked and some still lie, in Pompeii and Herculaneum, the tug of human suffering will always reach those who are open to feeling, those who possess imagination.

And – Larius was right, of course – painters would be drawn to that place where painting had once been so important, to capture the visual wonder of violent destruction and to suggest what it ought to say to us. As long as art exists, artists will collect their pigments and take up their best brushes to paint *Vesuvius by Night*.

Invitation to Die

Rome:
the Capena Gate and Palatine
November AD89

I

'In your city –' The speaker paused slightly. 'Rome,' she said, as if forcing her lips to form a distasteful word. From her very slight accent, she must be foreign. 'In your Rome, is it normal for a dinner invitation to be brought by *soldiers*?'

'When it's from Domitian!' snapped back the man in charge. His name was Taurinus, though he did not feel obliged to give it. He was a lean type, battle-hardened: lips slightly compressed, eyes slightly too fixed. Anyone familiar with soldiers who had experienced too much war might suspect he was liable to run wild.

Taurinus was wondering why calling it his Rome lumbered him with personal blame. Something wrong with Rome, was it? Hades, how would he know? He was a provincial-born legionary; he'd had fifteen years in the army, fighting for this city, yet had never been here before. Yesterday he marched in from the Danube among the Emperor's suppos-edly triumphal troops; today they had him out delivering post. Banquet bids. Bit of a comedown. You never got anything like this when you were stuck in a fort on a remote frontier. Even with winter closing in and the beer running out, there were limits. Thank the gods, this morning he had a man who could map-read – and, amazingly, one of the wily bureaucrats had thought to give them a map.

'I am not sure . . .' havered the snooty woman on the doorstep.

'Lady, we have hundreds of these to deliver, I'll have to ask you to look lively. If the senator is not around, any responsible person can take this in. Here you go, "noble Camillus, First Region, the Capena Gate". Sign there.'

He had a list. For heavens' sake, this was imperial Rome. Of course he did.

'*Sign?*' The woman was astounded.

Their eyes met. The officer knew that any wife of a senator would be able to read and write. Even though, just his luck, on this particular doorstep he'd run up against one who sounded foreign. That was tricky; Hosidia Meline might appear polite and only mildly baffled, yet every stage of their interview felt dodgy. It was as if one of them, or even both, could not understand the rules.

All his confrontations today had been a struggle. He could only hope this woman was frowning because asking for a signature implied the respectable household of the noble Camillus could not be trusted to take in a letter and then actually give it to him. Which was true: the officer had been told to make bloody sure he got his list initialled every time.

'We don't want any unfortunate losses, do we?' he explained, in what he meant as a helpful tone. According to the custom of her home country, the lady gave him the evil eye. Taurinus, who had been doing this all morning, spelled things out: 'Suppose, madam, this evening at the function your husband was missing, so Our Master queried where he was – believe me, Domitian will be counting empty couches. If Our Master were to ask, "Oh, where is the noble Camillus?", then I don't want anyone claiming he never received his invite.'

'That would be unfortunate,' the wife agreed. Suddenly, she became more feisty. 'You mean, if somebody made an excuse not to go? Refusing the Emperor? How shameful would that be! Believe me, my husband—' This time she gave an odd emphasis to the word 'husband'. It was not clear why. With many homes to visit, the soldier had already run into marital tension of many kinds, including one bronze vase flying out from an upper window that had painfully grazed his forehead. 'My husband,' said this woman, now sounding proud, 'will be honoured to dine at the Palace. Of course he will!' she then added, which somehow imposed a note of satire.

Impatient, the soldier gave his list a slight shake. The senator's wife looked on politely, but still did not take the document.

It was an unusual situation. She had been called to the door by a slave who was too nervous to accept anything from the military. Domestic staff were jumpy. Yesterday, the Emperor had returned from a season of frontier wars, bringing a rumbustious procession of legionaries. They were certainly campaign-fit, if not really as victorious as everyone pretended. They had 'won' once because a frozen river suddenly thawed, which stopped a rebel army reaching them; they ended their other war by paying off the enemy. Neat trick, if you can find the moolah.

Now they were here. A city full of soldiers acquires a different, more dangerous atmosphere. Large numbers of men spending their cash bonuses on drink can be vile. Doormen wanted to barricade the houses they guarded. Soldiers who brought letters from their dark commander were cause for deep suspicion and, frankly, fear.

Here, after an irritating delay with the porter, the lady

of the house had appeared in person, surrounded by elderly maids. They were all in dark colours, swathing their heads formally as they came into conjunction with men, all jingling with eastern-looking bracelets, all twittering behind their hands. In Greek. Taurinus knew Greek, it was part of basic training. He could tell when his physique was being discussed; he reckoned the senator's wife realised he understood what her women were jabbering. She silenced them with a sharp exclamation, before he had to.

The lady was on the young end of the spectrum, elegant and well presented in her silk drapes, yet neither pretty enough nor lively enough to interest a soldier. She had a hooked nose above a small chin, a highly superior attitude and no sense of fun. He had met worse today however, so he faced out her disdain. Calling a woman of this class from her household tasks was an imposition; he would be lucky if the worst she said was 'Remember who pays your wages'. A senator's wife, even one that the senator had picked up abroad and married to oblige her father, did not expect to conduct interviews with roughnecks in red tunics on her doorstep. Nor was it her domestic role to oblige officers who had found themselves acting as postmen, even if what they were delivering had come from the Emperor.

She had definitely decided not to sign for it. For one thing, she had spotted a key reason to say no. Her father, lately dead, had been Minas of Karystos, a master of jurisprudence. Minas, whose grasp of law was monumental even when he was tipsy – best of all when he was rolling drunk, her husband joked – her loud, florid father, deemed by many to be ghastly, had somehow found the time between riotous symposiums to make his youngest child a stickler. She signed nothing without reading it.

226

The officer pushed the letter into her hand. Hosidia Meline, wife to the noble Camillus Aelianus, inspected the address label. She stared at the receipt list that she was supposed to initial. Then she drew herself up so her fine bangles rattled.

'I cannot accept this!' She spoke as if she had been sucking grapeskins until the inside of her mouth dried up: 'I see you have my husband's name on your list, but that is immaterial. This letter is addressed to someone else.'

Then, sneering as if she had been passed a counterfeit coin by a money-lender but had spotted it coming, Hosidia Meline tossed the dinner invitation back.

2

'Oh shit!' said the soldier. This was and always will be the official military response to panic.

He managed to catch the invitation; he scrabbled at his scroll of names, could not find the right line, did find it, compared, saw what the woman meant, then said it again. '*Shit!*'

'My husband,' Hosidia Meline stated, making her sneer a touch more gentle, 'is the noble Aulus Camillus Aelianus.'

The letter was addressed to the noble Quintus Camillus Justinus.

'Mistakes can be made.' She was feeling sorry for the messenger now.

'On behalf of the Palace, *domina,* I must apologise . . .' Taurinus would need to send one of the lads running back to the bureaucrats – at least the Palatine was close, but delays in the labyrinthine imperial quarters were the last thing he needed.

The wrong senator's wife had made her point. She came from an ancient civilisation that had set fine standards of behaviour for the world, so she would help him out. She nodded to one of her women. The maid, bent with arthritis, began turning inside the house but Hosidia Meline clapped her hands. 'No, no. Be quick! Don't bother with the corridor, come out and knock on their door here. We must not keep these poor men waiting; they have a lot to do.'

As the maid scurried outside into the street and hobbled up the steps of an adjoining property, the soldier leaned back to survey where he was. A large building took up a whole block at the end of a stubby sideroad; it had been built as one dwelling originally, probably with land behind and a back entrance for deliveries. At some point the grand piece of real estate had been divided up. Now it was two adjoining homes, each with its own front entrance. You could see where the old central porch had been bricked up, a botched job with poor rendering.

The whole place looked rundown nowadays. This side had received desultory attention, but the other part was very neglected. Paint faded and peeled in the hot Roman sun. Urns lost their plants to drought. Senators were million-aires, they had to be in order to qualify. Many had trillions; those tycoons swanked around, spending freely to demon-strate their social worth. But a few, new men who barely made the cut, tended to have all their collateral invested in Italian land and consequently a poor cashflow.

The officer noticed a bunch of dark little heads craning out of an upstairs window then heard a young boy shout satirically, 'Mama, mama, *time for the jewels!*'

The other front doors jerked open partway as if a nosy porter had been peeking out. Hosidia's maid hauled herself inside. The tall double doors snapped shut, almost catching her stole between them. There was audible scuffling. A pause. Squeals. The doors reopened fully, though one side was sticky on its hinges.

What must be the aforementioned jewels now swanned

outside. Lopsidedly hung upon their tall owner, they dominated the scene with flash and sparkle. Their wearer was fastening an awkward clasp on her enormous statement necklace, while stooping low so a little girl who liked helping mama could attach a matching ear-ring to its customary dock on her lobe. These were huge pieces of kit. Weighty green gemstones glittered forbiddingly.

Announced by her treasure as a person of consequence, this new woman left her chaperoning staff in the doorway while she sailed forwards among a slew of interested, intelligent children. Two of her boys had found the time to throw on red tunics and grab their little wooden toy swords – as had her daughter. This girlie, only about four years old, seemed even more excited than her brothers to be meeting real soldiers. All three ran straight up to take a close look.

The soldiers shrank together. They only knew civilians as foreign scum, tribal trolls that they were allowed to plunder, curse and rape. Bold, rich Roman tots were new. They were worried.

'Leave them alone,' said the mother vaguely. She had a big nose and a distracted manner. 'You don't know where they've been.' Although this was presumably addressed to the children, it could just as easily be a warning to the soldiery about her offspring.

'Germany, Pannonia and Dacia!' replied her eldest boy calmly. This factual lad, who took an interest in current affairs, was about thirteen; too old to dress up and play with toy swords, he wore a white tunic with thin purple braid, over which a big gold bulla hung on a thong around his neck, supposedly to protect him from evil. In fact, he had the air of a lad who would punch evil squarely on the nose. Clearly accustomed to reassuring his mother, he announced, 'Don't worry, the men are not armed. Inside the sacred city boundary they are not allowed to be.'

A couple of the soldiers quickly altered the hang of their cloaks to hide weapons they were not supposed to have. Others merely played with their neckerchiefs self-consciously.

The two senators' wives plunged into each other's arms to formally kiss cheeks, even though the second one was still adding bracelets from her expensive set of gems. Next, even more costumed in bling, she turned to the officer. At that point, the Greek lady pushed in to explain coldly, 'Claudia darling, this man has brought Quintus an invitation; he is summoned to dine with the Emperor. Give her the letter, centurion!' He was not a centurion. His centurion was lolling in a flea-ridden bar, much too important to take messages.

Immediately fearing the implications, Claudia felt her mouth go dry. 'Oh! Meline dearest, why Quintus? Quintus and not Aulus?' Aulus was older, so slightly more senior.

Meline dearest made a high-shouldered *don't ask me, darling!* gesture; under her show of good manners she was clearly put out on behalf of her noble partner.

'Give it to me!' commanded Claudia. Despite her woolly manner, she now demonstrated how she habitually took it upon herself to sort problems. She sighed slightly, as if life was one long swathe of incidents that other people messed up, due to their hysterical incompetence. She alone took charge. Nobody else ever would.

Quicker-witted than anyone assumed, the unhappy Taurinus had already begun searching his documents again. Claudia whipped the invitation from his hand as if he were a naughty child, then confiscated his list too. Behind him, troops shifted anxiously; the rackety old lags were disturbed to see their empty-handed officer being bullied – which was supposed to be his role.

'Oh for heavens' sake!' Claudia reacted irritably, muttering it to herself as she read. 'This list is alphabetical by *fore-names*: secretaries are idiots.'

Agreeing, the officer managed to recapture the list, which allowed him to make his own search of many praenomina As and Qs. Rome had only twelve commonly used first names so bunching the entire Senate that way was decidedly unhelpful.

By now Taurinus, poor dog, was feeling desperate. Sure enough: among quite a few Camilli, a second was listed, also at the Capena Gate. 'A Camillus Aelianus, Decimifilius – plus Q Camillus Justinus, also Decimifilius.' Aulus and Quintus, the two sons of Decimus. Both members of the Senate, they both bloody would be. Both with tricky foreign wives and an almost identical home address. How was a soldier supposed to cope? He muttered to his man with the despatch satchel, who began burrowing inside. 'So, then, don't mind me checking – I've got *two* noble Camilli here-abouts?' he said gamely, to fill in time.

'Brothers!' chorused their two noble wives and some of the noble children. The three nippers with wooden swords were too busy posing confidently with the soldiers as if part of their detachment, while the nervous soldiers stared ahead and pretended not to notice.

'They are not here?'

'Bunked off, "to the courthouse",' Claudia said frankly. '—or, since we had a Triumph yesterday, to avoid being nagged about morning-after hangovers.'

A second letter was extracted.

'Shit!' said the officer again, glad to have the answer, yet needing to relieve his annoyance at this pickle. A couple of the children took up the word, noting the kind of occasion when you could officially use it. With sidelong glances towards their mother, they began trying it out together in undertones, testing it on the tongue like an exotic new fruit.

The two letters were handed over. Meline and Claudia made sure they had been allocated correctly. Finding they were not, they both sighed dramatically then swapped them.

The officer's clerk proffered an inkwell and reed pen. Meline inspected the pen for sharpness, heaved another sigh, then signed the receipt list. Neatly, but in Greek. When the clerk looked troubled, she gave him her Medusa glare then smoothly added her name again in Latin letters.

Claudia's eldest boy interrupted. 'I'd better have it next. I should do this, Mama.' His mother shrugged hopelessly; she was learning on a daily basis that her role was to be shoved aside by the assertive sprites her children were turning into. The young boy subjected the officer to a frank gaze, but spoke politely. 'I am Gaius Camillus Rufius Constantinus, eldest son of Quintus Camillus Justinus, grandson of Decimus Camillus Verus. I shall accept the letter for my father.' He looked at the close columns. 'I shall have to use abbreviations in order to fit my whole name in.'

'You do that, son!' said Taurinus.

Just scratch something on the bloody list so my lads and me can get on . . .

'What legion are you from, sir, if I may ask you?'

'Seventh Claudians. Viminacium – Moesia.'

'Are they any good?'

The officer managed to stay nice. 'The best!'

'That's very interesting. My papa served with the First

Adiutrix at Moguntiacum in Germany. Don't worry, I know what you think of them – he is the first to admit they were a shower of ex-sailors, crudely thrown together to beef up the legions. But he speaks of them fondly.'

'Oh, does he?' Taurinus remained deadpan, though with an effort.

'Will you tell us about this invitation,' instructed Claudia Rufina, reclaiming her position as the woman who took charge. 'We had the banquet last night of course, sharing it with the whole city at the end of the Emperor's Triumph.' That was the traditional street party held on such occasions. 'What is this extra meal about? What does Domitian want to say to the Senate? Is he up to something?' she cajoled. As the wife of a man who depended on her for money and as the mother of many self-willed infants, she knew how to squeeze; people faced with Claudia Rufina found they would weakly cooperate.

The officer's orders had been specific: no collusion. He tapped his nose, in a more-than-my-post's-worth gesture. All he would say was: 'It is a banquet for the fallen.'

'Oh!' exclaimed Meline, much too brightly. 'Claudia darling, Domitian wants to talk about death!'

'*Oh shit!*' whispered one of the little boys. He was about eight, but had correctly interpreted this as a situation when he was allowed to say it.

3

Claudia Rufina had lived in Rome for a few more years than her sister-in-law. Hosidia Meline sometimes uttered words of sombre prophesy, relishing doom like a tragic chorus in a drama festival. Meline might dare to assess the Emperor's secret motives, then even to show how much she despised the political regime she was now obliged to live in. Because Claudia was an anxious wife and mother, for her it had become second nature to pretend everything was all right – even though in Domitian's Rome, that no longer applied. 'I am sure it will be a lovely occasion!' Even to herself, she thought, *You're wittering! It won't be* . . .

Taurinus grunted. He recognised her meaning. He had served under many sarcastic centurions.

He gave a signal to the men.

'Be very careful how you step on the pavements at the corner, when you pass under the aqueducts,' Claudia advised the soldiers with genuine kindness, as they completed their errand, strapped up their satchels, prepared to depart. 'There are so many puddles from the water leaks, it is easy to slip over.'

'And watch out for the beggars!' snorted Meline. She spoke with less concern for the soldiers' welfare, more local outrage. 'The prisoners who built the Amphitheatre have been turned loose on us. My husband keeps writing to the authorities about the problem, but of course no one ever listens.'

Not bothering to be grateful for their advice, the officer turned away, intent on the next delivery. He led away his men, tailed by their downtrodden clerk. Their guide fixed his eyes on the street map, looking up their next address. The soldiers were marching more stiffly than usual, as they tried to ignore the fact that three children, one a very small girl, had fallen in behind and were marching with them. Fortunately, the eldest boy whistled to bring his siblings back home.

At the far end of the short road, two men in their forties turned a corner. They stopped and stood watching. Both were casually dressed in belted white tunics, which gave nothing away about their status; however, the belts were expensive – soldiers notice – while both men were easy in their skins in a way that actually said it all. One gave the passing officer a quiet salute, so he had military experience. In return, the troops snapped to attention as they went by. Neither party spoke to the other.

The two men strolled unhurriedly up to the Camillus property, where their waiting wives silently handed them their invitations. Each addressee looked down at his document. Each pulled a face.

'Domitian wants to have dinner with you.' Hosidia Meline made it a simple statement, watching for her husband's reaction; he gave none. That was husbands the world over.

'He is inviting the whole Senate,' added Claudia Rufina, sounding more anxious.

The brothers looked up and glanced at one another briefly. Still neither commented.

Aelianus reviewed the street behind them, where a few neighbours had – coincidentally, no doubt – found reasons to come outside so they could stare. Justinus did not even bother to look, sticking his imperial request under his arm like some routine note from his estate manager. Each family went inside its own home, the children jumping about their father excitedly.

Moving ahead of his brood with practised ease, Justinus strode immediately to his study on his own, then he closed the door after him very firmly.

It had been his father's room first. Now there were plenty of scrolls and note tablets that Quintus used in his work as a lawyer, although other containers and shelves still held material that had belonged to his father, Decimus. Perhaps he would sort through them one day. Dusty busts of poets gazed down from the tops of cupboards. Some were unidentifiable, so they might be corrupt politicians, though they all had noble brows and sturdy noses. Sculptors know what is required. So many of the unscrupulous are blessed with handsome features, Decimus would say; it helps them get away with it.

A bust of the Emperor Vespasian, unashamedly wrinkled and characteristically smiling, lurked lower down; his large bald head was sometimes sponged free of spiders' webs because he had been the old senator's friend. Vespasian fathered Domitian, though nobody held him responsible for Domitian's way of ruling. Tyranny is something you choose for yourself, Decimus said.

He had once ventured to say it to Vespasian, when he and the genial old Emperor were having a spat about the way the Camillus boys' careers had been blocked for political

237

reasons. Vespasian had allowed him to speak out, though their careers remained stalled.

Closing the heavy door immediately cut off this room from the rest of the substantial home, though it failed to mask all evidence of domestic life. An occupant would still hear low conversations among slaves who were using inane discussion as an excuse not to do anything. No door ever blotted out the trundling racket of Claudius, aged two-and-a-half, endlessly pushing his small horse-on-wheels around and around the colonnades of a nearby interior garden. From time to time he sat down abruptly on his sagging loincloth and fell worryingly silent. Then, with an unexpected squeal of delight he would suddenly resume rattling his toy along the uneven mosaic, earning himself the muttered nickname of 'right little Claudius'.

This pattern of everyday life formed a sensory background that was as familiar as the fading frescos on the walls. From the clank of the man filling buckets at the tap from the aqueduct, through the maid singing to herself as she beat bedcovers before slinging them over the upstairs balcony rail to air, to the scents of new bakery bread and the first stirrings of oil sizzling in pannikins for lunchtime snacks, this was home. Its routines were not consciously noticed; they seemed unremarkable, yet if those sounds and smells ever stopped for some reason, the shock would jar. A possible reason had just been delivered today.

Quintus dropped into the chair his father had used when he dived in here to escape family stress. It was a straight-backed armchair, easy to read in, that looked as if it had been borrowed from a schoolteacher. Perhaps it was left behind by the decaying specimen who used to be employed here, a wheezy grammarian the family now thought of recalling for their next generation of sons; he still needed to work and had always been cheap.

Quintus leaned forward, elbows on his knees, head bent, and buried his face in his hands with a groan. Anyone who knew them both would have said he resembled his father more than usual at that moment. Though taller and more lithe, he had the same sprouting hair and now the same air of rueful domestic dread. He straightened up again just in time. Instinct warned him: his elder son had sneaked into the room.

Gaius closed the door behind him with the same firm click Quintus had used, the 'keep out; I'm working until dinner' gesture that Decimus had employed to maintain the myth he was master in his own house – or at least within this sanctum. The boy was probably unaware of what he did. Heredity is wonderful.

Gaius was tall, like both his parents; tall for his age. At thirteen this meant he was still wearing tunics with a narrow purple stripe, although next year he would formally exchange them for plain white, plus the toga of manhood. By Roman tradition, he would then have to suffer with a rhetoric teacher, which was why Quintus was vaguely wondering who to hire. It would be a significant moment. Quintus liked to explain with cheery guffaws that if a boy who reached manhood committed an offence, he would be deemed to have full criminal intent, whereas now, anyone who came complaining about him would have to prove Gaius had known what he was doing. No more riding away on a neighbour's donkey if it was foolishly left tethered in the street, then saying you had just thought it looked lonely.

As his mother Claudia often noticed grimly, Gaius would soon be even more good looking than his father; once he gained his confidence, he would have the same attractiveness and charm. So far he had no idea about women. He scarpered if one looked at him. Claudia knew that would not last. The easy-going charisma that had made her fall in love all those years ago was likely to be repeated. Weeping girls would beg her to intercede for them . . .

'Hello son. Come to see me? Pull up a seat.'

Gaius did so, unearthing a stool from piles of untidy documents, which he carefully lifted and placed on a side table, trying to keep them just as they were. He knew Quintus would remember all that was in this apparently haphazard mound; while he was working, he would be able to go straight to anything he wanted.

Moving the stuff gave the boy an opportunity to look around until he spotted where his papa had tossed Domitian's invitation, still unopened.

'Don't look so worried.' That was how Quintus often began conversations with his children. And with his wife. Claudia had originally felt patronised, but she learned to live with it. Everyone eventually fell in with the strong, relaxed, comforting Quintus Camillus Justinus. He could calm anyone – even Claudia who, because she owned the money, sometimes tried to be her own woman.

Gaius nodded at the invitation. 'Aren't you going to open it?'

They had recently shared tentative political exchanges. The boy was bright, curious about the society he would soon be entering formally. He listened in on adult conversations, picking up that people around him thought that Rome was beset with problems. Quintus never disguised the truth. Even so, despite his liberal way of running his household, he had to be careful how much he said. An incautious statement could be passed on by slaves – that was obvious – but according to rumour, in today's Rome parents were even being betrayed by their own children.

As a practising lawyer, Quintus was close to the tense environment where political informers did their worst. Domitian listened to them. Being paranoid, the Emperor positively wanted to hear about bad behaviour. True or not, shocking tales of things that he reckoned he ought to stamp out found a ready audience. In Domitian's eyes, crimes, plots, adultery, having worked for his father, or simply holding intellectual opinions, all justified his paranoia. Then people told him what he wanted to believe. He guzzled it down and rewarded them. The whispers did not have to be true.

Reaching for the Palace's sealed note, Quintus shrugged to imply he saw it as unimportant. Then to satisfy the boy, he broke it open, read it, tossed the thing back on the side table. He flipped it with a casual air to show he had been right. It nestled between a peg calendar and a pottery oil lamp that was never used because it was cracked.

After a moment Gaius reached for it to read for himself. Quintus watched, then murmured, 'Just a request to attend a banquet, as Mother said. I suppose the soldiers must have told her who is going.'

'The whole Senate?'

'Not specified.'

Gaius was anxious. 'The Emperor hates the Senate, you say that all the time.'

Quintus moved restlessly in his wicker armchair. After he stretched, massaging his neck, he tried out his well-known winning grin but his son, who knew it of old, simply scowled. 'I suppose,' Quintus confided, 'I had better assign that statement to "questionable evidence" and cross-examine myself brutally: "Isn't the truth, Camillus Justinus, that you know full well the Emperor never *consults* the Senate, preferring to rely upon his own stunningly wise judgement? . . ." The thing is, Gaius, Domitian may wish he wasn't stuck with the Senate's existence, yet he will not openly reveal his dislike. That is because rulers such as him—'

'Tyrannical bastards?' Gaius suggested innocently, with a smile of his own. He was learning.

'Single-minded, self-assured, self-serving . . . devious, uncontrollable tyrannical bastards – but I never said that, Gaius – these rulers are a particular type. We have had them before. For some odd reason, they always claim to be extremely traditional. Rome has been run by a Senate since the founding of the city. How many years?'

'Eight hundred and forty-two,' whipped back the boy, as if answering his schoolmaster.

'Good stuff! Emperors may be new in that context – we've had emperors for less than a hundred years – but none has yet dismantled the Senate. That's mainly because, even though emperors control so much, they first acquire their power through the Senate voting to give it to them. This locks the Emperor into a relationship. Cull the Senate, and you undermine your own position. Besides, emperors whose actions are unpopular rely very heavily on saying they are following the rules. Blame the rules, not the man who finds himself stuck with them. Eight hundred years is a solid system. Domitian will not want to be seen to abolish it.'

'So he just lets you sit in the Curia on session days and make a few laws?'

'Exactly.'

'Unimportant ones?'

'Law,' proclaimed the noble Camillus Justinus, since he made his living by it, 'is always important.'

'Right! But the Emperor never has to be so friendly with the Senate that he feels obliged to ask you all to dinner?'

Once again the father attempted to put forward a line that would sound safe if an informer got hold of their discussion: 'No, he has no obligation, so it is very gracious of him. Our Emperor is known for giving civilised banquets, with fine food and delightful entertainment.'

Gaius sniffed. 'You don't believe that. I heard you say he winds things up too early. He doesn't enjoy the eats and drinks; he upsets guests by saying rude things about them, he chucks bread and flicks sauce at them because nobody dares object.'

'I should have known,' Quintus remarked to the ceiling in a man-to-man fashion, 'not to say that with children listening! No imitations, Gaius. *You* haven't been given tribunician powers by the Senate, so don't you try sauce-flicking at home.'

'Our mother would never allow it.'

'No, and I suppose if Domitian had not lost his mother when he was young, maybe *he* would have been brought up as nicely as you lucky bunch.'

During their last remarks, the study door had opened. Someone was leaning against the architrave, listening in. Fortunately it was not an informer.

Quintus, when he noticed, gave no hint of anxiety, merely cocking up one eyebrow to enquire why the visitor had come.

'So,' drawled his brother Aulus laconically. 'This dinner tonight. Are we going then?'

4

'What do you think?' Quintus consulted his brother. 'Are we?'

'No option.'

'It's only a dinner.'

'It's dinner with him.'

'As you said then – no choice!'

'Freedom of choice is for barbarians. Their luxury. We live in a regulated society, sadly for us.' Now Aulus spent a few moments posing like an orator, one arm extended; Quintus leaned back in his chair, listening. The elder brother, chunkier and very slightly shorter, spoke more satirically than usual: 'We get up, wash our faces, spend the day trudging those antiquated plough tracks that were dug out for us by our sturdy, porridge-eating forefathers. Honouring the national gods, obeying our wives, being very polite to our banker, rudely ignoring our doctor – then jumping, whenever our Emperor commands. Mindless automata. Mere mechanical toys.'

'He doesn't command us to dinner. It is neutrally phrased. *Titus Flavius Domitianus Augustus Germanicus, conqueror of the Chatti and Dacians, in the ninth year of his tribunitian power, fourteen times consul, imperator, pontifex maximus, princeps and Father of the Country, invites your attendance at a banquet on the Palatine.*'

'Nine bloody years, eh? Feels like a lifetime. Nice, to tell us who he is. Modest . . . You did read it, then?' scoffed Aulus.

'But of course. Had to check what it was. I was hoping some defendant was offering to bribe me on a case. Yes. I read it – and you are right, perspicacious brother, the wording is cordial though there is no helpful indication of who to reply to, in the event of our unavailability.'

'Unfortunate illness.'

'Death of favourite horse.'

'Allergic to aspic.'

'Don't want to get accidental shellfish poisoning from lukewarm nibbles.'

'Don't want *deliberate* poisoning . . .'

Both senators beamed at the boy. *Aren't we clever? Don't you love our merry banter?*

'Is he planning to do something?' asked Gaius, entirely serious. 'Something terrible?'

His father and uncle stopped beaming. Each seemed to be waiting for the other to come up with a neat answer.

'If he is, we shall have to be patient and see,' said Quintus.

Any father of six children will have learned to answer questions vaguely.

After a pause, during which Gaius was clearly brooding, the worried boy commented, 'Six hundred senators. That would require huge vats of poison. I believe that strong, very fast-acting poisons have been developed at the Palace in the past, but it would be a logistical nightmare.'

His father qualified the numbers: 'It is generally accepted that only about a third of Senate members are active. Discount all the ones who hold official posts so are legitimately in foreign lands – legionary legates and tribunes,

245

provincial governors and their young finance officers – forget the ones in exile for criminal activity, and those who are simply too ga-ga to be let off their country estates . . . Two hundred actual guests, call it.'

'Swords,' said Aulus, king of the terse rejoinder.

Gaius thought it through. 'Swords? So, two hundred men, Praetorians it ought to be, move in quietly behind the dining couches while everyone is reclining and off guard. Then at a signal, the troops all bring out their weapons, step close and in a synchronised movement they cut throats . . . Messy! There would be vats of blood, blood sploshing all over the place.'

'Two hundred slaves with sponges would clean up,' answered Quintus, sighing slightly. 'It's the Palace. They have maintenance teams. Besides, if it did happen and if they couldn't get the stains out, the Palace surveyor would just lay a new, more fashionable floor right on top. Nice opportunity to buy in something fancier. Domitian loves remodelling projects. His planning is so deliberate, he's probably chosen tonight's dining hall specifically because it's the one he is hankering to change: thinks it is due for a refit, never liked that décor anyway because his brother Titus chose it.'

'Let them bleed!' continued Aulus, with rather too much relish. 'Cover the tired old black and white geometrics with gore, then install gorgeous polychrome micro-mosaic, dressed up with twinkly gold bits.'

'You two are just larking about!' Gaius reproved them grumpily. The brothers did not dispute it, though they fell silent as if tired by their own joking. 'I am supposed to look up to you – a pair of idiots!' the boy complained. As one, Aulus and Quintus slowly nodded.

Gaius relaxed a little, aware that other boys thought he was lucky to be growing up in this environment. Increasingly these days, he was allowed to share in the humour. Nevertheless, his father and uncle could be serious; he understood that and when they were, he did admire them. They were well-read, clever men who worked hard, cared about the law and gave good advice to clients, some of whom were grateful to obtain their services. One or two, Quintus had told him, even followed the advice.

'So,' he challenged the brothers. 'I have another question for you. Uncle Marcus would say, in his cheery manner, if you are going out to dinner in Rome, you should write your wills before you go. Have you done it?'

Aulus and Quintus both guffawed. 'No, of course not; we are lawyers!' chortled Aulus.

'It doesn't apply? You tell other people to do it, but you never get around to it?'

'Exactly. Ever seen a doctor who never drinks and goes for healthy walks?'

'A banker who puts all his money in time-honoured, risk-free investments?'

'Or a slave at a public latrine who leaves the seat as he would wish to find it?' Gaius himself got in a rude one before they started lowering the tone. That stopped them.

His father went particularly quiet. That was because one evening a few weeks before, Quintus had been attacked on his way home from dinner with his niece. He was seriously beaten up, so badly hurt that Aulus (who had sewn up the worst gashes) afterwards made loud demands for a Senate edict against gangster behaviour.

Aulus, who rarely spoke in the Curia, was now regretting that; he hoped Domitian had been so busy arranging his return to Rome that he had not read the *Daily Gazette*, with its notes on the Senate's business. Aulus preferred not to draw attention to himself from the dark throneroom.

Quintus found himself under intense scrutiny from Gaius. 'Don't worry. There is a will. I was teasing. You will get your inheritance – bearing in mind that I must provide well for Mother, I shall have to supply a dowry for Aelia, and after that there are five more of you who must share.'

Now that he had dared to raise the question, Gaius thought he might as well press on. 'I am glad to hear it is done, but I would like to know, please, whom you have named as our guardian?'

Aulus was the more shocked: 'Back off, young man! Your patriarch isn't fifty yet; don't be too hasty killing him off. He is only going out for a Chicken Vardana and some flute music.'

'If anything ever happens to me,' Quintus broke in, somewhat stiffly, 'your mother will look after all of you.'

'You cannot name a woman,' Gaius reminded him. 'She does not have legal capacity.'

'Quite right. Uncle Aulus would be your formal guardian.' Aulus gave his brother a quick glance, as if this came as news to him. Having no children himself, the prospect of acquiring six all at once made him blanch. Besides, living next door, he knew what a handful these were.

Gaius retorted, 'That won't be much use. You're both dining with the Emperor; what if something bad happens to both of you? Who is the deputy after Uncle Aulus?'

'Uncle Marcus,' confirmed Quintus weakly.

Gaius cheered up. The substitute guardian was Didius Falco, their aunt's husband: a man who had mentored both Camilli in their time, and the very person who always said make your will before you go out into Rome's dangerous streets. It was safe to assume Falco would never be asked to a banquet at the Palace. He was an informer, a despised low calling, and an auctioneer, which earned him a lot of money so it was viewed as an even worse profession because money was dirty – unless it happened to be your own. He had been an imperial agent too, though acting for Domitian's father, which made Domitian suspicious of him.

Falco kept his head down, so if he managed to survive, he might be a gruff but amiable guardian. Jovial Uncle Marcus. He would expect them to work in his auction house, probably for nothing, and if Quintus did manage to leave them an inheritance, it might mysteriously vanish – but they would grow up sane, healthy, competent members of society who could hold their drink or dodge a fight, a new generation who revered women, despised corruption and loathed meanness of spirit. The best thing about him was that he had married Helena Justina, the strong-minded sister of Aulus and Quintus. Falco had known what he was doing. With Aunt Helena taking ultimate charge, Gaius reckoned everything would be all right.

'So you are definitely going?' he asked. 'Don't eat the mushrooms, then!'

This was a time-honoured joke about the Emperor Claudius, who supposedly died at the Palace from poison in his dinner. There tended to be fewer jokes about emperors who might themselves poison other people. It could be you next.

5

Back in the Aelianus house, the master confirmed to the mistress that he would be out for the evening as the Emperor asked, so he would not require dinner at home.

These two were a curious pair, recently living together again after some years apart. There had been no ceremony, no announcement. Aulus being Aulus, he had barely mentioned their decision to anyone – assuming they did take a deliberate decision, rather than simply drifting back into the same house.

The first time they married had been twelve years before in Athens, a union contrived by her father, Minas, he who so famously loved wine. He had achieved his object by giving Aulus quantities of drink; after months of this process, Minas reduced his hapless, homesick, headaching student to a limp blob, incapable of argument. Being lawyers, they should both have said Aulus lacked capacity to enter into a contract; neither did.

Typical lawyers, his brother-in-law would have said. Falco would have got him out of it, but they were in different countries at the time. Even Falco was not that clever. So Aulus was on his own.

Too late, though recollection was blurred, Aulus supposed Minas must have wooed him with promises, or at least a general suggestion that this was a good idea. For sure, Minas had wheedled out of him an admission that he was nervous about a young female relative who seemed rather too keen on him. The logic of Minas was: marry someone else then! Aulus blearily thought he had added: you would be well advised to do it quick. 'Well advised' was a legal term that Minas always said meant you could charge twice the fee for saying it. Or pay double the bride-price if he made you get married.

Perhaps Minas had offered as a lure that Meline was a shy, well-brought-up Greek homegirl, traditionally confined to the women's quarters, who would be no trouble. If so, he overlooked how generations of Greek women had decided that if they were to be penned up at home while their men went out to party with scantily clad flute girls, then the home was *their* domain so they would rule it. To be fair, Aulus thought this was reasonable. His mother was an influential woman, who had given him this attitude. Partly because of it, Meline had taken to her new mother-in-law. Towards Aulus, she then *almost* had the submissiveness he had been promised in a well-brought-up Greek woman. Almost.

Aulus and Meline had not known each other well; they had not even spoken much because she was such a sheltered young girl, who only mingled with her father's students when Minas had some scheme in hand. At first sight it seemed surprising that her own mother, left back on Karystos, had ever allowed her to come to Athens, though behind a vague mention of keeping house for her father, the intention was perfectly obvious: Minas was to marry her off. Linking his island-born daughter to the son of a Roman senator was beyond the dreams of Minas, even in his wildest post-symposium delirium. But then Aulus had turned up, literally fresh off the boat, innocently seeking to be taught law in the home of democracy – well, that was his fad that year; there had been others. Once he dropped into the clutches of Minas, his tutor saw himself as a made man. Aulus was doomed.

Nobody pretended theirs was a love match. It was never a disaster, simply awkward. The couple rubbed along until, soon after they arrived in Rome as newlyweds, towing the ambitious, unshakeable Minas, Minas discovered that the Camillus family barely registered on the social scale. Though senatorial (for one generation), they had little money and no influence. He would never make it to the top of the pile through any connection with these people. As soon as he could, he had his daughter divorced – which, in Roman law meant simply that he removed her. Being a good Greek girl (who had always known that Aulus was sorry he married her), Meline did as Father said. Minas made unsuccessful feints among the snobbish Roman aristocracy, then married her off to a cousin, a banker, who was Greek too, but at least filthy rich. Meline never got on with him, yet could not escape because he was family. This time, Minas would lose face by ending her marriage. It mattered. The mutterings back in Karystos would have been intolerable. Minas refused to allow it.

In the intervening years Aulus married twice more. Neither coupling worked; two more wives divorced him, each expensively. One was scornful, one quite bitter. Though he had been brought up to be polite, clean around the house, witty when he was in the mood, still nothing could change his core personality: he was a gruff loner. Women found him hard work. Having a brother who was effortlessly charming made them feel it more. His one consolation was that, oddly enough, he remained on good terms with Hosidia Meline. Even after she remarried she took a strange responsibility for her ex, consoling Aulus during his various troubles. Her new husband thought it was safe – for one thing, if he ever found out it wasn't, he would have a good excuse to beat her, which would suit his Hellenic manliness. It did cause more hostility from the other two wives of Aulus as they battled to leave him. He, being Aulus, didn't care. Being him, he showed it.

Eventually, Minas of Karystas died. It was an accident. He fell off a ladder. Nobody even bothered to ask if he was sober at the time.

Hosidia Meline struggled to cope with all that must be done when someone whose personal affairs are very disorganised dies suddenly, in a foreign country. As the Greek husband left her to it, she wished even more to escape her unhappy marriage. So it seemed natural to seek help from Aulus.

Professionally, he was good. People were surprised that Minas had taught him well. Faced with a tangle of family problems, Aulus had a calm, thorough approach. The personal stubbornness that people shied away from made him an excellent organiser.

He found a will – or so he said; certainly one turned up in a liquor closet used by Minas. Aulus, 'My dear trusted student', was named as executor – how lucky was that? – and Aulus executed it speedily. He reassured Meline that she had no need to return to Karystos, where relatives would despise her failed marriage and her unhappiness with their kinsman. Aulus found her a small apartment to rent while deciding what to do next. He somehow persuaded the husband that *he* was anxious to marry a more attractive woman, then even convinced him to be generous in a settlement. Meline had never known the man could be so decent. Nor had she realised Aulus had such wily skills. He had been trained by her father until she could have passed him off as Greek.

One evening, after they had been to his niece's wedding, Meline returned with Aulus to his house, in order to discuss the events of the day. They had seen more excitement than usual: the bridegroom had been struck by lightning. Aulus, grinning for once, said his relations were a tribe where an event like that seemed normal. The bride was the same young woman who had once hankered after Aulus, despite the fact he was her uncle. Meline was interested to know whether this wedding had affected him.

Apparently not, for he kept telling Meline how grateful he was for her support that day among his rather tiring family.

She kept telling him how grateful *she* was for his help with the Minas will and her divorce.

He said ah well, they would always be special friends, wouldn't they? She said yes of course they would. Very dear ones.

Then, staying safely with Aulus seemed an obvious solution to a stormy night where she would be at risk in Rome's dangerous streets. After all, Meline had lived at the Capena Gate in the past. If the bedroom that had once been hers as a bride was now tainted by two subsequent wives, women she frankly regarded as stupid predators on her old friend, perhaps that made Aulus offer the comfort of his own; perhaps Meline accepted. Slaves in the house must know. Slaves always did. Otherwise, it was never mentioned.

That was a month ago. Meline had remained with Aulus

ever since. Nobody knew on what terms they were now living. Both were people who liked keeping things to themselves. If Aulus was seen as sombre and imponderable, so was Meline. They were reticent, yet they were a mature couple, who had known each other a long time. They seemed content, possibly even happy. So everyone just let them get on with it.

A month of amicable living was too short, Meline thought sadly. So much of her life felt wasted, and now her unexpected hopes of better were dashed. They sat together in wintry sunlight in the colonnade of a peristyle garden. If they wanted anything they could call, then slaves would appear, but as a couple they were not demanding. This interior garden was their place – out of reach of visitors, sheltered even from the gaze of their own household.

A fountain would have been of benefit to cover any private conversation, but the tap on the connection from the aqueduct was sited in the house next door. It dated from when Aulus' father Decimus lived there, a senator while his brother was only middle-rank. Uncle Publius, and now Aulus, shared access to the water but had to send slaves with buckets to fetch every drop. Aulus had been known to joke dryly that this leaky old tap could explain the entire motivation behind his black sheep uncle's political scheming, as if jealousy over the water connection was what had plunged the family into disgrace ... *Don't mention the plot!*

So there was no fountain here. Quintus had one. Aulus did not. Sharing a property, with a never-locked connecting door, is bound to bring moments when one or other party will be seething with irritation. Aulus Camillus was a high-

255

class brooder; one of the tasks Meline was now taking on was to be a soothing influence. In fairness to him, he acknowledged it, and did not object.

Their routine was to sit here, almost in silence, each busy with something of their own. Aulus would be working, with a scroll or more likely a waxed tablet. He might be at rest, thinking, then perhaps he would make a quick burst of notes. At the same time, Meline occupied herself with her hobby: looping wool on a small gadget with pegs around the top, which she plied with a little pointed stick. As her fingers flew, a cord of knitted wool slowly emerged at the bottom. One day if she ever had enough, she could sew it together into . . . what? A mat, a cushion, a round hat, possibly a sock. Aulus thought she looked as if she were contriving a spell; he had once commented that he hoped not, for magic would be unlawful, so he would have to prosecute. Meline smiled. Generations of women in Karystos had shown her that a wife's role was to let her husband make pronouncements, which she should serenely ignore.

Today, they both simply sat.

At last, taking the initiative for once, Meline spoke: 'I thought that everything was now all right.'

'It will be,' he answered quietly. Her heart was full of fear for them, and he saw it.

Whenever they were alone together, they spoke in Greek. Every educated Roman could, in order to read ancient literature or attend religious drama – while thinking that their own literature or drama was better. Most Romans saw Greek as a secretarial language. Aulus Camillus had used Meline's native language to make his young wife feel comfortable when she first came to Rome; he continued the practice now, even though her Latin had become more fluent, because he liked to be different. He had studied in Athens. So, in his home Greek was his chosen way to feel civilised. Mind you, nothing would make him grow a Greek beard. There were limits.

He too had let himself believe his domestic life was settled now, at last.

'I don't want anything to happen to you,' said Meline, acknowledging her anxiety.

'I hope nothing will.' They never spoke of love, but after a moment he added unexpectedly, 'Your caring means a great deal to me.'

He was sincere. That might be all she ever got from him, but it was all she wanted.

She braced herself. 'What shall I do, Aulus Camillus – if you never come back from this dinner?'

'Go to my sister.'

It was the answer Meline expected. Yes, Helena Justina and Marcus Didius her husband were the right people – wise, capable, kind people; besides, if anything happened to Aulus, it was to be presumed the same fate would befall Quintus, so he would not be available.

It was the obvious answer, though he had given it too quickly. She knew, therefore: Aulus had been thinking about this. So, although all day they tried to avoid the darkness, the Emperor's invitation threw terrible dread upon their household, chilling their hopes for their new future together.

6

In the Justinus home, it was different.

Quintus and Claudia were long established. However rocky their partnership sometimes appeared, instability was the mode in which they had agreed to live. When young, they had eloped, travelling to North Africa, but both quickly saw that real life was no romantic journey. They came back; they stuck it out. That was what married couples did – relatives who followed them after the elopement had explained they had better consider themselves married. On returning to Rome, they had to live with his parents. That made sure of things. They had made a mistake but were stuck with it.

Quintus and Claudia had nothing to discuss. If something terrible was now to happen to him, she would pack up the children and return to her homeland, Hispania Baetica. There in the south of Spain, Claudia was the sole heir of majestic olive groves. She had grown up in that environment; her memories were bathed in sunlight, even though she had lost a brother there, a young man of great promise who was murdered. So Claudia had already known dread and danger. In the loneliness of being left behind when some-body vanished from her life, she had learned to be brave; she was forever stalwart. Her unspoken plan was that, if anything bad occurred this evening, she would take the children home – just as she occasionally threatened anyway, when exasperation with her husband made their stormy marriage feel too much to bear.

Quintus knew the escape plan. He did not tell her that if Domitian really turned against the Senate, finding refuge on her family estate might be impossible. The property would no longer be hers. When emperors despatched their enemies, the rule was that they confiscated those enemies' wealth. Grabbing the money was the main reason for making accusations in the first place. Being allowed to do it was a perk of emperors' fabled 'tribunician power'. In the legal sense, the precedent was horribly well-established.

'You will need a decent shave,' said Claudia, always practical. 'I asked the barber to come here this afternoon. I expect you will be going to the baths, but the man who does shaves there is so awful. Aulus will need his services too; a home visit will be worth his while.' Apparently lost in domestic trivialities, she stood up from her wicker chair and bent down so that she could gently move aside Claudius, aged two-and-a-half, who had been stubbornly bashing his beloved horse-on-wheels against the bronze leg of an expensive couch, a gift from her now-deceased Spanish grandparents.

This action allowed her to conceal any anxiety. Yet when she straightened, she found Quintus was behind her. He wrapped his arms right around her, resting his chin on her shoulder, the side of his face against her cheek. 'Try not to fret.'

He turned her around and held her gently, while the stalwart soul he had married tried to pretend she was not crying.

7

The rest of the day passed, too slowly for some, too quickly for others.

In most of Rome, people remained oblivious to the deep apprehension that oppressed the top tier of society. A cool but pleasant November day moved on from a quiet morning of recovery after the Emperor's official Triumph, through a subdued lunchtime, then into the diminution of the light that, even in the Mediterranean, already anticipated winter. While sluggish public slaves cleared up after the city-wide festivities yesterday, many stall holders were not bothering to do business, although by evening shops and artisan workshops began opening their shutters again. The public were weary. Trade would be slow. Hauling doors open and eventually lighting their tiny oil lamps was carried out more for social interaction than commerce.

Although the Triumph had held the whole city in its strident, colourful, relentlessly festive grip from dawn to dark, traces of it were cleared remarkably fast. The thing was over and done with. Domitian had wanted it, he had duly achieved it, but the event had seemed tawdry. In the absence of genuine victory, there was insufficient plunder; there were too few prisoners; nobody had heard of the alleged enemies who suffered ritual strangling on the

Capitol as a finale. Citizens and visitors had felt disappointed. Only the soldiery liked Domitian. For everyone else, this uncompromising man would always be less popular than his father and brother, and now that he was back in Rome, they were desperately afraid of whatever misery he might be intending for them. They cheered his procession, but the lack of empathy was ominous. He thought people wanted rid of him; some did. No one could prevent his Triumph, but the enforced jubilation soon died down. Today was quiet; tomorrow would be normal business.

So, this banquet on the Palatine, supposedly 'for the fallen': what was it about? Certainly, there had been fighting in various places along the Danube frontier. It had lasted for years and might never reach an end. The worst in recent years had taken place outside imperial territory, a disaster within the hostile land of Dacia, when an over-extended Roman army, including a large contingent of Praetorian Guards, was massacred at a dismal dunghill village called Tapae. But that was five years ago. It was now uncomfortably late to be honouring those men, even though they were élite troops, horribly butchered in a foreign land. Besides, the Roman attitude to military defeat rarely involved celebrating the unsuccessful dead.

Rome preferred to forget failure. Of course you did go and bury the bodies, if it could be done. You then spent years trying to fetch back military standards, because of their symbolic value. You honoured the commander and the units who managed to carry out that unhappy clear-up. So what was this? Who was it really for?

It was true that there had since been a more successful campaign; a new army had marched out, using greater care, because Domitian was supremely good at planning and desperately sore about failure. The new commander reversed the defeat at Tapae, supposedly at the very spot where his predecessor's force had been ambushed. Even so, he deemed it too risky to march on into the Dacian heartland, and so it could not yet be the right moment to overrun the Dacian capitol. Sarmizegetusa Regia: dear gods, even its name sounded threatening. And without taking the citadel at bloody Sarmizegetusa, they would never destroy the warlike Dacian king. That meant the big hairy brute in his exotic trousers and Phrygian cap remained, now diplomatically described as an ally, yet still potentially a foe: hovering, hostile, challenging, liable to be dangerous for years to come.

No one should forget that Tapae happened after this king's Dacian warriors had crossed the Danube, swarmed over the Roman province of Moesia, killed, ravaged, plundered, then even barbarically beheaded a Roman governor.

The dreaded king had been brought around to Rome with money. Eight million sesterces were to be handed over annually: a stunning pay-off. Domitian probably saw that as a genuine victory. No one else did. Even so, men who had died in the fighting were to be celebrated tonight. So as members of the Senate arrived on the Palatine, all except a handful who dared call themselves Domitian's friends – he did have friends, though they had to be courageous men – all the rest could only pray that honouring the dead would not involve further bloodshed: theirs.

The first misery they faced was a straightforward traffic jam. This always blights royal occasions. A good timetable allows for it. Security forces have to be deployed to keep

262

things moving, not simply to check arrivals' credentials (which they can do at the same time). Ideally, these men are hand-picked for tolerance, even if they are not exactly briefed to be polite. Traffic management cannot be achieved with a soft attitude.

Drawing a couple of hundred guests up a steep hill at a set time would never be easy. Many were elderly, or at least conscious of their dignity, so they insisted on travelling in fancy chairs or four-cornered litters. Bulky palanquins containing overweight cargo were being manhandled by staff who, in many cases, had not had much practice lately. It was also essential for anyone of noble rank to emphasise his public importance by having a crowd of attendants, the bigger the better. Some were just for show, though other slaves had jobs, tasks a refined senator could not be expected to conduct for himself, such as straightening the heavy folds of his toga and changing his footwear from outdoor shoes to party slippers on arrival. They had to carry his personal paraphernalia: his money, his fly whisk, his dinner napkin, any medicine he needed, a scroll he might decide to read on the journey, or perhaps a note tablet with the address a woman had given him, a house where he was on a promise if this dinner did not end too late . . .

To cope with such a high-flown mob, the logistics corps had set up a one-way system. People were supposed to arrive via the imperial ramp that climbed up the hill in seven switchbacks; the plan was for them to leave afterwards down the relatively straight Cryptoporticus, a covered corridor further over on the Palatine. A major cause of congestion was that many of the guests seemed unaware of this sensible arrangement, with self-willed

263

senators insisting that nobody had told them, so when they arrived at the wrong entrance in the Forum, there were loud altercations that had to be sorted out by Praetorian Guards, who were not gentle. Scenes of chaos choked the area. Even after they were manoeuvred into the long queue creeping up the ramp, these senators' outrage was still audible.

Among the het-up throng, Camillus Aelianus and Camillus Justinus were quietly making their way together. Both were on foot – hardiness was a traditional virtue. Besides, Justinus' wife had asked him not to let their carrying chair be bumped around in the fray, to save damaging its paintwork.

They looked smart and smelt better. They wore long white tunics under heavy white togas with wide purple detailing. Nielloed belt buckles, silver and black. A battery of signet rings. Fancy shoes. Barbered to a sheen. They were travelling the short distance from the Capena Gate in a haze of unguents: boys' ploys. They owned the where-withall; tonight they had splashed it on. Quintus always received fancy flasks of manly lotions from his children at Saturnalia and on his birthday. Aulus liked to treat himself at a secretive apothecary called the Transformer, who imported high class resins and balms. These were prepared by an unguent-cooker, with claims that they removed wrinkles and hints about helping sexual prowess. His iris water steeped in ginger grass was in fact basic, and clashed with his brother's splash; Quintus had no idea what was in his, only that it made him cough.

Aulus brought a small group of male slaves in plain tunics and sandals. Among them was Toutou, a tiny black boy from North Africa who was supposed to light the

264

journey home. Though an odd acquisition by the conservative Aulus, it was fashionable to park a curly-haired lantern-bearer outside any dinner party you attended, where the child would cutely fall asleep. Toutou, who could only be about four, was so loved in the household, one of the other slaves was actually carrying him in his arms up the ramp.

Quintus came with his regular bodyguards, booted men from his old legion. These were battered specimens who had been invalided out – so by definition they were missing various body parts, though they were mentally tough, with a deep loyalty to Justinus because he was unusual; he had given them a home and a job. Normally if the legions signed you off early, you were finished.

All these attendants had a po-faced air tonight; for once, it was their masters who might be done for, yet that had horrible implications. Other senators in this crawling line brought people who had failed to work it out, but the Camillus staff realised how badly the situation could affect them. Domitian might intend to confiscate assets: if this dinner went wrong, for victims' retainers it might soon mean the slave market or begging under a bridge. They were not happy.

None were armed. Before they set off, one or two suspicious bulges under tunics had been in evidence, but Justinus had reviewed the men, including his brother's escorts. He made them ditch anything that could be classed as a weapon. 'I know you are always up for it, and there have been times when I was grateful – but please, lads, no set-tos with cudgels on the Palatine tonight!'

They concurred because they had to. He made it plain he wasn't letting them go anywhere unless they would pass if they were officially searched. So now the brothers were strolling side by side at a gentle pace up the imperial ramp, with slaves and veterans simply packed in a close formation behind them on the narrow slopes, making sure nobody else jostled or overtook them. Toutou's lantern was dark so far, because the covered entrance was lit with flares that gave off a tickling smell of bitumen, with eerie shadows on the tall walls.

Aulus and Quintus paced up the long drag without complaint. Unlike many of their colleagues, they had endured plenty of situations that needed patience. For one thing, they had worked with their informer brother-in-law, Falco. His junior assistants were given the worst jobs, in investigations that often called for boring waits in doorways, sessions on watch in lacklustre bars, endless keeping warm of stone benches outside imperial offices. As young men, both brothers had been in the army for brief periods too, and Aulus once acted as a runabout for a provincial governor. Nowadays, if they absolutely could not reach a private pact for a client, they would appear in court. Tedium was nothing new.

Eventually, they reached the summit. Emerging through a tall arch onto the flat area in front of the Palace, they found it thick with soldiers.

'Here we go!' muttered Aulus.

Many of the troops were Praetorians. Normally even the Emperor's men obeyed the rule that nobody bore arms within the city boundary, showing respect to the heart of Rome, which had been regarded as sacred since Romulus and Remus were suckled by the she-wolf. The Guards wore togas. It never disguised their military boots and belts, or their unmistakable swagger; anyway, it was presumed swords could be had in a moment if an assassin struck out at the Emperor. The Guards tended to be tall, hard and visibly aggressive. They were old lags who loved the army life, ruled by long-term chief centurions who revered discipline as a mystic art. They were all on personal contracts with Domitian, top froth creamed off from the legions – and paid twice as much, with all that brought.

Tonight, although some still honoured the no-weapons law, ceremonially armoured men were seeded among them. In tribute to the dead, these surviving colleagues were allowed their kit, which meant spears as well as swords and daggers, plus some shields, and even full-face parade helmets that gave them a mysterious passionless look. Officers were equipped with heroically moulded breastplates. Every scrap of metalwork was buffed to a high sheen.

As always, along with so much armour came constant chinking, creaking sound effects. In war, soldiers needed to be silent, but their accessories created an aural background once their normal groin guards and segmented corsets were enhanced with ceremonial tackle – medallions, miniature spearheads, helmet crests in screw-on holders, cloak fasteners, wrist grips, belts and sheaths with fancy tangs. As might be expected, weapon-maintenance scents clung to them: the vinegar, oils and waxes they used for daily rust-prevention. Then, as a slight breeze riffled over the Palatine heights, the men themselves brought gusts of wine and garlic, tonight mingled with bathing, breath-freshening and barbering products.

Their main contribution, surely intended, was menace.

The atmosphere was heavy with the Emperor's power. Rome knew how to use an honour guard to imbue an occasion with threat.

The long line of senators disgorged from the narrow ramp into an outside audience space. After passing through the ornate garden, they made themselves known to civilian palace chamberlains, while silent soldiers stood and watched. Means of transport, chair-bearers and torch-carriers were ordered away from the arrival point; guests blinked at the swiftness with which they were peeled off.

As each senator arrived, he was crossed off a list. Top-grade secretarial clerks were using the full pen and ink, not waxed boards and styli.

'Looks bad!' joked Camillus Justinus affably, as a thick, straight line was ruled in black through his name. 'I am deleted!' Camillus Aelianus had chosen to say nothing.

Then, under the pointed stares of the military, they filtered indoors. Once through the immense marble entrance, there was an awe-inspiring audience hall, with several possible dining rooms that might have been used tonight, not least a grand salon with huge picture windows that gave splendid city views. However, that was not the venue.

As they passed into the vestibule, they were told their remaining attendants must stay behind. For some, this was a facer. Normally wives would have been invited too, competent women who would assist with matters of etiquette and who could be relied on to keep conversation going. While other senators milled around in distress at this new separation, the Camilli calmly let themselves be parted from slaves, bodyguards, even little Toutou and his lantern. Each guest now found himself stranded. Men who could not blow their noses without bothering a slave felt helpless. Alone, their disorientation had begun. The rich never moved anywhere unless surrounded by their slaves, their own people. This formed a private cocoon – so now, they found themselves forced to make eye contact and even speak nervously to colleagues. Aulus and Quintus were all right; they had each other.

Following flunkeys, their path was made through lines of soldiers – not so closely spaced as to threaten, but close enough to prevent wandering. To seat a large banquet always takes an age. A snack beforehand is advised.

Eventually, while they queued outside a curtained room, Aulus persuaded a doorman to explain that progress was so slow because everyone had to be assigned his very particular dining couch. They were to enter the room single-file, one guest at a time. There was a reason, which they would find out. Another chamberlain with another list was matching them up, then calling out each name as the senator in question was passed in.

The Camilli were allowed to enter together. The city of Romulus respected brotherhood. *Don't talk about Remus . . .*

Dark, heavy drapes were eased aside by unseen hands, allowing space to admit them while hiding the room from everyone queueing behind.

'Aulus Camillus Aelianus, Quintus Camillus Justinus – Decimifilii!'

As soon as they crossed the threshold, the curtains immediately dropped back. By then they were paying no attention to the world they had left.

They had stepped into blackness.

They expected a blaze of lights but met gloom so deep

they nearly staggered off balance. It took a moment for their eyes to adjust. Their jaws dropped; it seemed to be their turn to enunciate that trusty old swearword: the response to panic. Nothing came out. This darkness was throttling. Aulus and Quintus stood elbow-to-elbow, too stunned to speak.

Their fears were right. The Emperor was planning something – and here he was. Spotlit within a pale caul of light, Domitian stood in full triumphal regalia. Here was a one-man receiving line, awaiting each guest's reaction to his stunning design. One by one the Senate members would enter. The Emperor barely bothered to greet them: he wanted to observe their shock.

8

The niceties passed quickly. The party would never have
started if every guest had tried to hold a meaningful
conversation with their imperial host. His notion of manners
never involved tactfully bringing shy guests out of themselves or making everyone feel welcome; he did not care
whether they said something about themselves, because he
had invariably decided already what he thought of them.
To be fair to him, most senators normally needed no help
and would warble away bombastically; yet, dear gods,
tonight was hardly normal.

Afterwards, Justinus thought he had honoured Claudia's
instructions to say, 'Thank you for having me'; he would
tell her he did, even if it made him croak with insincerity.
Aelianus was completely reticent. In company, he always
looked remote, as if he had just remembered a walnut cake
he had left in his bedroom, so he wanted to go back to stop
his body-slave eating it.

Someone murmured in the imperial ear. Standing there
in near darkness, the Emperor repeated their names, as if
memorising them for an execution order. He held their gaze
briefly, letting them know he forgot nothing. It was twenty
years since their uncle disgraced the family. Domitian was
remembering it now.

In the slurry of plots and counterplots at the end of the

Year of the Four Emperors, even after Vespasian was acclaimed, the transition had not been seamless. Ambitious men continued schemes to install different candidates. Even among Flavian supporters, it was said that Vespasian's relative, a man called Cerialis, had wanted to lure Domitian into supplanting his father, although Cerialis had always had questionable judgement and Domitian was an untrained youth of eighteen. The Camillus uncle stupidly helped to organise a plot with similar intentions. After it was uncovered, he vanished, known to be dead, though the family could never claim his body. Publius had had no memorial. He was never mentioned at family gatherings. But he had blighted their lives.

The young pretender at the centre of such plots had shown no gratitude to those who promised to back him. Now, with his elder brother Titus dead – perhaps even poisoned by Domitian himself – the throne was his. The Praetorians supported him, since he was Vespasian's son; the Senate acquiesced for the same reason. His succession did not help the Camilli, though to date nor had it damaged them further. With Domitian, though, that could change at any moment. He might or might not have been a willing participant in the old plot. He had seemed to ignore it ever since, but they knew he would never forgive the crucial fact: it failed. At the time, Domitian had been admonished by his father, forced to accept his elder brother defending him, tainted with non-performance, demoted to running poetry competitions instead of sharing in government like Titus. Nine years into his eventual reign, resentment still burned like stomach acid. That was him: famous for brooding.

'Camillus Aelianus! Camillus Justinus!' Domitian intoned,

staring. He named them thoughtfully as if he had just discovered a crime they had committed.

They had grown more used to the dark so could make him out more clearly. In his glimmering purple the Emperor was a solid shape, with massed gold embroidery slithering over the full-length robes of a conquering general; he had a big, square forehead, above which lay extremely regular curls – known to be fake. Below a hooked Sabine nose inherited from his father, his mouth was the most defining feature of his face. It was oddly soft. Perhaps it had a suggestion of overbite, with the upper lip curved and protruding slightly.

'Connected to Didius Falco.' That was it then. 'You want to be careful there!'

The Emperor made their association a shameful issue, yet he could not even know how closely they had sometimes worked with the man. Trained and moulded in Falco's image as they were, strong family affection went both ways. That should be private – but had whisperers been passing information to Domitian?

Something bothered the Emperor, something to do with that old plot. Falco, their anarchic brother-in-law, had carried out missions for Vespasian, including some mopping up operation; he even occasionally snarled that Domitian was a killer, not just an innocent puppet used by others. This was dangerous. Falco still possessed an item of evidence – no one was sure what, no one knew where he kept it. To this day his wife, their sister Helena, who was normally a strong woman, wept if anybody tried to talk about that time.

Quintus thought the Emperor was well aware that he was better informed than them, and was relishing his advantage. They had had nothing to do with whatever had happened.

Like so many in Rome, however, the brothers were damned by the past. If the story was revived, nothing would save them. They were catalogued in the unforgiving archive of Domitian's dark mind.

New arrivals were pressing in behind them. Having made his threats, the Emperor lost interest. He had others to bully. He let the Camilli go.

Finally, they became fully aware of this piece of theatre. A few lamps, of the kind used at funerals, allowed them to follow an usher. Faint pools of light hardly made an impact because, bloody hell, the whole room had been painted black.

It was not the elegant black of fashionable frescoed rooms, where a glossy background would be relieved by fine white borders and exquisitely coloured picture miniatures. Plain black. No fantasy garlands or candelabra, no naughty winged cherubs having fun in cute pursuits, no theatrical masks, tripods or torches, no myths, no monsters, no airy figures strewing flowers. Nothing. Just black walls, floor and ceiling. Black marble columns. Black drapes covering any windows. A black dais for the host.

It was set out like a mausoleum, the old-fashioned kind where a family could enter their personal tomb to feast with their ancestors. Within the vast space stood couches. Devoid of the usual coverlets and banquet cushions to make reclining comfortable, these were in an uncompromising hard material; on the bare floor, they had been positioned like endless lines of graves. There was no doubt why: each position was marked by a dark rectangular slab. These were modelled on tombstones.

Each slab carried a guest's name. Dear gods. There was

a lamp for each man, which lit his name. Each diner had to lie on his couch beside his own gravestone.

Although plenty of others had entered ahead of them, no warm buzz of conversation rose, only anxious silence. The brothers passed through the banks of dining couches, not meeting the eyes of their fellow guests, not even greeting those they knew. It was every man for himself tonight, even though they all feared sharing one terrible fate.

After the Camilli reached their places and grimly noted their memorial slabs, things began to happen. Around them, the other places quickly filled. Although they never saw the Emperor go past, Domitian had now stationed himself at the central part of the gathering; from there he was able to glare at his guests – or victims – as his black joke played out.

Last to arrive, the two consuls joined him. Guests who were near enough witnessed a formal embrace between the Emperor and his leading men: a curious mix of supposed affection and ill-concealed indifference. Vicirius Proculus and Laberius Maximus, who were they? Domitian barely greeted them.

Best to be nonentities. The consuls would serve their term – not even a full year but on a speeded up rota, deputed only for the period of September to December so the deserving could all get a chance to hold office. Afterwards, best to subside into oblivion, grateful to have escaped the top man's suspicion, relieved to still be alive. Now it was November: a month to go. Pray no informer named them for something they had done – or more likely some imagined slight they had never even thought about. It would soon all be over . . . Scuttle back to their estates.

275

Hope to get a province out of it, so they could spend a few years far away. Try not to catch his attention again.

Into the darkness bled sounds of funereal flute music. A long train of young boys slithered out in a sinister dance, like ghosts emerging from caverns of the underworld. They were exquisite creatures, totally naked, painted black from head to toe. They writhed among the lines of couches, beckoning like slant-eyed satyrs. Old beyond their years, their sly gestures and smiles seemed an invitation to debauchery. Eventually, one by one, these pitch-black boys peeled off from the dance until each was positioned at the foot of a dining couch, where they offered an unspoken introduction: *My name is Doom, I am your server today . . .*

Under cover of the dolorous flutes, Aulus snarled to his brother across the gap between their couches, intending his assigned creature to overhear: 'I don't care where we are – if that little bugger gropes me, he'll get a backhander he'll never forget!'

Quintus managed a half-smile. He extended an index finger, simply warning his own creepy attendant to note what his brother had said.

The boys must have been chosen for their prepubescent beauty, under their black paint. They held themselves like professional dancers, chests out, feet pointed, arms at rest with hands together. There were men in the room who would normally have loved it, but even they were being very careful at this banquet.

At some signal, these attendants bent gracefully to help the guests remove their outdoor shoes, then their heavy togas. Irritated, Aulus shook his little monster off; he shed and bundled up his toga himself, stashed it at the end of

276

his couch. He kept his shoes. Everyone else was in the process of reclining. Aulus remained upright. Making a rude gesture to his server, a mime of a man peeing in a lavatory, he glanced quickly at Quintus although no words were spoken. As brothers, with barely two years between them, they had shared a lifetime of unobtrusive code, dodging the attention of parents, sister, nurses, pedagogues, tutors, women they fancied, men they loathed . . .

Unobtrusively, Aulus Camillus sauntered back to the entrance.

'Call of nature,' Quintus explained to those around him. His brother's one-handed shaking gesture had left no room for doubt. Still, someone had to raise the tone.

As Aulus made his retreat unobtrusively through the lines of couches, Quintus remained in position. He was holding their place, though a small enclave of revolt had been established. The Camilli had taken a joint decision. Since they were done for anyway, they would not be intimidated. Nobody would steer them. They would do as they liked.

Because it was expected no guest would dare to leave, or certainly not at that point, Aulus was never intercepted by staff. It would be a long evening and many guests were elderly, so in fact a few slaves had been positioned outside the room, holding pots and with towels over arms. Aulus walked past as if he had failed to notice them. He was pretending to head for the large public lavatory that lay beyond the clatter and glimmer of a massive ceremonial fountain.

In truth he was on reconnaissance. Quintus knew why. They had both been military tribunes, stationed in frontier forts. Aulus was inspecting the lines, reviewing the watch, listening to the night: he wanted to learn in advance exactly

277

what was being set up outside the sinister chamber where the Senate was confined. If preparations for mass killing were in hand, he would spot them. At least he and Quintus would know.

What he found amazed him.

All the enormous audience rooms were now empty. When he walked beyond the vestibule, the wide space fronting the Palace lay deserted. Previously crowded with soldiers, supervising officials and mobs of attendants, it was now hushed, oddly empty. Normally, even at night, there were members of the public wandering about but today sightseers had been stopped from coming up here. Petitions would have to wait.

What had happened to the huge crowds of slaves who escorted the guests here? Gone. Completely gone. All dismissed.

Camillus Aelianus stood motionless, feeling the cold breeze of coming winter on his grim face and bare arms. It was night on the Palatine, possibly his last night on earth.

Only a plaintive wail from beside the grand fountain bowl let him know the empty outside areas still had a presence. He recognised the unhappy snivel. It was his own tiny slave, clutching his lantern. With him Aulus saw another small figure, a dwarf Domitian used to keep with him. The diminutive personage had been born with a head that was even smaller than it should be for his size. Toutou was so scared he was crying, though the imperial dwarf appeared to be offering kind words. 'He got separated.'

'He's mine. Toutou, come here to Master. Bring your lantern. Nothing to cry about.'

Quietly, Aulus retraced his steps to re-enter the black-painted dining room. When a chamberlain moved to prevent him bringing in the child, he made a grim joke about not losing valuable property. 'He lost the others. I can't leave him. He'll get pinched. Anyway, he's black enough! He'll fit the décor.'

In Rome, property counted for everything. Toutou was a valuable commodity, so he was allowed to follow. He stuck so close, he was bumping against his master's calf as they progressed back down the darkened room to the Camillus couches.

9

Nothing seemed to have happened while he went out for his look around.

Aulus lifted Toutou, then put him down on the floor between the brothers' couches. 'Sit quiet. Dry your eyes; you're safe with us. No one will even know you're here.' As he bent to do this, he mouthed to Quintus what he had seen. 'Bare terrace. All on our own. No transport, not one attendant left.'

Stuck, thought Quintus. Helpless. He wants us helpless.

Most senators would not be able to find their own way home, if they were ever allowed to leave here. Few would be carrying money for a fare; one or two probably could not even tell a hired litter-bearer their home address. On the streets of Rome at night, if men of this rank started asking for directions, muggers would descend like a flash flood. There would be no kindness for strangers; claiming to have a powerful place in society would mean absolutely nothing without bodyguards to back you up. Stuck.

The two Camilli would survive. They had acted as informers. Their streetcraft was fine. They would make it back to the Capena Gate – though they would have to get out of here first.

It was now the younger brother's turn to leave his couch, defying protocol. He had spotted that aediles had been invited, even though two of their number were always plebeian not senatorial. He only counted three, so he went across to enquire about the missing fourth man, who was their niece's husband. In the family, she was regarded as a wild child yet she had recently married a magistrate. It baffled everyone how Albia had managed this, not least since any watching gods reacted so angrily that her bridegroom had been struck by lightning. A doctor's note had covered his absence tonight, apparently.

Quintus returned to report, casually flopping back onto his couch. Aulus commented that their nephew-by-marriage might be permanently singed, but clearly had his head screwed on. Weeks after the event, he knew how to deploy a good excuse.

A lightning strike in the middle of a wedding procession was sensational and the famous victim had let it be known that he was struggling with after-effects. This let him attend parties he liked the sound of, but when he chose to avoid something official he blatantly bunked off. The brothers discussed how long Faustus would be able to get away with it. They liked him. They were envious.

Insidious scents of incense became apparent. Fine oils and wine were being poured as libations. At funerals, ancient custom was to sacrifice a sow to the gods of the underworld, the so-called chthonic deities. The sow for Ceres was apportioned between the goddess, the mourners and the deceased. So, pork arrived, ready barbecued; the Emperor made an ostentatious religious gesture, offering choice morsels for the gods, before further pieces were brought to the guests as sinister appetisers.

Customarily, everyone shared in the last proper meal any dead person could partake of before they flittered off to be a shade in the underworld. So the fallen of Dacia, though their corpses were not present, theoretically participated in this dinner. Grim legionaries and Praetorians, hacked to death in a massacre, the men might have held crude views on how their deaths were being exploited for the Emperor's strange purposes.

A solemn line of servers, identical boys carrying identical platters, moved out across the banquet floor to deliver the sacrificial dainties. Crispy pork, still hot – well at least quite warm in mass catering terms – exquisitely cooked with a glaze that smelled of honey, though it looked like some much darker marinade. Meat was handed to guests, the stand-in mourners, on little black tridents. Neat touch.

Aulus gravely took his portion from his painted attendant. He pulled off a piece, leaned down and handed it to Toutou.

'See what this is like, boy.' Observing him, Quintus had paused. 'Give him some of yours too,' Aulus suggested, his tone sardonic.

'You are appalling!'

'I am looking after my slave.' No, he was using his slave. Aulus could be kind-hearted enough when he chose, but even in a good family Toutou's first role was to protect his owner; only then could he count on any protection himself. 'You're safe with us' was purely notional.

'What will you do, if he keels over?' demanded Quintus, who genuinely had more scruples.

Aulus shrugged.

Despite his conscience, Quintus followed his brother's example, dropping a piece of his meat to the little boy, who gobbled anything he was given. Who knew what had happened to this child before he was picked out at the slave market? He was now fed in the Aelianus household, but had failed to lose his fear of hunger. Perhaps he never would.

Some party, thought Quintus. Not only did the Emperor have his designated official who must routinely test everything before it could touch the imperial lips, but a guest had smuggled in his own taster. It would, of course, be seen as an unforgiveable insult if Domitian found out they too were checking on the food, his gift, in case *he* was intending to poison *them*. Etiquette ordained that you must always pretend to trust a host. Perhaps that was why murders at banquets were so common. And so successful.

'What shall we do, anyway, if Toutou groans and drops? We have to eat what we're given.'

'Shut up, bro! You sound like my mother.' However, Aulus thought about it. Yes, what would he do? If Toutou's small body succumbed, as it would do very quickly if a fatal drug was present, what alternative did they have? One thing: before he himself was carried off, Aulus Camillus would stand up and accuse their host. You only die once. May as well go out shouting defiance. Denounce the bastard. Make your own justice. Get your name recorded in history as crazily courageous.

Quintus saw it in his eyes. 'Make sure first! Don't say anything too soon, in case that grumble in your tum is only a touch of colic.'

'Trust me.'

'Fat chance! Look out – black plates on the horizon.' Sharp-eyed, Quintus had spotted the next treat: the black serving plates that would become famous. Each diner was allocated his personal heavy comport.

Aulus scoffed quietly. 'You have to admit, the theming

is superb. If we ever escape, I'm going to ask for the name of his orgy planner.'

'I only wish someone had told us the big idea, so I could have brought a black-dyed napkin to wipe my fingers on.'

The food brought upon the black platters had been coloured black. Black food is unappealing, many would say.

IO

Back at the Capena Gate, the Justinus home was as well-lit as could be, given that its mistress was an oil heiress. Claudia Rufina budgeted well, sitting for hours with a small abacus while she listed expenditure, carefully balancing their outgoings against future requirements plus the need to maintain and invest in those olive orchards back in Baetica. But once she saw the results, she was not mean.

Rome sucked up the precious olive oil. The rich commodity was used for so many purposes, demand was never-ending – luckily. Whenever amphorae from her estate were transported from Spain and brought to the city for sale, Claudia received a consignment. Growing up among family olive groves, she expected to use copious quantities, never troubled by the cost. Here in Rome, there was no shortage in her kitchen, nor did she stint on pottery lamps once twilight fell. Their run-down porch became a beacon after dark, the only entrance in the street with lanterns hung on brackets, lit every twilight. It showed up that the wood needed a repaint, not that anybody ever got around to that.

The house was quiet now. With their father out for the evening, the children would normally play their mother up, thinking it safe to be naughty. Not tonight. They were subdued. They knew.

Hosidia Meline came in through the communicating door,

in search of mutual support. Secretly, she found the Justinus children overwhelming, so she had waited until she could be fairly sure Claudia had sent her romping mob to bed. Nurses would watch over them. Claudia, a thoroughly good mother, would go up first to say goodnight. If any child was sickly, it would be her role to administer medicine and cuddles, but if not, she would soon return to her visitor. That was only polite.

On the surface, the two women shared little in common, apart from that they were both provincials and had, at different times and for different reasons, both experienced marital tension. Coming from outside Italy especially coloured their view of Rome. They were in a precarious position as overseas brides, having no family to fall back on. Marriage was supposed to make them Camilli too, but if Aulus or Quintus was difficult, Claudia or Meline were cut off from grandparents, parents and any siblings who might have argued for them. Claudia's relatives had all died, in any case. So within the Camillus family they had bonded as outsiders. Their niece, Flavia Albia, came from Britain, though they tended not to include her. To them, Britain was beyond acceptable.

Now they lived with their slightly unreliable husbands in a city that was growing ever more dangerous because of its cruel ruler. Both could only nervously acknowledge that. If the Camilli were disgraced, they might find themselves wobbling on their perch in Rome. There were wide, dangerous seas between Italy and Spain or Greece.

In fact, neither fitted in completely, even though Rome was fairly welcoming to all nationalities. Both had the disadvantage they were pointedly sober women. Each behaved with a gravity that could make them seem awkward. Italian women, as wives in Rome, might be reserved but would then be praised for modesty and quiet conversation. Foreigners were viewed differently, as wilfully standoffish. In a snobbish city with long traditions, foreigners were accepted if their rank gave them citizenship, yet they had to fight for equal treatment. Claudia and Meline coped, but they were grateful to live closely together.

Their mother-in-law had been a strong ally. Julia Justa was an intelligent woman with the rare quality of understanding why her sons, in their separate ways, might not be performing as perfect husbands. Before she died, her home had been an enclave of feminine control. Aulus and Quintus teased her, but they did as she said. Afterwards, when Julia and Decimus passed away within a week of one another, adjustments had been hard.

'I am glad their parents have not had to see the danger they are in tonight.' Claudia, who had known Julia and Decimus much longer, took the lead in speaking of them.

'Let's not talk about it.' For a moment Meline regretted coming across from her own side of the house. But she knew she could not have borne to be alone, waiting for hours for news, uncertain whether Aulus would ever return.

So, deliberately not talking about the danger to their husbands, Claudia and Meline toyed with stuffed honeyed dates for an hour. Their refined tête-à-tête was then broken when they heard sudden loud banging at the front entrance.

The two women pretended to hide their first alarm. It was, said Claudia, who was always so sensible, far too early for people to be released from dinner at the Palace or for news of trouble to arrive. They pretended to wait while the door porter answered – though by the time he roused himself and stumbled out of his cubicle, complaining under his breath at being disturbed, the women had been unable to stop themselves scuttling into the hallway and hopping about behind him as he peered through his grille.

They heard him grunt. It sounded an unremarkable response, as if a greengrocer had made a morning call offering a sack of curly kale, on special terms because he had somehow overbought . . .

With infinite slowness, the retainer unbolted bolts. He behaved as if he were ninety though in fact was in his thirties. Claudia would have pushed past him and unfastened the massive devices herself, but the last time she did so, she cut her finger on the metalwork. Meline was too good mannered; this was someone else's house. She did, however, hiss quietly to herself in a way that was plainly a Greek curse. The look in her dark eyes spoke of damage to the porter's anatomy. So strong was the vibe, he even turned around briefly to give her a reproachful look. Meline sucked in air sharply between her teeth. Greek might be a euphonic, elastic language of enormous antiquity, but when stressed, she did not bother with it.

As the double doors swung inwards, in poured all the attendants who had gone out that evening with Aulus and Quintus. Meline spotted they were without Toutou, from whom they admitted they had become separated. They swore that was not their fault.

From the ensuing babble of complaints and anxiety, the two wives extracted how Palace officials had dismissed everyone, steering attendants from the audience room along with any means of transport that came with them. It had been done in such haste there was no time for explanations or the agreement of their masters to them leaving. The women soon gained a fearsome picture of curt chamberlains, backed by heavy-handed Praetorian Guards. Escorts had tumbled away down the Palatine, almost tripping over themselves in the Cryptoporticus. Their masters still did not know what had happened.

'Nobody knew what was going on, or why they kicked us out like that. It was mayhem on the way down the Hill. All the escorts were in total panic. What are the masters going to do without us?'

Claudia and Meline looked at one another. They saw at once how separating senators from their entourages was a sinister ploy. It was Domitian's prelude to some nightmare. Meline covered her face with both hands, unable even to spit plosives.

'Dear gods, where are they? What has he done to them?' screamed Claudia, completely overcome.

'Nothing, tell yourself he has done nothing . . . but if he ever lets them go, how will they get home?'

'Go back out there!' Claudia commanded one of Quintus' ex-legionary guards. 'Run! Run at once to the Aventine; go round the far side of the Circus, not close to the Palatine. Go as fast as you can to Helena and Falco's house. Tell them everything that has happened, then ask them what we ought to do!'

I I

Back on the Palatine, the beautiful naked boys were serving cheesy pastries.

'Mmm . . . I always find funeral food so more-ish!' muttered Aulus, not even trying to sound guilty. It was all he could do to hold off long enough to let his little slaveboy taste the cheese parcels first.

Quintus was munching wheat cakes, even though they had been coloured black. This seemed to be achieved through charring, though the subtle palace kitchen staff had managed to avoid any taste of cinders. A crisp coating held together a luscious interior.

With his mouth full of spiced, honeyed cake, he could not answer. Both men had healthy appetites, despite the unnerving occasion; the imperial chefs had no problem enticing them with traditional graveside concoctions, rich in almonds, hazelnuts, sesame and pomegranate seeds, currants, cinnamon and cloves, parsley and bay. There comes a point for a nut-lover, Quintus thought, where funeral food is worth taking a risk, even when you are dining with a megalomaniac who wants to kill you.

'Dig in!' he managed to utter eventually, picking a grain from between his teeth with one fingernail. 'We are honouring the dead by sharing.' He began waxing lyrical, to keep his spirits up. 'Hypothetically there may be no corpses tonight, but we must imagine their presence. Just as, at a necropolis, spirits pass us unseen, a breath in the breeze that wafts by their teary mourners, we feel their unseen company as we remember them tonight. The poor sods who died at Tapae may have been buried miles from here, assuming anyone did ever collect the bodies up, but here we are, heaping upon them the reverence they deserve.'

'You are insufferable when you descend into mystic clap-trap,' was his elder brother's cool judgement.

Quintus gave him a grin that was honestly infantile. They could have been still precociously five and self-consciously seven. 'All right. If we have to go, better to die while chomping on the good flavours that have sustained our grief-stricken forefathers.'

'I remain unimpressed by your "remembering our roots" stuff. You wouldn't know a root if you stumbled over it and broke your ankle.'

'You're just so humourless.' Quintus continued, declaiming, 'Think of tonight as having a real purpose. Yes, it is dining with the dead in order to be at one with our ancestors, but at the same time, a good scoff in shared company provides solace for the unhappy, it anneals the internal stress of bereavement, it helps the living along the path of their recovery from grief.'

'That's a useful motto for a caterer!' Aulus dismissed the bombast. 'Actually I was talking to Genius, you know that famous cook Falco bought and quickly sold on because the man couldn't cook – in case you didn't notice, they had him back when Albia got married. Weird people. According to Genius, you would think happy wedding guests would tuck in with gusto – yet he said they eat far less than expected. It's mourners at funerals who scoff.'

'Because this is food as human comfort, plus respect for the national gods. We are one with our ancestors and one with our fellow mourners. Perhaps,' suggested Quintus darkly, 'this night on the Palatine, we are even one with the Emperor.'

'Our Master wouldn't like you saying that!' replied Aulus, lowering his voice. Domitian was not one for sharing himself with people. He thought everyone was against him, which in general they were.

The brothers had the sense to glance around to check, but their fellow guests were lost in fearful concentration on whatever the naked servers pranced up with. Cynics, who knew the ways of rough-end slaves, were keeping an eye on the boys in case they peed in the dish they were offering. If anyone looked up, it was only to squint nervously at what the Emperor was doing.

Domitian was not eating. He rarely did in public. It was said he preferred a hearty meal by himself at lunchtime. Tonight, he was simply watching. So, diners who dared turn in his direction found him staring at them, intent on how they received his strange banquet.

This was not a feast where people raised a beaker to compliment their host if they caught his eye.

There was wine, however. Dark red-black vintages, heavy in tannin, served in ebony goblets. Domitian was not drinking. His young eunuch cup-bearer, Earinus, spent more time preening than presenting drinks. Some world-rulers and empire-builders drown themselves in liquor until their reddened bloated bodies expire in alcoholic excess. Others never drink. They will not risk loss of self-control. Domitian was one of those. Inevitable, really.

Still, wine was one of the traditional beverages served

during feasts at tombs. At first, the Camilli tried sticking to water because wine was the obvious carrier for any poison with which the Emperor hoped to purge large numbers from the Senate. Eventually, Aulus reminded Quintus that when Nero murdered his step-brother, his young and popular rival Britannicus, the taster passed the wine as safe but Nero's fatal drug, reputedly supplied by the famous palace poisoner Locusta, was hidden in the cold water for mixing. One sip and the princeling was done for.

'Do we think Locusta is still alive?'

'If so, she would have to be about two hundred.'

'Sipping at the Fountain of Youth?'

'No, I think she was killed in the Year of the Four Emperors.'

'Poison?'

'Natural causes – execution.'

'Did she train up apprentices?'

'Yes, but the old crafts are dying. No one wants to be bothered. These days you can't find suppliers with the expertise, however big a bribe you offer. The fine art of removing enemies has been allowed to fade; commercial drug-dealing is all pastilles for breath-freshening and pods of wax to push up your arse for your haemorrhoids.'

'I wouldn't know!' Quintus demurely pretended, with a smile he intended to annoy his brother. Aulus ignored him.

They decided to move onto wine, taking it neat as a safety precaution.

12

Although the room had always been hushed, now an even denser silence fell. All the guests lay rigid with anticipation. Domitian began speaking.

The Camillus brothers listened to him with a quiet, respectful air, both wearing the faint smiles of men who had learned during various careers how to brace themselves to last out until the full story had been heard so the real truth behind it was revealed. Aulus had a fistful of funeral nuts, through which he chewed gloomily, screwing up his eyes. Quintus folded his hands and put himself into a private trance.

Dictators love to talk. It is remarkable how men who wield excessive sole power will be consistent in this: given a captive audience, they all drone on for hours. And hours. The human brain can only concentrate for twenty minutes, ask any teacher. Dictators have rarely been despatched on a training course to learn that simple fact. Many dictators are completely untrained; tyranny comes to them naturally.

When they speak, everything else stops. Nobody dares interrupt. Everyone sits looking rapt, hanging on these words of wisdom even while they are wondering what the flowing tirade really means. Clearly it is their own inadequacy if they are not transported into astounding inspiration by the demagogue's words of wisdom, so many words, so long in the delivery . . . No one can leave. Dictators never pause for a comfort break, nor may any listener abscond, not even with the anxious expression of someone desperate for the lavatory. Go before you come. Never was the adage so appropriate. Leaving the scene prematurely is the fast route to dying. It may feel like the anteroom to hell if you stay, but you'd better remain and look happy.

Dictators have no use for notes, for they are borne up by self-conviction. Besides, they wave their arms a lot for emphasis and to wind themselves up. They start, then continue until they have finished, which you know is going to be a long time later. They know what they have to say, and they most certainly will get through it. All of it, then any more that may come to them during the endless process of the speech.

Keep smiling. Keep smiling and whenever you have the chance, applaud enthusiastically. At one level, clapping will lengthen your misery by making the speech last longer – though of course it's extending your good fortune if you genuinely like their philosophy. That has been known. On the other hand, drowning him out with cheers provides a respite from the ceaseless continuance of the notable personage. He has grasped this gathering by the throat while he is telling you what he has done so gloriously, then, mentioning the foolish mistakes of others who are not favoured by history in the unique way that he is, and haranguing you with how the future will be glorious because he gives this speech, you listen to it, and that is how it has to be because he has his special understanding, which you are privileged to be sharing.

If there is a joke, laugh.

Do not get that wrong. Never laugh when he is serious. Absolutely do not get it wrong . . .

★

So Domitian began speaking that night on the subject of death. He addressed them in a careful manner, more as if he had thought long in preparing his words than as if he feared making an error. He had been called a good writer and orator, better even than his talented elder brother, though this praise was given by his friends. He never wavered from his theme. He paced the room, becoming in his triumphal robes a shard of glimmering purple and gold amidst the blackness. He spoke. They listened. That was it. There was no question anyone would dare challenge anything; at no point did any guest attempt to engage in a dialogue with their host, as would happen at a normal banquet. Even the old and doddery ones who had little idea where they were or why they had been brought here, somehow found enough self-preservation to lie still and keep quiet.

Domitian could do this because he had a captive audience, who understood his power. They themselves had given him all the rights that his father and brother had held. He was lord of the civilised world, Father of his Country, chief priest, chief lawgiving magistrate, and although he pretended to be too modest to accept it, people called him their Master and God. They did that, even though it was blasphemous for any living human to claim personal divinity. He brushed off the implication and never punished those who used the term. People around him soon got the hang of how to flatter him.

Flattery was the wisest thing. He had twenty-nine legions to protect his position, plus Praetorian Guards, Urban cohorts and even the vigiles. Soldiers liked him; he tripled their pay, awarding generous bonuses on top. He had also gone on campaign with them, facing dangerous enemies even if it was at a safe distance. Although his 'victories' were inglorious and his peace-terms little better, he had chosen wise commanders who overturned bitter defeat, recaptured missing standards, brought home rescued Roman troops – all in his name. One day a soldier would deal him his death blow, but that would be a long time coming.

There had been a mutinous revolt with a rival claimant to power, but Domitian reacted adeptly and survived with panache. The uprising was put down very fast; punishment carried out brutally, but that was the old Roman way. Afterwards, nothing is more dangerous than a dictator who survives a failed coup. He thinks himself invincible. He is out for revenge.

Domitian knew his strengths. He had made his mark on Rome with elegance and generosity. Unlike the raving maniacs of the previous Julio-Claudians, this Emperor's driven wish for control made him a perfect administrator. He could manipulate a budget. His building programme would astound future generations, even though much he had planned would be claimed by his successors. Since he dismissed officials for corruption even when they had not yet done anything corrupt, real embezzlement rarely happened. Having so few friends, he could never be accused of favouritism. He supported the arts; poets cloyingly spoke well of him. Historians quibbled – but would hold their peace until they had newer, safer men of power to flatter.

In the meantime, this cool, introverted, obsessive man in his forties was holding a banquet in his Palace, where he could dominate trembling guests. He held the right of execution; he was ready to use that power, if a grudge overtook him. His mind was dark, but clever. If he was mad, it was with a muscular kind of insanity, very self-aware.

Much of his paranoia was justified, borne of logic and experience. He faced his fears with sardonic courage. If assassins ever came after him, he would go down fighting to the end.

So, tonight he took the floor and said his piece to an audience he despised for many reasons, especially the way they were quaking. Most were transfixed. There was no doubt their fear pleased him. Whatever his ultimate intentions, he was enjoying this moment. He had them. They knew it. Brilliant!

But even as the Emperor relished talking to his audience about death, so ominously implying that the next exit from the world would be theirs, men who knew him to be whimsical still dared to hope. Perhaps this whole dinner party was a charade, sinister yet harmless. Might it all, they wondered incredulously, yet turn out to be nothing but a grim game: was the black banquet merely Domitian's spectacular practical joke?

13

The Capena Gate had a visitor from the other side of the Aventine. Tall, scathing and blunt, their sister-in-law had responded to the Camillus women's distraught appeal. Claudia wondered whether to run for her emerald set, but since Helena Justina was indifferent to matters of appearance, she decided not to bother. Meline found herself sitting up straighter in her basket chair, as if a more-than-usually caustic aunt had descended on them. The aunts of Karystos were legendary.

Helena Justina was the archetypal elder sister. Nobody called her bossy – no one dared – but she had supervised her brothers all their lives, which was absolutely for their own good. Now their parents were dead, it fell to her to take the lead in the family. The textbook verdict decreed that Rome was a paternalist society; the law gave men all the civic rights. This ignored a fierce tradition that went back to the city's founding. Romulus and his men may have raped the Sabine women;, but thereafter the Sabine women used their power as the mothers of the children who were needed to people Rome. The materfamilias was born.

An ancient king, Numa Pompilius, had laid down the laws Romans would follow; a practical nymph gave those laws to him. Vestal Virgins embodied the city. Women brought up the children. Women ran the home. Men might have a nominal right of life and death over their dependents, but in family councils strong female relatives spoke up and were listened to with meek respect, which often was not feigned. Never underestimate the power of a big dowry. Men held the purse strings; women spent then blithely sent their bills to the accountant. Even a whisper of divorce made husbands cringe. When men died, their widows had a riot. They married their appointed male guardians if they had to, or otherwise simply ignored them.

The materfamilias was typified in Helena Justina. She kissed her sisters-in-law formally; they kissed her cheek in return, respecting her enduring rights as the original daughter of this house. As soon as formalities were done, they burst out with their fears while she tried to calm them. Falco, she said, was at his warehouse conducting a stock take. Since there had been insufficient Dacian plunder for the Emperor's Triumph yesterday, the Didius auction house had lent a large quantity of 'treasures' to boost the carts of supposedly captured treasure. 'What's come back is not exactly what he sent, but if things have been pinched, other things have been sent. Auctioneers do like a good turnaround. He is in heaven with his inventory.'

'We are worried about the boys!' Claudia insisted.

'Of course you are. And so am I. I came by way of Albia's house, in case they know more, but they have avoided this fiasco; her husband had an invitation, but he made some excuse.'

'Snubbing Domitian makes Manlius Faustus a brave man!' Meline commented.

'He is. I don't think I have heard the half of what goes on there,' Helena murmured. Claudia and Meline knew she was trying to balance being a light-handed mother-in-law

300

against her yearning to know everything. They secretly laughed over how she always said she would not interfere. They knew she had brought up her children to be feisty souls, so they were bound to keep things from her. Helena could only pretend she was proud of their free will.

'Has Faustus, as a magistrate, heard anything about what the Emperor's dinner purports?' asked Melina in her slightly formal way.

'Not a thing. Domitian has kept everyone guessing.'

'He must be planning something! Something dire!' Claudia was losing her outer calm.

'There is no way to find out, sweetheart,' Helena Justina told her sternly. 'We'll just have to wait until the boys come back. I know the situation is worrying, so I came here to wait out whatever befalls. Will it help if I keep you company? I'd like to see my brothers safely home in one piece.'

'What does Falco think?' demanded Claudia.

'He has no idea. He only made a bet that Domitian will toy with a whole turbot, while everyone else is served wine-fried anchovies that have gone soggy on the route from the kitchen . . . No women are invited,' Helena then growled. 'I reckon Our Master is scared we would laugh at his antics, take over with our own funny stories, and spoil whatever sinister outcome he has planned.'

'I believe it used to be the custom,' Claudia speculated, 'that while great men dined at the Palace to celebrate a Triumph, the Empress would hold a simultaneous banquet for all the senatorial wives.'

'We may die waiting for that!' scoffed Meline.

Helena stretched on a reading couch, where she began to work her way through the remaining honeyed dates. Claudia and Meline had lost out there. Their sister-in-law looked innocent as she set about it, but they had seen her with a snack platter before. 'I can never decide,' Helena told them while she chewed, 'whether Domitia Longina is terrified of her husband and what he may do next, or whether her method is to lie low, avoid confrontation, and let him get on with being a paranoid maniac, if that keeps him happy. At any rate, it's obvious she won't try to upstage him by becoming more popular herself.'

'No, people say she is horrible!' Meline, who could be waspish, suggested the Empress might be glad to know Domitian was preoccupied with his party, so for one night she could do as she liked.

Claudia looked nervous at this, so to distract her Helena asked, 'How long have the boys been gone now?' They told her glumly. 'Juno, they will be hours yet! They won't be able to slip out before the end, saying terribly sorry, they have to see a client.'

A pause fell.

'I do not know,' complained Meline, 'why either of them ever wanted to be senators. My father always said that, given how the Emperor rules, the Senate is an irrelevance.'

'Social standing,' answered Helena. No snob, she sounded dismissive. She and Claudia exchanged a half glance, aware that Minas of Karystas had been perfectly willing to view this particular senatorial family as prey. The way he grabbed Aulus, first as a student then a son-in-law, had occasioned endless bitter debate. Aulus knew of it. Meline had been politely kept out of the Camillus family wrangling in theory – but inevitably Meline knew too; once she picked up the secret blame aimed at her father, it became one of the reasons her original marriage to Aulus was unhappy. Minas had seemed to be too sozzled to notice. His one complaint was that after he had drunk the senator's wine cellar dry, Decimus took much too long buying in new amphorae.

'They thought if they were senators, sheer reputation might bring them more work,' Claudia explained to Meline. '– which it has done, though probably not as much as they hoped. Yet you are right, darling; if they hadn't done it, we wouldn't be in this mess now. We would have more money,' she grumbled, 'and I would see Quintus here at home a *lot* more. Helena, I blame your husband for helping out when they decided to stand.' At the time, Falco had been in receipt of an unexpected inheritance. At first, he saw it as his role to act as benefactor for his numerous relations, though lately he had grown more comfortable with his wealth; he now guarded it more closely, which he openly said was the way rich men stay rich. *Hands off, you beggars. You can fight over everything after I'm dead. I won't care then.*

'They wanted to do it.' Helena brushed off any criticism, as if her brothers had simply demanded unfortunate toys to play with, asking to join the Senate the way they had once wanted model animals then, later, tickets to see gladiators. 'Too late now!'

The three women were all bored. Perhaps they were not sufficiently fond of one another to enjoy an evening of simply waiting around for their menfolk. Or perhaps the tension as they feared for Aulus and Quintus was becoming too much.

They could do something about the wait. None of these were passive women. Helena suggested that in the absence of proper entertainment provided by the Empress, they should hold their own party. Meline might be used to the Greek idea of being stuck at home in the women's quarters mending tunics, while men went out for drink and debauchery, but Meline was the daughter of a legendary boozer so she knew how a symposium worked. Claudia even liked playing the good Roman housewife; a bride receiving the keys to all the store cupboards formed part of the wedding ceremony.

'Then we should raid the wine cellar.' Taking the point instantly, Meline was showing herself to be a pragmatist. 'If Domitian kills our husbands, he will confiscate their property.'

'No! Surely he won't, darling, will he?' On the property point, Quintus had been less forthright with Claudia than Aulus with Meline. Claudia was now shocked.

Helena played peacemaker. 'No, no. Vespasian admitted them to the Senate. They never draw attention to themselves by speaking in debates; they just go for a snooze in the Curia. The present Emperor doesn't even know who they are.'

'That is not what I have heard!' Suddenly Meline rounded on Helena. 'My father said, Decimus Camillus told him in deepest confidence that your husband, Falco, possesses some evidence against Domitian. Domitian wants revenge for it, he is that type of person.'

Helena tried to avoid this conversation. 'Domitian wants revenge against so many people for so many slights, most of them pure imagination on his part. He cannot wreak his warped judgement on everyone. People close to him are at most risk, because he sees them frequently and it gives him ideas about them.'

'Is your Falco a threat to him?' Meline persisted.

'Marcus keeps his head down.'

'Do you have a plan? If Domitian ever turns on him?'

'Retirement to a farm in Britain – it's a pretty desperate plan!' Helena answered, laughing.

Meline growled. She kept digging. 'Domitian will see Aulus and Quintus tonight! Palace protocol means he will be told their names. Nobody knows what evidence your dangerous husband has, but if the Emperor fears it seeing the light of day, that will be fatal. Helena Justina, you should do the honourable thing by your family and divorce Falco!'

Helena looked surprised, but then she laughed again, more gently.

Claudia was amused too. She had known Helena and Falco long enough to reproach Meline: 'That will never happen! . . . Anyway, I have been told there was a plot by an uncle that still reverberates. It's their uncle who remains dangerous to Aulus and Quintus. Helena, you ought to tell us why.'

'I can't.'

'You don't want to!'

Helena merely shrugged. Her stole slipped off one shoulder so she busied herself with that classic gesture of fielding the cloth then rearranging it gracefully in new folds. Her gold ear-rings twinkled. Bracelets on one arm chimed. 'Old scandal. We survived. When Vespasian received my brothers into the Senate it was his signal of forgiveness. We should not harp on a past error as if we felt guilty. Let it lie.'

Claudia knew when to give up. 'This woman will not budge. We may as well stop asking . . . Meline, you and I had best consider our escape plans.'

Meline also capitulated. She too lifted and replaced the silken folds of her wrap, so that light from an overhead chandelier glistened on expensive embroidery along its edges. This was a formal way to punctuate a change of subject, an unspoken gesture that all women understood. 'So, before the Emperor's agents come to seize our goods, we must drink the wine – to keep it from them.' Claudia and Helena exchanged mock-humorous glances again, pretending to be nervous that she might follow in her father's inebriated foot-steps. Claudia deployed the stole gesture to imply unspoken disapproval. 'In moderation!' Meline assured them affably. She knew how people had viewed Minas. 'I believe it is appalling for Roman wives to be drunk?'

'That never stopped any of us,' Helena reassured her.

'You have been listening to Roman husbands,' Claudia added. They deserved a treat, she said to encourage her companions. Stuck at home, with nothing to do but wait to hear that the Emperor had murdered the men they loved . . .

'Well, "love" is a word to drive anyone to a wine goblet!' Helena giggled with Claudia, then she smiled at Meline, so lately returned to Aulus, who was looking perturbed. 'Irony, dear girl!'

So, while Claudia Rufina, best of housewives, toddled off to the cellar, Hosidia Meline took herself to Claudia's kitchen to persuade slaves to rustle up snacks and nibbles.

Left alone in the salon, Helena Justina, who ought to have been their role model, a woman of gravitas, realised she had polished off all the honeyed dates. For a moment she sat motionless, considering love: her love for her husband and children, then the love they all bore for her endangered brothers. Then, since she was still unobserved in the room on her own, she started the night's descent into decadence by licking clean the empty snacks plate.

14

It was over.

On the Palatine, quite suddenly, the Emperor stopped speaking. Before anyone could take in what was happening, Domitian had left them. He was famous for losing interest in dinners. He did not bother to say thank you for coming; after all, they had had no choice.

A brief period of confusion raged in the dim chamber, as the concerned senators tried to work out what they were supposed to do next. It was clear that the naked dancing boys had finished serving food and drink. They must have been told to stop. So, the meal had ended. Such music as there had been was funereal; it now ceased, so there was nothing to listen to, and therefore no reason to stick around as if taking an interest in culture. Sometimes on other occasions Domitian provided entertainment: a troop of comic dwarves, acrobatic displays, even stylised indoor gladiating. Nothing like that had happened. Nor would it, that was evident.

Murmurs began. Disbelief at the possibility of release gave way to anxiety about what was expected of them now. Men risked turning to their neighbours to enquire what anyone thought. They had to be circumspect. Nobody wanted to talk too freely, since any gossip about the evening would without doubt be noted by Domitian's staff and immediately passed on to him.

Perhaps some remembered how Titus, the golden boy, used to act as Vespasian's hitman; he would invite people who had caused offence to dinner, give them a good meal, then at the end they were executed . . . If an attack was planned, this could be the moment.

Camillus Justinus stood up, stretching his tall limbs. At scattered points around the dark room, others nervously followed suit, though no one was sure whether or not they could evacuate the black dining room without imperial permission. Camillus Aelianus stooped between their two couches, to gather up his slave. When he straightened, with the now sleeping Toutou securely in his arms, the brothers exchanged a practised glance, their signal.

Moving with smooth, unobtrusive steps, they passed down the rows without stopping to chat, aiming for the main door through which they had originally entered. Whenever they passed an usher they murmured false thanks for the evening, like good-mannered boys whose noble mother had brought them up in the right way.

They reached what they hoped was the exit. Their path remained unimpeded. A slave opened the heavy black curtains for them. Another operated the doors. They passed through to the outer audience chamber.

There, lines of officials were waiting for them, ready to surprise them with what Domitian had planned next.

15

In the Camillus Justinus house, proceedings had reached the stage that happens at all the best parties, where nobody remembers the original point. Once this occurs, the party *is* the point. Why quibble?

There were only three participants, plus a handful of Claudia's closest slaves, those who had stayed awake, stolid elderly Baeticans who proved the claim she and Quintus always made that their slaves were family members. For Rome, the Camilli were liberal. They lived up to their stated ideals, which high-minded people will not always bother to do.

Nevertheless, the slaves were on duty, so they were serving. They were allowed tots of their own. At least, half-full ones.

Since the group was so small, it was all fairly quiet. Besides, children were upstairs, hopefully sleeping. It was thought best not to disturb them, in case they came scampering down in their sleeping tunics, to investigate what exciting times their elders were having. In the absence of incense and garlands, not to mention the lack of imported goodtime boys (who organised this shindig?), a trio of respectable housewives was hardly going to raise the roof. As Helena said, the roof on the Camillus house was not in a good state, and never had been in all her memory; they needed to treat it gently.

The truth was that the effects of the wine hit them so fast mainly because they were unused to it. Not in such desperate quantity. Respectable women, some of them mothers, were no strangers to a warming nip during festivals, a medicinal draught for sickness (one for the patient, one for the exhausted nurse), or a small glass on somebody's birthday (to reward themselves first for keeping a calendar, then for remembering to look at it in time to fix up a suitable gift). But they did not drink to forget often enough to know that drinking to forget only makes you forget that someone is likely to turn up unexpectedly and find you at it.

In this case it was a small boy. He ran into the room barefoot, sweetly tousled, nervously het up. Claudia mentally went through the list of her children; this was Constans, her seven-year-old. He was prone to anxiety, sometimes suffered with his chest, had had trouble with his reading but was now catching up . . . His birthday, she knew without consulting, was next month. They had to make a special fuss of him, or he always lost out to Saturnalia . . .

'Constans! Why are you out of bed, darling?' burbled the fond mother ineffectually.

Meline had mellowed so much that although she was wary of children, at least Roman ones, she actually held out her arms and took the boy on her lap. Since he was prone to anxiety, he sat very still, staring out at the others, owl-eyed.

'Constans, don't look so frightened; you are not in any trouble!' his Aunt Helena soothed him. He liked her. She bought good presents. From what Helena had heard about Constans, she supposed there had been bed-wetting, although Quintus had recently assured her that the lad seemed to be

310

over that stage now . . . Helena had an introverted son of her own. But dear heavens (thought Claudia) our son is nothing like her crazy Postumus! 'Tell us what the matter is,' Helena went on kindly, 'and we can do something about it for you, sweetheart.' That was debateable at this point in the party, but they could send a slave to the nursery.

'Someone is coming! I was looking out of a shutter to see if my father would soon be home.'

'Coming down the street?' demanded his mother.

'No, they are here.'

'*Outside?*'

'The doorman has gone, but I don't think he wants to let them in.'

Claudia was on her feet in an instant. Silverware flew in all directions as she knocked a tray off a side-table. Meline caught the falling flagon, even though she was holding the little boy. The container she fielded was actually empty, but this was a superb hand-eye co-ordination. Helena clapped her effort, before they all made a wild stampede to the front doors.

The porter had refused to open up. He did not recognise the transport that had turned up on the doorstep; he became deaf when reminded that Quintus had not taken the family chair out that night, anyway. It was late. It was dark. Even by the standards of Roman porters, this one had always been intransigent. They only kept him because they were too soft-hearted to sell him on. He was taking a stand, nothing new in that. Despite increasingly frustrated banging, he would not risk letting danger in.

'This is the first time you have shown such regard for us!' snapped Claudia. 'It could be Quintus Camillus. Get out of my way.'

She herself withdrew the mighty bolts. She cut her finger again, like the last time she tried it. She would not care about that, because she could hear her husband in a rage, bawling about how it was iniquitous for a man to be locked out of his own house.

16

By the time they staunched the blood that was oozing from Claudia's finger, and wrenched open the doors, one of which always stuck inconveniently, Quintus and Aulus had disappeared. Tipsy female shrieks occurred. Little Constans covered his ears. Back in the house, two of his brothers had appeared on the stairs, wailing because they thought something was wrong. Children need a quiet routine. They never got it in this house, but since even Mama was now behaving oddly, and quite loudly, tonight struck them as worse than normal.

A curtained litter that no one recognised was already making an exit. Halfway down the road, almost under the aqueduct, it must now be empty, judging by the jaunty way the bearers were picking up their feet as they swung it along. They were in white, Domitian's Palace livery. '*Shit!*' exclaimed Gaius, running out into the road to look.

'Gaius!'

'Oh, he's right. Shit and double shit!' Giggling, Aunt Helena conspired with Gaius. The children perked up, intrigued by this variation on their newest phrase. They always regarded Helena as one of them, which their parents could only tolerate patiently. Helena had grown up here. Once she discovered a mind of her own, she had never changed.

When everyone piled back into the house, they met Quintus and Aulus in the hall. They had come through the communicating door after Quintus abandoned swearing at the recalcitrant porter, then Aulus simply used his key to his own house. Two shaken senators had returned – to find, oops, two unexpectedly merry wives. As the night's story began to be told, the uncontrolled mirth stopped.

There were intense hugs all round. Tears were shed, not always by women. Justinus loped off upstairs, where he did the rounds of his children, reassuring those who were awake, tucking those who had come downstairs back into their beds, gently kissing the warm heads of those who slept. He laid a hand upon each child, reconnecting after the threat of loss.

In his absence, Aulus gave a swift account of the dinner. 'He meant it to be horrible – the supposedly most important men of Rome reduced to gibbering wrecks, all of us trapped in that nightmare of confusion about his intentions, with the monster gloating over our discomfort. It did not end when he left. After we emerged from the Palace, he continued the process: screwing us with more anxiety. Instead of the familiar retainers most people were expecting to find, palace staff forced us all into transports they summoned up, with escorts that none of us had ever seen before. It was unclear where these unknown men were taking us. Nothing was said. We still thought we might never see our homes again. Everyone had to live through further dread on the journey, imagining we would be dragged off down an alley, then murdered on the city streets.'

'But you're not. Here you are.'

'Here we are,' said Aulus, though his face was drawn.

'Safe and sound,' added Quintus, as he returned. He

sounded subdued, looking like a man who might have been praying somewhat intently to his gods. Normally he had no time for such niceties. The lares and penates of the Justinus household would have been rather surprised he acknowledged them tonight.

Then, for once not scrapping but in earnest, he and Aulus came together. The brothers suddenly embraced: lumps in their throats, ordeal over, choking with relief.

17

Even their narrow escape from death left Aulus and Quintus silent and depressed. Neither could even find the spirit to complain about coming home from their great adventure to women who had spent their time carousing instead of weeping with fear for their men. Quintus had not even noticed yet that the wine Claudia pulled from the cellar had been his father's favourite Caecuban.

With little more ado, everyone took themselves off to bed. Helena Justina had been offered her old room by an elderly slave. 'Little Aelia has it nowadays, she decided she wanted her own place, but I can move her in with her parents . . .'

'No, let their parents have time together.' Helena, convincingly sober by some sleight, wanted to go home to her own family. She needed the kind of reassurance Quintus had sought earlier. To count them. Touch them. Tell them they were loved. To make sure for herself that everyone was there, and safe . . . Besides, she knew that her husband, left in charge, would be waiting for news of the situation. She could imagine him prowling about unhappily without her, pretending not to feel worry while he drove himself mad with it.

Night lay upon the Capena Gate. There was a period of rumbling commercial activity as delivery carts inhabited

316

the road system, but after yesterday's Triumph things were still slow. No one who lived in Rome noticed the familiar racket, anyway. Once their tasks were done, the wheeled vehicles evacuated the city. A quieter time ensued, where partygoers sometimes whooped or thieves yelled at the vigiles. Then there was peace. Stars. Near stillness. What passed for silence in a city of a million people, a city that was never entirely at rest.

Still wound up, Aulus and Quintus found sleep hard to come by. Their crazy evening on the Palatine reimposed itself, chuntering around in their heads obsessively as they tried to escape. Aulus and Meline, who sometimes kept to separate rooms, lay in each other's arms tonight. Quintus, the tragic traditional husband, had his back to his wife, though he was comforted by Claudia pressed up against him and had she needed, he would have turned to her. She, exhausted by wine and fearfulness, had collapsed, unable for once to listen out for troubled children. Quintus was doing that, until he too at last found sleep.

Only Aulus lay awake for some time longer. Aulus, the grim brother, the one who had always been most likely to harbour suspicions about situations where everyone assured him there was no need. His teeth clenched. He could not relax. Aulus Camillus had heard his relations congratulate each other that they had survived, that the threat had come to nothing, that the misery was ended. But Aulus assessed this as a crisis that was not yet over. To him, the black banquet's climax seemed to be missing. Domitian, he reckoned, had unfinished business. So he lay on his back, staring up at the ceiling, trying not to disturb Meline, while he waited alone for the crunch to come. Yet even he succumbed to weariness eventually and sank into a deep slumber.

Just before dawn, the time when raids are carried out and sudden arrests are made, two households were woken by thunderous, protracted knocking.

18

More terror.

Stumbling down to see who was attacking their doors, all the Camilli were horrified. As soon as they saw the soldiers, they were sure this time they really were done for. Just when they dared to believe they escaped last night, loud messengers from the Palace had arrived at their homes. They were, after all, being brought a death sentence.

'Morning! Let's be having you.'

This was a cheery cry from Taurinus, that hardened, diligent officer, still stuck with acting as postman, still subtly troubled by his task. Now he was in charge of wagons. He had two hundred doors to knock on, each time greeting a man who would think that this racket heralded his executioner. There was always a chance, Taurinus knew, that some noble senator, still with sleep in his eyes, would grab a weapon and come running out to spill blood. Nothing to lose. Go down fighting, like his hairy ancestors. Horatius Cocles holding that bridge single-handed. Now some victim of Domitian might finally choose to say no to a polite death. Blood all over the flower urns. Nasty incident. Horribly public.

From various directions, neighbourhood dogs could be heard barking. In other houses, shutters had been discreetly opened.

'Presents!' announced Taurinus. He had been told to keep them guessing until the last moment. 'Nice ones,' he added, pretending this was irony. Taurinus had no truck with mothers so he ignored Claudia Rufina, but he winked at Hosidia Meline. She was younger and, in her light sleeping tunic, almost lustworthy. He had taken to her. 'These your husbands, are they? Noble A Camillus, noble Q ditto?' He sounded chippy. 'So, aren't they the lucky boys!'

The noble A and noble Q pushed their wives behind them for safety, not that either of their wives was having it, so the two women moved back out beside them. The senators occupied their home doorsteps, arms folded, knowing that they were probably doomed but ready to turn truculent.

No need for heroics, Taurinus assured them pleasantly. Our Master just wanted to give them treats, mementos of his lovely banquet.

'Oh, he shouldn't have. The heartburn is enough!' quipped the noble Quintus.

'Nice one, sir! Now look lively, if you please. Sign here!' ordered Taurinus in his now-practised don't-give-me-any-trouble voice.

'I shall do it,' said Aulus Camillus, acting the elder brother.

'For what is he signing?' demanded his wife, true daughter of the famous jurist Minas.

Taurinus recited: 'Delivered goods. *Item*: one tombstone. That is, one per person.' The black painted name slabs that had stood beside each dining couch had been cleaned up, revealing an unexpected constituency. 'Very desirable, very expensive, *very* generous of Our Master!' Taurinus congratulated them, as the startled beneficiaries noticed that under the dark goo of last night, the tombstones were in fact substantial blocks of solid silver. 'What a merry trickster he is . . . *Item*: one serving platter each, elegant comport, seemingly onyx, will look delectable in your display cabinet!' The wives grabbed them. '*Item*: one slaveboy, cleaned up, personal attendant with high-end dancing and serving talents, just watch their habits and their language, which to my mind are both absolutely filthy.'

Aulus used the military response to panic, though he said it quietly. Taurinus responded, with sympathy. 'Don't blame me, sir. I am just the messenger. If anybody asks, I'll say you was both utterly delighted to get this stuff, shall I?' Aulus and Quintus nodded weakly. Children were crying now – and that was just the two appalling slave boys from the banquet who had been dumped here, almost certainly as spies.

Taking their gifts, the Camillus brothers turned into the Justinus' house, intending to share more raw mirth at the malevolence of the Emperor's 'joke'.

'I am not having that horrible pervert slave in the same house as my children!' stropped Claudia; 'Quintus, I shall give the dirty little beast to your niece Albia. She is setting up a new household and she doesn't stand for nonsense.'

'She can take ours too,' agreed Meline tartly. ' "*We thought you could have them, Albia – you are so scary, you can make them run away . . .*" Then my ex-husband, the moneychanger, will turn those hideous tombstones into cash. I shall ask him today, before the silver market crashes due to overload.'

'And maybe today for once,' they chimed fiercely at their husbands, 'you noble pair will stay at home for breakfast among your loved ones.'

'All we ever want!' promised the Camillus brothers, sounding meek.

It was too early, but no one would be able to get back

to sleep, so Claudia had her Baetican staff bring breakfast now. Appetites returned. The nightmare was over; they had emerged from it unscathed. Everything was all right.

As they ate, light-heartedness coloured requests to pass the chickpeas. Both men were freely teasing their wives over whether they needed a cabbage cure for hangovers; Claudia and Meline acted out disinterest, cradling small cups of mint tea with refined gestures. Wily children snatched slices of Lucanian sausage from other people's plates. When a saucer of olives was placed on the serving table, a wit cried, 'Black food!' so everyone collapsed laughing . . .

But perhaps, as their eyes met over their bread rolls, Aulus and Quintus were thinking. As brothers, they knew how to communicate privately. Each could see the other suspected Domitian had miscalculated. He had shown how much he despised the Senate. Yes, he had made clear that his return to Rome would have a cruel tone, while last night he clinched his intention to rule through tyranny. But this relied on his premise that the Senate was composed of cowards.

In fact, Rome had checks and balances. There had always been honourable senators, and the Camilli were not the only ones who were capable of resistance. They, and others at the black banquet, had refused to submit to fear. These dinner guests were all part of a strong network that stretched throughout the empire: relatives, colleagues, contacts in trade and politics, old ties to the legions in which they had served, new ones in provinces where they owned estates. Any emperor relied on the Senate to validate him. They were not moribund: they could vote in a new one and obliterate the predecessor from history.

It had been done; it would be done again. Plotting was a

tradition in their family, and they were permanently scarred by it, so what had the brothers to lose? All over Rome that morning, other men who had been made to suffer at the Emperor's dinner would start to share their mood. It would be slow. It might take years. There would be no oaths, no funny handshakes, no secret notes in code, yet it would happen. Domitian had invited opposition to begin.

The Bride from Bithynia

Part one

Aelia Camilla was eleven when her brother let her drive his four-horse chariot.

The hippodrome where he took her was a small private park enclosed by trees. Grooms stood about amiably. 'Enjoy it!' warned Publius. 'This is your only chance.' In the First Century Roman Empire a respectable girl travelled in a closed litter, guarded by family slaves. She never sat on a horse or drove herself.

'You will come in with me?'

'My word, yes!'

At nineteen, Publius was seen as a trial. He drove too fast; he knew a strange set at the public baths; he gambled; he wrote political slogans on private walls and even signed his name on them. Risking his little sister's neck in a quadriga was typical.

'Just decide you're going to do it, and we'll go. Once you start to twitter, you'll be lost.'

Camilla nodded. She would never be a twitterer again.

They examined the chariot, which had a great oaken axle with lions'-head finials, thrust through eight-spoked, iron-rimmed wheels. Camilla reached up to pat one of the four roan horses. Then her brother sprang lightly aboard the chariot car and lifted her in. There was not much room. She squeaked as the tiny car shifted under them when the trace horse stallions strained forwards.

Camilla held the reins. Publius stood behind, his own hands covering hers. 'There are three disasters to avoid – a scrape, the pole breaking, or losing the reins. In a race the reins would be tied to you, so you would take a dagger to cut yourself free in a spill –' The grooms loosed the horses. 'Now you're driving. We won't go too fast.'

Once they started properly, she felt safer than she had expected. It was bumpy; a patch of clods lifted the chariot right off the ground. They turned, passing around the white post with a screech of wheel hub on stone. 'Hold tight!' Publius cracked his whip; Camilla jumped. As the reins slithered through her fingers, he snatched them back, laughing. 'Round again?'

'Ooh yes!'

She was so small she was thrown about violently, but still loved every minute. Faster and faster they went, until her screams of delight were lost in the drumming of hooves on the hard-baked ground.

'Now grip tight on the front!' To pull them up, Publius threw the whole weight of his body backwards. The chariot base dragged along the track. Grooms rushed to hurl buckets of water on the smoking wheels and seize the horses' heads. Stopping a chariot was highly dangerous.

Aelia Camilla slid to the ground, trembling but ecstatic. She was covered with dust; her white maidenly gown was now uniform brown. Her face was dry with the fine powder, her hair and eyebrows clogged with it.

'Oh dear!' chortled her brother, unrepentant. 'Jump up and down,' he suggested. He pulled her hair about, uselessly. 'You look like a grub. We may have trouble explaining this at home . . .'

★

At home, there was certainly trouble.

'I shall have to beat you, Aelia Camilla,' her father declared; the worst part was his own distress at the thought.

Everyone knew he could not do it. Even Camilla felt reasonably certain that her father – who rarely beat his slaves, let alone his wife or children – would discover that instead of attending to her punishment, he was wanted on the farm. In fact, Lucius Camillus beat her brother instead.

Publius, startled, promised to behave more conventionally. Rubbing his bruises, he added, 'Well, I shall try – but Camilla may find it harder.'

Their father declared defensively, 'Aelia Camilla is a good girl!' This news even startled her.

Their father's confidence did have an effect: she vowed she would dedicate her life to being dutiful.

The best and most dutiful women, she knew, were the six Vestal Virgins in Rome. They lived with traditional simplicity, serving the city's gods in their temple in the Forum and setting a high example to the community. They also had power and privilege – something Camilla did not overlook. She decided to become a Vestal and, ignoring the convention that you were meant to be *chosen*, she wrote to Rome to apply.

At that time the family were living in a province on the Black Sea called Bithynia and Pontus. The Chief Vestal Virgin did reply to Camilla, sending her letter in the care of her cultured friend Valeria Flavia, who also knew Camilla's parents. 'So this is Bithynia! What a wonderful sanctuary from the turmoil of Rome.' Valeria Flavia was a polite woman. You had to be, to consort with Vestals.

In Bithynia there were peacocks and roses, angora goats

and thin-skinned aromatic figs. There were seas teeming with fish. There were sweet yellow grapes that were harvested, dipped in potash and olive oil, then laid out in the sun for five days until they became sultanas. Had it stood anywhere in Italy, the Camillus villa would have made an ideal retirement spot. Its position in a remote eastern province was regarded as too private to be true. Civilised people lived in Rome. There could be a faint suggestion the Camilli had gone so far away because they were somehow under a cloud.

It was not an enforced exile. They did have high social status but were lacking in resources. It was possible that, feeling the pinch in Rome, they retreated to their Bithynian estate. At this period the pinch was substantial, caused by putting the elder son, Decimus, into the Senate, an honour which had to be achieved by bribing voters. The move to a cheaper province weighed heaviest on his mother, who then warned Camilla and her two elder sisters against marrying men who owned estates in far-flung provinces.

When the Chief Vestal sent her letter about Camilla, her father called a family council. Valeria Flavia decorously withdrew. Lucius Camillus surveyed his offspring anxiously: Publius who, since his elder brother joined the Senate, had become a byword in the neighbourhood; Martina and Lucilla, two proud girls who worried him with enormous bills for yellow German wigs and gold ear-rings that rattled like small chandeliers; and now the little one. His children: he could sell them into slavery or give them away for others to adopt. They could not marry without his permission and he controlled all their property. He owned them; they owed him every respect. For fathers it was ideal.

Ideal if you could get their attention. He coughed, diffi-dently.

'None of this would have happened,' his wife, Lollia Aelia complained, 'if we had not lived in Bithynia! All my children will be ignorant provincials –'

'One of your children is already a senator,' her husband reminded her tetchily. 'I shall civilise the others eventually.'

'Even Camilla?'

'Especially Camilla.'

'I doubt it,' chortled Publius.

Lucius Camillus struggled on. 'Aelia Camilla, the Chief Vestal Virgin has taken time from tending the sacred flame and swilling out the Temple of Vesta with traditional mops to extend her wisdom all the way here.' His wife, who always pretended he was master in their home, flicked a glance at him. He knew what she meant but continued to ramble. 'It is a fine ambition. Ten years learning the sacred mysteries, ten years of service, ten more years teaching novices . . .'

Everyone stared at her. Aelia Camilla stood her ground.

She was hardly a child to be the apple of her parents' eyes; still parents are required to show loyalty. Camilla was tall, bony, dark and tended to glower. She had been moderately educated for the sake of her own children; each morning she was packed off before dawn to school in Heraclea Pontica, then spent her afternoons reciting to her mother whatever she had been told. Lollia Aelia had no faith in Greek towns, or their primary schools. Publius had books he could not be bothered to read so Camilla borrowed those.

'I am intrigued,' remarked her father, 'by your capacity to surprise me. But, Camilla, it is not the role of a decent Roman lady to surprise her paterfamilias!' She liked the way he always addressed her as if she were grown up. 'I tend to imagine you becoming the wife of some shy little man, into whose eye you might put a new twinkle . . .'

'Nonsense!' snapped Lollia Aelia, folding her ringed hands grimly. She respected her husband, as custom demanded, but his imagination went too far. Camillus sometimes had a twinkle in his own eye, though there was no reason to suppose his wife had put it there.

Aelia Camilla now felt ashamed that she had not told her parents what she had planned. 'There is,' continued her father, trying to sound stern, 'an obstacle. You are, I fear –' He paused, wickedly holding the stage. 'Too old!'

Everyone looked at Camilla again. 'How old are you?' Publius demanded. Perhaps he should have asked, before risking her life in his four-horse chariot.

'Eleven.'

'They only take new entrants up to ten,' her father gently explained.

Afterwards, Camilla took her letter then stomped up through the pine trees, breathing in air aromatic with the needles she was crushing underfoot. She sat down to read the heavy papyrus scroll. The Chief Vestal suggested she must learn history and geography, honour the gods, respect her parents, and accept with good humour whatever Fortune bestowed. The Vestal Virgin did not state that this was for the benefit of some man with twinkly eyes, but Camilla knew *exactly* what she meant.

Someone came down the hillside behind: Valeria Flavia, who smiled and said, 'Don't hate me for being the messenger.' Since Camilla was silent, the lady tried to win her round. 'What a glorious spot!'

'I expect you miss Rome!' Camilla sneered grumpily.

'Rome is so frantic; I much prefer travelling.'

Valeria Flavia had been widowed twice by husbands who redeemed their other failings by leaving her extremely wealthy. She now spent her time avoiding new suitors and visiting her grand estates. She was cultured and very beautiful, so the suitors were many and so were her adventures while travelling. 'Luckily all my farms lie near the Mediterranean. My poor nephew Gaius is in Britain at present. I worry about him dreadfully.'

Flavia shuddered. Camilla knew that the Emperor, Claudius, had a scheme in hand for conquering Britannia. Everyone thought it ludicrous. Absorbed in her own problems, she listened without hearing. Valeria Flavia tactfully left her alone again.

Camilla noticed she had placed her sandals in a sinister trail of blood-red ants so she leapt up angrily. 'I hate it here!' she shouted, as if she wanted to be heard all the way to Pontis and the Sea of Marmora.

But she did not hate Bithynia. She had merely begun growing up. What she hated was the sudden current of loneliness that had swept across her world.

Three thousand miles away, a young soldier tightened his neckerchief as a shiver ran down his spine. Valeria Flavia's nephew Gaius had never been so frightened in his life.

Above him reared hillfort ramparts which must be a hundred feet high. Huge embankments bulged outwards or followed the long, contoured curves so the tribesmen could strike at attackers from two sides. Each earth wall was topped by magnificent timber palisades, all alive with warriors brandishing slings and spears. The entrance gates were protected by complicated outworks, lined with gleaming white limestone and massive black timber baulks. There were ways to take these forts. Gaius knew his legion would struggle up the ramparts, keeping their shields over their heads against the rattle of the slingshot and would overcome the hillfort like many before. But this one looked hard work.

'What are we doing here?' muttered his friend Felix, as they began toiling up. 'Oh for an amphora of best Campanian wine, in a sun-drenched city full of theatres and girls!'

'Bear up!' gasped Gaius. 'A few more years of being heroes, then we can all go home.'

In Bithynia time moved only slowly. On the Camillus estate, the next four years brought few changes. The fountains gurgled more eccentrically; trelliswork faded; statues grew lichen.

The family scattered. Publius went into the army; he would be kicked out, then go into trade. The elder girls were married – Martina to a thin, nervous senator (well he might be, said her father) and Lucilla to a fat angry one (him too, added the father). Their mother lived in Rome with them. Their father was always intending to rejoin civilisation, or so he pretended, yet never got around to it.

Camilla stayed with him in Bithynia. They were both eccentric; that suited everyone. She had no sense of waiting for something to happen, since she believed that for her nothing would. She reached the age at which it was possible for her father to betroth her to some good Roman of free birth and noble mind. They both saw this as a joke. To pacify his wife, he made vague arrangements with an obliging cousin.

Meanwhile the Emperor's northern invasion had been an unexpected success. After four years of subduing woad-painted tribesmen, the troops came home to a celebratory Triumph. Far away in Bithynia, which was now seen as a less peculiar province, Camilla and her father, like most people in the Empire, found the new province of Britannia just another joke.

'Camilla,' warned her father, 'our province is just as queer as that wilderness of mist and fog.'

'But Britannia has painted blue men and druids.'

'While Bithynia is hot and packed with Greeks.' The Roman view of Greek achievements was sour. 'Painted men may be thin on the ground here, but painted women are everywhere!'

A year later the cousin Aelia Camilla was supposed to marry married someone else. Her mother sent urgent instructions that she was to be brought to Rome. Camilla was twenty; this was the year when she said with a scornful laugh that she was not interested in men. It did not stop her wondering what it would be like to be a girl who was.

When, still in Bithynia, her father collapsed with a stroke, Camilla sent for every Greek doctor in Heraclea Pontica, but she knew his time had come. 'Do everything you can that does not disturb him.'

Her father seemed to be grateful. She sat with him, talking quietly, until he died. At twenty, it was a hard burden alone.

As soon as possible, though it took weeks, her brother Decimus arrived to rescue her. She had not seen him for years and had never met his family in Rome. He was coming up for thirty, with an amiable wife, two sons and a lively little girl. Their father's death made him Camilla's keeper.

'I realise everything will have to change,' she reassured him glumly.

337

'I am responsible for you. I have to do what's best.'

'Father always said, *Aelia Camilla is a good girl.*'

'As a father myself,' answered Decimus, with unexpected dryness, 'I know the value of occasional self-delusion.'

Camilla liked him. She found him surprisingly fond of her. She frightened him but he intended to arrange her fate with care, like a co-conspirator. She realised she was fortunate.

'You are coming home,' her brother told her kindly.

But her journey across the Empire was to take her much further than that.

Rome. This was her parents' city; it was hers. She had to accept it was where she belonged, yet Camilla found it horrid.

Rome was crammed with humanity. Decimus owned a detached mansion, but poorer tenements rose seven storeys high, leaning over streets that were choked with carrying chairs and litters, all vying for space with tanners, flower-sellers, copper merchants and sausage men. Camilla hated the crush. And everyone seemed so angry all the time.

She found it hard to keep occupied. Staying at home was tedious. Going out was worse. Always chaperoned, she had to sit behind drawn curtains while bearers struggled up and down the hills and through the crowds, abused and jostled against shop fronts. How could she fit in? She had arrived as a foreigner, with no proper place. She was handed around her family, most of whom found her too serious and pinch-faced, while they all worried what to do with her.

A hiatus occurred when her sisters' friend Pollius Priscinus hove in sight. He was supposed to be a poet, which gave him access to ladies' salons. He enjoyed a reputation as a talker, though Camilla felt uneasy at his jokes. She did not really like him. However, he was always polite when he noticed her. 'Hello! You look as if you're needing some attention.'

People rarely fussed over Aelia Camilla. She seemed so capable. She forced a rueful grin. 'I warn you: I am the unconventional one in our family.'

'Yes; I heard you once caused a riot by arranging a religious career for yourself.'

He reclined on a couch next to hers and talked to her pleasantly. Next day it was not entirely a surprise when Priscinus visited, choosing a moment when she was at home alone. Only some time afterwards did she realise that someone must have helped him with his timing.

He stayed a short while only, made her laugh a lot, then took his leave with charm. Camilla, who distrusted attention, felt privately amused. She mentioned the visit to no one. Apparently no one noticed that she had acquired a friend.

The relationship developed. Camilla bloomed. She waited to find it all a sour mistake, yet daily grew in confidence.

He kissed her once. 'Mmm! Thank you.' Though she pretended to stay calm, she carried his murmur like a medal in her heart.

When she allowed him to seduce her, she coolly withdrew from a dinner party and he followed discreetly. It was more or less satisfactory, certainly interesting, and Camilla wondered why people made so much fuss. Privately she felt exultation that she, who was supposed to be so unworldly, now possessed a secret lover; that this man had, for some reason, chosen her.

She realised why quite suddenly. It ended then; she ended it herself. She had come into a room at Lucilla's house, to see Pollius Priscinus talking to her sisters in his suave way;

they were all laughing, but stopped immediately she appeared. Now she understood: her sisters had encouraged him to take her up. She experienced more anger than hurt. The worst aspect was, she felt not in the least surprised.

He continued his attentions, so she was forced to see him about it.

'Have I done something to distress you?'

'I just want you to go.' Her voice was dangerously level; she was finding out how easy it was to frighten men.

'Aelia Camilla, I would not offend you for the world!' He sounded so humble she could have scratched him. Why the need for pretence? 'Are we still friends?' he begged.

This was incredible. 'We were never friends.' He was frowning in honest puzzlement. 'Friends then,' she conceded wearily.

As he left, he kissed her cheek, like some unsatisfactory youth bidding farewell to a strict grandmother. Camilla felt soiled, the more so because she could see he genuinely wished to show respect.

'You are a special girl, Aelia Camilla; always believe it.'

It was that, knowing he had never wanted her, that nearly broke her heart.

She decided she had to change her life. She would not let other people make any more wrong choices on her behalf. Even allowing her brother to find her a husband filled her with foreboding; Decimus had a great affection for her, yet he did not understand.

Then, just as she had to make up her mind to act (but how?) the Fates brought her first invitation to visit Valeria Flavia.

The elegant lady whom Camilla vaguely remembered lived

in a smart new residential area of the Esquiline Hill. 'A small and mean apartment. Camilla, as you see.' Well, it was small.

In Flavia's 'mean apartment' there were exquisite frescos, reclining chairs, beds inlaid with tortoiseshell, and a huge maple-wood table cut from a single trunk. There were caskets of books, swansdown pillows, pillars of black Lucullan marble and mosaic floors of green porphyry and red Spartan stone. The silk curtains were not the rough, wild unravelled silk from Cos, but pure, fine cultivated Chinese thread imported through Phoenicia and worth nearly its own weight in gold. 'Fortunately, silk is light,' smiled Flavia. 'I married well. Welcome to Rome, Aelia Camilla. Your mother must be so glad to have you here.'

'My mother finds me difficult.' Camilla had decided she would become a blunt old battle-axe. 'I cannot manage being fashionable. I seem to live in a world of my own.'

Valeria Flavia thoughtfully crossed her knees, so her linen gown draped in simple but expensive folds. 'You must still miss your poor father. A fine man – much under-rated in his time.'

Camilla had assumed the lady was a friend of her mother's; it was a shock to discover the attachment was to her father all along. 'Part of me still expects to go back to Bithynia soon and find him still there.'

They spoke more about her father, then of nothing in particular. Not until Camilla was leaving did the subject of the nephew arise. At the door she had noticed a small table. It was a three-legged piece, with unusual slate grey feet. 'Eccentric, isn't it?' giggled Valeria Flavia. 'A variety of shale which is found, I am informed, on the British coast.' She turned to Camilla with an unrepentantly fond smile. 'A present from my nephew Gaius!'

That was all she said, or needed to say. Camilla suddenly knew why she had been invited here today. It was not unwelcome. 'I remember you telling me you had a nephew who took part in the British invasion. You were worried about him. Are you still?'

'Sometimes. In common with you, he was born in a wild province – Dalmatia. He was orphaned young, and left with a disinterested guardian, so he has to make his own career. As a woman, of course, there is not much influence I am allowed to wield . . .' Really?

'Didn't the British officers all come home hung about with medals?'

'Oh yes. And his commander was Vespasian –'

'This year's consul?'

Flavia looked approving. 'You are well informed! However, Vespasian's idea of helping Gaius was to have him sent back to Britain as a governor's assistant . . .' She smiled her smile, as if she would not trouble a stranger with her personal concerns. Yet it was understood that the subject of this nephew would certainly arise again.

The next time Camilla called, she brought a good Spanish tablecloth to adorn the British curiosity. 'And what news of your nephew?' she asked, just as she was supposed to.

His aunt sighed proudly. 'Gaius has been promoted to a special post – controller of the British mines!' Her voice dropped. 'Whatever that means.'

Camilla answered seriously. 'Extremely important. The mineral deposits in Britain were the main reason for Rome going there.'

Flavia blinked. 'Well, I cannot visualise Gaius tapping rocks with a mallet, but no doubt he will surprise me!' That was when the aunt of Gaius Flavius leaned forward confidentially. 'Aelia Camilla, would you be *very* cross if I said I had written to my nephew about you?'

Camilla wondered if her mother's warnings to avoid men from peculiar provinces should be activated, but she asked, 'Will he be interested?'

'Indeed yes! His guardian has proved incapable of finding him a wife. I saw the main suggestion; she was terribly small and like a pipeclay doll. She had nothing to say for herself, but Gaius believed that once she was married, she planned to blow into a hurricane. I'm afraid I agreed when he beetled back abroad.'

'So what happened?' asked Camilla.

'I told the miniature betrothed a few untruths about my nephew's personal habits.'

Camilla giggled. 'She backed out?'

'She gave me no trouble. I had made up some shockers . . . But he needs to marry. He promised that if I find someone I approve of, as he said, "in possession of a good temperament and all her teeth", then I may write him a description, in not more than half a sheet of papyrus.'

'So, Valeria Flavia, describe *him* to *me*.'

An aggravating vagueness struck his normally crisp aunt. She shrugged helplessly; she shook her improbable turrets of shining hair. 'Camilla, you will like him; I am sure of that.'

Camilla asked dryly, 'Is that a good thing in a marriage?'

Valeria Flavia thought it best not to answer. Even so, Camilla said without bashfulness, Gaius Flavius could be told that he might write to her.

If letters for Camilla came from a foreign province with a government stamp, questions might be asked. Luckily,

343

Decimus was at the Senate so his secretary brought the letter to her privately. Since Decimus did not know that Camilla was arranging her own marriage, it was as well.

She liked the tone. Gaius Flavius was direct and polite, but she detected character breaking through. His handwriting was extremely neat; she guessed this indicated nervous redrafts.

His first sentence said plainly that he would like to be assured by *her* that she was willing for the match. She liked that; not everyone would bother. He described his career and claimed to have no bad habits. He then asked her to involve her brother if she wished. Camilla decided she would.

Her family behaved badly. She could not blame them; they were badly surprised. To find her own husband – not a rogue, but a hero of the British invasion who had a consul as his patron – was vaguely indecent. Only Decimus steadily took her part. Faced with domestic turmoil, Decimus went out to the public baths. A man could do that.

His negotiations with Gaius Flavius were businesslike but not prolonged. Soon Camilla was posting off a ceramic betrothal medallion purporting to portray Gaius and herself. By return came a British silver ring. *'I have been told that you are sensible so you will not insist on gold from a man who is in charge of a silver mine. Wash your green finger every day and think touchingly of me. Thanks for the medallion. Are you the character with chickenpox or the one with a wince and no ears?'*

Camilla's family, in the sweet way of families, congratulated themselves on what *they* had achieved.

Camilla told Gaius she would like to join him in Britain. Gaius replied hastily that Britain was too primitive. It had few roads and fewer towns, and there was civil war among the tribes: no place for a cultured young lady. Her friends, he said, would confirm he was right; of course they did.

But Aelia Camilla decided to ignore her friends.

A light chill mist of rain, too slight to drive people into shelter but enough to be troublesome, blew in her face as she stepped ashore at Chichester, a British township on the south coast. Rain hung about the quayside, drifting unpleasantly. After a rough crossing, Camilla felt desperately ill. She had been travelling for weeks, with plenty of time to start dreading what she would find when she arrived.

A man was waiting. She disembarked and sat on a bale, too queasy even to look at him. 'Aelia Camilla?' He was devastating – broad, black-haired and handsome, with knowing eyes. She hated handsome men. 'Welcome to Britain. It feels better once your stomach settles.' Fortunately this hero was not who she had come to see. 'I am Volusena Felix.' Her troubled eyes never left him. Felix wondered if she ever smiled. 'Gaius Flavius is at Exeter. That's –'

'In the far west.' Camilla had studied British geography. Exeter was a hundred miles away.

She felt deeply humiliated. She had come fourteen hundred miles, all by herself. And Gaius was not here.

Her mother had warned her that husbands could be like this.

Gaius had also failed to mention that he lived in a villa farm with his slightly raffish friend.

The farm lay in a flat-bottomed valley. The low hills were clothed with tall forests, deep in centuries of leaf litter, with a dim light where deer slipped along mysterious paths and frightening fungi grew to enormous size on fallen trees. There was a sense of some Celtic god anxiously watching.

Astonishingly, though a Roman of some standing, Volusena Felix had married a British wife. Camilla could see why. Commia's beauty was natural, fierce and true. Her skin was gloriously fair, most translucent over her high cheekbones. Those bitter blue eyes glared down a straight handsome nose. She held her head high, flaunting a netted mass of golden-red hair. More than her shining good looks though, she was plainly in command of herself in a way Camilla never would be. Commia was a devastating woman.

'Welcome to our house,' said Commia, though Camilla could see that Felix was her life. She neither wanted nor needed a friend.

Camilla began to feel utterly demoralised. Men at the edge of empires lived by looser codes. His best friend's flamboyant marriage hinted darkly that Gaius might want something exotic too. Camilla knew she could not provide it. She had walked into the classic fatal situation of the stilted and lady-like bride from home; her best hope was that Gaius Flavius would take one look at her and send her back.

'When is Gaius expected to return?'

'No one quite knows,' Felix confessed. 'He stays at Exeter while he oversees the silver mines and explores for minerals in other areas —'

'Areas outside Roman control?' Camilla broached quickly. 'That must be hazardous?'

'I am sure he uses agents.' Felix paused. He felt sudden doubt. He was constantly surprised by how seriously Gaius took his work. 'A true bureaucrat. He can keep talking all day without ever being so discourteous as to get to the point . . .'

'It sounds as if he does more than talking!' Camilla insisted. 'I gather I may not see him for some time?'

Felix drew a cautionary breath. 'There is that possibility.'

Camilla began to feel a deep unhappiness, as bad as anything she had experienced in Rome, where at least she had been among her own family. 'Was Gaius aware I was coming?'

'Afraid so,' admitted Felix. 'Gaius is very shy . . .'

And that man had written to her *think touchingly of me*! To do him justice, he had told her not to come.

Several weeks of awkward existence passed at the villa farm. To Camilla it seemed much longer. Then one day came her chance to hasten events. 'Gaius is having his boat's keel scraped at the port.' Felix spoke with jovial gallantry, though his efforts to reassure her always made Camilla feel he was unreliable. 'Like to come and see?'

'My brother used to sail, at Heraclea Pontica . . .' Thinking of Publius, her resistance reasserted itself.

Felix hated boats. It was Camilla who pleased the master by asking interested questions. It was she who discovered the boat was tacking up to Exeter to meet Gaius there. It was she who suggested thoughtfully, 'I should think if you took me to Exeter on his boat, Gaius Flavius would be greatly surprised?'

No one disagreed with that.

He was not at Exeter either. He had gone to the Cornish tin mines. But outside the military fort, he kept a tiny house, a bachelor den with one living room, a kitchen and space for a servant, then two bedrooms upstairs. There, as the controller of mines' official bride from Rome, Camilla was allowed to install herself. And there she waited, with intense trepidation, for the controller's arrival home.

'I'd better warn him you are here,' the tribune at the fort had told her. He spoke warily, for Roman ladies did not normally turn up at forts unannounced. Theirs was a closed world, closely vetted by the masters of their households. Hard to say who was this headstrong lady's master; clearly not yet the controller of mines. 'He won't want to appear with mud on his boots and in need of a haircut, when he meets his future wife for the first time!'

'Oh really?' Camilla held back a terse retort. 'Well, if things are going to be formal, I'd better invite him to dinner,' she then said – before she wondered how on earth she was supposed to prepare an impressive meal in a province which grew no basil or marjoram. No cucumbers, no apricots, no olive trees, no figs . . .

'Don't worry, we'll clean him up and put him in a good mood before we send him round!' the tribune assured her jokingly – leaving Camilla to wonder more than ever just what sort of man she had acquired.

Next morning Camilla received a message that Gaius Flavius had returned and would accept her invitation. She heard no more all day, but properly at the ninth hour, he emerged from the fort.

It was not quite what she had come to expect.

Gaius was delivered to Camilla in a decorative chariot. He was escorted by cavalry in full parade armour over body shirts of deep blue. Their sturdy little horses stepped out in figured bronze with winking black enamel, rich saddle cloths, mysterious eye guards and harness hung with roundels that glittered and swung. The men carried light shields,

348

lances, and long swords slung from the shoulder. They wore helmets with full-face masks, gilded and plumed.

The illustrious Flavius had been barbered at the fort's bath house, shaved and splashed with disturbing unguents. He was steamed and scraped and pumiced until every pore of him glowed. He wore an immaculate toga. Hung upon him were his medals from the British invasion. On his chest too, the ceramic betrothal medallion from his bride.

Aelia Camilla came uneasily to the doorstep, neat and slender in red, with a massive pair of ear-rings – her mother's gift to bolster her during domestic stress. From behind her wafted the sharp salty tang of dried fish sauce and the bubble of good things steeped in imported wine. Her heart pounded helplessly.

She acknowledged the escort. Forty lances raised aloft; forty voices roared a warlike salute. 'Thank you,' replied Camilla, trying not to wince.

She looked up at Gaius. To her surprise he was a perfect Roman official. His bearing was upright and confident, his manner entirely respectable. Yet the quiet hazel eyes held a gleam of irreverence. 'Are you the brave young woman who has consented to be my wife?'

'I am afraid so,' she said, with a strict look.

'After Bithynia you must find Britain a very wild place!' Their eyes steadily met. 'So, Aelia Camilla, will you be sorry that you came?'

'The point is,' reproved Camilla, 'will *you* be sorry that I came?'

He looked shocked. 'How can you suggest that?'

'You have been hiding, Gaius Flavius!'

'Oh, I have not!'

'Then where were you?'

349

Gaius jumped down from the spectacular chariot with a good-humoured hint of self-mockery. 'Planning how to make a really good impression when I met my bride!' His voice dropped. 'Have I succeeded?'

'Things are better than I expected,' agreed Camilla rather boldly. Then she lifted her cheek for him to kiss her formally, and led her future husband indoors to dine.

Part two

Gaius Flavius appeared to be enjoying the strange circumstance of his first meeting with Camilla. Reclining on a dining couch, he served himself to chicken, brightening visibly. 'I am proud to have a bride who bravely came so far to find me – and who came from Rome equipped with aniseed and lovage to season my roasts!'

They discussed neutral topics, mainly her childhood in Bithynia. Finally Gaius asked abruptly, 'Now you've seen me, will you stay?'

Camilla toyed with a mushroom. 'If you want me to.'

'Then I need to know where we shall live. I hope you liked my friend Felix? And his wife?' She nodded, trying to be polite. Evidently sensitive, he grinned. 'Perhaps we should live on our own, and not share a villa with them?' Camilla did not bother to hide her relief. 'Well I'm going next week to the silver mines. Would you like to come?'

To reach the mines they left the blue ridges around Exeter and went north into green crags where a light rain fell gently from overcast skies. There were not many women who would visit these lonely hills. Camilla liked the hills. And Gaius observed he had acquired a bride who turned up at silver mines sensibly shod.

He showed her around, with likeable pride, pointing out

the military fort, the workings, the forges and the small civilian settlement. 'We are right on the frontier here but well-guarded. It's lonely but safe . . .'

His spirit had soared at Camilla's own sense of adventure. 'Perhaps we could live here?' she offered, knowing Gaius was steeling himself to ask. So they made arrangements for the troops to build them a house.

They had intended to be married quietly, but the entire fort at Exeter was yearning to join in. It was obviously their duty to provide a public spectacle.

The evening before, Gaius crouched on the floor unpacking their wedding gifts. Felix had presented them with pottery lamps, each depicting athletic couples in bed. 'This one is disgusting. I'm not sure it's even feasible . . . no; don't look!' He blushed and covered the lamps with a cloth.

Camilla murmured, 'Gaius Flavius, I hope you realise: I am prepared for us to have children.'

'I'm sure we'll both do our duty,' Gaius replied shortly. She could not tell whether he was joking or not.

All night it poured with rain. Lying awake, Camilla heard water trickling endlessly off pantiles and chuckling down drains. At dawn she squelched out into the countryside to pluck her wreath of sacred herbs. Unable to find marjoram, she pulled any wet sprigs from a hedgerow, brushing off snails. Back indoors she assumed her white dress, saffron shoes and the short flame-coloured veil. But when Gaius arrived, she found herself overwhelmed by despair. 'Gaius, whatever are we doing here today?'

'Being good citizens!'

'But we are strangers!'

'We're perfect,' he answered gently. He had kind eyes, eyes whose brightness made her heart lurch unexpectedly. The more she knew about him, the more she longed to know. 'Trust me!' he said.

In the absence of her own family, Aelia Camilla was married from the fort commander's house. The commander himself sacrificed a rather jumpy sheep and pronounced good omens – as priests at weddings invariably did. A marriage contract was formally signed, then Gaius took her hand, surprising her with his firm grip. They recited the ancient formula: 'Gaius Flavius, are you willing to take this bride?'

'I am willing.'

'Do you give your solemn pledge?'

'I give my pledge.'

'Aelia Camilla, are you willing to be given to this man?'

'I am willing. I give my solemn pledge.'

Then they carried around a ceremonial cake, supposedly baked on bay leaves though those had had to be improvised.

At dusk, everyone assembled in the porch. The commander's wife stood in for Camilla's mother, as Gaius rushed up and made a splendid show of wrenching his bride away by force. Camilla squealed, then furiously blushed as everyone laughed. Her procession formed in utter confusion. Three shy little boys were produced to lead her; she herself set a whitethorn torch in one reluctant fist. Gaius flung nuts to the waiting soldiers as they moved slowly through the fort, jostling and shouting, with torch smoke streaming in the lively wind.

At the house Gaius had owned as a bachelor, Camilla bound his doorposts with wool and anointed them with sluggish oil, while he fetched fire and water to symbolise his welcome. He was lifting her over the threshold with a ceremonial grunt when someone called out 'Kiss the bride!'

Gaius – her husband – held her suddenly close. Before she was prepared for it, he kissed her, very calmly. The crowd went wild, Gaius lobbed his garland at random – then he slammed the door smartly on the racket outside.

The crowd were beating at the door.

'You are supposed to let them in,' Camilla whispered. 'They ought to lead us to our bed.'

Gaius murmured, 'I'd like to lead you there myself!'

Then he kissed her again. Only this time, neither of them was calm at all.

So Camilla and Gaius gave their pledges. Later, they moved to the silver mine where they seemed destined for the perfect fate: a noisy wedding, followed by a quiet marriage.

They stayed at the mine for five years. It was isolated and dangerous, a testing environment. However, they lived in some comfort and style. Their house was full of ribbed eastern glass and handsome red pottery. In summer they bravely sat in the garden. In winter, when the oil lamps gleamed on their elegant silverware, they clung to the downstairs rooms with their heated floor-tiles and internal wall-flues, then scampered to bed and slept close.

One night the settlement vanished under bright swathes of deep snow. Aelia Camilla had never seen snow close at hand. 'Gaius! It's lovely. Can we go outside?'

'Just pray for it to melt before the food and fuel run out. Come back here . . .' He hauled her back into bed then looked thoughtful. 'Still, a few snowballs down your neck and snow in your hair – that should get you ready to be warmed up again by me . . .'

They did go out. They built a snowman, leering over their front gate. It caused a great stir in the community, which expected its Roman officials to be more sedate.

Their house had been built apart from the rest. When Gaius was away, Camilla had to remain secluded. As the only lady of rank, her position was difficult. The tradesmen who worked under licence – bakers, potters, blacksmiths, taverners – brought female company, for whom she set a standard of Roman family life. Yet she was not supposed to mix too closely and had no close women friends. Indeed, she had only one friend at all. Since that was her husband, he was not supposed to count.

Gaius, according to him, was a model husband. He brought home interesting tableware from business trips. He was kind to their slaves. He was reasonable over money – though, as Camilla pointed out, he had a reasonable wife and there was not much very extravagant she could buy.

Camilla liked him for other reasons: his honesty, his dedication; his sense of fun. His absences left her miserable; his return revived her life. Her love for him ran deep. She had never told him that and his feelings for her remained a mystery.

After five years they still had no children. There was no obvious reason for it, but it was one of the things that began to lie undiscussed between them in a worrying way.

In the fifth year, their relationship reached an abrupt crisis.

'I did not know,' said Gaius one day with an effort, 'that you had once wanted to be a Vestal Virgin!'

It was lunchtime. Lunch had been eggs in fish pickle sauce, which always gave him indigestion. He had also spent the morning grappling with a letter to the new governor, who had a knack of missing the point.

357

'Oh that!' Camilla laughed. She sensed an intriguing mood in Gaius. 'It was our family disgrace. I wrote and put forward myself, but the Chief Vestal turned me down. It broke my little heart.'

Gaius was reclining on his left elbow in a classic pose, spoiled slightly by his tousled brown hair and ink all down his arm. 'So why did she refuse you?'

'Too old, dear! I was eleven . . .' Gaius did not laugh. 'Gaius are you quarrelling with me?'

'No.' So he was!

'Who told you about the Vestal Virgins?'

'I read it in a book.'

'Be serious, Gaius!'

'Oh, I am! I've just found this touching allusion to my wife, in a scroll of poems written by someone else.' Gaius sat up. He swung his legs against the couch, scuffing the striped coverlet angrily. 'It came from Rome. My secretary failed to realise it must be for you. From the poet.'

Pollius Priscinus! Camilla could hardly believe that her old, unsatisfactory lover had surfaced in this irritating way. She stared at Gaius, not yet understanding how he was racked with bitter jealousy. 'You never told me about the Vestals, though you obviously told *him!*'

Camilla retorted, 'My religious career, like the poet, was something I had chosen to forget!' Then she demanded in horror, 'What sort of poems are they?'

'Love poems.' Camilla was appalled. Hating to see her so distressed, Gaius explained, 'Turgid odes addressed to someone unnamed, who is supposedly in Britain – woad-stained men – bad poets love that sort of stuff.'

'The man should have asked my permission!'

'He certainly should have asked mine!' Gaius blazed.

358

Then his voice dropped painfully. 'Aelia Camilla, why did you come so far to marry me? Was I merely a refuge from an unhappy love affair?'

Camilla went white. 'That's untrue and unfair. I wanted a worthwhile husband —'

'What more can a plain man ask?'

That was when, to his astonishment, Aelia Camilla jumped up, seized her footstool, and threw it at his head.

She broke the stool, a bronze lamp, and a black pottery vase. Gaius, with his military training, safely ducked. He was horrified – glimpsing for the first time how much he had underestimated her feelings.

'Are you divorcing me, Gaius?' she cried, ignoring all the havoc. Running footsteps approached. Dazed, Gaius shook his head. 'Then you may send back the poems from me with a very rude husbandly letter!'

She stormed from the room. Gaius did not follow her at first. Then, as the house stayed silent, he jumped up and rushed to look for her.

She was standing in the garden, staring at the new currant bushes they were trying to introduce to this desolate spot. Gaius stroked the warm angle of her arm. Goosepimples raked from her shoulder to her wrist. 'I was afraid you had run away.'

'This is Britain – nowhere to go!' Camilla bent her head. Gaius gently kissed her neck.

'I'm glad you stayed.'

Camilla let him draw her close, no matter who might be watching them. 'So am I,' she admitted.

But neither of them thought of saying why.

★

After that they were extremely careful with each other; yet it seemed to make things worse.

It was while they were watching the tightrope-walkers that Camilla realised she had been here too long. The acrobats were not daring enough. She could glimpse their woolly underwear. They would not need those winter drawers if they livened up their act: perhaps just occasionally pretended to fall off the rope . . . The crowd clapped, but mainly to keep warm. The performers had brought a well-fed, over-friendly lion that padded around with a fixed smile. A smile that was much like Camilla's own in public, come to that.

She watched her husband. Troubled thoughts moved behind those deep eyes. Gaius was struggling with politics. The Emperor Claudius, who was so proud of conquering Britain, had died and his successor Nero mounted an exercise to decide whether Britain was an asset Rome should keep. Gaius was intensely involved, assessing the potential of the mines, yet he never now discussed the reports he was so busy writing. She expected to be her husband's confidante. So his intense silence was something she saw no reason to forgive.

He had however bought them a light pony trap. He said he was looking forward to driving them into the countryside; Camilla suspected he would never find time. 'I could learn to drive the pony myself,' she said, benignly smiling at the acrobats. Gaius said no.

Aelia Camilla folded her hands and looked at him sideways. The furious set of his chin was unutterably dear, yet she felt terrified that the downhill drag of their marriage would make her lose his goodwill.

Abruptly he relented. 'You may drive. If you must. I will teach you myself.' She knew he never would.

360

He was staggered when Aelia Camilla said in reply, 'Gaius Flavius, I have decided to go home to Italy.' In fact, she had surprised herself.

For Gaius the world, which was already in a different turmoil, broke down completely. Conscious of their public position, he controlled his voice carefully: 'If the province is too remote . . .'

Camilla had closed her eyes. 'It is not the province.'

'Oh! Only the man?' He was very quick.

Camilla spoke equally rapidly. She was leaving. There was nothing he could do. 'Everything is over. I don't know why. You don't need me.' Gaius moved slightly. If he had only turned to comfort her . . . She should have been prepared. Her mother had warned her: men never know what to do.

'I wish I had done better for you.' Gaius addressed her in a formal undertone. She could not tell him her feelings. She had left it too late to start.

She abandoned her seat in the makeshift wooden theatre and went home alone. Gaius, who had paid to provide the acrobats, stayed to the end of the performance, as he must.

It began to rain. His mood, already bleak, turned to honest self-pity as he strode to their house.

Camilla sat hunched in her chair before her dressing table with its litter of bone pins and pink glass bottles. She heard furious thuds as Gaius flung down his boots and belt, heavy with rain. 'I want to speak to you.'

'Phryne is doing my hair.'

Gaius snatched the double-sided ivory comb and zipped his thumb along it. 'Then Phryne can stop.'

Foolishly impressed, her maid scuttled away. Camilla quietly moved her chair to face him.

Gaius, soaked to the skin, was peeling off several tunics. She knew all the lines of his wiry torso and sunburned limbs. He was part of her now. She breathed a small moan of unhappiness, which he ignored.

Pulling on a robe, Gaius dropped onto her footstool. 'I know what I have done.' There was a wary excitement in his tone now they were alone. 'Thank you for speaking out. It helped me face my own anxieties. We are so far from home. You need my confidence, and never imagine that I don't need yours.'

'I doubt that, Gaius!'

'Please listen. Things are going wrong here. Nero has decided to keep Britain within the Empire but is neglecting the province badly. I can't bear to watch . . . You and I are going home,' Gaius announced earnestly, ' – together!'

Camilla was shocked. 'Your place is here.'

'My place is with you.' His eyes met hers, with their own special gravity. 'I will give the governor my resignation, though I can't leave immediately. He wants to make his name expelling the druids from Anglesey. There are copper deposits, so I feel obliged to accompany him there . . . Oh I do wish my work here was going to last! I have given too many years to the province not to care. Besides, Britain was,' said Gaius quietly, 'where I met you.'

Camilla choked back a sob. He reached for her hand; she moved; he missed; he grabbed her wrist instead. 'What I gave you the day we were married was my true pledge.' He had not intended that it would make her cry. '*Oh my dear sweet precious soul!*' Her head spun. They had never exchanged endearments. Camilla felt completely bewildered as she realised how hard he was fighting to win her back. 'If I have to go to Anglesey, will you wait for me?'

She nodded, deeply shaken by what she had exposed.

Approaching tentatively to light the lamps, house slaves found them still sitting there, so silent and still they appeared to be asleep.

Camilla agreed to wait for Gaius, staying with the wife of his old friend Felix. Travelling to London, Gaius taught her to drive. He was brutally thorough. 'I want you to be safe. You drive too fast – *Slow down!*'

They went by sea around to Colchester. There, an ancient British stronghold had been made the Roman capital, crowned by a vast new temple to the Emperor Claudius. Shops sold imported ceramics and fine candelabra. Roman bread was baked. Roman taverns provided familiar Roman wine. There was a colony of Roman military veterans who were supposed to set an example. Camilla could tell even Gaius found the presence of the arrogant old soldiers upsetting and threatening. They were relieved when Felix met them in his dashing two-horse wagon.

Felix had broadened into an imposing figure, whether in his country clothes or a glittering toga in town. He was wealthy – his great hands barnacled with heavy rings. He and Commia were solid Roman citizens; they led the community and possessed every Roman convenience in their home. Even their child, five-year-old Felicia, seemed an asset to be proudly shown off.

New arrivals were taken at once to the dining room, to admire their new wall fresco of Leda and the Swan. The noble bird resembled a large duck with a dislocated neck. Leda had big feet, puny arms, and very untidy hair.

'Looks as if wall painting has yet to reach full British flower!' scoffed Gaius, offending his hosts deeply.

Next their dreadful tot. Gaius had brought Felicia a bronze goose for her model farm. She already had poultry. What she wanted was a lion killing a roebuck. She kept an adventurous smallholding. 'Next time, Uncle Gaius, ask me the proper thing to get!' Uncle Gaius glared.

The governor was coming to dinner; Gaius became even more unhappy. Then it turned out he and Felix were to depart with the governor the very next day.

That evening, Camilla sat glumly waiting to be fetched. (It was a house where servants constantly announced where you had to be next.) Commia herself knocked. Camilla's heart sank; it prophesied womanly chats of a kind she had never liked while Gaius and Felix were away.

Commia was now matronly, in the way odd, angular Camilla never would be.

'Are you pregnant?' she demanded.

Camilla jumped. 'No. Why?'

'Gaius has a look . . . obviously not what I thought.'

To cover awkwardness, Camilla said, 'My father always prophesied I would marry a shy man, and put an interesting twinkle in his eye.'

'Oh you have!' Mollified, Commia offered, 'I am sorry if my child was rude about your gift.'

Camilla replied calmly, 'And I am sorry if my husband was rude about your wall fresco.'

Commia burst out laughing, just as Gaius came in. 'Gaius Flavius, I do like your wife!'

'Actually,' said Gaius with disturbing stillness, 'so do I!' Commia laughed again, then rather primly left them alone before dinner.

Gaius was upset by something. 'Camilla, I must tell you–' He had brought it to share, doggedly rebuilding their friendship. Love washed over Camilla; she did not want him to go on the coming campaign. 'Listen: the king of the Iceni has died; he willed half his estate to the Emperor, the rest to his two daughters. Catus, our upright Roman finance officer, sent a troop of soldiers to claim Nero's legacy. The upshot was, the entire Icenean nobility were violently robbed, and during what Catus would no doubt call "restoring law and order", Queen Boudicca was flogged then her teenaged daughters were handed around the military to be raped.'

As she analysed this brutality, Camilla felt her own temper heat. 'I may raise it with the governor,' scowled Gaius, seeking her approval.

'I hope so!' she encouraged him angrily.

It was a good dinner. In April, in Britain, all the more creditable. There were Thames oysters, wildfowl, Gallic venison, Spanish hams, imported olives and wine.

Afterwards, music. Little Felicia played her tibia. She stood on a stool, necklaced in amber, and she blew with all her might down her double-piped flute until she faltered to a stop, rosy-cheeked and completely out of puff. Even Commia had to see the funny side.

Time for polite conversation. Commia weighed straight in unconventionally: 'Will we be safe, sir, during your campaign in the west? In view of recent events in the east?'

The blunt question jarred the governor, Paulinus, but his public speech on the atrocity was already well-oiled: 'The Iceni were disarmed years ago and the Ninth Legion will provide you full protection. I regret events, but the finance officer answers directly to Nero, not to me . . .'

Commia scoffed, 'And of course natives do not count!'

Felix stretched, an imposing sight. 'Leave it, love.'

Paulinus murmured soothingly, 'I don't condone what happened, but tempers should soon cool now.'

That was intended to close the matter, but Camilla broke in: 'We have an old treaty with the Iceni. The tribes must feel Rome's attitude has changed very oddly.'

Gaius strongly backed her up. 'Roman law makes rape a capital offence. The Iceni should be given legal redress.'

Camilla enjoyed argument; she particularly enjoyed sharing common ground with Gaius. 'We offered the British our civilisation. If we tolerate this, what rights does a Briton have?'

'I hear what you say,' Paulinus conceded. 'When I've dealt with the druids, I'll certainly consider it.'

'What if the Iceni will not wait for your return, sir?' Camilla asked finally.

No one could answer her.

Next day, at dawn, the governor took his leave.

Gaius was on his horse. Every time Camilla tried to approach, she found herself staring into its wild teeth.

'Be careful!' With a kick of his studded boot, Gaius forced the mount closer. 'If there is any trouble, go south; go immediately –' She nodded frantically. Then Gaius called out in a steady voice that cut straight through the hubbub, 'I love you; you will always know that.'

'You know I love you too!'

His slow smile spread; he knew.

The governor signalled. Gaius straightened. And Camilla

366

was left in the thin morning air with nothing but a faint persistent feeling where his fingers had stroked her cheek.

At Anglesey, grey mountains marched down through a grey mist; the island merged into the sea. The wind snatched and shoved. The younger troops were shocked by black-robed shrieking women, railing at them with torches from the dark shore opposite. But, though the fighting was bitter, the sanctuary fell. The sacred groves were hacked down. Over the long white sands and reedy hollows fell the stern mantle of Roman order and peace.

Almost immediately it was broken. A ship came tearing up the strait for the governor: the Iceni had dug their hidden weapons out of hayricks and were rioting all over the east.

From Anglesey to London was two hundred and fifty miles. Riding hard with a scratch escort it took the governor barely four days, but he came too late. Colchester was lost. After a ferocious two-day attack, the Roman capital had been burned to the ground. No one survived. Racing to help, the Ninth legion had been butchered in a trap.

The governor paused at London. Paulinus wrestled with a heart-rending choice, but his only hope of saving the province now was to leave London to its fate. Its wealthy merchants had already scrambled into boats and fled. Anyone else who could ride might follow the army to the military zone, but the weak, those without transport, those who could not bear to leave their home of twenty years, must stay and face the worst.

Paulinus retreated, hoping to draw the Iceni away from their home ground. Behind him, Boudicca's hordes freely rampaged, falling upon Romanised hamlets and farms. No prisoners were taken. Everyone the rebels caught was

367

massacred. Whatever could not be looted and carried away was burned.

Before they went west again. Gaius and Felix approached the governor. He looked at their ashen faces and let them go. They rode as fast as they could. When they hared up the villa's approach road the first thing Gaius noticed was the acrid smell. Then they had to slow their horses because the drive was churned into a morass where the Iceni had been here before them, and used it for a chariot race.

They stood in the garden. There were roses on a pergola, reflected in long ornamental ponds. Of the house, only charred clinker remained. There was no sign of human life.

The two longtime friends turned to grip one another, their hearts erratic with grief. Then there was nothing to do but abandon hope, and ride after the governor.

Yet Gaius Flavius had reckoned without the sense and courage of his Bithynian bride.

For Camilla and her hostess, it had seemed a quiet summer. Too quiet. Eventually they began to be told of wild portents in the capital: how women had fainted as ethereal voices cried out in the Temple of Claudius, how the statue of Victory had crashed to the ground on its face. 'Do we believe these rumours?' asked Commia thoughtfully.

'No,' Camilla replied. 'But someone has gone to a great deal of trouble in making them up!'

Then Commia pointed out how all the tribal farmland had remained unploughed: 'As if the farmers are planning to seize next year's grain from bulging Roman granaries . . .'

That was when, although as women they were not supposed to take decisions, they began to send the household slaves with wagonloads of valuables to safety in the south.

But they themselves had stayed too long. The slave who went to book their sea passage from Colchester fled home, describing a huge red glow and a pall of smoke, visible for miles. They sent another to London, who never returned. All the remaining household deserted them one night.

'Right!' Camilla decided briskly. 'Commia, harness the mules and put Felicia in the wagon while I pack food and water. I shall drive us myself!'

She was nearly too late. When they emerged from the estate road, they ran straight into an advance party of British warriors. Camilla did not hesitate. For a moment she glimpsed angry faces, wicker chariots with bare-chested drivers, and tribesmen in chequered trousers wielding huge broadswords. Cracking her whip furiously, she turned the wagon and fled, driving not as her demure husband had taught her, but as she once raced with her brother such a long time ago. More eager for plundering property, the startled tribesmen let them go.

Forced to turn north, and hoping to take refuge with the Ninth legion, Camilla drove through damp forest paths, frowning as she smelled smoke on the chill summer air. They reached a potters' settlement. They still had no idea of the scale of the rebellion, but now they learned how the Ninth had been ambushed and cut to pieces. Camilla's heart raced. 'All the other troops are with the governor in the west!'

She sought safety at St Albans. Luckily she knew the province's rough geography, for they had neither map nor guide. But St Albans was deserted, its covered market roughly boarded up, its prosperous houses silent and stripped.

At an almost empty villa, the British landowner, who scarcely paused in packing his last mule train, told them the governor had raced through and left, not daring to state his plans. 'We expect the worst. The tribes hate us for cooperating with Rome. You take care too!' the man warned, glancing at Commia who was so obviously British with her fiery red hair. He let them fill their water jars at his well, then they took the military highway, hoping to turn south across the downs towards friendlier areas.

This road was jammed with fugitives. Families stared, sombre-eyed. Some people had abandoned everything. Others urged on oxen, laden under bales and sacks, caged chickens, upended beds. Old women towed little cows on rags of string. It took a day to move five miles.

'The Iceni will be travelling very fast,' Commia told Camilla grimly. 'Except when they stop for entertainment. If they catch us, you and I will be the entertainment.'

'Let's turn off,' Camilla said.

They spent the night in a sheep-cote. It was cold, dirty, uncomfortable, but next day they were able to move more freely, on into drab watercourse country where they were soon quite alone.

By now, Camilla knew the province must be lost. She watched Commia; soothed the child; tried to eke out their food. She was pacing herself with a frightening restraint. Whatever happened they would be out in the open for a long time and she had to keep her strength.

The ways were lonely now. Fright and insecurity affected Felicia; she became ill; they had to stop. Now Camilla slept, comforting herself with the warmth of the sweating child in her arms, while Commia watched.

When they set off again, hunger, exhaustion, soiled clothing, panic, all began to take their toll on Camilla herself. The road she had chosen became much less good. In the morning they found themselves travelling an ill-repaired local track with no milestones. 'I believe we are going north again,' Commia groaned. Felicia started whimpering. 'Camilla, we have to give up!'

'Hush, Felicia. I'll tell you a special story. When I was a little girl like you, I lived in a far country called Bithynia. I had a brother, a bad one called Publius, who one day let me drive his four-horse chariot . . .'

'Just decide you're going to do it and we'll go,' said Publius. 'Once you start to twitter, we'll be lost . . .'

'We shall keep going,' Camilla said firmly.

'The army will rescue us,' Commia reassured her white-faced child. Staring at her, Camilla saw that Commia believed in Rome unshakably; without Rome, she would be utterly bereft.

Camilla could no longer bear her responsibility. Neither she nor Rome would survive in this province; it was all hopeless. Abruptly, she stopped the mules and let herself cry. Suddenly Commia held her, stroking the dark tangle of her uncombed hair. 'Camilla, we are in danger here. Think how Gaius will feel if he loses you . . .'

'I'll take us to the next crossroads,' Camilla decided. Dazed with tiredness, she drove them on. The track meandered aimlessly for miles, then ended at an unfortified tribal settlement. Silent faces stared at them and they knew they must not stay. But there was, as Camilla had hoped, a good road back south.

Also another. It was set above the fields, gravelled on packed foundations with flagstone kerbs. A Roman road. A road built to last forever. It came straight as a spar across the landscape: the great high road from London that she had tried to leave behind. It was the way to the frontier.

And it was the road, they discovered, on which the Roman governor had recently ridden back west.

All Camilla could think now was that wherever the governor was, she might find Gaius. Something in her revived a little. 'We must be right in the path of the Iceni again – Hold tight!' said Camilla. 'I am going to take us to the army and I shall have to go very fast!'

She turned the wagon onto the military road. She whipped up their weary mules, trying not to listen for the low rumble of pursuit behind, and she drove until she had brought them onto the central plain. They were further north than she could bear to think. If this failed, it would be fatal. The air seemed colder. It was danker, greener country, with forest, fruit trees, more cattle, fewer sheep. And eventually a Roman fortress lay ahead.

More than a fort. There were rows of leather tents beyond, as far as the eye could see. 'The army!' She drove right to the gate. She called to the sentries but realised at once that she and Commia were two ordinary women with a grubby child. The sentries ordered her merely to join the other desperate refugees. Camilla stood up. 'Apparently, I shall have to make a fuss.'

She stated ranks; she mentioned officers; she named public men. She declared she would not budge unless she saw the governor, Paulinus, himself.

Somebody ran to fetch a tribune to deal with her.

It was Felix who first reached them. Felix who bawled at the gatemen. Felix whose outstretched arms lifted down his child. Then he was lost in his wife and family, while Aelia Camilla could only wait. Finally, she spotted Gaius.

She could no longer move. She stood, one ache from skull to heel. He reached the gate. His walk quickened. He passed through one of the double entry ports, under the overhead rampart walk. Then he saw her, standing on the footboard of the wagon, alive, and Camilla watched all the panels of his stricken face fill out with joy.

She just managed to stay on her feet. She had always been brave. Therefore she said, speaking out so the soldiers would laugh too, 'Gaius Flavius, I have to confess, I drove here a great deal faster than you said you would allow.'

Then her knees began to buckle, but Gaius caught her in his arms.

At the legionary altar, Gaius stood for a long time with his palms raised. Camilla could not pray. She had no need to. The gods and the whole camp knew her heart.

Gaius fed her and washed her, then they clung together listening to the constant activity of the fort. 'Gaius, what will happen now?'

'The tribes are expected tomorrow. We shall be vastly outnumbered, but our soldiers are rested and we have found a good battle-site. There is a narrow gap, where we may just be able to draw them in until they are too tightly packed to fight.' He did not say what would happen to the tribesmen then, or to Boudicca. 'It's slim, but we do have a chance . . .' In the light of a single oil lamp, he cradled her, lying close on his camp bed. 'I should never have brought you here.'

She shook her head. 'We chose this province. We knew it was dangerous.'

'If we survive, I shall take you right away.'

'If we do, the worst will be over. With you, I can bear everything.' She laid her palm against his cheek. There would be work for him; she would rally him when the time

373

came. 'We should stay, Gaius. There will be mistakes to be righted. We must not only civilise the province, but show that Rome can civilise itself.'

Gaius lay back, smiling at how they gave each other love, comfort, and somehow hope. After a while, at peace together, they both slept.

They awoke in the same moment. A trumpet was sounding the watch, but the fort lay still. For some moments they did not move, until Camilla became aware of an intense desire for Gaius which he obviously shared.

Perhaps it would be the last night that Rome governed Britain. Perhaps it was the last night they would ever be together. Yet however short their reunion, however desperate their plight, she knew that there was nowhere else that either of them wanted to be. 'Dear gods!' whispered Gaius. 'No wonder the rules forbid women in a military fort . . .'

Then by lamplight she caught the flash of his grin as he gathered her even closer, while she met him in the passion and adoration of his kiss.

RECEIVE
THE LATEST
NEWS FROM
LINDSEY DAVIS

Go to
https://www.hodder.co.uk/contributor/lindsey-davis/
to sign up to Lindsey's email newsletter

Visit Lindsey's website at www.lindseydavis.co.uk

Or head over to the official Facebook page
f /lindseydavisauthor

HODDER &
STOUGHTON